NIGHTMARE

Chief Saylor opened his mouth as if to say something, changed his mind, stood up, and held out a hand. "Well, I'll do my best to find out what happened to your wife, Mr. Duran. You can count on that. Come on, I'll show you out."

Duran's car was wedged in between two black-and-white patrol cars. Saylor gave the Jaguar an admiring look. "Nice wheels. What year is it?"

"1975."

"It looks like new." He peered into the window. "They knew how to make them then. How about the backseats? Much space?"

Duran dutifully opened the back door for the policeman, who bent down and swept his hand across the car's carpeting. "You mind if I look a little closer?" Saylor asked, not waiting for an answer. He leaned and pawed under the front seat, his hand coming out with a cluster of rosary beads.

"Are you a religious man, Mr. Duran?"

Duran stared at the chief's hand in wonderment—they were his wife's rosary beads. "I . . . I don't know how those got there!"

THE SUSPECT

Jerry Kennealy

ONYX
Published by the Penguin Group
Penguin Putnam Inc., 375 Hudson Street,
New York, New York 10014, U.S.A.
Penguin Books Ltd, 27 Wrights Lane,
London W8 5TZ, England
Penguin Books Australia Ltd, Ringwood,
Victoria, Australia
Penguin Books Canada Ltd, 10 Alcorn Avenue,
Toronto, Ontario, Canada M4V 3B2
Penguin Books (N.Z.) Ltd, 182–190 Wairau Road,
Auckland 10, New Zealand

Penguin Books Ltd, Registered Offices:
Harmondsworth, Middlesex, England

First published by Onyx, an imprint of Dutton Signet,
a member of Penguin Putnam Inc.

First Printing, February, 1998
10 9 8 7 6 5 4 3 2 1

Printed in the United States of America

PUBLISHER'S NOTE
This is a work of fiction. Names, characters, places, and incidents either are the product of the author's imagination or are used fictitiously, and any resemblance to actual persons, living or dead, events, or locales is entirely coincidental.

For my sons, Frank and Steve
Thanks for dragging me away from the computer
for some fishing, golf, dinners,
and fine, fine, cigars.

ACKNOWLEDGMENTS

Once again, sincere thanks to my literary agent, Dominick Abel, for guiding this one over some rough waters, and to my editor, Todd Keithley, for coming in midstream and doing such a great job.

And special thanks to Larry Del Bucchia, for filling me in on the hazards in Pelican Bay.

Prologue

Cabris, France

Even at his advanced age, Claude Bresson had not relinquished a bit of his admiration for the female figure. He felt somewhat like a Peeping Tom as he watched the young artist go about her work.

But it wasn't Anona Stack, as beautiful as she was, despite being outfitted in paint-smeared khaki shorts and a man's blue button-down-collar shirt, that held Bresson's attention.

The forty-by-forty-inch canvas, which had been nothing more than a blank white square six hours earlier, was now an intense splash of colors, the artist's impression of the view from the terrace of Chateau Bresson.

That panoramic view looked out over the rolling carpets of violets, mimosa, lavender, roses, heather, and patchouli. All of these were processed, then distilled, the *effleurage* used in making the essences for perfumes, perfumes that since the eighteenth century had made the Bresson family one of the richest in all of France. The chateau, with its multiturreted roof and coarse-hewn granite walls, had been constructed in the twelfth century and had once housed a Benedictine monastery.

Bresson, short and bulky, with a napkin-length gray beard, had been impressed by all that he had seen and heard of Anona Stack. It was highly unusual for someone who was so young to have the love, the passion, the drive, and discipline needed to become a great artist, especially someone who had been worth millions of dollars long before having daubed that first paint onto a canvas. He had often wondered if it would have been different for him, if he had not been born a Bresson.

He had seen her work in the galleries of Paris, London, and New York, and had been delighted when she'd accepted his offer of a two-week sojourn at the chateau. It was considered an honor to be a guest at Chateau Bresson, joining the illustrious list that in the past had included Cezanne, Renoir, Chagall, Dufy, Matisse, and, of course, his mentor and dear friend, Pablo Picasso.

Anona Stack was the first American to whom the privilege had been extended. She had arrived with her family, the tall, cruelly handsome husband, Jason Lark, and a beautiful daughter and son. The children had turned out to be charming, the husband not so. A *bon à rien,* good for nothing.

Prior to his marriage, Lark had been an interior decorator, of all things, and had the nerve to suggest some changes for the chateau's grand dining room. Luckily, he was seldom seen, having discovered the topless beaches of nearby St. Tropez and the casino at Nice.

Bresson had watched Anona paint, first at the flower markets in Cours Saleya, then the wedding-cake Hotel Negresso, then the beaches of the Côte d'Azur. Color. God, she was so good with color! The canvas was ablaze with rich pinks, blues, yellows, and greens. The blends, the contrasts, were magnificent. She had the gift, as Monet would say, and even more important, style. Her own unique style. She copied no one.

Anona reached around with her free hand and massaged her back, then chose a clean brush, dipped it in the small well of black paint and scrawled her signature across the right top portion of the canvas.

Claude Bresson clapped his hands together when she was finished with the ritual and said, simply, "*Magnifique.*"

Anona swiveled around, her golden hair veiling her eyes momentarily.

"Ah, Monsieur Bresson. I didn't know you were there."

"*Pardon,* Anona. But I could not help myself." He approached the canvas slowly, as if wading through water. "I must have this one." He pulled his eyes from the painting and smiled at her. "Name your price," he insisted. "I must have it."

Anona's face glowed. "It is yours, Claude. A thank-you for your wonderful hospitality."

"*C'est impossible,* out of the question. It is a great painting. Your best," he assured her, then added, "at least so far. I must pay you."

Anona wiped her hands on a clean rag, then raked her fingers through her hair. "No arguments, Claude. The painting is yours." She leaned against the scrolled-iron railing, looking out across the valley, then glancing at her watch. "It's almost five. I didn't realize it was so late. Where are Johnny and Lisa? Pestering your horses again?"

Bresson grinned within the nest of his beard. "No, today your children are on my boat. Jacques is teaching them the waterskiing." He could see a look of concern cloud her face. "They are safe, believe me."

"And my husband. Have you seen Jason?"

"No," Bresson admitted. "I'm sure he'll be back shortly," he said with little confidence. He reached out for the canvas. "You are sure you will not accept payment for this?"

"I'm positive," Anona said firmly.

Bresson gently removed the canvas from the easel. "All right then. Since this is your last night at the chateau, I shall arrange a special dinner."

Claude Bresson waited until Jason Lark returned to the chateau, well after eleven o'clock—he had missed many dinners during their stay.

He heard the scream of the Alpha Romeo's engine, then saw a spray of gravel spurt from beneath the car's tires as Lark skidded the borrowed convertible to a halt in front of the chateau's massive stone steps.

"Monsieur Lark," Bresson called out as Lark started up the steps.

Lark stopped in midstride. The yellow illumination of the flame-shaped streetlights revealed a tall, thin man, the face narrow, the dark hair thick, parted on one side and falling over his eyebrow. He was wearing a tuxedo, the tie undone, the red carnation in the lapel beginning to wilt.

"Who is it?" Lark asked sharply.

Bresson stepped into a pool of light. "I am sorry that you missed your family's last dinner at the chateau."

Lark feigned a faint smile. "The roulette tables kept me busy, I'm afraid." He turned to go up the stairs, stopping when Bresson tapped him on the shoulder.

"Jason, Anona was kind enough to give me her latest painting, 'Perfume Fields.' She would not let me pay her for it. I would appreciate it if you would take this." He pulled out a brick-colored manila packet. "Give it to her when you are back home in America. It's a small token of my appreciation."

"What is it?"

"Some sketches. A few of my early efforts . . . and those of a friend."

Lark undid the packet's ribbon and riffled the edges of the linen sketching paper. "All right," he said impatiently. "Where is my wife?"

"In your room, monsieur. *Bon soir.*"

Lark ascended the stairs slowly, his fingers digging in the packet again. The first two sketches seemed to be of the Bresson Chateau. Harsh, straight lines. No depth of field. Obviously amateurish. Claude Bresson may have been born to money, but he obviously wasn't born with talent.

Lark shoved the bedroom door open without knocking. Anona was sitting on the bed, dressed in a foam-green nightgown, brushing her hair.

"It's about time you came back," she said angrily.

Lark responded by waving the packet at her. "That old fool Bresson tells me you gave him one of your paintings. In return he's giving you some old drawings he made of his precious chateau." Lark carelessly tossed the packet into an opened compartment of a Louis Vuitton traveling trunk.

"Where were you?" Anona demanded.

"Out. Having fun. I didn't come over here to be cooped up and watch you paint. Hell, I could do that at home." He sneered.

Anona pushed herself to her feet. "It seems your idea of fun includes getting lipstick on your shirt. And that powder under your nose, Jason. I'm sure that it isn't—"

Lark's open palm streaked in a long, curving arc, landing flatly on his wife's cheek, knocking her to the floor.

Anona cried out and the connecting door opened. Five-year-old Lisa, dressed in teddy bear pajamas, came running into the room, dropping to her knees alongside her mother.

"Don't hit Mommy anymore," she screamed. "Don't hit Mommy!"

Lark rocked back on his heels. He looked to the doorway. His son, John, just eighteen months older than his sister, was standing there, holding on to the knob with both of his hands, the knuckles white, his eyes wide, his mouth gaping.

"Get out, Jason," Anona said, struggling into a sitting position and pulling Lisa to her chest. "It's over. Get out!"

Chapter 1

Sixteen Years Later
Crescent City, California
Pelican Bay State Prison

"Well, well, well. The last night for the artist." The pot-bellied guard smirked, pronouncing the last word of his sentence as "arteest." "We're going to miss you, Michelangelo." He slipped the anodized telescoping baton through the cell bars, then flipped his wrist, sending the baton's tip out toward the man in the lower bunk.

"You bc a good boy out there, artist, 'cause if we get you back here again, we ain't going to be so nice."

The man waited until the guard's sharp heel clicks were a distant echo before jackknifing into a sitting position.

His cellmate Ken Firpo's shaved legs were dangling down from the upper birth.

"He's right. You come back and they'll put you in solitary confinement again," Firpo predicted. "You couldn't handle that. Are you sure you still want to go through with it?"

"Definitely," he vowed, pushing Firpo's legs out of his way. "Anona Stack's going to die, the same way Arlene died. And on the same day. And Duran is going to take the blame. October twelfth. Nothing's going to stop me." He slipped his right hand, his lithe, long-fingered painting hand, under his armpit, then pushed his nose between the cell bars, inhaling deeply, as if the air on the other side of the bars was cleaner, purer. "Nothing."

Firpo slithered out of the upper bunk, his feet hitting the cement floor with a thud. He was wearing nothing but gray prison-issued boxer shorts—fifty-four years of age, with a power-lifter's build, his corded muscles rippling under fish-belly white skin that had been decorated with numerous hot-tipped ballpoint-pen tattoos. His head, like his legs, armpits, and pubic area, was shaved, his face that of a heavyweight fighter who had taken too much punishment, his large nose broken and skewed to one side. He slipped his thumbs into the waistband of his shorts and pushed them down to his ankles. "That doesn't give you much time. Well, I taught you how, and told you where. Now, since this'll be our last night together, get over here and give me a good-bye kiss."

Firpo drop-kicked his shorts toward the lower bunk. "And don't tell me you're having one of your fuckin' headaches."

Jamaica

A sudden gust of warm, sea-scented wind ruffled the palm trees, awakening Robert Duran from a tranquil nap. He yawned lazily and swept a hand out across the towel, reaching for his wife.

He blinked his eyes open and rolled over onto his stomach, the brightness causing him to search the warm white sand for his sunglasses.

Duran put the glasses on and scanned the Jamaican

Inn's private beach for Anona. There were several dozen oil-coated bathers, the women young, beautiful, in wispy string bikinis; the men older, thick-bodied, seemingly more interested in the newspapers, books, or laptops propped on their stomachs than their companions or the cobalt-blue waters of Sandy Beach Bay.

Duran had never been happier. His business was booming, so much so that it had been difficult to find the time to squeeze in this vacation. He and Anona had recently celebrated their wedding anniversary. Six marvelous years. There were times when Duran would wake up in the morning, stare at his wife's beautiful profile and wonder why Anona had picked him. With all of the rich, talented, and famous men chasing her, why had she settled for a widowed insurance investigator whose only claim to fame was locating stolen works of art from time to time?

An enormous, triple-stacked, *Love Boat*–style luxury liner caught his eye. Rainbow-hued, butterfly-winged sailboats rode the wide feather of the liner's wake, bobbing up and down like toys in a bathtub.

Duran got to his feet and stretched his hands over his head. He was of medium height, with a lean, athletic body. His black hair was flecked with gray. His face was angular, well cut, the coppery skin set off by a pair of blue eyes that somehow didn't seem to belong with the rest of the package. A thick scar weaved through his left eyebrow, then curled down in a comma to his cheekbone. He was about to run down to the water for a swim when he spotted Anona. She had changed from her swimsuit to a canary-yellow basket-weave dress.

Tall, slender, her hair shades lighter from a week's worth of sun, she had a regal way about her. Although she was in her forties, a good many of the male population on the beach dropped their reading material long enough for an appraising glance as she strolled by.

Duran always marveled at the way she could command attention. His mind flickered back to a luncheon at a three-star bistro just outside of Paris. They'd sat on a balcony with a view of the Monet–inspired garden. Anona, using a ballpoint pen, a lipstick, and an eyebrow pencil dipped into her wineglass, drew a rough outline of her latest painting on the white linen tablecloth. The meal, which included several bottles of wine and after-lunch cognacs must have been quite expensive, but the proprietor wisely told Anona the lunch was on him, if only she would sign her name on the tablecloth alongside the drawing.

"Had enough sun for the day?" Duran greeted her cheerfully. Anona's fair skin required massive doses of sunscreen, while Duran could lay on the beach for hours and not worry about getting burned.

Anona slid gracefully onto the beach towel. She took off her hub-cap-sized dark glasses and gazed at her husband, her azure-tinted eyes narrowing against the strength of the sun. She dropped her head, causing her hair to screen her eyes. "It's been a wonderful week, hasn't it?"

"Wonderful. We can stay another day if you want, I can put—"

"No. I've had my fill of sun and sand for a while. I miss the city, Bob. Let's go home."

Duran had noticed that Anona was getting a little edgy. It was always that way when she was away from her painting, from Stack House, her children, and her dog—she and her terrier, Andamo, had become almost inseparable.

"Sure, darling, anything you want." Duran got to

his feet, brushing the sand from his legs. He wrapped his arms around her shoulders. "I'm getting the feeling that you've got an idea for a new painting. Am I right?"

"Well," she admitted, "I have been thinking. Before we left on the trip, when I went to the cemetery, to the Stack mausoleum, to put some flowers—"

"You're going to paint a cemetery?" Duran asked skeptically.

"Yes. There's something special there. Early in the morning. The light. The trees, it just struck me. A garden. God's garden. God's backyard."

Duran buried his face in her hair. It was wonderful being married to a genius. A beautiful genius. "I'll tell the concierge to book us a flight home."

Chapter 2

from *The Los Angeles Times,* October 1

The Santa Barbara mansion of movie producer Alan Fritzheim, whose latest film, *Lethal Confession,* has grossed over one hundred and forty million dollars, was burglarized last night.

Neither Mr. Fritzheim, or his wife, the former actress Danielle Altray, were at home at the time of the robbery.

Mr. Fritzheim's attorney stated that the only item taken was a Vincent Van Gogh painting, "Sun and Sky," which was purchased four years ago for twenty-eight million dollars.

Police say they have no suspects at the present time.

It was a classic case of the barn door being shut long after the horse had taken off. There were two black-and-white police cars parked in front of the entrance to Alan Fritzheim's house.

Duran showed his credentials to the uniformed officer guarding the gated entry, then drove into the compound, following an S-shaped cobblestone path that skirted neatly trimmed topiary hedges.

The large-scale two-story structure was all white rolling adobe stucco with circular windows. Bright orange bougainvillea spilled over a low escarpment bordering the front of the house.

He parked alongside yet another black-and-white, the heavy-jawed officer checking his ID before taking a walkie-talkie from his belt, mumbling a jumbled message, and grudgingly allowing Duran to go up the black-tiled steps.

The man waiting for him inside the front door was in his forties, with thinning brown hair, wearing a tan poplin suit, and rep tie.

He extended a hand. "Mr. Duran? Lieutenant Beeler. Come on in, I'll give you the guided tour."

Duran shook the policeman's hand, noticing his rigid grip and the resentful expression on the lieutenant's face. It was a look Duran was used to, and he was not unsympathetic to Beeler's frustrations. The police took the heat for the crime taking place in their territory, then were often left out of the picture while the insurance company representatives negotiated with the victims—and the thieves.

Beeler led Duran through the house. The walls were dotted with vintage movie posters: *Casablanca, King Kong, Bambi, The Wizard of Oz.* They passed by the dining room, the long table set between two narrow pools of water. The table top was of granite, matching the floor. An orange-and-yellow Mark Rothko oil hung on one wall.

Beeler moved into a large room, pointing out the numerous jade statues and figurines encased in a ceiling-high glass case. The adjoining room held a collection of Western memorabilia—saddles, hats, rifles, pistols, and at least a half dozen Remington bronzes of cowboys on horseback.

Duran followed Beeler up the stairs to the master bedroom. Here the floors were of gleaming ebony. A round bed dominated the room. Above the terra-cotta-tiled fireplace, in a hollowed-out alcove, under a spotlight, sat a gold statue. An Oscar presented to Alan Fritzheim three years ago. Framed posters from several of Fritzheim's movies hung from the walls. The ceiling-to-floor windows looked out on a quarry-stoned patio. A woman with ash-blond hair was stretched out in a padded lounge chair on the patio, reading a magazine.

"The Van Gogh hung right over there," Beeler advised, "over the bed." He slapped a clipboard against his thigh. "Do you want to take photographs?"

"No, thanks, Lieutenant. I'm sure you and your crew have taken care of that," Duran granted. "What about the alarm system?"

"It was off," Beeler said, the disgust in his voice obvious. He peeled off a page from the clipboard and handed it to Duran. "This is a diagram of the alarm system. It cost Fritzheim close to three hundred thousand bucks. If it was on, it would have activated as soon as they touched the Van Gogh."

"Was anyone at home during the theft?"

"Just the Mexican housekeeper, Eleana Fuentes. She's in the kitchen now if you want to talk to her."

"I do, and—"

The glass doors leading to the patio slid open and the blonde strolled into the room. She looked to be in her late thirties, though Duran knew that she had to be at least fifty. Her hair was layered back at the sides, her makeup artfully applied. She was wearing a glimmering red silk dress carved deeply at both the neck and back and stiletto heels.

"Who are you?" she demanded, pointing a red-tipped finger at Duran.

"This is Robert Duran, the man your insurance carrier hired, Mrs. Fritzheim," Beeler informed her. He turned to Duran. "Do you need anything else?"

"Just to talk to the housekeeper and Mr. Fritzheim."

"I'll take him to my husband," the woman said dismissively.

Beeler jumped at the opportunity to leave. "Let me know if I can be of any help," he called over his shoulder.

Duran turned to the woman and said, "Where is your husband?"

She tilted her head to the side and sized up Duran as if he were a side of beef that she was contemplating purchasing for a barbecue. "You dress too good to be just an insurance investigator. What are you? Someone like Banacek? The guy on the old TV show who solved all those tricky cases?"

"No, Mrs. Fritz—"

"Danielle," she said batting her heavily mascaraed eyelashes at him. "You know they offered me a role in that show, but I never did TV. Just movies."

"Yes, I've seen your pictures," Duran lied amiably. "They were wonderful. It must have been a shock for you, coming home and finding the Van Gogh gone."

She shook her bare arm, the string of gold bracelets on her wrist making a jangling sound. "I'm just glad they didn't take my jewels." She jutted her chin toward a door on the far wall. "All they had to do was go in there and scoop 'em up." She tilted her head to the side again and said, "You want to take a look?"

"No. I'm not interested in what the thieves didn't take. Maybe I better talk to your husband."

"Alan's in his library. He stays there all day, sometimes. When he's not at the damn studio. The library's downstairs, just across from the kitchen."

Duran thanked her. "I think I can find it."

She headed for the patio, her stiletto heels digging into the hardwood floor. "Yes, but can you find the painting?"

Duran checked the kitchen first. Like the rest of the house, it was all white, with a vaulted ceiling and arched walls. A round-faced girl dressed in a dark skirt and a ruffled off-the-shoulder blouse sat at the butcher block table, nervously drumming her fingers on her lap.

"Buenas dias, Señorita Fuentes," Duran greeted her formally.

"¿Habláis español?"

"Sí."

Duran conducted the entire interview in Spanish, confident that he had gotten more information from the housekeeper than the police had. He learned that she was nineteen, or at least claimed she was. She had been working at the house for less than three months. The doorbell had rung shortly after noon. She had looked through the peephole and saw two men in coveralls carrying a couch. She had opened the door and let them in. One of the men spoke Spanish and asked her who was home to sign for the delivery. When she told him she was alone the man had pulled a *"grande pistola"* from his pocket. She was tied and gagged, and not set free until Mrs. Fritzheim came home later in the afternoon.

Duran went over the incident with her several times, but couldn't get a better description of the two men other than they were both *flatco,* skinny, possibly in their thirties, and looked enough alike to be brothers.

They wore white coveralls and Los Angles Dodger baseball hats. She had not seen their vehicle.

The kitchen door was swung open and a short, balding man with a rounded back and caved-in stomach, dressed in light blue shorts, a matching shirt with shoulder tabs and button-down pockets, and shower thongs clomped into the room.

He skidded to a halt when he saw Duran. "You with the cops?"

"No." Duran gave him one of his business cards.

Alan Fritzheim glanced at the card, then snapped it with a fingernail. "Lost Art, Inc. You're the guy those morons at my insurance company hired."

"The manager at Pacific Indemnity hired me," Duran confirmed.

Eleana Fuentes tiptoed silently toward the door. Fritzheim gave her a quick look, then shook his head. "She let them right in the house." His eyes bounced up to Duran. "And don't give me a ration of shit because the alarm system wasn't on. And what makes you and those assholes at Pacific Indemnity think you can get the painting back and the cops can't?"

"I don't think the police are going to be of much help. The thieves knew exactly what they wanted. Your wife's jewelry wasn't taken. That Rothko hanging in your dining room is worth over a million dollars. The Remington Western bronzes are very valuable, as are the jade items. They left your Oscar behind. They wanted the Van Gogh, period, which means there are two possible scenarios. Either they already have a buyer for the painting, or they'll sell it back to the insurance company."

"Scenarios." Fritzheim glowered. "You sound like a fucking scriptwriter."

"The Van Gogh's too well known to peddle on the

open market. Either they've got a buyer who'll freeze it, or they'll come to us with an offer."

"What'd you mean, 'freeze it'?"

"Put it in storage," Duran explained. "For a long time, twenty, thirty, fifty years."

"You'd have to be nuts to do that," Fritzheim said angrily.

"No. Just patient. Over time a phony provenance could be carefully detailed—so-and-so bought it from so-and-so, who passed it on, and on, and on. In the meantime, the buyer has the Van Gogh. He can enjoy it all he wants, as long as he doesn't show it off to the wrong people. Fifty years from now 'Sun and Sky' could surface in Europe, South America, or Asia. Your heirs would have a tough time getting it back."

"Heirs! You mean I'm never going to see the fucking thing again?"

"It depends. As I said, if the thieves don't have a buyer, they'll contact us. Do you want your Van Gogh back, Mr. Fritzheim?"

Fritzheim squared his shoulders and puffed out his chest. "What the hell kind of a question is that? Of course I want my painting back. I love that fucking painting! I kept it under plexiglass, to protect it. I even had a curtain across it. I covered it every goddamn day so the sun wouldn't touch it. I treated that fucking thing like it was my kid, and you want to know if I want it back!" He waved an arm around his head. "People like you just can't understand what it's like to own a painting like that—a masterpiece. A flat-out goddamn masterpiece."

"Oh, I understand, Mr. Fritzheim," Duran assured him. "And I'll do my best to get your Van Gogh back for you."

* * *

It had taken two hours, but the wait was worth it. He'd found the right van. The couple were young, the man blond, muscular, the girl dark-haired with a heart-shaped face. They were smiling and laughing at each other like honeymooners—like he and Arlene used to.

The courtesy bus pulled up and the young man reached down for a bulging black vinyl suitcase.

"Can I give you a hand with that?" he asked.

"Yeah, I'd appreciate it," the blond man said with a chuckle. "We're going away for three weeks, but my wife's got enough stuff to last us for months."

The girl wrinkled her nose and stuck out her tongue at her husband, picked up one of the bags and lugged it onto the bus.

"Where are you two off to?" he asked, once all the luggage was stowed away.

"Mexico City, Puerto Vallarta, then Baja."

"Sounds great," he said enthusiastically. "Three weeks, huh."

"Yeah. How about you?"

"Oh, nothing quite so exciting. I'm going to New York for a week on business."

The young blond man nodded, then said, "You're traveling light. No luggage?"

"I dropped it off at the terminal." He twisted his neck around and looked back at the long-term parking lot. "I hope my car will be there when I get back."

"It'll be there," the blond man predicted. "I've used the lot before and never had a problem."

He nodded and folded his hands in his lap, watching the outline of the San Francisco Airport terminal come into view. Long-term parking lots. A prison lesson. Not from Ken Firpo, but from Darien, a young, Aryan skinhead who had murdered two black men who had made the mistake of scratching his car in a supermarket parking lot.

Darien's lesson was simple: never steal a car. Stealing a car leads to too many problems. Get stopped for a speeding ticket, the cops had you. If they questioned you and your ID didn't correspond with the vehicle's registration, they had you.

Always take a truck, or a van. A business vehicle. If you get stopped, your story is that you're driving your boss's rig.

The second part of the lesson was just as instructive. Spare keys. Darien claimed he could find a spare key hidden somewhere on the chassis of half the vehicles parked on the road. If he couldn't find a key, he'd move on to another vehicle. "Never break into a car and hotwire it," Darien had preached.

When he got back to the parking lot, it took him four minutes to find the blond man's spare key—taped behind the rear license plate.

He hummed to himself as he switched on the ignition and familiarized himself with the van's controls—another litany from Darien's gospel of do's and don'ts. "Know where everything is, the wipers, the lights, the radio. Cops see you fumbling around like you don't know what you're doing, they'll jump on you."

The registration papers were conveniently located in the glove compartment. He switched on the ignition, his thin lips pinching in a smile when he noticed the gas gauge. Full.

The young lovers would be in Mexico for three weeks. That would give him enough time. If not, he'd just steal another van.

Chapter 3

Danielle Fritzheim slowly raked her fingers over Jason Lark's face.

"You're so damn good looking, you should have been an actor, Jason." Her thumb and forefinger traced the outline of his nose. "Who did this? Hassend? Do you know he's married to that stupid bimbo who does that spy show on NBC? Forty-two-years old and she claims she's never had anything done to her. She's married to the best plastic surgeon in Hollywood and she acts like a virgin."

Lark pushed her hand away. "Tell me about Alan. I suppose he's upset about the stolen Van Gogh."

"Upset?" She laughed. "He's furious. The insurance company is stalling, so he's hired an attorney to sue the bastards."

"What's the insurance company's position?"

She got to her knees and leaned over Lark, her hardened nipples brushing across his lips. She dragged her Gucci purse from the nightstand, her fingers digging inside until she found the circular gold compact. "They say it was our fault. That the security system should have been operating. As if we have to live like we're in a third world country or something."

Her fingers went back into the purse, this time coming out with a tiny silver spoon. "It's that little bitch

Eleana's fault for letting them in the house." She dipped the spoon in the compact, then shook a line of the powder from the middle of Lark's stomach down to his belly button.

"I think Alan's fucking her," she said.

"Who?" Lark asked, pressing the back of his head into the bed pillows.

"Eleana. Did she ever make a move on you while you were decorating the house?"

"The maid's name was Sonia when I was at the house."

Danielle bent over and vacuumed up the cocaine with her nose, her tongue licking up the remaining granules. "Well, Alan probably fucked her, too. I can't think of any other reason for him to keep them around."

Lark reached down and grabbed Danielle's mane of ash-blond hair. "So is the insurance company going to pay or not?"

"Oh, they think they'll get the painting back. An investigator was at the house yesterday." Her fingers reached out to his penis, slowly stroking it. "He was from San Francisco. A real hunk. He said it was obvious the thieves were interested in the Van Gogh, and nothing else. In cases like this they usually always sell the stolen items back to the insurance company."

"What do you mean 'cases like this,' Danielle?"

She jiggled her wrist. "My jewelry. They left it all behind. The jade collection. Even Alan's Oscar. They could have taken everything, but they didn't."

Lark pushed an extra pillow under his head so he could watch Danielle's hand. "The San Francisco investigator. What did he look like?"

She dropped her head to his stomach, her tongue exploring his belly button. When she came up for air, she said, "He was cute. Dark, but with blue eyes. Paul Newman eyes."

"Did he have a scar over one eye?"

Danielle pulled her hand away, satisfied that Lark's manhood stood at attention on its own. "Yes." She squinted up at Lark. Without her contact lenses his face was a hazy blur. "Do you know him?"

"Perhaps. Robert Duran, right?"

"Right. Like the fighter. The one that quit in the ring." She picked up the compact again. "This one doesn't look like a quitter. I hope he gets Alan's painting back. He's been a fucking bear." She swirled her finger in the cache of cocaine, coated her lips with the powder, then leaned down and engulfed Lark's penis with her mouth.

Lark lay back and stared at the ceiling. Robert Duran. Of all the luck. Of all the rotten fucking luck.

The area was just as Ken Firpo had described it: Thickets of pine, oak, redwood trees, and head-high scrub bushes soaked up every sound of movement.

The road was overgrown by low lying vegetation. A rusting iron gate held together by an equally rusty lock had been the only barrier.

He had sawed off the lock, replacing it with a new one that quickly achieved a patina of rust from the thick, salt-drenched fog that coiled in from the nearby Pacific Ocean.

A warren of trails used by small animals led him to the caves. There were at least a dozen, and the one he had chosen was perfect—and within walking distance of the cabin.

The cabin wasn't much, but it was better than anything he'd lived in in a long time. It had taken him four full days to clean it out, hook up butane for the stove, and install a new water heater.

The only piece of furniture worth keeping was a redwood kitchen table. He'd bought some odds and ends at a Salvation Army store—a comfortable old couch, two sturdy wooden chairs, curtains, and some pots, pans, plates, cups, and silverware.

He took a deep breath and looked at his project. He had considered several vehicles: trucks, moving vans, campers, but had settled on the bakery truck after his cellmate Ken Firpo convinced him it would be the easiest to convert into a likeness of the SHU at Pelican Bay.

The truck's blue-and-white checkerboard coloring was faded. The Kilpatrick's Bread lettering was chipped and had oxidized. The engine's front cowling was missing and it tilted to the right, the result of two tires being almost flat. But that didn't matter. It had just a short trip left.

The cave was hollowed out deep enough to engulf the entire truck. He hit the ignition switch and eased the clutch in, inching the vehicle over the plywood boards leading into the opening. He butted the bumper against the dirt wall, then edged himself out of the driver's seat and observed the results. Not bad, not bad at all he surmised. Nothing like the real thing of course. His cell, called the SHU for solitary housing unit, was six feet by ten feet—no windows, just raw concrete walls and floor, the door of perforated steel sheets, with a small slot for the passing of food, fresh linen, and blankets. He had counted the bullet-sized holes in his cell door—a total of 3,864. He had counted them over and over, outraged when he was off by a number or two, determined to pinpoint just which holes he had missed. There had been no television, and books or magazines weren't allowed. No one to talk to, to touch. No view of neighboring prisoners. Dark, cold, desolate. Not a ray of sunlight ever reached his SHU. The three daily meals were delivered by a close-mouthed guard—starchy prison food: potatoes, rice, beans, overcooked meats, white-bread sandwiches, fruit, potato chips, stale pieces of cake or pie. A hard plastic cup and an unbreakable spoon were provided. If the spoon was not returned with the cup and tray, four of the guards would enter the cell, batons and stun guns flying.

He had saved pieces of dessert—crumbs of cookies, cake, or pie—and sprinkled them around the floor, hoping that something, anything: an ant, a spider, a fly, something alive would visit, if only for a short time. But nothing ever came.

His options had been limited to praying, masturbating, or exercising. He had long ago given up his belief in a god. He opted for masturbation and the exercises, and since he was not allowed access to weights or machines, he built up a regimen of running in place, sit-ups, and isometrics, contracting one set of muscles against another.

He had endured the SHU for eighteen months. Five hundred and forty-seven days. And nights. Now Anona Stack was going to have a taste of it: the loneliness, hopelessness. He wanted to watch her, see how she reacted, see if she would last until October the twelfth. Stare into her eyes when she realized that she had no chance, no hope—that death was her only avenue of escape from the SHU.

His hand massaged the back of his head, behind his right ear. That was where the migraines started. First the dazzling light, then the blurred double-images, followed by the pain that echoed throughout his head.

Pain that the prison doctor claimed was nothing more serious than headaches brought on by anxiety. Not the batons, or the guard's steel-capped shoes, but anxiety.

He selected a pick from the tools littering the area and eased his way back into the cave, sweating from the effort it took to swing the pick in the narrow quarters, aiming at the tires, listening to the air hiss out as the truck's rims settled ever so slowly down into the damp ground.

He examined the truck's interior. The half-inch steel plates bolted to the walls had a wet, silvery look. He'd found the toilet at a dump site. It wasn't connected to plumbing pipes. It sat over a hole in the floor. Anona Stack would have to put up with it. The single bunk was nothing more than strips of angled iron, welded together and bolted to the wall. No sink. No shower. They had always watched him when he showered, as if they were afraid he would somehow try and escape through the drain. They'd watch, laugh, and make crude jokes.

A donut-sized eye bolt had been welded to the ceiling. He reached back and removed a garment from his back pocket. A black brassiere—size 36 C. Arlene's size, her favorite color of lingerie. He wrapped one end of the bra around his neck, stretching the opposite end toward the ceiling, threading it through the eye bolt. The nylon expanded under the strain. But he outweighed Anona Stack by at least seventy pounds. Would it hold her? Would it do the job? He slipped the brassiere free and stuffed it back in his pants pocket, deciding that he might have to add a small section of rope to Anona's bra for reinforcement.

A mattress, a blanket, a pillow, and it'd be finished. Except for the new doors, of course. He still had to work on the doors. He walked over to the sawhorses holding the heavy steel sheeting. It would be too much work to drill 3,864 holes. He decided to compromise: four rows of holes, three in the first row, then eight, then six, and finally four.

Danielle Fritzheim dressed hurriedly after showering.

"I've got to get home. Alan's bringing some people over to the house. He's thinking of making a costume flick. One of those Three Musketeer type things." She looked around for her shoes.

"Put your glasses on," Lark suggested, already dressed and waiting impatiently at the door.

She gave him a nasty look, found her shoes, then patted Lark gently on the cheek. "Give me a five-minute head start, Jason. It was nice seeing you again. It's been too long. Get some rest. You tired out awfully fast today."

Lark watched as her liposuctioned fanny sashayed toward the elevators. Once she was out of sight, he closed the hotel room door and took the stairs to the back exit.

No one was taking advantage of the inviting sky-hued swimming pool, but the surrounding beach chairs were overflowing with vacationers and the flight attendants who used the hotel on a regular basis.

It was there at the pool that he'd met his last wife, Ilsa. His fourth and, he swore to himself, positively last wife. He crossed through the lobby and out onto the street. The hotel was overpriced and beginning to look a little seedy. Its appeal was its location, less than two blocks from his office.

Adam Sheehan, his assistant, a pale-skinned, pale-eyed man of fifty who wore tweeds no matter what the weather, was showing a customer swatches of wallpaper.

"Ah, here's Mr. Lark now." Adam approached Lark cautiously, his voice a whisper. "Mrs. Quiller. She's driving me crazy."

Mrs. Quiller was a dimple-chinned woman with a diet-hard body and a mansion overflowing with valuable antiques. Lark gave her a friendly wave, then told Adam, "You'll have to handle her. I've got an important call to make."

Lark weaved his way through tables covered with upholstery and drapery fabrics. The showroom walls were festooned with oil paintings and ornately framed mirrors. He heard Mrs. Quiller call out something to him, but he ignored her. He reached his office, entering quickly, slamming the door behind him.

He flopped into the Eames leather desk chair, slipped a black-lacquered cigarette case from his jacket pocket, extracted a ready-rolled joint and lit up.

He held the smoke in as long as he could, then let it stream out his nose—the nose that Danielle Fritzheim had rightly diagnosed as having had reconstructive surgery, the cartilage having been chewed up by cocaine.

He flipped the Rolodex to the letter *M*. There was just the single letter—and a Las Vegas telephone number. He often wondered just where the telephone that Mario Drago always answered so abruptly was located. His home? Office? Do men like Mario Drago have homes? Lark's only meeting with Drago had taken place in an empty room in the basement of the Sandbar Casino. He took another hit from the marijuana, then dialed the number.

"Yes."

Drago. As abrupt as ever.

"It's me, Jason."

"What did you learn about the Fritzheim robbery?"

"Fritzheim has hired an attorney. He's threatening to sue the insurance company."

"Yes, we know about that. Have the thieves contacted Fritzheim?"

"No, and apparently the cops don't have a clue."

"The police are useless in cases like this," Drago imparted.

"The insurance company has hired someone who has a good track record in recovering these types of things."

"Yes. We know that, too. Robert Duran. And that's bad news for you. He's married to one of your ex-wives, isn't he?"

"Yes, Anona Stack," Lark confirmed.

"Duran lives with her, and your two children, John and Lisa in San Francisco, doesn't he?"

Lark felt his throat muscles tighten. He had been debating about whether or not to even bring Duran's name up.

"You seem to know all about it, Mario."

"I do. I do indeed. What kind of relationship do you have with your ex-wife?"

"We're on speaking terms. Why?"

"I want you to go to San Francisco. Find out what Duran's up to. If he negotiates with the thieves and finds out the Van Gogh is a fake, he'll start making inquiries about who had access to the Fritzheim's house, Jason. And he'll find you there. It won't take him long to put it all together. And once he targets you, he might get to me."

"Can't *you* find out who stole the damn painting?" Lark asked hopefully.

"I'm working on it. But if Duran gets to them first, someone will have to be eliminated."

Lark didn't like the way Drago emphasized "someone." He knew the bastard wouldn't think twice about killing him if he thought it would blunt his connection to the Van Gogh.

"I've got something that looks very good," he said quickly. "A woman in Beverly Hills. She's in her eighties, doesn't remember her name half the time, and has no relatives living close by. There are some real treasures in the place. A Renoir that I'm sure you'd like."

"Solve the Van Gogh problem first. Take care of Duran. Then we'll talk."

The phone line crackled a moment, then purred. Lark crashed the receiver on its rest.

"Shit," he said aloud, then flopped back into his chair. He had done four jobs for Drago—each time switching a forgery for a valuable painting: a Paul Gauguin, a Botticelli, a Matisse, then the Fritzheim Van Gogh. Alan Fritzheim. It had seemed so easy—almost too easy. Alan was at the studio all day, every day, and Danielle went shopping every afternoon. That gave Lark all the time he needed to allow Drago's man to photograph and laser scan the Van Gogh. The forgeries had always been perfect.

It had seemed like such an amazingly safe scheme. Foolproof. Most people held on to works of art like the Van Gogh for years. For lifetimes. There had never been a problem. Until now. The damn thieves took the forged Van Gogh.

"Take care of Duran." Meaning that Mario wasn't going to be much help. If Duran did somehow tie the phony Van Gogh to Lark, he'd check his other clients, find the other forgeries. "Take care of Duran." Why the hell didn't Drago take care of Duran himself? It was his kind of business.

Lark moaned inwardly. He would never forget meeting Drago. He had been at the roulette wheel when a man with a beach-ball face and chunky body tugged at his sleeve and told him that the casino manager wanted to talk to him.

Lark had expected to be escorted into a plush office, but instead the goon had taken him to the elevator and pushed the button for the basement, then shoved him down a narrow corridor to a cold room, the ceiling criss-crossed with air ducts.

Drago had been seated in a canvas-backed chair. He got to his feet slowly, a short, pudgy man with wispy, receding gray hair, carefully combed across his scalp. Unimpressive, was Lark's first impression. The well-cut tuxedo did nothing more than make him look like a waiter in an upscale restaurant. It was when he started speaking that Lark's impression changed. Drago kept his face frozen, using no facial muscles when he spoke, like a ventriloquist. But the words were cold, hard, blunt.

Drago waved Lark's gambling debts under his nose, then began telling him what he was going to do to him, pulling a pen from his tuxedo pocket and placing it on the areas of Lark's body that would be fractured first.

When Lark was sweating sufficiently, Drago widened his deep-set eyes and explained how "things could be straightened out. To the advantage of both of us."

Lark didn't need much convincing. The work was easy. He'd get a redecorating job and tell Drago of the treasures available. The gambling debts were canceled after the first job, then he was paid for his efforts.

And the money was good. Always in cash. Cash, that somehow didn't last long. His last divorce had cost him a bundle. Most of his marriages had cost him a bundle, he reluctantly admitted. He should have stuck it out with Anona.

Robert Duran. Lark had convinced himself he could have gotten Anona back if it hadn't been for Duran. He had started visiting the kids in San Francisco. Seeing Anona. Taking her out to dinner. She was coming around, her attitude toward him softening. Then she came to Los Angeles to testify against some bungling forger. Some bungling forger that Duran had caught. Anona was infatuated with this "rugged art cop." Infatuated enough to marry the bastard. Now Duran was sleeping in Stack House. With Anona.

Duran had made it clear that he didn't want Lark around. Didn't want him near Anona, and that he was more than willing to make life physically unpleasant for Lark if he "ever touched Anona or the kids again."

Lark flipped through the Rolodex, then dialed San Francisco.

The all-too-familiar voice of George, the pompous butler, greeted him formally: "Stack House. To whom do you wish to speak?"

"George, this is Jason Lark. Is Johnny there?"

"No, sir. He is not."

"What about Lisa?"

"No, sir. She is not."

"Well, then let me speak to Anona."

"I'm sorry. She's not in at the moment."

"Well, I'm coming up, George. Tomorrow, or the day after. Prepare a room for me. And let my son and daughter know I've called."

"Yes, sir."

Lark broke the connection. Somehow he had to get Drago to go after Duran. Get rid of him, and then he could—

A knock at the door interrupted Lark's thoughts.

It was his assistant, Adam.

"Mrs. Quiller is becoming impatient. What shall I do with her?"

Lark was about to suggest in a most vulgar way what Adam do to Quiller, what he had done so often to Danielle Fritzheim, but then he realized that given Adam's sexual preferences, it wasn't possible.

Chapter 4

It had been a break, Stack House being located so close to the heavily wooded Presidio, the sixteen-hundred-acre former army post that was now a national park.

He found it easy to hide among the pines and eucalyptus trees. The stolen van was parked a block away. As long as he moved it every few hours, the police wouldn't bother with it—and he certainly didn't have to worry about paying parking tickets.

He kept a camera and a sketch pad with him, so if anyone spotted him he could start drawing. Have a prop, Firpo, his cellmate had preached to him, a prop of some kind to validate your reason for being where you are. The sketch pad was perfect, and it gave him something to do while waiting for his quarry. Anona Stack had not changed much. She was still an attractive woman, a little older than the vision in his jail-cell fantasies, but still beautiful, aloof, full of herself.

He remembered Robert Duran from Duran's visit to the gallery seven years ago. He had barged in with the police—the day he and Arlene were arrested.

Marrying the rich and famous Anona Stack and having access to all her money hadn't seemed to have changed Duran. He looked what? Tough? Competent, he decided. A "stone" was what he'd be called in prison. Someone not to fool with—until the time was right.

He smiled, his upper lip riding over his teeth. The time was coming. Soon, very soon.

Duran had not testified or made an appearance at the trial, but the prosecutor had mentioned his name, mentioned how Duran had been responsible for identifying the gallery and the forged Anona Stack painting, "Blue Leaves." Responsible for him and Arlene going to prison. That was seven years ago. A lifetime ago. An eternity for Arlene.

The surveillance at Stack House had been tedious, but ultimately rewarding. Every morning, starting at seven o'clock, a series of women arrived: Some were dropped at the side door by men driving battered cars and pickup trucks; others parking similar vehicles on the street. Day workers: cooks and maids, he correctly assumed. Then, a few minutes before or after ten o'clock, a straight-backed, white-haired old man would emerge from the house and deposit some letters in the brass mailbox attached to the ornate wrought-iron gates bordered by towering privet hedges. Within fifteen minutes the mailman would hurry by, pick up the outgoing mail, and deposit the day's delivery.

It was dangerous, but too tempting to pass up. He had beat the mailman to the box twice, quickly grabbing half of the outgoing letters. It had been worth the risk. There were two letters from Lisa, Anona's daughter, to a friend. Those letters didn't provide him with any interesting information, other than the fact that the daughter had either a vivid imagination or a very active sex life.

So far, the closest look he'd gotten at Lisa was when she raced out of the driveway behind the wheel of a red convertible.

The letter that had made the mail theft worthwhile was one from Anona Stack to her attorney, Hugh Stringer, advising Stringer that she approved of his strategy to sell thirty thousand dollars worth of securities and transfer the proceeds to her son, John's, account.

He had no interest in the son, or the money. It was her stationery—a pale lavender, thick linen with ragged edges, her first name only, ANONA, in calligraphy on the letterhead.

The envelope was of the same quality. He had to go to a half dozen stationery stores before he found the exact duplicate in a small shop on Union Street. He then drove to San Jose, a good fifty miles from San Francisco and had an Asian who barely spoke English print up the letterheads.

Each morning, an hour or so after Duran returned from his morning run in the Presidio woods, he would take off in his fancy green Jaguar sedan. He had followed Duran several times, the Jag had always ended up in a parking lot alongside Duran's office on Taylor Street, near Fisherman's Wharf.

Some days Anona Stack didn't made an appearance at all. But the last two days she appeared to be on a schedule. A schedule he liked. She'd driven out of the garage in her white Land Rover about the time Duran was starting off on his jog. He followed her to a cemetery in Colma, where shc parked the Rover, using the vehicle's hood as a drafting desk as she sketched. A small dog sat at her side, or wandered around the cemetery grounds.

Then, just after noon, she drove back to San Francisco, to what he thought at first was an abandoned building on the Embarcadero. A small brass placard on the door announced STACK STUDIO. Then it was back to Stack House in the early afternoon.

A cab pulled to the curb in front of Stack House. He lowered his sketch pad and picked up the binoculars that dangled from a cord around his neck. A tall man with silvery hair exited the taxi, a raincoat draped around his shoulders like a cape.

He zoomed in on the man's face. Handsome, arrogant. He'd seen that face before. At the trial. Who was he? Someone who had been with Anona Stack. Sat with her in the courtroom. It came back to him. Jason Lark, Stack's first husband. The father of her two children.

He hadn't paid any attention to Lark while he was in Pelican Bay. Ken Firpo's job in the prison library gave him access to the Bay Area newspapers, so he was able to keep track of Anona Stack—her gallery showings, the sales of her paintings at Christie's and Sotheby's. The bitch had divorced Lark years ago. What the hell was he doing showing up now?

"Help the driver with my bags, George," Jason Lark ordered when the butler greeted him at the door of Stack House.

Lark stood with his hands on his hips, surveying the entry hall while he waited for his luggage. He shook his head sadly. Stack House was a massive, half-timbered English Tudor designed by Bernard Maybeck in 1911 for Anona's grandfather, Sean Stack. It stretched out some 19,088 square feet, with twenty-two rooms, twelve bathrooms, an indoor swimming pool, a game room, and a media room in the basement.

Old Sean had arrived in America from Ireland with little more than his confirmation suit. He'd started his life in the New World as a blacksmith, worked his way into the steel business, eventually building ships and bridges. Very large ships and very large bridges.

His son, Conrad Stack, wasn't quite the businessman his father had been, but he carried on the family enterprise, marrying a young secretary, Grace Hanlon, who died just two days after their only child, Anona, was born.

While Bernard Maybeck may have been a genius in his time, back in 1911 he hadn't had to worry much about garage space. Later on, it just wasn't fashionable to leave those Dusenbergs and Rolls lined up along the sidewalk, so in the 1960s, Anona's father did what he thought was the sensible thing. He bought the property alongside, tore down the house, and built a garage.

The garage was hidden from the street by a fifteen-foot privet hedge and was designed to resemble an English countryside stable—but instead of gravel, mud, and straw, the flooring was of precisely laid herringbone-patterned brick.

Early Twentieth Century, Lark had dubbed the interior of Stack House when he first saw it—20th Century-Fox. It looked as if old man Stack had brought in Cecil B. DeMille or some other Hollywood dinosaur to furnish the place. Jason had tried to lighten it up, bring in some color, some life, but Conrad Stack would have none of it.

The mail was bundled neatly on a Regency-period mahogany table. Lark glanced over his shoulder to make sure the butler was out of sight, then quickly thumbed through the mail, hoping to find something addressed to Duran. He was disappointed. It was all for Anona. One envelope caught his interest. The return address was for the Gerhow Gallery in Zurich, Switzerland, perhaps the most famous and influential gallery in the world. He slipped the envelope in his coat pocket, then strolled into the living room and was pleasantly surprised at the changes. The dark coffered ceiling was now pale yellow and backlit under frosted glass. The walnut paneling was painted a light beige. The massive carved-oak furniture was gone, supplanted by a hodgepodge of brightly upholstered chairs and couches.

The fifteenth-century tapestries were gone, too, replaced by one of Anona's paintings.

"I'll take your bags to your room, sir," George said in his clipped baritone. "You're on the third floor. You may remember the guest room."

Lark's jaw flexed. Old George reminding him of the times he'd spent in the guest room during his marriage to Anona. Impertinent old prick!

"Is my son home?"

"No, sir. Master John has purchased a houseboat in Sausalito. He spends much of his time there."

"What about Lisa?"

"Not in at the moment, sir."

"You told them I was coming?"

"I did indeed, sir."

Lark slid the coat from his shoulders and tossed it over the luggage at the butler's feet. "What about Bob Duran?"

"I believe he's at his office, sir."

"Well, I'll go and see Anona." Lark edged up close to the butler. George had to be in his seventies now—tall, gaunt, a seemingly emotionless man with a thick cowl of billowy white hair. He had been in the Stack family's employ since before Anona had been born. Lark and George had taken an immediate dislike to one another. Lark had tried to persuade Anona to fire George several times, but she wouldn't hear of it.

"You don't mind if I visit with Anona, do you, George? I remember the way to her room."

"I'm afraid she's not receiving anyone at the moment, sir. She's taking her afternoon nap."

"Still getting her beauty rest, is she?" Lark said with some nostalgia. Almost every day of their short, tumultuous marriage, she'd found time to take a catnap. "All right, George. Bring the bags to my room, and let me know when John or Lisa arrive."

Chapter 5

"You look exhausted," Peggy Jacquard advised Bob Duran when he came into the offices of Lost Art, Inc. "How was Santa Barbara?"

"Hectic." He walked over to the fax machine. "Any developments on the Fritzheim heist?"

"No. Nothing. Are you expecting the bad guys to give us a call?"

"It's a strong possibility." Duran took off his sports coat and hung it on a rack near his desk. He poured two cups of coffee and handed one to Peggy.

Peggy Jacquard was a sleek-figured Jamaican with jet-black, close-cropped hair. She was graceful in her movements and had a delightful singsong accent. She favored brightly colored blouses and black tailored business outfits. Today's blouse was a solid cyan blue. She had worked with Duran at the Centennial Insurance Agency and had left to join him when he opened his own office. Mocha-colored skin and coffee-brown eyes, was the way one hopeful office Romeo had described her.

"Tell me about Alan Fritzheim," she urged, settling into her chair.

"He's short, bald, and pissed off," Duran said. "He was ranting and raving the whole time."

"What about his wife? Danielle. How does she look now? Tell me all the juicy details."

Duran grinned. Peggy was a devotee of *People* magazine and supermarket tabloids. "She's blond, flashy, and likes to flirt."

"Hmmm. What's the house like?"

"Unbelievable. It looks like a beached ocean liner. All white, half of it hanging over a cliff."

"I read where it cost over thirty million dollars," Peggy disclosed.

"I wouldn't argue with the estimate. Everything was state of the art—including the security system."

"So how did the burglars get away with it?"

Duran sipped his coffee, then smacked his lips in appreciation. It was a strong French roast. And he needed a jolt of caffeine badly. "They showed up in the afternoon," he said. He went on to tell how the heist had been pulled off. "The local cops showed me the blueprints for his security system. And the price tag. Two hundred and eighty-nine thousand dollars. He's paying the housekeeper seven bucks an hour."

Peggy made a clucking sound with her tongue. "Was anything else taken?"

"Nope. Just the Van Gogh, and there are plenty of valuables throughout the house. That's why I think they'll contact either the Fritzheims or the carrier, Pacific Indemnity, who will pass them on to us."

Duran watched Peggy saunter back to her desk: the liquid movement of her hips made it look as if there was a samba playing in her mind. Maybe there was, he thought. She was currently dating a halfback who played for the Oakland Raiders.

He logged the computer on to the Art Index, a database set up by the museums, auction houses, and galleries in the United States. When a major work was stolen, it was reported to AI, which then listed it on their "missing" bulletin board, along with a description of the work, a color photograph when available, and the name of the last registered owner.

Over nine thousand works of art were listed as stolen in the last twelve months. About seven percent were recovered. The going fee for recovery was ten percent of the insured value, so it certainly gave investigators like Duran an incentive to go looking for them.

The problem was that there was nothing close to the Art Index for Europe, Asia, or South America, where most of the stolen items eventually ended up.

Duran scanned the latest items listed on the bulletin board. At least a dozen new ones since yesterday, but there was no mention of the painting stolen from Alan Fritzheim. The insurance company was holding off for ten days. If the thieves didn't contact them by that time, the information would go on line.

Jason Lark showered and changed clothes. George had left his luggage on the bed. Lark remembered the wretched bed, and the room with its pot-bellied, bow-legged French Provincial pieces. The print on the wall was of Van Gogh's "The Night Cafe." It made him think of the original Van Gogh from Alan Fritzheim's collection, "Sun and Sky," the one he had helped Mario Drago's man scan, photograph, and, when the forgery was complete, switch. The one that was causing him so much trouble.

"Goddamn thieves," he murmured under his breath. He unsnapped his suitcase and began hanging up his garments. He remembered the letter from the Gerhow Gallery to Anona he'd pilfered from the morning mail. He slipped it out of his raincoat pocket.

The envelope was creamy white, heavy cotton. He slit it open with his fingernail. He glanced at the first paragraph, then began reading carefully.

Dear Madame Stack:
We have been hired by the Bank of Zurich to catalog and evaluate the paintings and sculptures of the estate of Claude Bresson.

One of your paintings, "Perfume Fields," is among the items in question. There seems to be no bill of sale, or mention of payment in the personal records of Mr. Bresson, other than a handwritten diary notation—showing the date and the words "A gift."

There is a further notation in Mr. Bresson's diary—the same date—" 'Cinq Putains.' Pablo's Paris studio, and my sketches of Chateau Bresson to Anona."

We would appreciate it if you could enlighten us as to whether or not "Perfume Fields" was given by you to Mr. Bresson, and your estimate of its approximate value at that time.

In addition, would you please clarify whether or not Mr. Bresson presented Monsieur Picasso's "Cinq Putains" and studio sketches to you.

Our research shows that Mr. Bresson obtained these sketches from the artist, Pablo Picasso, in approximately 1925.

Your earliest attention to these requests would be appreciated.

Very truly yours,
R. G. Gerhow III

Lark groaned and flopped down on the bed. Claude Bresson! He vaguely recalled Bresson having given him a packet of sketches for Anona. He remembered the ones he'd seen were amateur drawings of the chateau. There had been others, but he hadn't bothered to look at the damn things. What was it that Bresson had said to him? Something about the sketches being some of his early works and those of a friend. Friend! Pablo Picasso! "Cinq Putains."

Lark's knowledge of French wasn't extensive, but he knew that *cinq* was five and *putains* was slang for whores. Five whores. Picasso was a known whoremonger in his youth. He pounded his bunched fists into the mattress. Why hadn't he looked at all the drawings? He could have easily kept them. What the hell had become of them? What would five Picassos, Picassos that had no doubt never been on the market, be worth now?

He went to the bathroom, ran a comb through his hair, sprinkled on some aftershave, then took the stairs to the second floor. To Anona's room. The hell with asking George's permission to see his ex-wife. He eased the door open a crack. He could see her silhouette on the bed.

"Anona," he whispered, then entered the room and silently closed the door behind him.

A large-screen TV was situated in front of her bed. The sound was off, the screen showing an old movie. Lark recognized the figure of a young John Wayne on horseback.

He crept around to the side of the bed, his eyes surveying the walls. One of Anona's paintings hung over the bed. The rest of the walls were bare, except for several mirrors.

The brass four-poster bed was tented, with a half dozen silk-covered orange pillows scattered on it. He remembered the bed well, and the pillows. They had been pale blue when they were married. Or was it yellow? The figure on the bed was wearing jeans and a white cashmere sweater. Anona's golden hair was splashed across one of the pillows.

He was about to whisper her name when something dark darted at his feet and began barking and biting at his shoe. He kicked out at the small dog. "Get away, get away, damn it!"

Anona's eyes popped open. When she saw Lark, she frowned. "Andamo, no! Come, Andamo, come!"

The black-and-tan Welsh terrier backed away slowly from Lark, his teeth bared. Anona patted the bedspread. "Here, Andamo, come."

The dog leaped onto the bed, his teeth still bared.

"When did you get that goddamn killer?" Lark swore, stooping down to look at the teeth marks in his Allen Edmonds loafers. "These shoes cost three hundred bucks!"

"Well, you shouldn't just barge in like that, Jason." She stroked Andamo behind the ears. "George told me you might be stopping by." Her eyes narrowed to slits. "You look as handsome as ever. I've lost track. Are you still married?"

"No. I'm single again. Ilsa left me months ago."

"Ilsa? Was she the blonde or the brunette?"

"It depends on your vantage point," Lark disclosed.

Anona laughed lightly. "Have you seen the children?"

"No. I just got in."

Lark looked up at the painting over the bed. "I've been thinking about you a lot, lately. About us. Remember when we were in France? The Riviera. Claude Bresson's magnificent chateau."

"What I remember is you casino crawling and chasing all those naked girls on the beach."

"I acted stupidly, I know. I never really thanked Bresson. He died recently, didn't he?"

Anona swung her legs over the bed and stood up.

The dog jumped down and took a position right beside her. "Yes. Poor Claude. I didn't find out about it until days after his death. I would have liked to have attended the services."

"I remember you giving Bresson a painting. What was it called? 'Perfume Fields'? Something like that. And he gave me some sketches for you. Remember?"

Anona shook her head slowly. "I remember the painting—those beautiful fields of flowers. But sketches from Claude? No. What were they like?"

"They were of the chateau and some young women. Bresson did them himself. Don't you remember seeing them? I must have given them to you, or I may have put them in our luggage."

Anona pushed the sleeve of her sweater back and checked her watch. "No, I don't remember anything like that. But if Claude gave them to me, then they must be around somewhere. I wouldn't have gotten rid of them. He was such a wonderful man. So what is it you want this time, Jason? More money?"

"No, no," Lark assured her. "I'm doing great. I may have a job over in Tiburon. A big new house. I just thought it would be nice to see the children." He gave her a wide smile. "And you. It's time to let bygones be bygones, don't you think?"

Anona looked Lark right in the eyes. "Three days, Jason. You can stay three days. But if I hear that you're pestering the children for money, I'll boot you out of here."

"Don't worry," Lark protested. "I'm flush. I just want to be . . . more of a father, I guess. I thought all you Irish Catholics believed in redemption."

"Oh, we do, Jason. We also believe in the devil."

Lark bowed his head solemnly, said "*Mea culpa*" and made an exaggerated sign of the cross across his chest with his forefinger. "How is John? The last time I talked to him, he was thinking of opening some kind of club."

"Yes. One of those places with bad food and loud music, I'm afraid."

Lark lowered himself onto the bed, bouncing up and down slowly on the foam mattress. "I don't know if that's such a good idea at his age, maybe—"

"Don't start trying to act like a father at this late stage," she cut in icily.

Lark held up his hands in a gesture of surrender. "You're right, you're right. What about Lisa? How's she doing?"

Anona strode to her dresser and picked up a hairbrush. The dog dropped to the carpet, resting his head on her bare feet.

"She's fine. She has a new boyfriend every few months, but no one she's serious about." Anona paused to look at herself in the mirror. "At least that I know of."

"God. She's what? Your age, when we were married."

Anona swiveled to face Lark. "Yes. And I certainly don't want her making the same kind of mistake."

"Me either. How about Bob? Is he tracking down lost treasures?"

"Yes, and quite successfully."

"I'll bet. Is Hugh Stringer still the family attorney?"

Anona tapped the hairbrush against her thigh, causing the dog to jump up to try and snatch the brush from her hand. "Why all the questions? What are you up to, Jason?"

"Nothing. Just curious, that's all. I remember old 'Uncle Hugh' hanging around all the time."

"Hugh is still my attorney. Do you need legal advice?"

"No." He laughed. "Though I could have used help when Ilsa divorced me. What do you say we get together for dinner tonight? You, Bob, and me. My treat. You pick the spot."

Anona turned her attention back to the mirror and began stroking her hair with the brush. "You haven't got much time, Jason. Perhaps you should concentrate on your children."

Chapter 6

Duran carried the tray with the iced cocktail shaker and the crystal glasses into the bedroom. He could hear the shower running.

Andamo greeted him with a wagging tail and flurry of barking.

He set the tray down on the nightstand, dribbled the iced Ketel One vodka into the glasses, added a lemon twist, then edged open the bathroom door with his shoulder just as Anona turned the water off.

Andamo yelped and tried to sneak in, but he nudged him back into the bedroom with his foot, then closed the door behind him.

Anona's long arm snaked out from behind the frosted-glass shower door, groping for a towel.

She blotted her face and smiled. "Hi, handsome, how was your trip?"

"Not bad." Duran filled his wife in on the details of the Fritzheims' robbery as she dried herself off. "I've got a hunch the thieves will be calling Pacific Indemnity to unload the Van Gogh."

"Bastards," she hissed, then wrapped a towel around her waist and blew him a kiss when he handed her a martini.

They toasted each other, saying *"Siempre"* in unison. She took a long sip, then said, "Bless you, kind sir. I needed that."

Duran perched on the edge of the toilet while Anona used another towel to wipe the steam from the cabinet mirror. He watched the sway of her breasts as she moved the towel from side to side. The outline of the bikini she'd worn in Jamaica was visible on her light-golden skin. "George tells me that Jason Lark is here."

"Yes. I gave him a time limit. Three days. He says he just wants to visit with the children." She took another sip of the martini. "Though he asked about you, and Hugh Stringer. And he invited you and me out to dinner tonight."

The thought of dinner with Jason Lark caused Duran to gulp down half of his drink. "You declined, I hope."

"Yes. Unfortunately we can't very well kick him out, love. He is their father. He looks disgustingly well. I bet he had his face tightened with a little surgery." She reached for Duran's arm. "I'm sorry he showed up. I know Lisa's never forgiven him for the way he's neglected her all these years. He's unscrupulous. And Johnny's vulnerable. So vulnerable."

"Don't worry about Jason. I'll handle him," Duran promised. "Now, tell me about your day."

Her face lit up. "Oh, it went quite well. I think I'll get three, maybe four paintings out of it. I love it there at the cemetery in the early morning. The fog spreads like mercury though the tombstones. Then the flowers come to life when the sun breaks through."

Duran dipped his head to her neck, running his tongue across her shoulders, his hand groping for the shower faucet. "You missed a spot. Hop back in. I'll get it for you."

Anona undid the towel knot, then her hands began unbuttoning his shirt. "Did anyone ever tell you that you have sexy blue eyes?"

George informed Duran that, "Mr. Lark is in the game room."

The game room had both a regulation-size billiard table and a pool table. A rectangular-shaped Tiffany lamp hung over each table, and above the circular oak table, where Conrad Stack and his cronies reportedly had indulged in high-stakes poker marathons. The walls were paneled with thick French walnut, the floor covered by overlapping three-hundred-year-old Bahkshayesh Oriental rugs.

Lark was leaning over the pool table, lining up the cue ball on the three ball when he heard Duran's footsteps.

He waved the cue stick in Duran's direction. "Hello, Bob. Long time no see."

Duran nodded, making an effort to disguise his feelings toward Lark. Lark was an imposingly handsome man, with a narrow-shouldered body, a movie-star face, and silver hair worn long and winged at the sides. He was wearing a brass-buttoned blue blazer and gray cashmere turtleneck sweater. His twill slacks were creased saber-sharp.

Lark extended a hand and Duran grasped it by the fingers and gave an extra hard squeeze, taking satisfaction in knowing that it was the same hand that Lark had struck Anona with.

"What are you doing here, Jason?"

"I have some business in town. I thought I'd stop by and see the kids."

"How long is your business going to take?"

"Oh, just a couple of days. Johnny's coming over

and we're going out to dinner," Lark said, turning back to his shot. The cue ball hit the red ball, then banked off the cushion, and rolled into the corner pocket.

"I never was any good at this," Lark confessed with a frown. "John tells me he's opened a nightclub. Have you seen the place?"

"No. Not yet." Duran knew that Anona had been the prime backer of the project, but John had made it clear that Duran would not be welcomed. Duran had never gotten as close to Johnny as he would have liked. The boy was already spoiled rotten when Duran married Anona. Bright, good looking, and headstrong. There was no way that Duran could have disciplined a sixteen-year-old who had his own Harley-Davidson motorcycle and an allowance of several hundred dollars a month. Duran had tried to form a bond: fishing trips, golf lessons, Forty-Niner football, and Giants baseball games. But John wasn't interested. When he got kicked out of Stanford, Anona came down hard on him, cutting back on his allowance, taking away his car for a time. John had blamed Duran for those decisions.

Lark racked his cue stick, picked up the eight ball and rolled it slowly down the green felt. "Look, I know you don't think much of me, and . . . well, there were times when I didn't think much of myself," he admitted genially. "But, I'm still fond of Anona and though I know I've had a funny way of showing it, I love my kids. But, if you want me out of here, I can understand that. I—"

"You can stay for a couple of days," Duran proposed, knowing that Lark would put on a martyr scene if he was asked to leave now. "Have you seen Lisa yet?"

"No. She hasn't been home since I got here." Lark pointed to the fully stocked bar on the far side of the room. "Have a drink with me?"

"No thanks."

Lark selected a bottle of Glenfiddich thirty-year-old Scotch malt whiskey and dribbled an ounce or two into a cut-crystal goblet. His eyes circled the room. "Did Old Man Stack ever get you in here and give you the third degree?"

"No, he chose the wine cellar for that session."

Lark barked out a laugh. He pointed to the poker table. "He sat me down right there and put me through the wringer. He was a tough old bastard. But he was right. That time. How's business, Bob? Still an art gumshoe?"

"Still working at it," Duran confirmed. "How about you? How are things in the interior-decorating world?"

"It's a living. Nothing exciting, like what you're doing. I was wondering if—"

"Hey, Jason." John Stack entered the room with a swagger. Duran noticed that whenever he'd seen John or Lisa with Lark they'd call him by his first name. Never Father, Dad, or Pop.

John was twenty-three now, with reddish-brown hair worn earlobe length. His mustache, all of six months old, was slightly darker than his hair.

Hc slapped his father on the shoulder. John was wearing blue jeans and a black shirt with a silk-screened Grateful Dead caricature across the chest. "Good to see you. Come on, let's get out of here. I want to show you my club."

"Sure, John. I was just having a drink. Join me."

Johnny gave Duran a strained look. "No. Let's go."

Duran said, "Your mother's upstairs. I'm sure she'd like to see you."

"Yeah, well I'll look in on her later. Come on, Jason. Let's go."

Lark gave Duran an exaggerated shrug, took a long sip of the whisky, then slipped his arm around his son's shoulders.

Duran watched and wondered what that little scene had been all about. Jason Lark was acting like a long-lost sheep ready to come back to the fold. The rich fold of Stack House.

From what Anona had told Duran, Lark was less than happy with the annulment settlement her father had reluctantly bestowed upon him. Lark thought that he was worth more than what Conrad Stack was offering, but Stack was a persuasive man. Lark had given in to all of Conrad's demands, including that of legally changing the children's name to Stack.

Conrad Stack had offered Duran a settlement, too. Before their wedding.

Every detail of that meeting was still vivid in Duran's mind. Conrad Stack had invited Duran for a "man-to-man" dinner at Stack House in Conrad's favorite room, the wine cellar, a vast, brick-floored vault catacombed with long racks of expensive, dust-coated wine bottles. Conrad Stack was a heavy-shouldered man, with shovellike hands. He had worn a formal business suit and somber tie in contrast to Duran's casual slacks and sports coat.

Stack was a meat-and-potatoes man with a complexion that rivaled the prime rib they dined on. It had been an elaborate, but tension-filled meal, Stack snobbishly explaining the vintages of the wines that accompanied each course of their meal.

When they'd finished dinner, Stack lit up a long

Cuban cigar, smiled at Duran through the smoke, then pulled an envelope-sized leather notepad from his well-tailored suit coat. "I made a terrible mistake by not doing a better job of checking out that bastard Jason Lark. I'm not going to make the same mistake with you." He locked his eyes onto Duran's. "Do you object?"

"Damn right, I do. But I don't suppose that makes much difference to you."

Stack snapped open the notebook. "Robert Duran. Born in Otay, just south of San Diego. Father, Mexican, born in Tijuana. Mother, Danish, born in Copenhagen. Father a salesman for a paper goods company. Mother worked in a . . . ah, bakery. Mother deceased. Father? Unknown. Just sort of disappeared, did he?"

"Yes. He had a habit of doing that. One day he took off on a business trip and never came back."

"You did make it to college, for a short time. A city college down there, wasn't it?"

Stack pronounced "down there" as if it were some terrible disease.

"Yes."

"But you didn't graduate, did you?"

"No."

"Why not? Your grades weren't all that bad," Stack conceded.

"I was restless. Uncle Sam called. I listened."

Stack drew deeply on his cigar, fanning the smoke away with the back of his hand. "Restless. Did it have anything to do with your being arrested?"

"Yes. It did. I got into a fight with a man. I hit him a little too hard and I ended up in jail for a few months. When I got out, I joined the army."

Stack smiled knowingly. "You seem to have been

quite restless, Robert. There was more than just the one fight. Is that how you acquired that scar?"

"I grew up in a barrio, Mr. Stack. Near the border. I was a half-breed to most of the kids. The Mexicans didn't like the blue eyes, the whites thought I was an uppity Latino. If you didn't fight, you didn't survive. If your investigator did his job thoroughly, then you know that my mother committed suicide. She was very beautiful, and didn't speak either English or Spanish very well. Most of her time was spent waiting for my father to come home from his sales trips. He'd be gone for weeks at a time, then finally he just never came back. I suppose that's when she decided to kill herself. With his shotgun. I was seventeen years old. I found her in the bathtub, a plastic laundry bag around her head and the shotgun." He paused a long moment. "My mother was always very neat. Even in death."

Conrad Stack flicked the pages of his notepad. "United States Army. Fairly distinguished record. You were in for six years. Then you went to work as an insurance investigator. What pointed you in that direction?"

"The army. I spent some time in the Intelligence Division. I liked the work, so when I was discharged it seemed a natural choice."

Stack made a noncommittal humming noise. "Then you were married in New York. Your wife's name was Teresa, wasn't it?"

"Yes."

"And she died quite unexpectedly."

"An aneurism. There was no warning. She just felt ill one day, complained of a terrible headache. I took her to the hospital and she died shortly after we got there."

Conrad Stack slid the notepad back into his suit pocket. "I'm not saying that you aren't an honest man, Robert, and in many ways I admire your grit. Your work record at the insurance company is quite good. However, I don't think that you are the right person for Anona."

"You're wrong," Duran replied bluntly.

Stack worked the cigar thoughtfully from one side of his mouth to the other. "Let's get down to business. How much?"

"I'm not marrying Anona for her money, or your money," Duran declared, knowing that the statement, true as it was, sounded trite.

"Then you won't mind if there's a prenuptial agreement?"

"Not at all. You have the document drawn up, and I'll sign it."

Stack dug out his notebook once again. He thumbed though the pages. "You have a few dollars put away. Close to sixty thousand dollars. I'll double that amount. In cash. It's my one and only offer."

"Keep your money," Duran advised him, annoyed that Stack knew his financial worth. He leaned forward. "Anona was a very young girl when she married Jason Lark. But she's a woman now. A strong woman, a mind of her own. Don't try to make me into something I'm not. I'm thinking of leaving the Centennial Insurance Company and starting my own business."

"Are you really?" Conrad Stack scoffed. "Starting your own business. Your business will be squandering my daughter's money."

Duran stood up, the legs of his chair making a screeching noise on the brick floor. "I love Anona, and I'm going to marry her. Get used to it, Mr. Stack. It's as simple as that."

Conrad Stack stared at Duran a long time, then pushed his chair away from the table and stalked out of the room without saying a word. Duran had made his way out of the mansion on his own, deciding not to mention her father's offer to Anona. Two months later Duran and Anona flew to Mexico and were married. Three months after that, Conrad Stack died from a stroke.

Chapter 7

Seven quarters, fourteen dimes, and more nickels and pennies than he bothered to count. All scattered across the base of the modest old tombstone, as if it were some kind of wishing well. The worn inscription read: WYATT EARP 1848–1929.

He wondered how the notorious lawman had ended up with his bones interred in a graveyard in Colma, California. A famous man like Earp, with nothing more to show for his life than a cheap cement slab.

He knelt down and picked up one of the quarters. "For luck, Wyatt. Just for luck."

He stood, pocketing the quarter, and hitched up his pants. The air smelled of freshly cut grass. A soot-colored sky blanketed the horizon. He tilted his hat and hummed a tuneless song as he strolled toward the spot Anona Stack had picked for her work, a narrow dirt road at the far east end of the cemetery.

She had parked her Land Rover under a stand of cypress trees, their long branches spreading out like interlocking hands. She used the car's hood as a drafting board, leaning across the fender, her dog at her side.

The dog could be a problem. He never did like dogs. He unconsciously looked at his right hand, his painting hand, thinking back to the day a dog had bitten him. The mate sharp teeth had broken the skin. He'd needed seven stitches and was unable to paint for almost a month. The dog was a mongrel, who had easily slipped through the broken pickets of her owner's fence. When his wound had healed, he'd gone back to the house at night. He wore gloves for that occasion. Thick canvas construction worker's gloves that reached to his elbows. He'd lured the bitch through the fence with some hamburger meat, then strangled it.

Anona Stack's dog was a small terrier. Smaller than the mongrel. Off the leash, the animal roamed amongst the cypress, but never strayed farther than twenty or thirty yards from his mistress. Once it had meandered over to a row of cross-shaped headstones, but she'd scolded him, calling out his name: "Andamo, come," and the dog had scurried back to her side.

He discounted the possibility of Anona recognizing him. He'd worn a beard and his hair had been shoulder length when she had testified against he and Arlene. He was clean shaven now, his hair short, slowly growing out from the prison buzz cut.

He tugged the misshapen straw hat down on his forehead as he approached the Land Rover. He'd been careful to dress in the same manner as the cemetery gardeners with a hat, faded jeans, and a soiled field jacket.

The dog spotted him first and gave a low growl.

He unconsciously slipped his right hand under his armpit, as Anona Stack turned toward him. She was dressed pretty much as she had been yesterday: khaki pants, a men's style button-down light blue shirt under an olive-colored fisherman's vest. Her cap was tan, a long-billed fisherman's cap that reminded him of the type he'd seen in photographs of Ernest Hemingway. Her suede desert boots looked brand new.

"Morning, ma'am," he greeted her warmly, putting a slight southern drawl on his words.

"Good morning," she replied with a smile. "There's no problem, is there? I told the cemetery manager I'd be here a few days."

"No problem, ma'am." He bent down, again sliding his right hand under his armpit, holding his left hand, palm up, toward the dog. "Well maybe a little problem. Someone complained about your dog here. There's some rule about domestic animals not being allowed on the grounds."

The terrier gave a low growl and Anona leaned down and ruffled his fur. "Andamo. Heel."

He straightened up and peered at the sketching paper spread across the Rover's hood. Even in just color pencil, the drawings were unmistakably Anona Stack's—organic, a raw blend of Abstract Expressionism with amorphus shaping of nature: trees, flowers, and sky. She was wonderful with colors. He and Arlene had found her style difficult to duplicate.

"It looks like you're doing something real pretty."

"Thank you," Anona said with resignation. "What if I just left Andamo in the car? Would that be all right. I'll be gone by noon."

"I'm sure that's fine, ma'am. For today. As far as I'm concerned he could have the run of the place. But you know how people are nowadays. You plannin' on coming back tomorrow?"

"Yes. I'll be here at least two more days."

He smiled in relief. Two more days. One was all he needed. "Well, maybe tomorrow you best leave him home."

Anona snatched the terrier up in her arms. "Andamo, it's time for one of your naps anyway." She rolled down the passenger-side window of the car for air, dropped the dog on the leather bucket seat, then gave him a final pat.

He tipped his hat to her. "Sorry for the trouble, ma'am. Hope to see you tomorrow."

Anona used one of her pencils to point toward a group of small gray stone buildings. "See that one on the end? The larger one. That's my family mausoleum. I noticed there are a lot of weeds cropping up. Could you cut them down? I'll be happy to pay you for your time, and—"

He smiled at her, his lips riding up over his teeth and gums. "I'll attend to it personally. Can't get to it 'till tomorrow, but you've got my word I'll clean it up real good. See you tomorrow."

He turned on his heel and sauntered away, taking the quarter he'd removed from Wyatt Earp's grave from his pants pocket. The Stack family mausoleum. Within walking distance of where he planned to take her. He flipped the quarter in the air, like a character in an old gangster movie. Tomorrow. October sixth. That would give her six full days in the SHU. Not as long as he'd hoped for, but enough—especially when she realized she was never going to get out alive. "Wyatt," he said out loud, "it turned out lucky."

Jason Lark had waited until Anona had driven off and Bob Duran had left for work, then used the phone in the library to call the Gerhow gallery in Switzerland. He decided to use Hugh Stringer's name.

He was put through to R. G. Gerhow III almost immediately after identifying himself as Anona Stack's attorney.

"We received your letter yesterday, Mr. Gerhow.

My client does recall giving her 'Perfume Fields' painting to Mr. Bresson. It was purely a gift."

"I understand, monsieur. It was very generous of her."

"Quite," Lark concurred. "I am afraid there is some confusion regarding the Picasso sketches. Anona remembers Claude Bresson giving her some sketches—but they were ones he himself had done. Of the chateau."

Lark could hear the shuffling of papers over the long-distance line.

"Claude's records show that in addition to his drawings, there were the Picasso sketches, six of them, one of his old flat in Paris, the other of five women: *putains*," Gerhow said with a polite chuckle.

"I assume these would be quite valuable."

"Monsieur, I know that Mrs. Stack's canvas is worth a great deal now, but the Picassos, ah, these would be special. Very special."

"How so?" queried Lark.

"Two of Monsieur Bresson's nephews, as well as several friends had seen the Picassos. They are unique in that they are signed *in verto,* on the back—just the initials—P.R. P., for Pablo Ruiz y Picasso, but there is the name of each of the young ladies there also, and, according to the those who have seen them. . . . a toast to the earnestness in which they performed their duties."

Lark involuntarily sat up straight and squared his shoulders. Five unknown Picassos with a ribald history!

Gerhow seemed to be reading Lark's mind from the distance of over six thousand miles. "It is almost impossible to estimate the monetary worth of these sketches, Monsieur Stringer. The originals, as well as the value of the reproductions."

"I'm an attorney, not an art dealer, Mr. Gerhow. If I suddenly walked into your gallery now with the Picassos, what would you give me?"

"First, a heartfelt thanks, then, oh, something like twenty million dollars, Monsieur Stringer." Gerhow paused. "Do you think that such an event is possible?"

"I wish it was, but as I say, Mrs. Stack has no recollection of the sketches."

"Perhaps if I spoke to her?"

"I couldn't allow that right now," warned Lark. "She is ill. Nothing serious we hope. Perhaps in a week or so, I'll discuss this with her again, and then I'll get back to you."

"A speedy recovery for Madame Stack, monsieur. Please do everything you can to locatc those sketches. Your cooperation will be greatly rewarded, I assure you."

Lark bid Gerhow good-bye, then leaned back in the chair.

The Picassos. He remembered throwing the packet that Claude Bresson had given him into Anona's huge Vuitton traveling trunk. He decided to search the basement first—the storage area adjacent to the wine cellar.

There he found a jumble of lawn furniture, old toys he remembered as belonging to Johnny and Lisa—a wooden rocking horse, a white doll's house that Lisa had played with hour after hour, golf clubs, tennis rackets, fishing equipment, all neatly lined up against the brick walls. Sealed cardboard boxes reached to the ceiling, and luggage—mounds of luggage. Lark dug his way through the pile until he found the Vuitton trunk. He ran his hand across the distinctive patterned fabric and the brass hardware, then unsnapped the locks and began digging through the drawers. Empty. All of them empty.

He stood back and dusted his hands off. He hadn't really expected the Picasso sketches to be there, but it was an obvious starting place.

Anona certainly would have recognized anything by Picasso. He had questioned her again late last night after he returned from dinner with John. He was sure now that she'd never seen the Picassos. Could they have been discarded? No. Anona was certain that she would have never gotten rid of a gift from "wonderful old Claude."

He wondered about Duran. Did he know anything of the Picassos? Lark doubted it. If Duran knew of them, then so would Anona. He'd have to find them. Find them fast.

So where were they? Stuck in some bureau drawer in the house? At the bottom of a pile of magazines in some cupboard? They had to be here somewhere.

"Is there something I can help you with, sir?"

Lark whirled around, almost losing his balance. "Oh, George. It's you. No, I'm just . . . chasing memories."

The butler nodded solemnly and did an abrupt about-face.

Lark waited until George was safely out of sight, then took a closer look at the cardboard boxes. Most were neatly labeled: XMAS LIGHTS. XMAS ORNAMENTS. TAX RECORDS. SILVERWARE. CHINA SETTINGS. There were at least a dozen with no labels. It would take time to go through them. Time when George wasn't around peeking over his shoulder.

The Picassos could be his salvation. He'd leave California, leave the States, maybe go back to the South of France. In style. Far away from Mario Drago. But there was still Duran to consider. Drago was right about Duran. He'd start digging into the Fritzheim job, and it would only be a matter of time before the trail led right to the doorstep of Lark's interior-decorating shop. The Picassos wouldn't do him any good in jail. He'd have to take care of Duran, get rid of him, then find the Picassos.

Chapter 8

Peggy Jacquard stuck her head into Duran's office. "Telephone. It's Harry Lawson."

"Lawson." Duran gave a curt laugh. "It looks like we're in business." He picked up the phone. "Good afternoon, counselor."

"Robert. Good to talk to you again." The attorney's voice was smooth and oily. "I had a call this morning. The caller was quite cryptic. He mentioned that he had come into possession of a painting. A rather valuable painting, he thought."

Duran reached out gratefully for the cup of coffee in Peggy's hand. "Let me take a wild guess. A Vincent Van Gogh. 'Sun and Sky.' "

"That's an excellent guess," Lawson admitted. "My impression was that the gentleman was thinking of shopping the item around."

"And what did you advise him to do, counselor?"

"My advice was that if the item was obtained illegally, that it should be returned to its proper owner or turned over to the police."

"I bet that went over real big with your client, Harry."

"The gentleman is not my client. Yet. However, if in fact he does contact me again, what do you suggest

I do, Robert? I'm told that you are handling the Fritzheim incident."

"You're well informed."

"The newspapers reported that Pacific Indemnity is the carrier. Pacific confirmed that you've been hired to get the painting back. And that's a very wise choice on their part, if I may say so. We've been able to solve these problems together in the past."

Duran was tiring of the verbal sparring. Harry Lawson was a criminal attorney who was known in the trade as the "Holy Redeemer." He was the connection between the thieves and the insurance companies. Neither Duran nor anyone else could ever prove that Lawson was directly involved in any of the thefts.

"I think you should do what you usually do, Harry. Tell the crooked bastards that we're ready to deal and take your cut."

"My, my. You're a little testy today, Robert. Wrong side of the bed?"

Duran took a deep breath and sighed. He wasn't in much of a position to give Harry Lawson a "holier-than-thou" speech. They both dealt with the same clientele. "Sorry, Harry. If the gentleman calls again, tell him I am interested."

"Yes, I'll do exactly that, Robert. The usual conditions?"

"Yes, I think that can be arranged." The usual conditions were that the payment would be in cash and that once the painting was safely returned, the owner would advise the police that he would not press charges.

"This may take a couple of days, Robert. Give my love to Peggy and your wife," Lawson urged before hanging up.

Duran dropped the phone on its cradle and turned

to see Peggy's smiling eyes. "Lawson says to give you his love."

"I know what his idea of love is. A room-service dinner in his hotel suite. I'd rather he tempted me with a percentage of his profits. What do you think he makes on these deals?"

"A bundle, Peg."

"I wonder how Harry's clients knew the Van Gogh was hanging on Fritzheim's bedroom wall? You think he or his wife were splashing the word around?"

"Probably. That's Hollywood. Run a Nexis check on the Fritzheims and their purchase of the Van Gogh. Let's see how much press it did get. Who do you think we should use to authenticate 'Sun and Sky'?"

"How about Wendy Lange?"

"Good idea," Duran agreed. There were at least a dozen experts in the Los Angeles area that he had used on a random basis. He never used the same one too often, in fear that the thieves would anticipate his selection. Lange's reputation was as good as anyone's in the field. It had been at least a year since he'd done business with her.

He clicked the computer over to his address list and dialed Lange's number.

"Wendy, it's Bob Duran. How's your schedule for the next couple of days? I've got an item I may want you to look at."

"It depends. What's up?"

"The Fritzheim Van Gogh."

Lange's voice rose appreciably. "I'm definitely available for that, Bob. When and where?"

"I just heard from Harry Lawson. He was not very specific, just mentioned that he's heard from the thieves and they want to deal. Sometime in the next few days, I would think."

Lange laughed lightly. "Good old Harry. 'The Holy Redeemer' strikes again."

"Yes. I haven't advised the insurance company yet. Give me a price for the authentication."

Lange paused. A Van Gogh would be a real feather in her cap. She'd almost do it for free. Almost. "Ten thousand, Bob."

"That sounds fair to me. I'll talk to Pacific Indemnity and fax you a confirmation. I'd like to have Lawson bring the painting directly to your place."

"That's fine with me. I'm anxious to get my hands on 'Sun and Sky'."

"So is Alan Fritzheim," Duran assured her.

"Hey, where you been, buddy?" the tall black man in the long overcoat asked.

"Out working, Justice. Open up."

Justice yanked the gated entrance to the hotel open. "You being good, buddy?" he said over the screech of the un-oiled hinges. "I told the probation officer you were. Don't make a liar out of me." He smiled, showing a keyboard of over-sized teeth.

He halted halfway through the door. "The probation officer was by today?"

Justice bobbed his head in confirmation. "Left about half an hour ago. I told him you was in and out. Probably having dinner 'round the corner."

He dug his hand into his pants pocket and came out with a loose pile of bills, selected a twenty and dropped it in the black man's palm. "Thanks, I appreciate that."

The accordion-wire gate squealed as Justice pushed it shut. "You should, buddy. I could get in trouble, you know." He flashed his teeth again. "Hardly worth it for a lousy twenty bucks."

"There'll be more tomorrow," he promised, then turned away and walked to the check-in desk, rapping his knuckles on the grimy countertop.

The manager, a short, dark, angry-faced man in his fifties shuffled into sight.

"What do you want?" he demanded.

"Mail. Any mail for me? Room 704."

The manager turned to look at the pigeonhole boxes, then shook his head in disgust. "No!" he shouted, then hobbled away.

He was hoping for a letter from Ken Firpo. Firpo had said he'd write. He took the stairs, two at a time up to the seventh floor, wondering how Firpo was doing. If he had a new cellmate.

The foul odor in the stairwell was only slightly better than that of the elevator. Rancid food, urine, with cigar and cigarette butts ground into the threadbare carpets.

His breathing was normal when he reached the seventh floor. That was one thing he could credit Pelican Bay for. He was in excellent physical shape. He used his key and entered his room.

Just barely better than a cell. Uneven wood floors. A lopsided, unfinished pine dresser, a single bed. But it had a window. With a view. He dragged a chair over to the window and pushed the thin, tattered curtains aside.

The small, dark figures on the street below were up to their usual tricks. The drug dealers boldly waving cars to the curb, negotiating their fees, then casually bumping into the fast-moving pedestrians who passed them the dope, which was in turn given to the customer, who quickly slipped the tiny cellophane bag into their mouths, ready to swallow it whole should the seller turn out to be a narc, or if an undercover cop suddenly loomed up from an inky doorway.

He recognized several of the garishly dressed, slack-mouthed whores—some of whom took their johns to the Excelsior—their provocative strides hugging the curb, circling the one-way streets, always going against traffic so the desperate johns would have no trouble spotting them.

He smiled at the sight of the "crack man," a cadaver-thin junky who claimed he was a Vietnam vet and spent his waking hours walking the streets, dropping to his knees, a magnifying glass in one hand, a pair of tweezers in the other, probing at the cracks in the sidewalk, looking for a few grains of stray rock cocaine.

He watched the bizarre parade for a few minutes, then flopped down on the bed.

The cabin was better than this, but he had to follow the rules. And be patient. His probation stipulated that he had to reside at the halfway house for three months.

Patience. It was one of the most important lessons he'd learned from Firpo. He still woke up in a sweat, dreaming he was back in prison. The first four months in jail hadn't been bad. It had been almost a country-club atmosphere. Dormitories instead of cells. Tennis courts, a fully stocked library, unlimited access to art supplies. There was a fear in the beginning, the fear of sexual attack, expecting to be gang raped at any moment. He soon learned that it was the young ones, the pretty ones, who were at risk. If a man minded his own business, made his intentions known, and kept some kind of weapon with him at all times, he had little to worry about. For some the loneliness became too much and they went looking for sex, became one of the predators, or one day woke up and decided there was no sense waiting any longer and willingly joined the scene. He'd seen men who had succumbed to the pressure, the temptations, and late at night pulled lipstick and mascara from beneath their pillows and went "cruising for a train."

Everything had changed after Arlene's death, after he'd hit the guard and been transferred. The transfer to hell—the Pelican Bay State Prison. A cold, clammy hell. Just fifteen miles from the Oregon border. His first eighteen months there had seemed an eternity. Twenty-three hours alone in the SHU. Every afternoon the guards would come. Three of them. Then the handcuffs, a humiliating strip search, a short march to the cramped confines of the exercise yard and an hour alone in the fresh air, surrounded by a twenty-foot-high concrete wall. The yard floor was cement, too. There were no trees or shrubs. The few weeds that dared show through the cracks were quickly uprooted. Nothing to see except the sky, and that all too often was gray, threatening, bursting with rain clouds. He remembered a movie he'd seen as a child. *The Bird Man of Alcatraz* with Burt Lancaster. At least Lancaster had birds to talk to. To hold, to fondle. The few birds he'd seen had been high up in the sky. Free wheeling, soaring. Once in a while a flock of ducks winged by. They never got close. Even the birds were wary of Pelican Bay State Prison.

It was different once he was released from the SHU and placed in the main yard, where he was able to mix with the other prisoners. Many of them were lifers: murderers, rapists, career criminals with sentences stretching out far past their life expectancies. But he could talk, communicate, touch.

The main yard had two-man cells. His cellmate, Ken

Firpo, was a professional criminal, a man who had followed his grandfather and father into a life of crime and who had taught him how to "beat the clock." Don't count the minutes, the hours, the weeks, or the months.

The guards utilized his painting skills—first with elementary chores like painting bathrooms, the galley, then more personal jobs for their offices, canvases for their homes.

Once his forgery talents had become known to the other inmates, he'd found himself in demand. He joined the "staff," passing on his skills in return for learning new ones: lock picking, breaking and entering, survival techniques. It had been a long, grueling education, and now that he was out, it was payback time.

The pounding in his head started again. He reached into his jacket pocket, his fingers rooting around for the capsules. He quickly swallowed three of the painkillers and closed his eyes.

Patience. All those years of patience were finally going to pay off. Starting tomorrow morning.

Robert Duran was sliding his feet into running shoes when Anona came out of the bathroom and gave him a kiss.

"You're up and raring to go already," Duran said, trying to stifle a yawn.

"I want to get an early start. Maybe I can finish up today." She gave him another kiss and, as she pulled away, said, "I've got a favor to ask."

"No wonder I got so many morning kisses," Duran accused.

Anona pointed at Andamo, who, as usual, was sitting right beside her feet, his tail wagging, his upturned face focused on his mistress.

"I'm not taking him with me today."

"Why not? He's not digging up any bones at the cemetery, is he?"

"No. But one of the gardeners told me that someone complained. There's a no domestic animals rule."

"Keep him in the Rover," Duran suggested as he bent over and began tying his shoes.

"No, Bob. He'll start whining and I'll never get anything done. Why don't you take him with you on your run?"

Duran groaned. "Because if I keep him on a leash, he'll lag behind and I'll end up carrying him. If I let him run free, I might lose him." He flipped the dog over and scratched him on the stomach. "Why don't you sneak out, then I'll take off? I'll ask George to walk Andamo around the block. Then this evening we'll take him down to the Marina Green and walk the promenade out to old Fort Point."

Anona stood with her arms folded across her chest, as if debating with herself over a serious decision. "All right. I told the gardener to weed around the mausoleum. It looks like hell. Weeds growing up all around it. He's going to take care of it today. I should give him something. Have you got some cash?"

Duran grinned and dug his wallet out of the armoire. Anona was worth millions, but never had any cash on her. Maybe it was a trick her father had taught her. It seemed all the really rich people Duran knew never had any hard money on them. He had made it a point from the very beginning of their marriage not to become involved in his wife's financial dealings. He handled his business, and Anona, with the help of her attorney, Hugh Stringer, managed the Stack family fortune.

He passed her several twenty dollar bills. "Maybe we should go out to dinner tonight. That way we can avoid Jason."

She kissed him lightly on the ear, her tongue making a quick, catlike lick before retreating. "Good idea," she whispered, tip-toeing to the door. "See you later, love."

Andamo's head followed her progress. Duran kept rubbing the dog's stomach until he heard the bedroom door click shut.

Duran got to his feet while Andamo raced to the door, scratching at the wood, barking loudly, his brushlike tail beating angrily.

"You're spoiled rotten, Andamo," Duran admonished. "But then so am I, pal."

A low-lying, wall-like fog obscured the Broadway Street pedestrian-only entrance to the Presidio.

As was his practice, Duran kept to a little-used path bordered by towering groves of pine, cypress, and eucalyptus trees.

He slowed his pace as the path skirted the golf course, then picked it up again as he found himself alone on a narrow dirt trail. The air was cool and so thick with the overpowering scent of eucalyptus that it felt as though he had a cough drop in his mouth.

He didn't hear the footsteps until they were almost alongside him. Something hit him hard on the left shoulder, knocking him off balance. He swayed for a moment, then there was another blow, harder this time, and suddenly he was tumbling over a cliff, his head twisting around as he fell, trying to see who had struck him, his hands grasping at shrubs and tree branches. He came to a jarring halt in a thick patch of ferns. He slowly got to his feet. His shoulder, back, and knee were sore and the skin on his right wrist was cut and bleeding. His hands were covered with nicks and scratches.

Duran cursed, then began climbing, flopping down to his knees once he reached the trail. He heard something in the distance. It sounded like someone laughing.

Duran scrambled to his feet and began running. The laughter started again. It now sounded farther away. To his left or his right? He came to a fork in the trail, pushing his way through some low-hanging pine branches, sprinting hard for some fifty yards, then pulling up short, his hands on his hips. He made a slow traverse of the area. The only sound was his labored breathing. He kicked at a pine cone in disgust, then jogged back to Stack House.

Chapter 9

The massive solid-oak dining-room table was capable of seating up to twenty-eight people. Jason Lark recalled many occasions when the table had been filled—mostly with stuffy guests of Conrad Stack. Now he sat by himself, in front of a setting of Wedgwood dinnerware and Gorham sterling-silver cutlery. John was at his houseboat in Sausalito. Lisa was obviously avoiding him, Anona was out painting somewhere, and Duran had gone off to work.

He cut into his eggs with surgical care, watching the yolk yellow the plate. The Picassos. Could they possibly be at Anona's cottage in Monterey? She used to spend a lot of her time down there when—

"A call for you, sir." George handed Lark a cordless phone.

Lark waited until the butler had left the room before picking the instrument up.

"Yes, what now?" he asked, assuming the caller was his shop assistant, Adam Sheehan. He was wrong.

"Well?"

Mario Drago. He had managed to insert a tone of impatience, arrogance, and menace in that single word.

"Nothing positive yet," Lark said. "But I'm making progress."

"How so?" Drago pressed.

"Ah . . . it's difficult to say from this location."

"Call me within twenty-four hours, Jason. If I don't hear from you in that time, I'll assume you've failed and I'll have to make other plans."

There was a click and the dial tone began droning.

Lark's hand was trembling as he looked up to see George poised over him with a silver coffeepot in hand.

"Bad news, sir?" the butler asked stiffly.

Lark held up his half-filled coffee cup. "Just before Anona and I split up, we stayed at Claude Bresson's chateau in France. I vaguely remember Anona having done some sketches over there, but I haven't come across them. You wouldn't happen to know what happened to them, would you, George?"

The butler's reply was, "No, sir. Will you be needing anything else from the kitchen?"

Lark dismissed George with a sharp shake of his head, then squirmed in his chair and fluttered his lips. He was running out of time.

Shreds of mist spread like fine gauze across the cemetery's low rolling hills. Stratus clouds dominated the sky, blotting up the morning sun.

Anona Stack was happy with her morning's work. She missed having Andamo under foot. She'd been working steadily since daybreak, capturing the stillness and beauty that only the early dawn knows. She was thinking of gathering her material and heading for the studio when she spotted the gardener, the same one she'd seen yesterday. He was carrying a rolled-up tarp over one shoulder.

"Howdy, ma'am," he said, tipping his hat. "How are you today?"

"Oh, just fine. You didn't forget about the weeds around the mausoleum, did you?"

He dropped the tarp to the ground. "No, ma'am." He peeked over her shoulder at the sketches on the hood of the Land Rover. "I sure like what you're doin' there. You're good. My wife painted, did you know that? Real good, too. Then she had to stop."

"Oh," Anona said with some curiosity, "why did she stop painting."

A long-blade knife appeared almost magically in his right hand, while his left hand swiftly wrapped around the base of her neck.

She struggled with him, stopping when he placed the point of the knife blade in the middle of her chest.

He watched her irises widen, drilling his eyes into hers. Once he had glared at a guard like that, the hate in his eyes so intense that the guard had reacted by shooting him with a stun gun, then clubbing his ankles and knees so hard that he couldn't walk for three days.

Anona opened her mouth to scream, but only a muted gurgle came out. She felt her legs go limp as she slumped to the ground.

He kept the pressure on her neck as he followed her body down to the dirt road. The "fuck 'em hold" was the name that a serial rapist had given to the technique of applying pressure to both the right and left carotid arteries of the neck. "You got to be careful," his teacher had advised him. "You keep the pressure on too long and she'll be dead, and won't be worth fuckin'."

He had practiced the hold on Ken Firpo in their cell, Firpo getting a sexual high from coming close to passing out, close to death.

He unlocked the vehicle's back door, then loaded Anona's unconscious body into the car. His head swiveled constantly, on the lookout for a gardener or a mourner, as he ripped off pieces of duct tape and bound her hands and legs. A final strip was plastered across her mouth. Then he covered her motionless body with the tarp.

When he was satisfied that no one had seen them, he swept all of her sketching materials from the car's hood, jammed them into her black-leather portfolio, and casually tossed the materials on top of her supine body.

He took a final sweep of the area, donned a pair of cheap cotton gloves, and slid in behind the Land Rover's wheel. He swabbed the sweat from his forehead with the back of his gloved hand before switching on the ignition and smiling at himself in the rearview mirror.

Jason Lark took the elevator to the third floor, then walked down a flight of stairs to Anona and Duran's bedroom. He backed up a few steps when he saw one of the maids exit the room, vacuum cleaner in tow, pushing a cart loaded with cleaning materials.

When she had disappeared around a corner, Lark hurried toward the room. The door was unlocked. He slipped inside, closing the door behind him, leaning against it, waiting to hear the latchbolt click into place.

Lark wiggled his feet out of his loafers and padded quickly over to the door leading to the closet.

A closet wasn't the right term. It was bigger than the bedroom in his own apartment. Anona's clothes hung neatly, sectioned off by dresses, coats, then suits. Rows of shoes, neatly placed in separate cubbyholes, lined the bottom of the wall.

Duran had a section of one wall of the closet for his garments and Lark felt a pang of envy as he fingered the suits and sport coats, most tailored by London's Savile Row—names like Cundy and Parker, Henry Poole, A. J. Hewitt, Ltd.

Anona kept her lingerie and jewelry in built-in cabinets adjoining the ceiling-high, three-way mirror at the far end of the closet. He checked every drawer, resisting the temptation to palm a diamond ring or expensive watch.

There was no sign of the Picassos. He went back to the bedroom and systematically went through the nightstands and two large bureaus. The final piece of furniture was a massive oak armoire that he hadn't seen before. He opened the drawers.

More of Duran's clothes. Shelves of sweaters, underwear, and a middle drawer loaded with men's accessories: cufflinks, tie pins, and a plain Ziploc bag stuffed with keys.

Lark's pulse surged. Spare keys. To Duran's office? They must be. And to Anona's studio? That would be a bonus.

He stuffed the bag of keys into his coat pocket, slipped on his shoes, and headed downstairs.

George was at the bottom landing, dressed in his usual immaculately pressed charcoal-gray suit, standing stiff-backed, staring at Lark through squinting eyes.

"I need a car, George," Lark announced coldly. "Anona said I could take my pick."

"Yes, I was told. Except for the Bentley," George qualified.

When Lark opened his mouth to protest, the butler added, "It's scheduled for service today."

Lark grumbled a reply and walked through the kitchen and out to the garage. So the Bentley was "scheduled for service." Goddamn George. Scheduled came out as "sheeduled" in his phony Eton accent. He'd never forgiven Lark for wrapping the Bentley around a streetlight on Lombard Street one late, wet night many years ago.

He surveyed his choices. Anona had taken the Land Rover. Duran his jazzy old Jaguar sedan. Johnny's ink-black, shark-jawed Porsche was no doubt parked by his houseboat in Sausalito. The leftovers were a gunmetal gray Lincoln Mark VI, a boring Ford station wagon, and Lisa's red Mercedes convertible.

The wagon and the Lincoln were both show-room polished. Lisa's Mercedes had a fresh dent in the grill, blackened whitewalls, and half-moon marks from the wiperblades visible on the gritty windshield. Lisa was hard on cars. She was hard on everything, Lark concluded.

He selected the Lincoln, and went in search of a locksmith.

Chapter 10

Once he was off the freeway and through the small community of Montara, he stabbed the accelerator. He enjoyed punishing the Land Rover, grinding through the gears. When he reached the turnoff, he pushed the selector into four-wheel drive, jammed the transmission into low gear, his foot grazing the brake only when absolutely necessary. The Land Rover's hood jounced up and down like a ship's bowsprit in heavy seas as he steered between the silent rows of redwoods and pine trees.

He hit a deep pothole and the 4x4 bucked under him, his head banging up against the roof-liner.

He pulled off his hat and slapped it against his thigh, and yelled a croak-voiced "Yahoooo."

He slammed on the brakes when he came to the locked gate, reaching over the seat and patting the bundled figure of Anona Stack. "We're almost there. Almost home."

Anona shivered under the thick tarp. There was a bitter-acid taste in the back of her mouth. Who is the madman? Where is he taking me?

The vehicle started up again, and she felt the Rover's undercarriage scraping the ground. Her father had always been worried about the possibility of her being kidnapped. He had George instruct her in techniques. "Survival- and evasion-techniques," was the way George explained it.

First it was simple things, like never getting into strange cars, never going anywhere alone, always walking in the middle of the sidewalk.

Then, as she grew older, different lessons. Dear old George blushing when he'd showed her the targets to aim for: "the golden circle," that most vulnerable spot between a man's legs. "If the need should ever arise," George had preached solemnly, "then use your fingers and fingernails on the man's eyes. Blinding an attacker is the most effective means of rendering him harmless."

For several months they'd gone through a series of exercises on a gym mat alongside the swimming pool. Anona hadn't been a bit surprised at George's expertise in the art of self-defense. He seemed to know everything about everything. Later, she'd learned that George had been a sergeant in the British Cavalry before an injury had forced him into civilian life.

Would any of George's lessons help her now?

The Rover skidded to a halt. She could hear him open the driver's door. Hear it slam shut. Hear the back door open, then feel him tugging at the tarp.

She blinked her eyes in the sudden light.

He was bent over, leering at her. His hat was off. His hair was short, cut close to the scalp, his eyes filled with rage. Who was he? Who in the name of God was he?

He grabbed her feet and dragged her out onto the ground. Anona fell to the weedy dirt in a thud. She lay there, facedown for a moment, then he rolled her over. They were on a flat, football field–size plateau ringed by towering trees. He reached down and effortlessly pulled her to her feet, shoving her up against the Land Rover.

She ground her spine into the cold metal of the vehicle when he pointed the knife at her face.

"Scares you, doesn't it?" he said, giving her a vulturelike smile.

Ken Firpo had told him to use a knife with a woman. A sharp blade intimidated women much more than the barrel of a gun. And this knife was an intimidator: a ten-inch, stainless-steel blade with a sawtooth backside. He had a small derringer stuffed in his boot, ready for the police. Or himself, should it be necessary. He vowed he'd never go back to prison.

He tapped the flat side of the blade against the tip of Anona's nose. "First I'm going to take the tape off your mouth. Then from your hands and feet." He waved the blade in front of her face, watching her eyes follow the motion.

"You try getting away and I'll gut you, right here and now. Understand?"

Anona nodded, and tried to keep from gagging.

He reached over and gingerly worked a corner of the tape from her mouth, then, when he had a tip of the material between his thumb and forefinger, ripped it free with one quick pull.

Anona gasped at the pain, then shouted, "Who the hell are you? What do you want?"

"Don't you recognize me? Go ahead and shout," he encouraged. "Scream all you want. No one can hear you up here. No one."

He grabbed Anona's vest and twisted her around, then cut through the bindings on her hands and feet.

She felt her knees buckle. She leaned against the Land Rover's window, seeing her breath cloud the glass.

Then his hand was on her shoulder, jerking her backward.

"That way." He jabbed the knife toward an old wooden cabin. "Over there."

Anona stumbled forward, falling to her knees. Her legs felt leaden, useless. He prodded her with the knife blade and she climbed back to her feet, her head rigid, her eyes swiveling back and forth. More trees. Pine needles made a rusty carpet leading to the small, dilapidated cabin.

There were three stairs leading to a small porch. The algae-streaked wood was a mossy gray color. The sagging stairs squeaked under their weight. The cabin windows were covered with crinkled aluminum foil. A windowless door with a corroded steel knob seemed to be the only point of entry.

"Go on in," he told her. "It's not locked." He laughed lightly, sending chills up her back. "We don't have to worry about burglars here, Anona."

"Why are you doing this? I want to—"

"What you want doesn't count anymore. Get in there!"

Anona was shoved through the door, into a large rectangular room. The floor was moldy planking, partially covered by a threadbare, brown-tone, oval braided rug. A table was draped with a blue-and-white checkered cloth. Bright green camp lanterns were spread across the table. Alongside the table was a familiar item. An artist's easel partially concealed by a plain white sheet.

"That's your chair, right there."

She dragged her eyes away from the easel, recoiling at the sight of the chair. Dark, heavy wood, with a straight back. A two-foot-long piece of shiny steel chain hung from both of the chair's sturdy arms—a pair of handcuffs was linked to the end of each of the chain lengths.

She started backing away and he grabbed her by the shoulders and rammed her into the chair.

"Snap those cuffs on your wrists," he ordered.

Her hands fumbled at the chain and cuffs. Keep calm, she told herself. Keep calm. "I know you want money. My husband will pay you."

He tested the handcuffs, then glided the butt end of the knife along her jawline. "You're going to pay. And so is your husband. But not with money, Anona. You can't buy your way out of this." He backed away a few feet. "Don't go away, now," he taunted.

She strained her neck to keep track of him as he disappeared through the door. Her eyes quickly searched the room. There was a curtained doorway that partially shielded an old-fashioned wood-burning stove.

A grimy stone fireplace sat in the middle of one wall. The smell of charred wood hung in the air. Another wooden chair like the one she was cuffed to, was tucked under the opposite side of the table. A faded green upholstered couch with amoebalike, dark brown stains was positioned in front of the fireplace.

Then the easel. What was under that sheet?

Her throat was sandpaper dry, her lips raw from the duct tape, and she had an urgent need to use the bathroom. She bit down on her tongue—fight it, fight it, she encouraged herself. Another of George's old lessons: If someone should abduct you, appear to do what they say, don't provoke them. Don't threaten them. Your father will always pay whatever is necessary. Don't panic.

He said he didn't want money. What does he want? His face—long, narrow, sharp-featured with bushy black eyebrows over acid-blue eyes. Pale, scaly skin, and stubby, mottled teeth. When he smiled, his lips rode up over those teeth, exposing blotchy pink gums. She couldn't remember ever seeing that face before, yet he acted as if she should know him. Why had he mentioned his wife? And the fact that she had to stop painting?

Her eyes drifted to the easel. He must be a painter. Why had—

She jumped at the sound of the door crashing open. He was back, her leather purse looped over his shoulder. He was still wearing gloves. White cotton gloves. Funeral-type gloves, she realized.

He pulled the purse free, upended it, dumping the contents on the table.

"What have we got here?" he asked, fingering through her possessions, examining her wallet, checkbook, her compact, and rosary beads.

He picked up a silver Bulgari pen that Bob had given her for her last birthday. "Ah, this is what I was looking for. This will be perfect."

"Can I have something to drink?" she asked, working at keeping her voice clear and level. "And could I please go to the bathroom?"

He pressed his lips into a kiss of disapproval. "Please? You'll have to learn. You never say 'please.' They just think you're a pussy, if you say please."

She watched as he went through the curtained doorway. She could hear the sound of cabinet doors opening and closing, then water running. She pressed her knees together.

He placed a glass of water on the table, out of Anona's reach, even if her hands weren't shackled to the chair.

"I'm going to let you have a drink, but before you can go to the bathroom, you have a little chore to do."

He disappeared through the curtain again. When he came back, he had a sheaf of paper in hand. Pale lavender paper. He held it in front of her face, rifling the pages. She could see her printed name. Her letterhead.

"Where did you—"

Suddenly the knife blade was back, the tip less than an inch from her eye. "I'm going to undo the handcuffs. Then you're going to write a letter. To your attorney." He slid the rough, serrated backblade over her shoulder, down the pebbly goosebumps of her arm, scraping the skin. "If you don't do it right, I'm going to cut off the thumb of your right hand." He applied some pressure with the knife blade. "You'll never be able to paint again if I do that, Anona. You wouldn't like that, would you?"

"What do you want me to write?" she asked, her voice trembling.

He patted her head, as if she were a student who'd just given the teacher the correct answer to a difficult question.

He moved the glass of water to where she could reach it, then fished in his pockets for the key to the handcuffs.

"You can have the water after you write the letter and address the envelope. After that you can go to the bathroom. And when you're in the SHU, you'll be fed."

Anona rolled her fists into balls as he worked on the handcuffs. Shoe? What was this madman talking about?

Chapter 11

Carmel is some 120 miles south of San Francisco and, like much of the Bay Area, owes a great deal of its existence to the City of St. Francis. Many of the artists and writers who were left homeless by the 1906 earthquake migrated south, finding a home in the small, seaside community.

It had become a tourist mecca, the narrow sidewalks bordering its quaint shops and galleries jammed elbow to elbow with upscale visitors trying to appear casual while they cruised the area, hoping to get a glimpse of Clint Eastwood, Carmel's most famous resident.

Anona Stack's cottage was on Carmelo Street, just a short block from the beach, near the Carmel entrance to the famed Seventeen Mile Drive.

Jason Larks' first impression of the place had been that Snow White would open the door and the Seven Dwarves would troop out, hi-hoing their way to work. "English Cotswold Cottage" was the correct description, Anona had informed him. Two stories, cream-and-chocolate colored, with a steep, wave-laid, shingled gable roof, eyebrowed on each side of the chimney with small dormer windows.

The front garden was a melange of free-growing fuchsia, yellow flowering marguerite, and jasmine. The carport was filigreed by an overreaching weeping willow at the north side of the house.

Jason Lark hadn't been to the cottage in years. It hadn't changed at all. Johnny had told him that a front-door key was kept under the doormat. Lark lifted up the dusty coco mat. It was there, all right. How trusting of Anona.

He searched through each room, then the small garage. There were some old clothes, garden tools, and golf clubs, but no sketches of any kind, let alone the Picassos. Where the hell were they? They must still be somewhere in Stack House. There were so damn many sealed boxes in the basement, and additional boxes in the attic. The problem was the omnipresent butler.

He'd checked the game room, Conrad Stack's library, and most of the bedrooms, including Lisa's.

He'd tried questioning Lisa, but it was obvious she wanted nothing to do with her father. Their conversations were brief, her responses to his attempts at starting a dialogue futile. She still hates me, he conceded.

Johnny seemed indifferent. He knew nothing of Bresson's sketches. All he was concerned about now was his nightclub.

Lark found a dusty bottle of Chivas Regal in a kitchen cabinet. He poured himself a stiff drink, then leaned against the sink.

He took an appreciative sip, then slipped his hand in his pocket and removed the set of keys he had made from the ones he'd found in Bob Duran's armoire. Eight keys. One of them must fit the lock to Duran's office. He'd go there tonight. After dark. Duran would have a file on the Fritzheim Van Gogh. He had to find something that would keep Mario Drago at bay, and he had to find it fast.

He jangled the key chain, hoping that one of the keys was to Anona's studio on the Embarcadero. He knew she kept a lot of her old sketches there, and it was just possible that the Picassos had somehow been lumped in amongst them.

It took Anona Stack four attempts before she wrote out the letter to the madman's satisfaction.

"What makes you think Hugh Stringer will believe this?" she asked, reluctantly passing the pen back to him.

"He'll believe it. So will your children. And more importantly, so will the police. The only one who won't believe it is your husband."

He slid the glass of water over to Anona.

She fought back the urge to gulp the water down, instead taking a series of sips, all the while looking him straight in the eye.

"More, please," she said when she'd drained the glass.

"I told you, please don't work. Take off the watch. And the ring," he ordered.

She unclasped the Rolex, setting it carefully down on the table, then twisted her gold wedding band off, placing it alongside the watch.

He spiraled the watch around his fingers, then slipped it in his pocket.

"You can use the bathroom now. And shower."

"I don't need a shower," Anona protested firmly.

"Yes, you do," he insisted. "Enjoy it. It may be the last one you ever have."

She wrapped her arms across her chest. "No, no, I—"

"I said yes!"

He cupped her elbow with one hand, the other

brandishing the knife, and shepherded her through the curtained doorway.

The kitchen was small. Shutters in bad repair hung drunkenly alongside the one small, filmy window looking out to a stand of trees. An ancient, black-iron cook stove. Wooden cabinets that had once been painted white, and were now a yellowy-gray color, as was the speckled Formica kitchen counter that sloped down to rust-stained sink. Two black-handled kitchen knives lay in the sink. A half-window Dutch door led out to the woods. To freedom.

"That's the bathroom door there," the man instructed.

Anona opened the door cautiously, pinching her nostrils at the overpowering scent of disinfectant.

There was no window. No way for her to slip out. Just the toilet, and a metal shower with a lime-green plastic shower curtain.

He prodded her with the butt end of the knife. "I'll be right outside the door."

She bobbed her head in agreement, stepped into the room and closed the door behind her, noticing that there was no lock.

She undressed quickly, her shaky hands fumbling at the buttons and zippers.

The shower water was ice cold at first, but gradually warmed up. She closed her eyes and tilted her head back, letting the water flow into her still-parched mouth.

She froze when she heard the rasping sound of the shower curtain being pulled open. She swung around in a crouch, bringing her hands up in a defensive posture. Rape. He's going to rape me. Why did—

"Hurry up," the man commanded.

Anona turned her back to him. "Just another minute, please."

He reached in and turned off the water. "I told you, please don't work."

He held out a towel. His eyes traveled up and down her body, which she hastily covered with the rough-textured, plain white towel.

He snatched the towel away and she recoiled back against the cold metal shower wall.

He smiled again, one of those over-the-gum smiles. She looked different than she had in his prison cell fantasies. Not as young, not as beautiful. But just as frightened. Just as vulnerable. His early fantasies had included detailed sexual confrontations, where she would be bound, chained, forced to submit to him, to anyone he chose. But those fantasies had faded as time went by. The sex wasn't important anymore. Fear. That was all that was important.

And justice. Justice for Arlene.

He stooped down and picked up all of her clothing, with the exception of her shoes. "Dry off and I'll give you your uniform."

She waited until he was out of sight, then scrubbed herself off with the towel. A weapon. She needed a weapon. Could the towel be a weapon? She could snap it in his face. Aim for his eyes.

His heavy booted steps announced his return. He was too big. Too powerful. She needed more than a towel. A knife. There were knives in the kitchen.

He tossed her a pair of denim pants and a chambray shirt.

"Your uniform," he informed her.

"My . . . my underwear. What about my underwear?"

"You'll have to make do. Hurry up!

Anona slipped into the jeans, turning her back to him as she buttoned up the shirt. The clothing felt new and was over-sized and baggy.

"Don't forget your shoes," he said when she spun around to face him. His eyes were less angry now, but his face was creased, as if in pain. When he'd pulled the shower curtain open, she thought for sure that he had planned to rape her. Then and there. The way he looked at her, while she was naked. It wasn't a look of lust. More a look of satisfaction, as if he had already had his pleasure.

He led her back to the chair, securing the handcuffs. She stiffened when he rolled her shirt sleeve up and couldn't hold back a scream when he nicked her arm with the tip of the knife.

"Relax," he scolded. "I just need a little of your blood."

He pinched the punctured skin between his fingers as he rubbed her fishing vest over the wound.

"That ought to be enough," he conceded as he examined the bloodstains. He folded the vest neatly, dropped it on the table, then went through the pockets of her pants and shirt.

He held her bra in both hands, stretching it across his chest as if it were an exercise device. He tossed the bra on top of the vest.

Anona cleared her throat, then asked, "Why am I here? Can't you tell me what you want? If you don't want money, then what do you want?"

"I've got what I want," he said with a lopsided grin. "Half of it, anyway. One more chore, then you go in the SHU." He carried her pants, shirt, socks, and underpants over to the fireplace, threw them on a burned-out log, poured on some fire starter, then scratched a wooden match on the hearth and set them ablaze.

Anona watched the flames leap upward with a

whoosh, then settle down and steadily consume her clothing.

It was a little after six o'clock when Robert Duran notched the Jaguar into its parking slot at the Stack House garage. He noticed that Anona's Land Rover was not in sight.

He had hoped to be home sooner, in time to take that promised walk with Andamo down to Fort Point, but Harry Lawson's phone call had delayed him. Lawson's clients were ready and willing to deal. The exchange was going to take place in Los Angeles. All he needed was the final okay from the insurance company to pay Lawson the negotiated fee. Harry said his clients were firm on three million dollars for the Van Gogh.

Anona must have gotten tired of waiting for him. Or more likely, Andamo had.

George was pacing back and forth in the main hallway, his face set, looking serious as a mortician.

"What time did my wife leave?" Duran asked the butler.

"Miss Anona hasn't been back since leaving early this morning, sir."

Duran stopped short, his hand resting on the stairway balustrade.

"You haven't heard from her all day?"

"No, sir. She had a luncheon at the Museum of Modern Art at one o'clock. She never arrived. We had scheduled a meeting to go over the house accounts at four o'clock."

Duran gnawed at his lower lip. Anona was a member of the museum board. She wouldn't miss a lunch without calling them. George had full rein of what went on in Stack House—ordering food, liquor, the hiring and firing of household help. Once a month George presented the itemized monthly accounts. It was a tradition that dated back to Anona's grandfather, and one that Anona went along with, more to appease George than for any other reason. Duran was sure that Anona kept Stack House for George's sake, too. The house was way too big for them, especially with John gone most of the time and Lisa making noises about getting her own apartment.

"Maybe she's at the studio, somctimes she gets to painting and—"

"I took the liberty of calling there, and when there was no answer, driving over. The studio door was locked. Her Land Rover was not there."

George had always been very protective of Anona. At first he'd thought that Duran was nothing more than another fortune hunter. Marrying one was a mistake commonly made by rich women in their middle years. Someone who would be gone after a year or two. But after a while, George seemed to grudgingly accept Duran.

"This isn't like Anona, George."

The butler nodded in agreement. "Not at all, sir."

"Is Lisa home?"

"In the swimming pool. With a friend."

"What about Johnny?"

"I haven't seen Master John all day."

"How about Jason Lark."

"He left after breakfast, sir."

Duran's forehead knitted with concern. "Anona said she was going to the cemetery again this morning, George. I'll call and ask them—"

"I've already done so. She was not on the premises when they locked the gates at five o'clock."

"There's probably nothing to worry about, George,

but just to be sure, you start calling the hospitals in the area. She may have been in an accident. I'll check with Lisa. She may know something."

"Yes, sir." George rolled his eyes questioningly at Duran. "What happened to your hand?"

Duran held up his right hand. A bandage was wrapped around his wrist. "Some nut bumped me off the trail when I was jogging this morning." He stared at the bandage. That incident couldn't have anything to do with Anona not being home yet. "It couldn't," he said under his breath to assure himself.

Chapter 12

Jason Lark fiddled with the key ring. Finally, the fourth key turned the lock on the door of Lost Art, Inc.

He was worried that there would be a burglar alarm, so he opened the door a crack, then backed off, walking briskly back to Taylor Street, checking his watch every few minutes, anticipating that the police or an alarm company would respond. Neither did. He made his way back to the office, and once the latchbolt clacked into place, he donned a pair of leather driving gloves and snapped on the lights. There were three rooms, one crammed with file cabinets, and shelves bowed under the weight of books and document-sized boxes.

He approached Duran's desk cautiously, walking on the balls of his feet. For once, Lady Luck was smiling at him. The Fritzheim file was right there, sitting squarely on the green-felt blotter. He eased himself into Duran's chair and began paging through the papers and photographs, cursing when he read that the thieves had already made contact. There was a letter to the insurance company, Duran advising that attorney Harry Lawson would broker an exchange for "Sun and Sky" in Los Angeles, probably in the next couple of days. The price was going to be three million dollars. Three million for a phony Van Gogh.

He scanned the fax message Duran had sent to an appraiser named Wendy Lange. He'd never heard of her, but she no doubt was an expert. She had agreed to examine the Van Gogh and authenticate it. He'd have to alert Mario Drago right away.

A small stack of papers sat alongside the Fritzheim folder. A scrawled note lay on top: "Bob—Nexis search on Fritzheim's house."

Lark flipped through the computer printouts of stories culled from newspapers and magazines. Shit! He knew it would be there. And it was. The article that had appeared in the spring issue of *Architectural Review*. The architect, Richard Weufer, a puffed-up, egotistical, New York prima donna had gotten most of the ink, but his name was there: "Weufer used the talents of local interior designer Jason Lark to assist in completing the project."

Duran would jump on that. He slipped the page out, rolled it into a ball and jammed it in his pocket.

He searched through the rest of Duran's office with a vengeance, but the Picasso sketches weren't there.

Which left Anona's studio, or those boxes in the basement of Stack House.

Duran took the stairs rather than the elevator to the swimming pool, which was situated in the lower level of the house. The smell of chlorine intensified as he descended. Someone yelled an indistinguishable chant, followed by giggling, then a splashing sound.

The pool area had been fashioned after the famous Randolph Hearst indoor pool at San Simeon, with azure and gold mosaic tiles arranged in a variety of intricate patterns on the walls and ceiling. Old man

Stack had been wealthy, but he was not in Hearst's league, so the pool was much smaller than the massive eighty-by-forty-foot one in Hearst's castle. Duran remembered reading somewhere that Hearst had used tiles faced with real gold. Stack had settled for colored tile. Anona's acerbic wit had chronicled the room as "Faux Turkish whorehouse."

Lisa Stack stood, beautifully posed, balancing herself on the end of the diving board. She was wearing a bikini that was nothing more than a trio of dayglo orange triangles tied at the neck, back, and hips. She curled her toes over the edge of the board, stretched her arms above her head, and dove into the crystal-blue pool.

She broke the water with hardly a ripple, surfacing with a shake of her head, spraying water in all directions.

"Hi, Bob," she called out when she spotted Duran. "You know Eric Marvin. He works for Johnny at the club."

Duran didn't know Marvin. He looked to be older than Lisa—late twenties, lanky, ruddy skinned, his long, stringy hair plastered to his scalp.

Eric waded out of the shallow end of the pool, picked up a towel and buried his face in it.

Duran shouted a hello, and Eric's face appeared briefly.

He nodded, looped the towel around his shoulders, said, "Hi," then turned his attention to Lisa. "I'm going to go change." He gave Duran a nervous look, then disappeared up the stairs.

"What happened to you?" Lisa asked, pushing her wet hair away from her face. "Cut yourself?"

"No. I took a spill on my morning jog." Duran bent

down, his knees making popping sounds. "Lisa. Your mother isn't home yet. Did you talk to her today?"

Lisa swung around and effortlessly glided through the water to the shallow end of the pool. She climbed out slowly, turning to face Duran, shifting her weight from one hip to the other.

"Can you get me my towel?"

Duran scooped up a fur-thick, gold-colored beach towel and tossed it to Lisa, instantly aware of her body, the bikini top seemingly glued onto her skin, the bottom backstring buried in her buttocks.

He tilted his head toward the ceiling. "I'm a little worried about your mother. Do you have any idea where she might be?"

Lisa's voice was soft, mocking. "You can look now, Bob."

She had tied the towel sarong style around her hips.

Duran knew from their first meeting that Lisa was a first-class prick-teaser. One of the pricks she took exceptional delight in teasing was Duran's.

"George already asked me about Mom. I haven't seen her since last night."

Lisa reached her foot out to the pool and wiggled her toes in the water. "Maybe she's—"

A harsh voice interrupted. "Lisa, are you coming, or what?"

They both turned to see Eric now dressed in slacks and a white dress shirt, his hair wet-combed back from his forehead.

"In a minute," Lisa said angrily. "I really don't know where Mom is. I do wish you'd get rid of Jason. I don't like him hanging around."

"Neither do I, kid. He'll be gone in a day or two. What about Johnny? Do you think your mother could have—"

"Lisa!"

Eric Marvin again. This time the look he gave Duran was one of pure hatred.

"What's your boyfriend's problem?" Duran asked, glaring back at Eric Marvin.

"He works for Johnny. Maybe Johnny's been telling him about you."

"Telling him what?"

"I don't know. I've got to go." Lisa strode off, then turned on her heel, her shoulders shrugging, almost pulling her breasts free from the bikini. "Maybe Mom's somewhere with Jason. Get rid of him, Bob."

Anona Stack pulled the blanket around her shoulders and shivered. It was cold, but that wasn't what was causing her discomfort. It was him. The madman. He had a cool, fanatical way about him, as if he was completely in charge of her and she could do nothing to stop his plans. Whatever they were.

What were his plans? Why the bloodied vest? He must be going to plant it somewhere, to make it look as if Bob had . . . done something to her.

The letter he'd dictated, forced her to write to Hugh Stringer—saying that she was leaving Bob, that she wanted Hugh to file for a separation. And he had photographs of Bob hugging Peggy Jacquard. The madman wanted to implicate Bob. Those photographs might look incriminating to Hugh, but not to Anona. She trusted her husband.

She rubbed her hands together, hoping the friction would bring some warmth. The photos, and the stationery, identical to her stationery, proved that he had been planning this for some time. The statement that she was going away for a while. He wanted Hugh Stringer to think that. But what of Bob? He'd never believe what was in the letter. He'd know that something was wrong. Bob would search for her. But how could he find her?

The madman. She couldn't think of a better description. "Don't you know who I am?" he'd taunted her again after her clothes were burned to a crisp. He'd leaned over her, brought his nose to within inches of hers—his eyes, the, bulletlike, piercing pupils, the whites webbed with red, his breath warm, fetid. "Don't you remember me?"

Before he released her from the chair, he'd placed cuffs on her feet, leather-lined cuffs with a small length of chain between them, the same size chain attached to the chair. She was able to walk, shuffle really, out of that dismal cabin.

The jeans he'd given her were so loose that she had to hook her thumbs in the belt loops to keep them from slipping down.

He'd marched her across the field and into the woods, some fifty yards from the cabin.

Down a rocky dirt trail to this . . . this . . . makeshift prison cell. The back of some kind of truck. He'd called it a shoe. Why a shoe?

She'd watched him closely as he unlocked the cell's two doors. Each door was secured at the top by a stout-looking padlock. He kept the lock keys in his pocket.

She stood up and paced the dimensions of the cell. Twelve feet in length, eight feet wide. There was a grungy porcelain toilet. A mattress and pillow were the only furnishings. The door had a series of holes drilled through the steel and a rectangular cutout, some eight inches high and two feet wide. She was able to look out through the cutout—watch him stroll away into the trees, then disappear.

She didn't know how long she'd been left alone. It could have been ten minutes, it could have been an hour. She was lost without her wristwatch.

She heard someone humming and went to the door, peering through one of the holes. It was him. He was carrying a tray. The leg cuffs were draped over one shoulder.

He slid the tray through the cutout. "Dinner, Anona. Eat all of it," he advised. "Always eat when you get the chance. You never know when they'll stop feeding you."

They. Who were they? How many were there?

The tray held a peanut butter sandwich on white bread, an apple, and a small carton of milk.

She had put the entire tray under the bed. She was too cold, too scared too sick to eat.

He then opened the door and threw the leg cuffs at her. "Put one on your leg, attach the other to the bed frame."

She held the cuffs in her hand a moment. The chain was a weapon. It could be a lethal weapon.

"I know what you're thinking," he chided, then pointed a small, silver handgun at her. "Do what I said!"

After she was harnessed to the bed, he climbed into the cell, taking her bra from his back pants pocket, humming again as he threaded one end of the bra through the hook in the ceiling and knotted it in place.

He slapped the bra back and forth, as if he was fanning himself. "This is for when you get tired of hanging around, Anona. I don't want you trying to untie it, hear? I find it untied, and I quit feeding you." He slapped the bra again and grinned. " 'Course you could find some use for it, couldn't you?"

Then he left. She heard the sound of a car's engine

start up and drive away. Her car. That had been what seemed hours ago.

Now it was dark, and she was hungry. She got on all fours and groped under the bed for the tray. For a moment she considered the possibility that the sandwich or the apple were poisoned. Just for a moment. The madman wouldn't kill her that way. When he did kill her, he'd be there to watch. She was sure of that.

She finished the food, all except for the milk, figuring that she had better keep some liquid available. There was no telling when he'd be back. Her shoulders wracked with a sob.

She got to her feet, feeling around in the dark for the toilet. Something soft brushed across her face and she let out a yelp, then realized what it was. Her bra, hanging from the ceiling.

The madman. He was a subtle bastard. "In case you get tired of hanging around." He was going to try to break her. Drive her insane. Drive her to hang herself. "No way, buster," she said aloud, glad that he wasn't there to hear the quaver in her voice. She held her hands out like a blind woman, taking short, mincing steps until her legs bumped into the bed frame. She lowered herself slowly, lay down, and curled her knees up to her chin.

The madman said he had half of what he wanted. If I'm one half, the other half has to be Bob, she reasoned.

She closed her eyes, focusing her energy on the image of her husband in her mind. Get him, Bob, she prayed. Get him.

Chapter 13

He was uneasy driving Anona Stack's Land Rover. It was a point of vulnerability. Robert Duran may have already reported his wife missing, although according to Ken Firpo and the other jailhouse lawyers, the police would not take a missing person's report on an adult unless he or she had been missing for at least forty-eight hours.

Still, an accident or a speeding ticket now could ruin everything.

He drove north on Highway 1, past the small coastal communities of Linda Mar, Rockaway Beach, and Pacifica, then onto the freeway, heading into San Francisco, where the fog thinned and the bloody smudge of a dying sun could be seen sinking into the Pacific Ocean.

The letter he'd forced Anona to write was safely snuggled in his jacket pocket. Her blood-speckled fishing vest and rosary beads were jammed under the driver's seat. The vest he'd plant in the Stack family mausoleum—the beads in Duran's fancy Jaguar.

He wanted to make sure that the letter was delivered to the attorney's office in the morning mail. A call to the main post office in San Francisco informed him that the best way to guarantee a one-day delivery would be to post the letter from the Napoleon Street Carrier Complex.

The San Francisco map showed that Napoleon Street was situated in the Bayview District, which he found to be a dismal, industrial area of the city.

He posted the letter, then drove down Evans Street. There were old, clapboard houses wedged between small industrial buildings housing everything from jalopy-strewn auto wreckers to meat packing plants.

The few pedestrians walking the garbage-littered streets were young blacks who followed the Land Rover with hard, hate-filled eyes.

He spotted a corner liquor store that looked ideal, and parked in the triangular-shaped parking lot and left the Land Rover there, unlocked, with the key in the ignition.

Another jailhouse lesson—the best way to dispose of a vehicle is to simply leave it in a high-crime area. He had no doubt that Anona Stack's luxury 4x4 would be on its way to a chop shop by the time he walked back to the post office to call for a cab.

Jason Lark looked over his shoulder as he unlocked the door to Anona's studio on the Embarcadero.

He entered quickly, listening to the pulsing beat of the burglar alarm. If he remembered correctly, he had thirty seconds to punch the alarm code into the keypad on the wall behind the door, or the piercing alarm sirens would activate and a signal would be sent to the alarm company and the police.

It had been a four-digit code when he was married to Anona. Would she have changed the code by now? If so, he was ready to run like hell for the Lincoln, which was parked around the block.

He pushed the pad buttons, zero, five, two, five, for

Anona's birthday, May 25th. The pulsating beeps continued.

"Shit," he said out loud. She'd changed it. To what? Something that she'd always remember.

He tried one, one, one four, Johnny's birthday, November 14th, and still the beeps sounded, ever louder in his ears.

He decided to give it one more chance before getting the hell out of there as quick as his legs would carry him. Zero, seven, two, one. Lisa's birth date: July 21st.

The beeping stopped. He heaved a deep sigh of relief and started up the stairs.

Anona's eyes pinged open when she heard the movement. A rustling sound. Someone was coming through the woods.

The madman was back. She leveraged herself into a sitting position, straining her eyes to make him out through the cutout in the door.

The rustling stopped. She slipped to her knees and wormed her way over to the door.

She could see the silhouettes of the trees. The black sky was frosted with stars. But he wasn't there. Where was he? Hiding in the trees? Why? Was it someone else?

The rustling sounds started again and she could feel her stomach muscles tighten.

Silence.

Maybe it wasn't him. Maybe it was a neighbor, a hunter, or a lost soul. Someone who could help her.

She decided to make the first move.

"Who is it? I'm over here!"

Silence.

She put her face at the cutout, her nose into the opening.

"Who's out there? I need help!"

Silence.

She kneeled in place, her face pressed against the cutout in the door, eyes sweeping back and forth, trying to pick up something in the shadow-dense foliage.

She slipped an arm through the cutout and waved. "I'm over here! Help me, please!"

More rustling. There *was* someone out there!

She pulled her arm back instinctively as the animal made a loud growl and leaped forward.

Anona fell on her backside as the beast pounded into the door, snarling and roaring. A big, black, silver-dollar-sized nose pushed its way into the cutout, then she saw the sharp, pointed teeth.

A large paw poked into the cell. She cringed backward, sliding on the slick steel flooring.

Finally the growling stopped and she heard rustling noises again.

Anona took a deep breath and inched her way toward the door. She got a quick glance of a huge cat galloping away into the trees. A mountain lion. A hungry mountain lion.

When her heart stopped pounding she rolled back onto the bed. Could the lion help in some way? What if he attacked and killed the madman? She pictured him walking to the cell, food tray in hand and the lion attacking him, ripping him apart, killing him.

The vision drained from her mind when she realized that if he was killed, she'd be left there. Alone in this cell. Alone to starve to death. She had to find a way out.

She clasped her hands in a prayerful pose and began reciting a rosary.

* * *

"Thank you," Robert Duran said, then dropped the receiver on its cradle.

Andamo huddled next to his leg, his wooly upturned face seemingly questioning Duran: Where is my mistress?

Duran had parked himself behind the desk in the library, calling everyone he could think of who might know where Anona was—friends, gallery owners, her attorney, Hugh Stringer.

Next he called the San Francisco police department. The Colma police department. The San Mateo Sheriff's office. There had been no reports under her name, no vehicle accidents in which her name appeared.

He called the cemetery, got the name and home number of the manager.

"I saw her . . . yesterday, I'm sure it was, Mr. Stack. But I don't think I saw her today. I could be wrong, of course, but I assure you she isn't here now."

Duran thanked him, not bothering to correct the "Mr. Stack" reference. He'd long ago given up on the idea that Anona would be known as Mrs. Duran, except on their marriage license. She was simply too famous, too admired as Anona Stack for people to call her anything else.

"How does Stack-Duran sound?" she'd asked shortly after their marriage.

"Like the announcement of a welterweight fight," he'd responded. "Let them call you whatever they want, love. It doesn't matter to me."

And it really didn't.

George entered the room carrying a cocktail shaker packed with ice, condensation frosting the outside, and a single, stemmed glass.

"I thought you might need a drink, sir," he said, carefully pouring the martini. "Any developments?"

Duran rapped his knuckles against the telephone with enough effort to make the bell tinkle. "Nope. How about you?"

"No, sir. I've called the hospitals and emergency wards again. Nothing."

Duran picked up the glass and ducked his mouth to it. Anona's recipe—vodka right from the freezer, a single drop of vermouth to make it legitimate, then a lemon twist. He tossed the rest of the drink down with a quick flip of his wrist, then got to his feet.

"I'm going over to check out the studio, George. I know you were by there earlier, but maybe she stopped in and left a message or something. Call me on the car phone if you hear anything."

"I will indeed, sir."

When Duran was gone, George used a napkin to wipe the glass, then refilled it from the shaker. He ran the drink under his nose, then took a sip, rinsing the vodka around his teeth like mouthwash before swallowing. "Where are you, Miss Anona?" he asked himself wistfully. "Where the bloody devil are you?"

The sky was velvety black, the moon a mellow shade of pumpkin. Late Indian summer. Anona had often said October was the best of all the months in San Francisco.

Duran drove east on Broadway, past some of the city's finest Pacific Heights mansions, through a brief commercial area around Van Ness Avenue, then through the tunnel and out to where Broadway divided Chinatown from North Beach, an area famous for beatniks in the 1950s, then the topless craze through the seventies.

He took a right on the Embarcadero, a street bordering the bay and once renowned for its shipping activity. The brawny, graceless Embarcadero Freeway had been torn down after the earthquake of 1989, and replaced by a spacious boulevard with a center-dividing strip of towering palm trees.

The shipping industry had long ago deserted San Francisco and moved across the bay to Oakland. The new tenants started with the gaudy Pier 39, a tourist-magnet complex of shops, restaurants, and a merry-go-round, then office buildings, upscale restaurants, the Ferry Building and, at the far south end, a yacht harbor and the site of the new Giants baseball stadium.

Anona's studio was located in one of the last remaining old industrial buildings in the area: gray concrete streaked with brownish rivulets where the rust from window frames had rain washed down the walls. The windows were painted black and barred on the outside, giving it the look of a prison.

The building originally had three interior floors. The first floor was a storage depot for paints, thinners, and various supplies. Anona had had the third floor removed, and the second-floor studio walls now rose some twenty feet straight up to the roof. Anona had roamed the woods and hills of nearby Marin and Sonoma counties for inspiration.

She'd come across a dilapidated, once-red dairy barn and used it as background material in one of her most famous paintings.

When she learned that the farmer was planning to tear the building down, she purchased it and used the rough, pink-gray, sun-sucked boards to panel the studio.

A massive black metal bearing beam spanned the

walls some three feet below roof level. The major portion of the roof was of slanted glass, spaced between black aluminum girders. Retractable shades of ribbed iron completely covered the glass. There was no rear exit. Anona had often joked that she preferred the studio that way. "Just like the Texans at the Alamo. There's no way to back out."

Duran found a parking slot a few feet from the studio. The night air was whisper still. He could hear music. Badly played blues came from somewhere nearby. It had to be live, Duran concluded. No one would bother recording those sounds.

He inserted the key and opened the door, pleased to find that the alarm was off and the lights were on.

"Anona. Where have you been? I've been looking all over for you." He rapped his knuckles on the walls as he walked up the stairs.

The heavy metal roof shades were retracted, revealing the dark night sky.

"Anona! What's going on?"

Duran approached the easel, picking up Anona's canvas, running his hand lightly across the painting—blues and grays against a ghostly white background. He estimated it to be three-fifths finished. She had been there, and left the lights on, and the roof open, but where was she now? He took a look around the room, hoping to find a note from her. Something to tell him where she'd gone. There was nothing.

A narrow table littered with cans and tubes of paint, brushes left standing in empty soup and coffee cans, crusted putty knives and palettes sat alongside the unfinished painting. He dabbed his finger against the brushes. Dry.

One wall was taken up entirely by a closet of sliding doors some ten feet in height. He slid a door open.

Neat rows of empty canvases and cans of paint and thinner silently greeted him.

He headed for the small room at the rear of the studio, where Anona kept her sketches and research materials.

He was reaching for the light switch when suddenly his head exploded in pain.

Robert Duran's Jaguar had cruised right past him as he approached Broadway. He made an abrupt U-turn and closed in on the Jag.

Duran was looking for her. He must be worried sick. Where is she? Where are you going to look, Duran? Wherever it is, she won't be there.

He dropped back a half block when he saw the Jaguar turn onto the Embarcadero. The studio. He was going to her studio. Not a bad guess, Duran. But a wrong one.

He motored slowly by when Duran parked in front of the studio, circled the block, then found a parking spot that gave him a good view of the building's entrance. The van's engine died with a jerk and noisy sigh. He stretched his long arms over his head, then reached for his sketch pad.

He had just finished his second version of the building when he saw a man burst out of the front door. He was carrying a large can over to Duran's Jaguar. It was the ex-husband! Jason Lark!

His body flinched at the sound of the explosion. There was a flash of light as the fire belched out onto the street.

Lark raced down the street and out of sight.

Lark! That son of a bitch was going to ruin everything!

* * *

Duran struggled to his feet, his arms out, groping in the darkness. He bent over at the waist, sucking in deep drafts of air. There was a stench. Paint thinner. He wiped the sleeve of his coat across his face. It was wet. With thinner! He patted his suit. The jacket, the pants were soaked with the thinner. He heard a crashing sound, then saw a yellow-white flash come from the direction of the staircase. There was an explosion, blinding light, and a rush of heat.

Duran ran toward the staircase, only to find it engulfed in flames. Dark, oily smoke veiled the doorway.

He backed away. He couldn't make it down those stairs. And there was no rear exit, no where to run.

The suffocating smoke was spilling into the studio. He tore off his suit coat, dug his handkerchief from his pants pocket and jammed it over his mouth and nose.

The fire was all the way up the stairs, working its way into the dry, barn-paneled walls. Once it reached the paint and cans of thinner, the whole room could explode. He looked around hopelessly. The glass roof. The roof was his only way out.

He dragged a table over toward the storage locker and used his arms to pull himself up, his fingers clawing at the slick, dusty locker's top. He hoisted himself up, rolling on one shoulder, then got to his knees, feeling dizzy, tottering, almost falling back to the floor. He was gasping and coughing, his eyes running. He jumped, reaching up to the bearing beam, his fingers curling tightly around the metal. The edges dug into his hands. He took a deep breath, then, wrapping his hands around the beam, pulled himself up until his head was above the beam, only a couple of feet from the window roof.

He heard a roar, then a series of explosions. He glanced down, seeing balls of orange flame bursting through the smoke directly below him. He draped an arm around the girder, dangling free for a second. The windows. He had to get out through the windows. The noxious smoke was all over him, in his eyes, his lungs. The beam, no more than six inches in width, had begun to absorb the heat. He swung precariously for a moment, gathering his strength, pulling his legs up, wrapping them tightly around the steel beam. He raised an arm. His hand touched the glass. He pounded on it with his fist. It wouldn't break. He pounded harder.

There was another roaring explosion from below. Panic motivated him. Urged him on. His fingers were clenched in a death grip around the warming angle iron. He swung his leg—toe pointed outward. One kick. Sweat blurred his vision and poured down his face, hands and neck like small rivers. The smoke was deep in his lungs now. He kicked again, and this time was rewarded with a cracking sound. Another kick and glass cascaded down on him, along with the sweet, cool feeling of fresh air.

The oxygen-starved fire leaped upward. He reached out blindly, his fingers gripping the edge of the window frame. Jagged shards of glass ripped into his flesh.

There was another series of explosions. He could feel the fire itself—hot, burning. He braced his foot on the angle iron and launched himself upward.

A sudden burst of energy swept through him as the fresh air surged into his lungs. His hands were slick with sweat and blood. He felt his grip loosening.

He pushed his right hand out, the fingers grabbing, wrapping around something round. Solid. He pulled himself up, letting go of the window frame with his left hand, praying as it joined his right hand: Don't slip, don't slip now. Do it! Do it!

His arms and back ached from the effort, but gradually he moved upward, his head and shoulders were above the roof, then his chest. Without warning his blood-drenched left hand slid free for a moment. He dug his elbows into the window frame, using every bit of strength he had left to hang on, to leverage himself forward.

He wasn't sure if it was his imagination or not, but his feet were getting warm, feeling as though the fire was burning the soles of his shoes. He shook away the images of the fire, of his falling, and being swallowed by the smoke, the smoke that was billowing out all around him through the broken glass. He focused his watery eyes on his hands, which were gripping a short pipe. Some type of air vent. He dug his fingers into the metal, willing his fingertips to impale themselves into the pipe, then gave a final pull, inching forward until his hips were through the opening, then his legs. He rolled free onto the gravel edge of the roof, landing on his back, his mouth open, gasping, staring at the black sky.

He lay there, sucking air into his lungs, trying to get his strength back, while he categorized his wounds. He hurt all over—legs, neck, arms, back, but nothing seemed to be broken. He held both hands in front of his face, saw they were smeared with blood, and wiped them on his shirt.

He heard the sirens and struggled to his feet. He skirted around to the edge of the roof, avoiding the window areas. There was no fire escape. He'd have to wait for the firefighters to rescue him. The red lights on their trucks were visible now. His feet were feeling warm again. Would the roof collapse? He saw a battery of firemen position a ladder alongside the building.

What little energy he had left drained from his body

as he collapsed to his knees, watching the frenzied activities of the firefighters.

He noticed one lone figure across the street. A tall man wearing a straw hat. He was looking up toward Duran and clapping his hands together, like a spectator at a baseball game.

Chapter 14

The paramedic was a serious-faced young man of twenty-five. He used a pair of tweezers to pull a sliver of glass from Robert Duran's palm. "I'd suggest that you see your own doctor, sir, though I don't think any of these cuts need stitches."

"Thanks. I'll do just that," Duran assured him. He was feeling light-headed, possibly from the elation of surviving the firetrap, or perhaps due to the pure oxygen that the medic had him inhale.

Duran was sitting on the rear bumper of an ambulance. He watched with interest as the firemen went about their duties. There was no sign of flames now, just smoke rolling out of the roof—charcoaling the sky, before sinking down to ground level.

Four brightly polished, red hook-and-ladder trucks surrounded the building, their silver-colored metal ladders extended into the air, a fireman clinging to each tip, directing a powerful stream of water onto the skeleton shell of the studio.

Fire hoses were strewn like spaghetti all over the street, which was Vaseline shiny from the water.

Duran winced as the paramedic sprayed a disinfectant across his palm, then began wrapping it with gauze.

A man in knee-high fireboots, a black-canvas turnout

jacket, and a battered leather helmet that had ARSON SQUAD stenciled across the crown, sank down next to Duran. He lifted the helmet from his head and tossed it casually toward his feet. He was a solid, weather-worn man in his forties with thick, sandy-colored hair, his face darkened by soot except for the areas around his eyes, nose, and mouth, which had been protected by an air mask. "We've got the fire licked. Are you the man who was on the roof?"

"Yes. That's right. Bob Duran."

"Lieutenant Jack Powers." He craned his neck to watch the paramedic go about his work.

Duran pointed his unbandaged hand toward the building. "That's my wife's studio. I went there looking for her. Did you find any—"

Powers's voice tightened. "Are you saying your wife was in the building?"

"I'm not sure. She didn't come home this evening, so I thought she might be at the studio. She's an artist. Sometimes when she's painting, she loses track of time."

"I just came out of there. There's not much left of the interior. Everything dropped to ground level, and we went through it real good—no bodies. I didn't see any, neither did the rescue squad."

"Thank God for that," Duran murmured as if conversing in church.

"What's your wife's name, sir?"

"Stack. Anona Stack."

Powers pulled his right foot from its boot and began massaging his arch. "Yeah. She's an artist all right. Did you see anyone else inside the building?"

"I didn't see anyone." Duran reached back and gingerly touched his neck. "Including the person who rapped me on the head."

"Are you telling me somebody hit you? Before the fire?"

"That's right. I was there just a few minutes. I was hoping to find Anona, or something to explain her absence. She's been down in Colma working on a painting, sketching out the area." His hand again drifted to the back of his skull. "I went back to the room where she keeps her sketches. Then someone hit me over the head. When I came to, I was drenched with paint thinner and the fire started."

Powers wiggled his foot back into the boot. "You arrived at the studio about what time?"

"I guess it was a little after eight, something like that. The lights were on, the ceiling shutters were open exposing the windows. That's why I thought Anona was there."

The paramedic climbed out of the back of the ambulance and both Duran and Powers stood up to give him room to close the doors.

The ambulance driver tapped Powers on the shoulder. "We've got another call. There's been a shooting over in the Fillmore District. We're taking off."

"Yeah, okay. Send me a copy of your report." He turned his attention back to Duran. "So, Mr. Duran. Let's go over this again. You're inside the building, then what happened?"

"Like I said, someone hit me over the head. When I came to, I was drenched in paint thinner. Then I heard a crashing sound, and saw the fire."

"A crashing sound? Like what? The door being kicked open? Something falling?"

"I'm not sure."

"And you saw the fire right after that?"

"Yes. Immediately. I still can't believe how fast it moved."

Powers stooped down and picked up his helmet. "Mr. Duran, I looked at the building entrance. There's some type of alarm system, isn't there?"

"That's right. A standard touch pad. The code must be entered within thirty seconds of opening the door or the alarm will go off."

"Was the alarm on or off when you went in?"

"Off."

"And you used your key?"

"Right."

"And who else has a key?"

"Well, Anona, of course. Maybe her son or her daughter."

"Anyone else?" Powers pressed.

"I'm not sure," Duran responded guardedly, not liking the way the questions were going.

"Her son and daughter. What are their names? Would they know the alarm code?"

"John and Lisa. I doubt if they know the code. I'm damn sure that neither of them knocked me out."

"When you entered the building, did you close the door after you?"

"Yes. It locks automatically."

They had to detour around a hose connection that was leaking, spurting a mini-geyser of silvery water in a ten-foot circle.

Duran was impressed by the amount of activity. There were over a half dozen fire rigs spread out on the street now, some with hoses connected to each other. The smell of their diesel engines merged with the soot and ashes from the fire. Scores of firefighters were uncoupling hose lengths with large brass spanners and carting blanket-sized carryalls loaded with ruptured cans of paint thinner from the building. A group of six were lowering the fifty-foot wooden ladder that they'd used to get Duran from the roof. "Then what happened?" Powers prodded.

"There was no other way out. I couldn't get back down the stairs. I climbed up on top of a cabinet, and broke through the glass ceiling, and managed to get out through the roof."

Powers jammed his helmet on. "The roof. You were lucky those steel ceiling shutters were already opened up, Mr. Duran. Real lucky. Did you see anybody in the street prior to the fire?"

"No. Not a soul. Was the thinner the only accelerant used?"

Powers's eyes hardened. He was surprised at Duran's terminology. Accelerant. A technical term.

"We're not sure yet, but that's my guess."

"There was a lot of thinner in the studio," Duran said. "Some of it was upstairs, and there were cans of it stored down on the ground level." Duran ran his hands over his still damp pants. Someone had tried to kill him this time. It wasn't a push off the trail. It was a calculated attempt at murder. "I want to thank you and your men for getting to the fire so quickly, Lieutenant."

Powers pointed to a phone booth down the street. "Someone called 911 or we wouldn't have made it in time. In time to get you off the roof, anyway. You're lucky there're two firehouses within a few blocks of this place. What are your plans now, Mr. Duran?"

"I'm going to go home, and I hope my wife is there, Lieutenant. I'm exhausted."

"Yeah. I'll bet you are. How are you figuring on getting home?"

"Oh, I'm all right. I can drive."

Powers waved his helmet at the Jaguar. "Is that your vehicle over there?"

The car was parked where Duran had left it. A fire engine had jumped the curb in front of the Jaguar, its hose bed empty, the fire hose coupled to the side of the rig, weaving a path like a child's scribble toward the studio.

"Yes, that's my car." He shoved a hand into his pants pocket, grateful to feel the car keys.

"Mr. Duran, a trail of the accelerant ran from the front of the building, along the sidewalk, to the rear end of your car."

"Lieutenant, whoever set that fire was inside when I entered the building. No one knew I was coming to the studio. Except George, our butler, and that was just minutes before I decided to stop by."

"Your butler, huh? Would he have access to a key, or the alarm code?"

"No. And there was no way for George to get to the studio before I did."

"So it wasn't the butler. Who do you think it was?" Powers asked.

"I don't know."

"Do you think that this might have something to do with your wife . . . not coming home tonight."

"I don't know," Duran repeated in a pained voice.

"And the inside lights were on?"

Duran shrugged. "I told you, Lieutenant, I thought it was Anona. That she was either there, or had stopped by earlier. I just assumed she'd opened the shutters and left the lights on."

"That's possible," Powers conceded. He rapped his knuckles against the Jaguar's fender. "Maybe whoever bopped you on the head was thinking of torching your car, too, is that your guess?"

Duran didn't have to guess. Whoever was responsible wanted to make it look like he had started the fire and then accidentally burned to death.

Duran unlocked the car door. "I have no idea, Lieutenant. I've got to get going."

"Would you mind if I took a closer look at your car, sir? Maybe whoever did this spilled some paint thinner on the tires or under the hood. You never know."

"Not tonight," Duran said with an edge to his voice. "I've got to get out of here. I've got to find my wife."

"I can call a cab, or have one of my men take you home, sir."

Yes, Duran thought. And go through my car, and maybe find a can of thinner in the trunk.

"No, thanks, Lieutenant." Duran hit the ignition and the engine growled. "Call me if you turn up anything." He gave Powers the number for Stack House.

"Sure. Have you notified the police about your wife? Told them that she's missing?"

"Yes, I've done that, thanks."

Powers stood back and watched Duran maneuver the Jag from the curb and around the fire engine. He was tempted to impound the car right then and there, but he just didn't have enough to justify it.

It had all the earmarks of a botched job. A sloppy amateur pouring paint thinner all over the place, spilling it on himself, then getting caught in his own trap. But not many sloppy amateurs were as lucky as Duran.

Chapter 15

Jason Lark's fingers moved slowly, methodically over the yellowing ivory keyboard. He was playing Gershwin, but in a manner he was sure Mr. Gershwin would not have approved of.

He had raided the wine cellar for a vintage bottle of Burgundy, and was reaching for the wine when he heard the front door slam.

Lark narrowed his eyes, making crow's-feet, when the tarnished image of Robert Duran entered the room. "Jesus Christ! What the hell happened to you?"

Duran's clothes were blackened and torn. His face was smoke-stained.

"There was a fire. At Anona's studio," Duran informed him. "I almost got killed."

Lark swiveled around on the piano seat. "Let me get you a drink, man. You look like you could use one."

"How long have you been here, Jason?"

"Oh, an hour or so." Lark went to the drink cart. The neck of the bottle of cognac rattled against the glass. He handed Duran the drink with a shaking hand.

"Here. I know you don't like drinking with me, but under the circumstances, you can make an exception."

"Where were you tonight, Jason?"

Lark ran a finger across his ear, pushing away an errant lock of hair. "Out seeing the town. Having a few drinks. One or two too many, perhaps." He straddled the piano bench. "You look like hell. What happened?"

Duran studied Lark's features. He looked shocked. Shocked at how I look, or that I had survived? he wondered. "I told you. There was a fire at Anona's studio. When were you last there?"

"Me? Oh, maybe ten years ago. Is it still on the Embarcadero?"

"Yes. Did you see Anona today?"

"No. I thought she was out somewhere with you." Lark settled his fingers back on the piano keys. "Where is she?"

"I don't know. What I want you—"

The butler hurried into the room, the dog at his heels. Andamo ran over to Duran, skidding to a halt, sniffing at his pants legs.

"Good Lord, sir. Are you all right?"

"Yes, George, I'm okay. When I got to Anona's studio, the lights were on. I thought she was there. Someone hit me over the head, tried to kill me. Whoever it was started a fire. The building's destroyed. A total loss."

George said, "Was there any sign that Miss Anona had been there today?"

"The lights were on. The ceiling shutters were open." His eyes swung back to Lark. "Someone was there."

Lark sliced the air with his hands. "What's all this about Anona?"

"She's missing," Duran answered between clenched teeth.

"Missing? What do you mean she's missing. I don't—"

"She not here," Duran shouted. "We can't find her! And someone tried to kill me tonight. All of this happened after you showed up, Jason. Is it just a coincidence?"

Lark jumped to his feet. "Hold on there, Duran. Don't you start accusing me of anything. I've no reason to harm Anona. None at all." He sank slowly back onto the piano bench. "She must be out with a friend, or something."

Duran drained the cognac and settled the glass on the grand piano, then pushed his grimy finger into Lark's pale gray silk tie. "If I find that you are involved in this somehow, you're a dead man, Jason. Do you understand that?"

Duran was dressed and in the kitchen by six the next morning. He listened to news reports and made a pot of coffee while feeding Andamo, who, as usual, turned his nose up at his dog-food mixture and begged for his favorite vegetables: carrots, broccoli stalks, cucumbers.

George entered the kitchen, looking as if he'd had a bad night, too.

The household staff began arriving—three Salvadoran women who did the cleaning and Maria, the Argentinean cook.

Duran questioned them, speaking in Spanish, hoping that one of them might have heard Anona mention something yesterday that could explain her disappearance.

He drew blanks from all four.

Maria, a heavy-set fifty-year-old with graying hair and clear olive skin, the cook at Stack House since shortly before Duran married Anona, had tears in her eyes as she made the sign of the cross. "I will pray for her, Mr. Duran."

Duran used the phone in the library to recontact all the Bay Area police departments and hospitals listed in the Yellow Pages.

The plate of choriso and scrambled eggs brought in by Maria lay untouched alongside the phone.

Duran took a sip of his sixth cup of coffee of the morning, then pushed himself to his feet, deciding he was going to take Andamo with him and pay a personal visit to the cemetery.

He was calling for the terrier when the phone rang.

He snatched up the receiver, disappointed to hear Hugh Stringer's voice.

"Robert. I received a letter from Anona this morning."

"A letter? What does it say?"

Stringer cleared his throat, like someone coming down with a cold. "I think you should come down to my office right away."

"Listen, Hugh. Anona's still missing. I've been worried sick and going crazy trying to find her. Someone burned down her studio last night. While I was in the damn place. He tried to kill me. Now what the hell is in the letter?"

Stringer's voice took on a professional tone. "I'd rather not say on the phone, Robert. But I strongly advise you to come down here. Right now."

The pounding noise woke Anona from a deep sleep. She'd been dreaming. She and Bob were back in Jamaica—warm sand, warm water, Andamo running between them.

"You slept well. You must like it in there."

She clutched the blanket tightly around her. "What time is it? How long have I been here?"

"Hand me your dinner tray?"

She groped under the bed for the tray and passed it through the cutout.

"Where's the milk carton?" he demanded.

Anona reached down to the floor for the carton, which was still half full. She handed it to him.

"Good. If you don't return everything—every item—then you don't get your next day's food, Anona. Those are the rules."

Another tray appeared through the cutout. A plastic cup with a steaming liquid and a plastic bowl of cereal, already doused with milk, a plastic spoon, and a napkin.

She sat down on the bed, balancing the tray on her lap, and sipped the coffee.

"More rules," he informed her. "You get an hour a day outside. Yard time. I'm busy today, so your yard time will start now."

She heard him undoing the locks.

He was dressed in gray slacks and a gray shirt. The leg cuffs dangled over one shoulder. The knife was sheathed on his hip.

Anona finished the coffee, then started in on the cereal. He just stood there watching her, his right hand clamped under his armpit.

She was hungry. She thought of asking for more food, but held back, knowing it would just give him the pleasure of denying it.

"Hand it over," he said, gesturing for the food tray.

"You said yard time. What is that?"

He looked at his wristwatch. "An hour. You can walk or exercise."

Anona got to her feet. Her legs felt cramped, her

neck and back muscles tight. Yesterday, in the shower, she'd been sure he was going to rape her. But he hadn't. Hadn't molested her in any way. Yet. But how long would that last? Her bra was hanging from the hook. Even that didn't seem to have a sexual connotation for the madman. His obsession seemed to be acting out the role of being a warden, and she his prisoner. The cabin. That was where the weapons were. Kitchen knives. A heavy pot, fireplace tools. She had to get back to the cabin. Had to risk it. "Can I shower? I'd like to take a shower."

He bulged his lower lip with his tongue while he considered her request. "All right." He tossed her the leg cuffs. "Put these on."

She followed his instructions, then awkwardly made her way out of the cell. The leather-lined leg cuffs chafed her ankles. She walked slowly, taking in the woods, looking at the surroundings. If she could get into the forest, even with the leg restraints, there were places to hide.

"I had a visitor last night," she told him.

He grabbed Anona's shoulder and yanked her to a stop and spun her around to face him. "What are you talking about?"

"A mountain lion. It came right up to the door." She pointed her chin at the path. "I think those are its tracks."

He pushed her up the trail, then bent down and examined the ground, his fingers flicking over the dirt.

There were tracks. Kenny hadn't mentioned mountain lions. Or was it a lion? Probably a bobcat.

Either way, she was lucky. An animal. He hadn't even had a fly to keep him company in the SHU. He stood up, his head turning full circle, looking into the woods, thick with fern, scotch broom, waist-high weeds. The trees and brush were so tight together in spots that a man would have to move sideways to get through. He cocked an ear. Listening. There was nothing. Complete silence. The forest soaked up every sound. He stared at Anona. She didn't look scared. Not as scared as she should be. Yet. Just one night in the SHU. After two or three, she'd change. The SHU changed everyone. He thought about shutting her back in, but a rule was a rule. One hour a day.

He slipped the knife from its sheath and jabbed it in her direction. "Get moving if you want that shower. Fifty-five minutes left."

Anona walked with as much dignity as the leg cuffs allowed. The pewter-colored sky pressed down on her like a weight. Dark smoke curled from the cabin's chimney, adding to the gloom. The cabin door was open.

The easel was there, with no sheet covering it. Anona paused, examining the canvas. An outdoor scene—an open area with towering trees. He was painting what he saw from the cabin porch. She could feel his eyes on her. She sensed that what she did now, right at that moment, her reaction to his painting, could determine how he treated her from now on. Determine her fate.

She swiveled her head back and forth as she scrutinized the half-completed canvas, then said, "Hmmmmm," and moved off toward the bathroom.

The bathroom door was wide open. The shower curtain was gone.

She looked over her shoulder. He was standing there blank-faced, his right hand under his arm pit.

His upper lip crept up over his teeth. "I have to make sure you don't slip through the drain." He tossed a bar of soap at her. Anona reached for it, but it slithered through her hands.

She stooped to pick it up and heard him chuckle.

"That's something you learn not to do real fast." His chuckle grew into a full-blown laugh and the soap once again slithered through her fingers.

"Tell me," he said once the laughter had wound down. "Why does Jason Lark want to kill your husband?"

Chapter 16

Hugh Stringer's office was located on the thirty-fifth floor of the 101 California Street Building. It was a sleek, graceful, forty-eight-story glass silo tainted by the fact that it was the site where a crazed gunman had wandered through the floors, armed with several semiautomatic weapons with extended clips, killing eight people and wounding six more hapless victims. The killer was upset at an attorney for allegedly cheating him out of a great deal of money in a real estate transaction some years earlier. Security at the building had been upgraded after the tragedy: armed guards, metal detectors, and patrol dogs.

Time had eroded the memory, and the fears, and there wasn't a guard or dog in sight when Duran passed through the glazed street-level atrium and boarded an elevator.

Hugh Stringer checked the wall clock as he waited impatiently for Robert Duran in his office, a long, narrow affair, expansively windowed, with oak wainscoting and matching molding rimming the coffered ceiling.

Anona's letter, the photographs, and the morning paper were spread across the top of his hand-carved mahogany desk.

His secretary buzzed and informed him that Duran had arrived.

Stringer remained seated behind his desk as Duran entered the room. The two men had never been anything more than civil to each other.

Before Jason Lark had come upon the scene, Stringer had actually thought of proposing marriage to Anona. But Conrad Stack would have never allowed him to marry her. An attorney. Not nearly good enough for his only daughter. The egotistical old bastard couldn't stop her from marrying a nonentity like Jason Lark. Later, he'd hired Stringer to handle the annulment—Conrad wasn't going to settle for a divorce. After that Stringer started seeing Anona, not actually dating, but he had taken her out to dinner, to theater engagements. Anona had never shown any romantic interest in him, but he thought there was a chance that she'd change as time went on. Then Duran showed up.

Robert Duran. Another nonentity. At least he'd kept his nose out of Anona's finances. Anona left the management of the stocks, bonds, and real estate she'd inherited from her father to Stringer. And now it looked as if Duran was going to be history, à la Jason Lark. Maybe it was Stringer's time now.

Stringer rose and extended a hand across the desk. He was in his early sixties, a burly man with a fleshy face and meaty chin. His pale gray eyes were buried deep under bristly black eyebrows. His shoe-polish-brown hair was combed straight back from a widow's peak. He was wearing a perfectly tailored, dark blue double-breasted suit, a white shirt so heavily starched it had scored a red mark around his neck, and a muted blue-and-maroon silk foulard tie.

"I'm glad you got here so quickly, Robert."

"Where's Anona's letter?" Duran asked bluntly.

Stringer picked up the two pages and handed them to Duran.

The attorney studied Duran as he settled into the dark green leather client's chair. His wrists was bandaged. His face was scratched and drawn, his eyes puffy, as if he either hadn't slept, or had been crying.

Duran shook his head slowly as he read the document:

> Dear Hugh:
>
> I'm sorry to have to drop this in your lap, but I just don't feel up to meeting with you personally. Bob and I have been having problems. He's been drinking a lot and there have been times when he's become violent. The last time was the final straw. I was afraid he was going to kill me. He has become extremely jealous, for no real reason.
>
> I hired a private investigator. As you can see from the photographs, it's I who should have been jealous.
>
> I want you to start separation proceedings right away. Handle it any way you think best. I just want him gone.
>
> I'm getting out of town for a few days. I don't feel safe with him living at Stack House.
>
> Love,
> Anona

"This is crazy," Duran protested loudly, bursting from the chair and waving the letter back and forth. "When did you get this?"

Stringer folded his arms across his chest and leaned back. "In this morning's mail. I'm quite disappointed in you, Robert. This other woman. And the violence Anona writes of."

"There's never been any violence," Duran protested strongly. "This letter's a fake." He picked up the two color photographs from Stringer's desk blotter.

"Christ," he moaned. He and his secretary, hugging in one, him kissing Peggy in the next. The shots were taken in the parking lot next to his office. He remembered the occasion, her birthday, over a week ago. He'd surprised her with flowers at the office and a long lunch at Scoma's. "This is Peggy Jacquard. My secretary. Anona knows that there has never been anything between us."

"Those photos seem to indicate otherwise," Stringer said, with an almost apologetic look on his face.

"Where's the envelope?" Duran demanded.

Stringer opened the desk's center drawer and plucked out the envelope.

"As you can see, like the letter, it's Anona's stationery."

The buzzing of his phone interrupted him. He picked up the receiver. "No calls. No interruptions."

Duran examined the envelope. It *was* Anona's stationery. The postmark showed it had been mailed yesterday, in San Francisco.

"Robert, Anona never mentioned that the two of you were having problems. I hope we can keep this—"

"We don't have problems. This is a fake, Hugh. I don't know what's going on, but Anona wouldn't write something like this."

"It certainly looks like her handwriting to me." He tapped a finger on the newspaper. "This story in the *Chronicle* about the fire at Anona's studio, Robert. It says you were there."

"I sure in the hell was. Looking for Anona, then—"

The phone buzzed again and Stringer's normally red

face deepened in color. "No calls, no interruptions," he shouted, slamming the receiver back in its cradle.

He took a deep breath to compose himself, then said, "Do you have any idea where Anona went? Perhaps to the cottage in Carmel?"

Duran kicked himself for not thinking of the cottage. But why would Anona go there? Why would—

The office door opened and a nervous-looking woman in an equestrian-style red blazer cautiously entered the room.

"I'm sorry, Mr. Stringer. But there's a call for Mr. Duran. It's the police. They say it's urgent."

Stringer shooed her away with a hand. "All right, all right. You better take it, Robert."

Duran picked up the phone. The man on the line identified himself as Chief Saylor of the Colma Police Department. Duran's face paled and his legs turned rubbery. He dropped into the chair with a thud, mumbling, "Yes," several times; then "No," and, finishing with "Right away."

"What is it?" Hugh Stringer bellowed, prying the phone from Duran's hand. "What's the matter, Robert? You look ill."

"That was the Colma police. They found a fishing vest splattered with blood in the Stuck family mausoleum."

Stringer's eyebrows rose toward his forehead. "Fishing vest?"

"Yes. Anona was wearing a vest when I last saw her. She often wore it when she painted. She liked to stuff the pockets with brushes and things."

"What else did the policeman say?"

"Nothing. He wants to see me. Now."

Stringer tapped the edges of the letter neatly together. "I'll go with you. Under the circumstances,

Robert, I should turn the letter and the photographs over to the police."

Duran leaned forward and buried his hands in his hair. He couldn't believe what was happening—Anona missing, this ridiculous letter, and now the call from the policeman.

He snapped his head back and looked up at the attorney. "Yes, I think you should, Hugh. But I want a copy."

"I don't know if that's the correct—"

"My prints are on them now, Hugh, and so are yours. I want a copy of the letter and the photos!"

Stringer opened his mouth to protest, then picked up the phone and ordered his secretary to return.

The Stack family mausoleum was the size of a small house, constructed of quarried stone in a Greek Revival style complete with Corinthian columns and grotesque, demon-headed gargoyle waterspouts. It stood on a small knoll overlooking a few similar, but less grand structures, and serried rows of tombstones.

A massive, time-stained brass door afforded the only entry. There were fresh, gold-colored scars around the lock and on the greenish metal at the edge of the door.

The interior floors were of variegated marble, laid out in a geometric pattern with scrolled inserts indicating the points of the compass. Benches of red-veined marble were built into the walls. The crypts holding Anona Stack's parents and grandparents were set in the east wall, their coffins entombed behind six inches of concrete.

"Are you Mr. Duran?" asked a tall, restless-looking man with dark hair and tightly drawn features, wearing a beige policeman's uniform.

"Yes. I'm Bob Duran. This is Hugh Stringer. The family attorney."

"I'm Chief Bill Saylor." He strolled over to the brass door. "Whoever did this had no problem breaking into the place. That lock had to be fifty years old. A simple, warded lock. Oldest and least secure lock there is."

"But Christ, man," Stringer growled menacingly. "Don't your men patrol the cemetery?"

Saylor pushed a pair of tinted, aviator-style gold-rimmed glasses up on top of his head. "We've got fourteen cemeteries under our jurisdiction: Catholic, Protestant, Greek, Italian, Serbian, Jewish, Chinese, Japanese—you name it, we've got it. There's even a pet cemetery. I haven't got enough men to make passes at all of them."

Stringer wasn't satisfied. "Maybe, but breaking open those doors had to make—"

"Enough noise to wake up the dead," Saylor interjected smoothly. "It could have happened during the night, when there's no caretaker on the property." He propped his glasses back on his nose and looked directly at Duran, like a prizefighter surveying his opponent before a fight. His eyes strayed to Duran's bandaged wrist.

"Hurt yourself?"

"There was a fire last night. At Anona's studio in San Francisco."

"Was your wife with you?"

"No. No, she didn't come home last night. I called the police. Your office included. She was here yesterday morning, painting."

"Yes, I know about your call," Saylor said, hooking his thumbs into the belt holding his holstered revolver. "When I got the word about the break-in here, I checked it out and called your house. The man I spoke to there told me that you were at Mr. Stringer's office. I spoke to the cemetery manager. Your wife was here for several days. Over by that knoll up there."

Duran followed the policeman's finger to a hill shrouded by a grove of cypress trees.

"This morning, one of the maintenance men noticed the scratches on the door and he saw what he thought was a rag. It was a fishing vest. There's blood on it."

Duran's chin dropped to his chest. "Anona was wearing a vest. Where is it?"

"At my office. We can go over and take a look," Saylor suggested.

Stringer wasn't pleased with the idea. "Robert, perhaps I should call someone with more experience in these type of matters than I have. I can get a—"

"It's not necessary, Hugh."

Stringer put his arm around Duran's shoulder and steered him out of the mausoleum. He gave Duran a quick, probing look. "Is there something you want to tell me? In confidence?"

Duran took a deep breath. The air smelled of freshly cut grass. He walked across a gravel road to a row of knee-high tombstones.

A primer-spotted pickup truck rumbled by. The back of the truck was loaded with powermowers, shovels, and hoes. The driver, a solemn-faced man wearing a straw cowboy hat, pulled the truck to a halt.

Duran turned back to the mausoleum. Chief Saylor was waiting patiently. The sunlight reflected off his glasses, making him appear sightless.

"Hugh, something's happened to Anona. She's not just out of town for a few days. I'm afraid she's been kidnapped. And someone's out to get me, too. The fire last night, and yesterday morning while I was out jogging, someone set a trap for me. I always take the same route. Yesterday someone came up behind me and knocked me off the trail, and over a cliff."

"Someone? Who?"

"I don't know."

"All I know is that Anona wants to divorce you. She claims you were violent and that you're seeing another woman."

"I told you, the letter's a fake," Duran replied hotly. "You better give Anona's letter to Chief Saylor."

Stringer stared at the ground. "I have to tell you, that as Anona's attorney, my first loyalty is to her."

"Mine is, too. Saylor looks like a capable guy, and the important thing is to find out just what the hell is going on. Give him the letter."

Duran watched the attorney walk purposefully over to the police chief. Saylor's eyes bounced back to Duran every few seconds.

Stringer handed the manila envelope containing Anona's letter and the photographs to Saylor. The policeman studied the contents briefly, then his head twisted toward Duran like a compass needle.

Chapter 17

Duran had driven Hugh Stringer to the cemetery in his Jaguar. Chief Saylor arranged for a uniformed officer to drive Stringer back to his office in San Francisco.

Duran followed Saylor from the cemetery to police department headquarters.

Saylor's office was located in a small, two-story Spanish–style building less than a half mile from the cemetery.

A cameo-faced woman seated behind a bullet-proof glass enclosure buzzed them into the restricted area. Duran followed Saylor past a small kitchen area, then up a cramped stairway to the second floor, and into a medium-sized room. Two desks abutted each other. Each desk was littered with file holders, pencil caddies, telephones, and rolodexes. A coffee machine sat in one corner, perfuming the air.

"Coffee?" Saylor asked, unhooking his belt and laying his revolver on the desktop.

"Thanks."

"I hope you like it black. It's all we've got."

"Black's fine."

Saylor handed Duran a chipped white mug with a Highway Patrol emblem on the side, then flopped down in his chair like a man who'd put in a hard day's work. "That's Sergeant Miller's chair," he said, waving a beefy hand. "He's off today. Make yourself to home."

"Before we get started, Chief, I'd like to call the police in Carmel, or maybe you should make the call. Anona has a cottage there. It's the one place I haven't checked yet."

"You think your wife may be in Carmel?" Stringer asked skeptically.

"It's a chance. I should have thought of it earlier."

"What's the address?"

Duran gave him the information, then added, "If the house is locked, there's always a key under the doormat."

"Pretty trusting, huh?"

"Carmel isn't exactly a high crime area, Chief."

Saylor nodded in agreement. "I'll be right back."

The chief was gone a good ten minutes, giving Duran a chance to absorb the morning's news. Anona's letter. It was her stationery. It looked like her handwriting. Obviously, someone had made her write it. But who? Why?

Whoever it was, had taken her from the cemetery grounds. But why go to all the trouble to break in to the Stack family mausoleum? Unless he had . . .

Saylor trooped back in the room, carrying two packages, one a plain brown paper bag, the other Anona's letter and photographs, now inserted in a clear plastic sheet protector.

"Saylor tells me that you handled the letter and the envelope and had him make you a copy."

"That's right, Chief."

"Is it your wife's handwriting?"

"It looks like it."

"Stringer's going to get me some samples of her

writing so I can have it verified." He upended the bag. An olive-colored fisherman's vest tumbled out onto the desktop. "The crime lab's already looked at this, and scraped off blood samples, Mr. Duran. There are paint smears as well as the bloodstains, and there were pencils, pens, erasers, a tape measure, and some peanuts, and half of a Hershey bar in the pocket. Does this look like your wife's vest?"

"Yes. It's Anona's vest," Duran confirmed. "She was wearing it the last time I saw her. Early yesterday morning." Duran's hands moved slowly toward the garment.

"You can handle it," Saylor advised him.

Duran picked up the vest, his finger circling the band of scallop-shaped drops of blood.

"That's one good thing," Saylor consoled. "There were just those few spots on the vest. No blood samples were found in the mausoleum or in the area where your wife parked her car. Do you know her blood type?"

"Yes, we're both A-positive."

Saylor drummed his fingers on the photographs. "Who's the lady?"

"My secretary. Peggy Jacquard," Duran responded, knowing that Hugh Stringer must have already given Saylor that information. "We're good friends. That's a birthday kiss I'm giving her in the picture. Nothing more."

"What do you think happened to your wife, Mr. Duran?"

Duran's hands moved as if to explain, then dropped to his side. "Someone's grabbed her. Made her write the letter."

"Why?" Saylor challenged. "No one's called with a ransom demand, have they?"

"No."

Saylor studied Duran over the rim of his coffee cup for a moment, then wheeled his chair around so he was no more than four feet from him.

He picked up a pen and pad of foolscap paper and started questioning Duran, speaking softly, probing like a dentist. "Tell me about the last time you saw your wife."

"It was yesterday morning. In our bedroom. She was getting ready to come down here—to Colma—to the cemetery to work on her next project."

"Besides the vest, what was she wearing?"

"Khakis, a bluc shirt. She usually wore a hat when she was outdoors. I don't remember seeing it. A baseball cap with a long brim. It was probably in her car."

"What kind of car?"

"A white Land Rover. I don't remember the license plate number, but I can get it for you."

"Was there anything unusual about yesterday morning? Anything different?"

"No, there— well, yes. She usually brought Andamo with her, but she said that—"

"Andamo?"

"Our dog. Her dog, really. A Welsh terrier. Anona said that a gardener at the cemetery told her that someone had complained, that domestic animals weren't allowed on the grounds, so Andamo stayed home."

Saylor made a clicking sound with his tongue. "Did your wife have any enemies?"

"No. None."

"Did your wife have anything valuable with her? Money? Jewelry?"

"Well, she was wearing a watch. I'm not sure which one, probably her Rolex."

Saylor jotted the information onto his notepad. "Anything else?"

"Her wedding band. A plain gold band. I paid about five hundred dollars for it."

"Was there an inscription of any kind on the watch or the ring?"

"The ring. One word. *Siempre.*"

"*Siempre.* Spanish for always, right?"

Duran nodded his head.

Saylor tugged at an earlobe. "Mrs. Stack. She's Irish, right?"

"Yes. I'm half Mexican, Chief."

"The blue eyes fooled me. I've seen a lot of blue-eyed Italians. My wife is one of them. But never a blue-eyed Mexican."

"My mother was Danish. That's where the eyes came from."

"Is this your first marriage, Mr. Duran?"

"No. I was married before. My first wife, Teresa, died years ago. In New York City. An aneurysm."

"What about a purse? Did your wife take a purse with her to the cemetery?"

"I'm sure she did. There wasn't much there of value. In fact she asked me to give her some cash. So she could pay the gardener."

"The one who told her not to bring the dog?"

"Yes. I think it's the same one. She asked him to clean up the grounds around the Stack mausoleum, knock back the weeds."

Saylor leaned forward in his chair. "Did she tell you the gardener's name? Mention what he looked like?"

"No. No, she didn't."

"Okay, the purse. What kind? Big? Leather?"

"Brown leather. She had her wallet, driver's license, credit cards, that kind of thing."

"Anything else?"

Duran closed his eyes to concentrate. "Just the normal stuff. Comb, compact, things like that. And her rosary beads."

"She's a religious woman?"

"Anona's Catholic. The beads were from Rome, blessed by the Pope."

Saylor added that information to his list, then said, "Tell me a little about yourself, Mr. Duran."

"I'm an investigator, Chief. I work primarily for insurance companies tracing stolen art." He dug a business card from his wallet and handed it to Saylor.

"An art investigator, huh? That must be interesting."

"Just a way to make a living, Chief."

Saylor drummed his pen against the legal pad. "Still, you must have learned some things about the criminal justice system."

"I worked for the Centennial Insurance Agency, or the CIA as they liked to joke. I was with them fifteen years, first in New York, then Dallas, then Los Angeles, finally in San Francisco. Thefts from museums, private galleries, and forgeries. After I was married, I started my own business. I handle art thefts and recoveries exclusively."

"Keeps you busy, does it?"

"You'd be amazed at the amount of forgery going on in the art world. It's so damn easy to do now, with computers and scanners."

"They use computers to forge paintings?" Saylor asked skeptically.

"Sure. Someone brings in an original, say for a cleaning, or a new frame. The forger runs it through a scanner. There's software now that will give you the exact measurements and, more important, the depth, thickness, the viscosity of the paint. You can—"

Saylor held up a hand. "I get the picture." He grinned at his own joke, then said, "You must have put some people in jail. Or at least made them surrender whatever it was they stole."

"Yes," Duran acknowledged. He had helped recover millions of dollars of stolen art, and in doing so had angered a lot of people, rich and poor. Professional criminals as well as not very clever amateurs. The Mafia in New York had been involved in a couple of his investigations. "But I don't think that any of my cases would have anything to do with . . . with this . . ."

"You never know, Mr. Duran. People harbor grudges for years and wait until their victim has forgotten about them, then they strike. Are you working on anything in particular at the moment?"

"Yes. Alan Fritzheim, the movie producer. His house was robbed of a very valuable painting. A Vincent Van Gogh, 'Sun and Sky.' "

"I read about that. Millions of dollars involved, right?"

"Right."

"Have you any idea who pulled off the heist?"

"Not yet," Duran answered truthfully. He saw no reason to inform Saylor that there was a good chance he'd be negotiating with the thieves shortly. The police hated it when they weren't involved in the transactions. Hated it even more when the thieves walked off scot-free with a bundle of cash.

Saylor said, "Is there a possibility that the Van Gogh heist has something to do with your wife's disappearance?"

"I don't know, Chief. I just don't know."

Saylor scribbled something on his pad, then said,

"You and your wife don't have any children together?"

"No. Anona has two children from a previous marriage. John, who's twenty-two now, and a daughter, Lisa. A year younger."

"Who's their father?"

"Jason Lark. Lark is an interior decorator. He lives in Southern California. He just came up here to visit. Two days ago, Chief."

Saylor's eyebrow cocked into a questioning arc. "You think there's a connection between this Lark showing up and your wife's disappearance?"

"I don't like coincidences. Lark is . . ." Duran paused, groping for the right word. "An asshole. He drank too much, and when he started getting violent, Anona threw him out. The divorce took place over fifteen years ago."

"That's a long time to harbor a grudge."

"Yes," Duran agreed. "But since he got here, I was pushed off a jogging trail, and then—"

"What trail?"

"I was jogging yesterday morning. Right after Anona left for the cemetery. Someone bumped into me, knocked me over a cliff and I took a fall."

"Where was this?"

"In the Presidio. It's not far from Stack House."

"Did you see who knocked you over the cliff?"

"No."

"The Presidio. That's the jurisdiction of the United States Park Police. Did you notify them?"

"No. At the time I thought it was just some jerk that was in a hurry and accidentally bumped into me."

Saylor's gaze settled on Duran's hands. "Were you injured?"

Duran held up his hands, like a surgeon waiting to

have a nurse slip on gloves. "They got scratched up a bit. Then I got a few nicks and cuts at the fire last night."

"Tell me about the fire."

Duran took almost ten minutes going over every detail of his movements, before and after the fire.

Saylor looked down to his polished cowboy boots, then brought his eyes up to interrogation depth. "If this is a kidnapping, there will be a ransom call. From what Stringer told me, your wife is quite wealthy."

"Yes. She inherited a good deal of money from her father, and her painting career has been very successful."

"Your wife is a very wealthy and very famous woman, yet you continue to work as an investigator."

"I tried retirement for a few months after Anona and I were first married. I didn't like it much."

The phone rang. Saylor leaned back in his chair until it creaked, reaching for the phone. "Chief Saylor."

Duran's gaze roamed the room as Saylor spoke, flicking over the photos on the wall, the bulletin board pin-cushioned with mug shots and lost children flyers.

"Okay, thanks, Sergeant," Saylor said, ending his call. "That was the Carmel P.D. They went to the cottage. No key under the front mat, Mr. Duran. But the front door was unlocked."

"Was . . . was—"

"The house was empty. No sign that anyone had slept there. A bottle of Scotch out on the kitchen table and a glass smelling of booze in the sink were the only signs that someone might have been there."

"Anona's a vodka or white wine drinker, Chief. She doesn't like Scotch."

Chief Saylor opened his mouth as if to say something, changed his mind, stood up, and held out a hand. "Well, I'll do my best to find out what happened to your wife, Mr. Duran. You can count on that. I'll be in touch. Come on. I'll show you out."

Duran's car was wedged between two black-and-white patrol cars. Saylor gave the Jaguar an admiring look.

"Nice wheels. What year is it?"

"Nineteen-seventy-five."

"I like the color. British racing green." Saylor ran the back of his hand lightly across the trunk. "It looks like new." He peered into the window. "They knew how to make them then. Leather looks like real leather. And wood trim, not that plastic stuff they put out today. I've got a classic 1958 MG convertible, but I'm getting tired of it. This is just what I'd like to move up to." He pointed to the rear of the car. "How about the trunk? Much space?"

Duran unlocked the trunk lid. He'd checked and made sure whoever had started the fire at Anona's studio hadn't stashed any paint thinner cans in the Jaguar. "Enough," he said. Enough for a reasonable amount of luggage, golf clubs, or for the chief's unspoken question: a body.

Saylor bent down and stuck his head inside the trunk. "You sure keep it clean, Mr. Duran. How about the backseats. Much room there? I'm tired of that cramped MG."

Duran dutifully opened the back door for the policeman, who bent down and swept his hand across the car's carpeting, his fingers coming in contact with what appeared to be a small pebble. "Beautiful piece of machinery," he said, scooping up the pebble. "Just beautiful." He held the pebble between his thumb and forefinger, squeezing one eye shut like a jeweler examining a rare stone. "There's a little hole in this thing."

He handed it to Duran. "You said your wife had her rosary beads in her purse, didn't you?"

Duran nodded, rolling the bead around in his palm. "Yes, yes she did."

Saylor plucked the bead from Duran's palm. "How do you suppose this got into your car?"

"I . . . I don't know, it could have been there for some time, perhaps it was a—"

"You mind if I look a little closer?" Saylor asked, not waiting for an answer as his hands explored the carpeted floors and the leather seating. He leaned and pawed under the front seat, his hand coming out with a cluster of rosary beads. "Are you a religious man, Mr. Duran?"

Duran stared at the chief's hand in wonderment. "I don't know how those got there."

Otto Kline focused the binoculars in on Duran and the policeman, his upper lip riding up over his teeth in a wolfish grin. It had worked out better than he had hoped.

Kline had had no trouble in slipping the rosary beads into the back of Duran's Jaguar, while Duran was visiting the attorney. The car had been left in a downtown parking lot, the doors unlocked, the key still in the ignition.

Kline had anticipated Duran finding the beads, or maybe the stiff-backed butler, who probably handled such mundane chores as washing the cars at Stack House. But the police! God, it was almost too good to be true.

Chapter 18

The sky was pale blue, with just a few scratches of clouds. The bay waters gleamed like dark ice. He sat on his camp stool and sketched a dusty-brown pelican perched on a rotting piling. A pelican. In all his years at Pelican Bay Prison he hadn't seen even one of the species. His eyes drifted over to the Jaguar, then to the pier leading to Duran's office.

Duran had stopped back at Stack House after leaving the police station, and after a brief interlude of pulling off the road and tearing through the car looking for anything else that might belong to his beloved wife. Then he'd driven directly to his office. He smiled at the thought of Duran worrying that her purse, watch, or wedding ring might pop up at any moment.

The pelican arched its neck and stretched out its wings toward the morning sun, rolling them slowly, like a matador taunting a bull.

After a few minutes, the pelican had enough of the sun, folded its wings and burrowed its head into its chest, hunched over like an old man.

He flipped back to the original drawing. Anona Stack hadn't figured it out yet. He enjoyed the look of puzzlement on her face as she stared at him, trying to figure out who he was. He'd have to help her—give her a few clues. She had to know. Had to know how Arlene died. Would Duran make the connection? After all these years? The odds seemed slim. So much had happened since that day in Beverly Hills. He and Arlene were in the back of the shop, working on a Piet Mondrian geometric oil "Composition in Red and Blue." It was one of the easiest works they had ever forged, simple squares of color bounded by black outlines. They'd been discussing where to go for lunch when the commotion started. The banging of doors, shouts, then Royce Breamer screaming in that high-pitched squeal of his. Before they could get to the back door, two policemen had stormed into the room, grabbed him, then Arlene, handcuffing them like common criminals. Duran had stood by the door, taking it all in, a satisfied look on his face.

"How much?" a voice asked from behind him.

He jumped to his feet and turned to confront a beer-bellied man wearing dark glasses, a flower-print shirt, and plaid Bermuda shorts.

A bell-shaped woman was standing alongside him. A sweatshirt with a stencil of Alcatraz Island barely covered her stomach.

The man pointed a pudgy finger at the sketch pad. "How much for the picture of the bird?"

"How much would you spend?" he countered.

"Put me and the little lady in with the bird and I'll give you ten bucks."

He laughed. Prison prices—except the guards always paid him off with cigarettes rather than cash. "All right. Stand over there, by the piling."

"Come on, Mama, and don't scare the bird."

Peggy Jacquard swooped by without paying any particular notice to the artist or his subject. Street artists were a common sight around Fisherman's Wharf. She hurried down the pier, as always careful not to catch her heels in the cracks between the boards.

She had spotted Duran's Jag in the parking lot, so she didn't bother looking for her key to the office.

Duran was hunkered down behind his desk, the computer on, a stack of folders at his side. His sleeves were rolled up, his tie undone. His forehead was a washboard of wrinkles. She walked over, gave him a peck on the cheek.

"Bob. You really took a beating in the fire," she said, glancing at his face and bandaged wrist.

"Nothing serious," he assured her. "Here, take a look at these."

Peggy's nostrils flared when she saw the Xeroxed copies of Anona's letter and the photographs of her and Duran.

"This is bullshit," she protested loudly. "It was at my birthday lunch, for God's sake! You and I never—"

"I know that, Peg, and so does Anona," Duran insisted. "Whoever took those photos forced Anona to write that letter."

"Are you sure it's Anona's handwriting?"

"If it's not, it's a damn good forgery. And the letterhead and envelope. Dead ringers for Anona's stationery."

"You think somebody could have snatched the paper from Stack House?"

"It's a possibility. But Anona is a compulsive letter writer—she writes to her friends, her fans. She'd rather write a letter than use the phone. Someone could have sent her a letter just to get a response, so he could buy the same type of paper, and have the letterhead printed. Whoever grabbed Anona planned this out very carefully, Peg. He stalked her, and me.

He followed you and me out to lunch and took those photographs."

Peggy brought her hands together at chest level, fingertip to fingertip, as if doing an isometric level. "Who the hell could it be? Have you any ideas?"

"Not really. The head Colma cop, Chief Saylor, asked me if I thought one of our cases could have something to do with Anona's disappearance. I've been going through some files, trying to find someone mad enough at me to pull a stunt like this."

"Any luck?" she queried, striding over to the window overlooking the lineup of colorful old wooden fishing boats. "Have you come up with any suspects?"

"A few possibilities. I know some people out there who dislike me, but not enough for someone to do this. It just doesn't make any sense."

"What about the police? Have they got any leads?"

"No, nothing. At least they haven't told me anything."

"Could the theft of the Fritzheim Van Gogh have anything to do with it?"

Duran massaged his chin. "So far, I can't see a connection, but I'm not going to rule it out."

"What about Jason Lark?" Peggy asked. "I don't like the timing. Him showing up, and then Anona disappearing."

"I gave Saylor his name. Jason's a no-good bastard who is capable of just about anything if the stakes are high enough. But this just doesn't fit Lark. He's more a steal-your-wallet-when-you're-asleep guy. This is too physical, too complicated for Lark."

"Maybe it's someone with a grudge against Anona. Someone whose toes she stepped on without realizing it."

Duran's brow knitted. "Let's take this one step at

a time, Peg. I'm shoved off the trail. Then Anona is kidnapped. Then I'm knocked out and left to die in the fire. That means someone had access to the studio—he must have gotten the key from Anona, and made her give him the alarm combination." He patted the folders on his desk. "You take a look at these and see what you think."

Peggy carried the files to her desk, then came back with a thick manila envelope. "This came in yesterday, from Fritzheim. It's a photograph and the appraisal for 'Sun and Sky.' "

Duran nodded his thanks. The appraisal was a duplicate of the one the insurance carrier had provided.

Duran glanced at the photograph of the Van Gogh, a pale image of the explosive power of the artist's well-documented imagination, his distorted images and "devil's furnace" coloring: blood-reds, mustard, and lemon-yellows applied with a strong, varied brush stroke.

He shuffled the photograph and documents together, then dropped them in his "in" file, and returned to the computer, accessing old cases, sifting through the reports on the blue background computer screen. There had been threats made against his life. They were the heated "I'll get you for this" cries of frustrated white-collar thieves, often first timers who really didn't consider ripping off an insurance company a crime. He concentrated on the more exotic cases, where a lot of money was involved, and where he had worked with the police, had testified in court, and where the suspect had gone to jail. A Monet recovered in Venice. The thief a mild-mannered security guard at a private museum. He'd been sent to an Italian prison according to the notes in the file. That was over five years ago. He was probably out on probation after a year or two. If so, with all the corruption going on in Italy, he might even have his old job back.

There were several more museum thefts, in New York, New Orleans, Santa Fe, Dallas, and Houston. The Houston case involved a Robert Motherwell abstract that had been insured for over two million dollars.

Duran had eventually found it hanging over the bar of a restaurant in New York's Little Italy. "Funny thing, just black circles and stripes on white, but I kinda like it," the thick-necked bartender had told Duran.

The owner of the restaurant wasn't all that happy about having to give up the painting. Threats were made, with obvious references to the Mafia.

Duran had had another run-in with the New York Mafia, over Peruvian artifacts smuggled in via a ship that docked in New Jersey. The Mafia was not adverse to killing two birds with one stone—the ancient statues were hollowed out and filled with cocaine. Duran figured that if the Mafia had wanted him killed, they would have done it right then and there, but he decided to print out the names and ID of the two mafioso who had been arrested, only to be found not guilty by a nervous, intimidated jury.

He worked his way through myriad fraud cases, then into the investigations where he dealt directly with the thieves—buying back the artwork at a tenth of its insured value—the thieves often actually working for the owner of the stolen property.

He made hard copies of the files that had even a remote possibility of a connection to Anona, highlighting the individual's name with a yellow marking pen.

"Coffee?" Peggy asked, drawing Duran's attention from the computer screen.

He rubbed his eyes and fought back a yawn. "I could use a potful."

Peggy set a cup on the desk.

"Did you find anything in the files?" Duran remarked, reaching for the coffee.

Peggy rolled her ergonomic, adjustable chair over to the desk and sat down with a sigh. Her nylons rustled when she crossed her legs.

"No. I was thinking. Maybe we're not looking back far enough. Maybe this is someone who's been holding a grudge against the *two* of you for a long time. When we were working at the Centennial Insurance Agency, there was a forgery case involving one of Anona's paintings. Remember that? You caught the people who forged her painting. Didn't Anona go to Los Angeles and testify against that old Swiss character?"

"Yes, but . . ."

"He went to jail," Peggy pointed out.

"If I remember right he was extradited to a prison in Switzerland."

"Well, it's a thought," Peggy said, getting to her feet and smoothing her skirt. "It might be worth checking out."

Duran took a sip of the coffee. It didn't sound very promising, but it was something to do. He'd go crazy if he just sat around waiting. Waiting to hear from Saylor. Or from the bastard who had kidnapped his wife.

He stood up and slipped into his suit coat. "Have Rachel run a criminal check on those names I've highlighted."

Rachel was a tough-as-nails bail bonds woman in Oakland, who was Duran's source for confidential records. She was a statuesque brunette with a tattoo of a snake coiled around one wrist. She got the rap sheets from her boyfriend, an Oakland Homicide detective. Peggy and Rachel sometimes went out on double dates. They made an intimidating duo.

He started for the door. "Peg, lock up after me."

"No one's going to mess with me," Peggy protested.

"Let's not take any chances. Remember those photos. Whoever's behind this knows what you look like."

Duran walked toward his Jaguar, nervously eyeing the milling crowds of tourists.

Chapter 19

Anona Stack nursed her second carton of milk, taking birdlike sips every few minutes. She had tried to judge the time of day by the way the shadows were slanting through the trees. But now that the sun was gone, there was just a thick gray mist. She could smell the heavy scent of the ocean.

She knew she had to be somewhere on the coast. North or south of San Francisco. She didn't know how long she'd been unconscious on the floorboard of the Land Rover the day before.

If they'd gone north, he would have had to drive across the Golden Gate Bridge. He'd abducted her in Colma. It would have been easier, quicker to go south. But how far south?

The almost constant fog, the cool nights. Her best guess was somewhere in San Mateo County. Somewhere not too far from the city, because the madman wanted to know all about Bob, all about Jason Lark. He'd want to be close to the city.

Was that where he'd taken off to? To San Francisco? What was he doing? Looking for Bob? Was he planning to kidnap Bob, too?

She slipped her hands through the door opening for the umpteenth time, straining, feeling around, but finding nothing but slick, cold steel. The padlocks were out of reach, and even if she could get her hands on them, she knew it wouldn't do her any good.

She needed a weapon. But she had nothing. Just her hands and her feet. She'd filed her fingernails on the edge of the rough seams of the bed's angle iron. They were sharp and ragged now. She dug the nails into her palms, disappointed when they didn't puncture her flesh.

She kept going over what the madman had said: "Haven't you figured it out? Don't you know who I am?"

Movement caught her eye and she edged backward thinking of the mountain lion. But it was just a pair of black squirrels rummaging through the pine trees.

She settled down on the mattress, forcing her mind to go blank—turning it into a big white empty canvas. Then she placed the madman's face on the canvas, studying it, focusing on each feature: hair, forehead, nose, ears, cheeks, lips, mouth, chin.

"Don't you know who I am?" her canvas mocked at her.

She fleshed out the face a little, gave some weight to the cheeks, removed a few wrinkles, lengthened his hair, had him turn his profile to her, with his lip curled up, exposing his gums. "Haven't you figured it out yet? Don't you know who I am?"

Anona added a mustache, and lengthened his hair. She gave him a beard, screened his hair out farther, hippy length. His altered image leered back at her.

Now! That was a face she knew! The forger! And his wife was a forger, too! But why now? That was years ago. Why now?

The Centennial Insurance Agency's receptionist, an attractive brunette who looked like a cheerleader fifteen years after leaving college, gave Duran a quick look, noticing the scratches on his face and the bandaged wrist first. Then she took her time, her shopper's eyes raking him professionally. Rugged looking, beautifully tailored suit, immaculate shirt, power tie, chunky gold watch. She flashed her best smile. "May I help you, sir?"

"I'd like to speak to Peter Fowler."

The receptionist hesitated a second. Fowler was a notorious grouch who had a standing order that he did not want to be bothered with unscheduled appointments. "Your name, sir?"

"Bob Duran."

"A Mr. Bob Duran would like to see you, Mr. Fowler." She tilted her head and cradled the receiver between her shoulder and neck. "That's right. Bob Duran."

After a moment she lowered a finger, breaking the connection. "He'll be right out. Would you care for a cup of coffee?"

The coffee and Peter Fowler arrived at the same time. "Bob Duran. It's been a long, long time," Peter Fowler said in a raspy, smoker's voice. "I never thought I'd see you back here."

They shook hands in that uncomfortable way old acquaintances, or at least coworkers did. People who worked together on a daily basis, got to know each other's habits, good and bad, and then drifted apart and became strangers.

Fowler was a tall, gangly man, his body curved in an academic stoop. Bald, but for some gray strands combed sideways across his scalp. He wore a floppy, polka-dot bow tie and baggy pants held up by bright red suspenders.

"Good to see you, Peter. Can we talk in your office?"

"Sure. You must remember the way."

Duran followed Fowler down a familiar, narrow hallway, the filled-to-the-brim coffee cup in one hand. Nothing seemed to have changed. It was the same honeycomb of offices, all with six-foot partitions—the top half of frosted glass. The hollow doors had slide-in signs with people's names on them. Names Duran did not recognize.

Fowler's office was different from its clones only because of the view. If you leaned just the right way, you could see the Ferry Building clock tower, sandwiched between the city's ever-changing skyway.

"Sit down, Bob," Fowler suggested, whisking out a vinyl, contoured chair. "I saw the story about you in the paper. It looks like you were lucky to get out of the fire alive." He collapsed into the chair behind his desk, the chair sighing luxuriously as he did so.

"Yes. The fire department is still trying to figure out what happened." Anona's disappearance hadn't made the news yet. He wondered how long it would take for the story to come out. He'd checked with George before leaving the office. There had been no ransom demands. No news. Nothing.

"I think there's a possibility that someone who I came across in an old investigation here at CIA could be responsible for the Fritzheim Van Gogh heist. I'd like to run through the old files."

Fowler pulled a bent-stemmed, briar pipe from his jacket pocket and tapped the stem against his freckled teeth. He grimaced slightly. There had been some hard feelings when Duran left to start his own firm. He hadn't taken any of CIA's clients with him at the time, but eventually many of them had gravitated his way. "Can't smoke in here anymore," imparted Fowler. "Damned environmentalists." He gnawed briefly on the pipe stem. "I don't know, Bob." He pulled back his sleeve cuff and examined his watch. "It's getting a little late, those files are in storage, and after all, you're no longer with the company."

"You must keep all the reports on the computer. Even way back then we were using computers."

"Yes, but—"

"Look, Pete. If I find anything, I'll be sure to mention your cooperation to the people at Pacific Indemnity."

Fowler sucked on his pipe for a moment. "I guess it wouldn't hurt," he conceded.

Fowler led Duran to one of the cubicles and showed him how to access the computer. Duran explored the index until he found the correct name: Breamer, Royce.

Royce Breamer. A small, foppish man in his sixties, barely five feet tall, with an upscale art gallery in Beverly Hills. He had been doing well, selling well-done forgeries to the rich and famous. He was part of the "in crowd." Cashmere and cocaine. Power seats at the Lakers games. All was going well until he was tripped up by a forgery of one of Anona Stack's abstracts, "Blue Leaves."

The Centennial Insurance Agency had been asked by one of Breamer's Los Angeles buyers to insure "Blue Leaves" for eight hundred thousand dollars. CIA was delighted to sell the policy, only they had already insured that very same painting for a woman in Tampa, Florida.

Duran had been sent to Los Angeles, where he picked up "Blue Leaves," then flew to Tampa. The two paintings were close to being identical. It was only when they were placed side by side and examined by a trained eye, that the subtle differences could be detected.

Anona Stack had agreed to fly to Tampa to personally check them out. That was their first meeting. The attraction was immediate. And mutual. She was in the prime of her mid-thirties, tall, willowy, her hair a soft, spun-gold color. He still remembered what she was wearing that day: a cool-looking white dress, alligator shoes and, dangling from her arm, an Hermés red calf-leather purse.

The owner of the original "Blue Leaves" in Tampa was a handsome, flaxen-haired woman who was obviously delighted to have the famous artist as a guest.

The paintings were displayed in her private gallery, a large, airy room with a barrel-vaulted ceiling studded with recessed lighting which pin-spotted her collection.

Anona Stack's original hung on the wall, between a David Stuart cubist and a John Singer Sargent watercolor landscape.

The painting that Duran had picked up in Los Angeles was propped up against the wall, directly under the original.

Anona Stack ran the tips of her fingers slowly across both canvases, moving to her signature, which, in defiance to tradition, was on the top right corner of her paintings. She stood transfixed, hands on hips for a good five minutes, studying both works before she spoke. "The miserable son of a bitch," she finally said. "I'd like to kill him. He's even got my signature down pat." She swiveled to face Duran. "Please find out who did this. I hate the thought of someone doing this to me."

The Centennial Insurance Agency required all of

their employees to fly coach, and the red-eye whenever possible. Duran had booked a flight back to Los Angeles early the following morning.

Anona Stack insisted that he travel with her, first class to San Francisco, where he could catch a commuter flight to Los Angeles.

They spent the flight sipping champagne, talking art and getting to know each other. Although the financial gap between them was of Grand Canyon size, they found that they had a lot in common: They liked the same artists, the same foods, and their politics clashed just enough to make it interesting. She was a wonderful raconteur, and had Duran in stitches with storics about the rich and famous. She in turn seemed fascinated when he told her of his background, and his first wife's untimely death.

After they landed at the San Francisco Airport, Duran accompanied Anona to her waiting Bentley.

"Go down to Lotus Land and bury this creature, Bob," Anona Stack said, her voice slightly slurred from the on-board champagne. "Do that for me, please." She dug a card out of her handbag. "Call me when you get back. I want to see you again. No matter what happens."

What happened was that Duran, cooperating with the Los Angeles Police Department's Fraud Squad, found that Royce Breamer's real name was Joseph Phelps, that he was a con man wanted in Switzerland and Italy for similar ventures. Breamer had a long record, all the charges relating to forged art: paintings, ancient manuscripts, and rare coins. But there was never any violence involved. He was sentenced to prison, then shipped off to Switzerland, where the charges were more extensive than those in Los Angeles.

Duran remembered Breamer's gallery. A beautiful layout positioned in a perfect Rodeo Drive location. There had been some really fine paintings on display. He no doubt could have made a good living operating it on a legitimate basis. But once a con man, always a con man.

Duran was chasing down a Paul Cezanne painting which had been lifted in broad daylight from the walls of a Boston gallery at the time of the Breamer trial. Anona went down to Los Angeles to testify.

Breamer's employees, who had done the actual forgeries, a husband-and-wife team, Otto and Arlene Kline, were also arrested.

Duran closed his eyes, conjuring up a fuzzy image of the Klines—she was short, very attractive, with long, dark hair. The husband was tall, with a wiry beard, his hair almost as long as his wife's. Neither had any type of prior criminal records and when convicted, were given minimum sentences.

Duran printed the entire file, then phoned his office. He caught Peggy just as she was closing up shop.

"I have a few more people for Rachel to check out."

Peggy reached for a pen. "Shoot."

Duran read off Breamer's name and statistics, then added the Klines'. "When will Rachel be able to get these to us?"

"Her boyfriend works the four-to-midnight shift."

"Tell her I'm in a hurry, Peg. Have her fax them over as soon as she can."

Chapter 20

Anona heard the car engine cough to a stop.

She picked up her blankets, threw them on the bed, then crouched down by the cutout in the door and waited.

She edged backward when she spotted him coming down the trail. He was dressed the same, all in gray. There was one thing different. He had a rifle in one hand.

Was this it? Was this the day he was going to kill her? She swallowed hard, raking her fingernails on her dungarees, feeling the sweat on her palms. His eyes, she told herself. Go for his eyes. She waited until the door locks were undone and the door swung open before speaking.

"I didn't think you were coming back today."

He tossed the foot cuffs onto the cell floor.

"You don't like being all alone in the SHU, do you?"

"Why do you call it a shoe?" Anona asked, bending down to attach the leather cuffs to her ankles.

"S-H-U. Solitary Housing Unit. Hurry up," he instructed. "You've been here two days. Does that seem like a long time?"

"How much longer will I be here?"

He poked at her bra hanging from the ceiling hook

with the rifle barrel. "That's up to you, isn't it? I did it for five hundred and forty-seven days."

Anona thought of calling him by his name, to see his reaction, but held back, thinking she could surprise him with the information, possibly catch him off guard. Somehow use the knowledge as a weapon.

If she could figure out who he was, then so could Bob. It was just a matter of time. Then Bob would find her.

She shuffled out of the cell, her thumbs hooked in her jean loops, her eyes examining the rifle. A lever-action carbine. Probably a .30-30 caliber. Her father had one just like it, and called it a "saddle gun." She started toward the cabin.

"You're getting the routine down, aren't you?" he joked.

She nodded in agreement, walking slowly, steadily to the cabin, up the steps and inside.

He stood back and gestured with his head. "To your chair."

Anona followed his directions, sitting down, and snapping on the handcuffs.

He left her there for what seemed a long time. She heard him rummaging around in the kitchen. When he came back, he was carrying her portfolio of sketches, the ones she'd had with her at the cemetery.

He spread her sketches across the table top.

"Too bad you'll never be able to finish these."

Anona shivered, then stretched her head toward the easel. Words. Fight him with words. It was all she had. "What I saw of your painting looked interesting."

He went to the easel, snapped the sheet off, and dragged the painting closer to the table.

"Tell me what you like about it."

Not too much, not too little, she told herself, he's

no fool. "I like the naturalistic style, mixed in with the shadings."

He sank into the chair across from her and asked, "What about the sky? What do you think about the sky?"

Anona was silent for a moment. "You're not finished with the sky yet."

The scraping of his chair legs made her jump. He gave her a long, hard look, then stomped into the kitchen.

He came back with her purse in one hand, a can of beer in the other. He shook two pills loose from a small bottle, took a long pull on the beer, then began trawling through the purse, coming out with her wallet.

He dropped the purse to the floor as he began flipping through the plastic foldouts holding her family photographs.

"This is your daughter," he announced, holding up a picture of Lisa in a floor-length gown. "Did you know she's sleeping with Eric? And was fucking a guy named Donald?"

Anona fought to keep her facial features emotionless.

"And this is your son," he said, fingering a picture of John in his swimsuit, standing in front of his houseboat in Sausalito. "I don't like his club. The music's too loud, and he charges too much for a drink."

Anona felt her left eye begin to twitch. He knew all about her children. About Lisa's friends. How could he? It wouldn't have been hard to find out about Johnny's nightclub. But Lisa. How did he know about her friends? She had dated Donald months ago. Had he been stalking them that long? What plans did he have for Lisa? For John?

He wiggled the next picture from the wallet holder.

Anona blinked back the tears as he shoved the photo at her face.

"Your wedding picture. The happy couple," he scoffed. "Where was this taken?"

"Acapulco," she said, dismayed at the sound of her own voice: cracked, wobbly, fearful. She strained her wrists against the metal cuffs, concentrating on the pain.

"Acapulco," he repeated. "How nice."

He trawled the photo in front of her eyes slowly, then rasped, "Take a good look, it's your last chance to see Duran."

He tore the photo in half, then went back into the wallet, extracting both Lisa's and John's photos and tore them in pieces also, all the while grinning, his lips riding obscenely over his teeth.

He molded the pieces into a ball and casually tossed it over his shoulder toward the fireplace.

"Poof. All gone," he said in a stony voice. "You'll never see them again. Never."

Anona bit down on her tongue to keep from responding. From cursing him, shouting out his name.

He watched her eyes closely, waiting for the flood of tears. She was tough. Tougher than he'd expected. He'd have to increase the pressure.

He slipped his knife from its sheath.

Anona braced herself for the blade, her muscles taut, straining at the handcuffs and leg restraints. Instead he stabbed the painting on the easel, slashing back and forth until it was nothing but a ragged, gaping hole.

His eyes were narrow slits and he was breathing deeply through his nose, his face creased in pain, his lips so tight they looked sewn together.

"That was shit!" he erupted. "My wife was the

painter. Yes, she was good. Better than me. Better than you!"

He drop-kicked the damaged frame, sending it flying across the room. "Better than you!" he repeated, then dropped down to one knee, so that his face was level with hers.

"Do you know how my wife died? Do you?"

Anona couldn't control her left eye anymore. It was twitching as if sending out morse code. "No," she said, feeling that he'd gone over the edge.

"You killed her! Damn you, you killed her!"

Anona flinched as if she'd been struck. "No, no. I—"

He ran the back of his hand viciously across his mouth, as if he wanted to hurt himself. "You drove her to it. She was in her prison cell. She never should have been there. You put her there. Where she hung herself. With her bra! Just like you're going to do!"

He pulled Anona's Rolex from his pocket, his fingers fumbling as he pulled out the knob and twisted it, adjusting the date. He shoved the watch in front of Anona's eyes, so close to her eyes that all she could see was a blurry gold circle.

He threw the Rolex to the floor, picked up the rifle and smashed the butt end furiously up and down on the watch.

"That's when you're going to die!" he ranted. "Either you do it yourself, or I'll help you!"

Duran was surprised to see both Hugh Stringer's silver BMW and Johnny Stack's black Porsche in the Stack House parking area. Lisa's Mercedes was in its regular spot.

He parked the Jag and hurried into the house, entering through the kitchen.

George was there to greet him.

"Any news, sir?"

"Nothing. What's going on?"

"A meeting, in the game room. They've been there for over an hour."

Duran found them seated at the poker table. Hugh Stringer sat at the head seat. Johnny and Lisa were at his right, Jason Lark at his left.

Johnny was dressed all in black—leather pants, cotton T-shirt, and a leather motorcycle jacket with zippered pockets and sleeves.

Lisa was wearing a butter-yellow, V-necked sweater and skirt. Her hair was tied back with a matching ribbon. Duran tried to make eye contact, but she tilted her head toward the ceiling, like royalty ignoring the crowd.

"Ah, here's Robert now," Stringer announced nervously.

John Stack pointed a finger at Duran as if it were a pistol. "I saw Mom's letter. What did you do to her?"

"Nothing. The letter's a phony, John."

John pounded his fist on the table, causing the liquid in the glass at his elbow to spill onto the heavily polished oak. "I can recognize my mother's handwriting, Goddamn it!"

"It's Anona's handwriting. I'm saying someone forced her to write it."

Johnny slammed his hand down again, knocking the glass over this time. "What bullshit! She wants you out of here, and so do I. Right now!"

"Easy, John," Stringer cautioned. "Easy. We won't get anywhere at this rate."

Jason Lark broke the strained silence. "Let's say for the moment that what you're saying is true, Bob. Who do you think would . . . make Anona write such a letter?"

"I was hoping you might have an answer. Everything's gone to hell since you got here, Jason."

"I'm just sorry I didn't get here sooner," Lark sneered. "I may have been able to prevent all of this."

Duran leaned over, his hands knuckle down on the table, the heavy blue veins standing out like ropes. "Where were you yesterday morning when Anona went to the cemetery?"

"Right here," Lark responded coolly. "Dear old George can verify that." He smoothed his tie and examined both ends to see if they matched in length. "Lisa tells us that you were all cut up before Anona's letter arrived." He gazed at Duran's bandaged wrist. "Before the fire at her studio."

Duran straightened up and glared at Lark. "Someone pushed me off the trail in the Presidio."

"Really?" Lark responded. "How convenient."

"Gentlemen, please," Hugh Stringer shouted, his normally red face deepening in color. "Let's be civil about this."

Jason Lark jumped right back in the skirmish. "From what Hugh tells us, there's more than just the letter. There's the family crypt being broken into. Blood on Anona's vest. That's what worries me."

Johnny Stack leaned across the table and shook a fist at Duran. "I'm going to hire a private investigator to find my mother. You've probably been stealing from her since you got married, you bastard! If you hurt her, I'll kill you!"

"John, calm down. I don't think hiring an investigator is necessary," Stringer counseled. "The police are—"

"Fuck the police! I want my mother found!" Johnny

shoved his chair back from the table, a look of loathing on his face. Saliva flew from his lips when he said, "If you've done anything to my mother, I'll kill you!"

Jason Lark followed his son from the room, pausing at the doorway to call to Lisa. "Are you coming?"

Lisa hesitated momentarily, then rose slowly to her feet. Her eyes flicked over to Duran briefly, then her chin dropped to her chest and she moved swiftly from the room, brushing Lark's hand away when he reached out to her.

Duran slumped into the chair just vacated by Jason Lark.

"Whose idea was this family gathering, Hugh? Yours?"

Hugh Stringer pursed his mouth for a moment, as though he was considering or rejecting a thought. "I thought the children should know. I am their attorney, as well as Anona's."

"And mine?" Duran queried.

Stringer shrugged and looked a trifle embarrassed. "You have to consider my position. Anona's letter directs me to start divorce proceedings. I sent Chief Saylor some of Anona's correspondence, so that he could verify the handwriting. The photographs of you and your secretary add credence to Anona's letter. You must realize that, Robert. Anona claims that she hired a private investigator. If so, he'll have to be found. Immediately."

"There is no private investigator," Duran argued. "Someone made her write that letter." He twisted the wedding ring on his finger. It was a plain gold band, a duplicate of the one Anona wore.

A rigging of yellow crime-scene tape sealed off the area in a fifty-yard circumference around the mausoleum.

Chief Bill Saylor ducked under the tape, his shoes making crunching sounds on the gravel.

"All finished, Chief," the crime technician, a bearish-looking man with a full beard informed him. He stripped off his rubber gloves as Saylor approached the mausoleum.

"Find anything, Tony?"

"Not much. Nothing in there except dust and spiders."

"Did you look for the rosary beads, like I asked you?"

"Yes. Didn't find a one."

Saylor ran a hand down the edge of the mausoleum door. "Nothing fancy here, huh?"

"No. It was simply pried open with a screwdriver or chisel. It didn't take much effort to break the lock."

"Were there any trace samples of blood?"

"We didn't find a drop, Chief."

The results of the blood samples from the fishing vest had come back. A-positive. Anona Stack's blood type. Her husband's, too.

Saylor rooted around in his pants pocket for the rosary beads. They were not worth anything as evidence now. Maybe he should have impounded the Jaguar right when he found them. But hell, he didn't even know if a crime had been committed, other than breaking into a mausoleum.

It was still possible that Anona Stack wanted to get away for a few days, just as she said in her letter. Divorce Duran. Leave him out in the cold. How would he react to that? The loss of all that money.

Duran was a cool customer. Or a damned good actor.

Saylor had run a criminal check on Duran. Two arrests in San Diego for the same offense. Battery.

Duran had been twenty years of age at the time. Nothing too serious, but they were crimes of violence. Then there was Duran's first wife. Teresa. Duran had said she'd died years ago in New York City. An aneurysm. Saylor had called in a request for the New York police to fax him a copy of the Teresa Duran file.

"Oh, there was one thing, Chief."

"What's that?" Saylor asked, zipping up his jacket.

The technician handed him a small plastic bag. Inside was one item. A quarter. A plain American Liberty twenty-five-cent piece.

Saylor carried the bag outside, examining the coin in the natural light. There was nothing special about it. Minted in 1973. It appeared to have seen its share of pay telephones, parking meters, and possibly slot machines.

"Where'd you find this, Tony?"

"In the corner. It was lying heads up," the technician explained. He rolled his shoulders. "I don't know if it means anything, Chief."

"Neither do I," Saylor admitted.

Chapter 21

Jason Lark tried to catch up with his son, but by the time he reached the garage, the squeal of the black Porsche's tires were echoing off Stack House's brick walls.

He sauntered back into the house and up to his room, flopping down on the bed. He placed his hands behind his head and stared up at the cream-colored ceiling.

Anona missing. And Duran. The hypocritical prick. All those years, Duran lording it over him, threatening to break his head if he ever touched Anona again. The black woman in the photos—Duran's secretary. She was a looker. Duran got caught dipping his wick. Lark knew only too well that Anona wouldn't put up with that. She had given him a few extra chances, but that was because of the kids. They were babies then; now they were adults. He applauded Johnny's idea of hiring an investigator.

Maybe Duran knew about the letter. About her dumping him. What if he . . . killed her? Where would that leave Jason? If Duran was responsible, he'd be out of the estate. In jail. The entire Stack fortune would be split between Johnny and Lisa.

Johnny had been pleasant enough, but there was no

love, no bond of any kind between them. And he had no doubts about Lisa's feelings. She still hated him.

If he wanted any of Anona's money, he'd have to beg for it from John.

He was angry with himself for not taking more of Anona's sketches from the studio before starting the fire.

He'd left behind outlines of some of her best paintings, and they went up in smoke. If Anona was dead, if Duran had killed her, the sketches and outlines would be worth even more money. Duran showing up like that was a shock. A shock he thought he'd turned into good fortune.

Killing Duran would have gotten Mario Drago off his back and solved a lot of his problems.

He closed his eyes, contemplating how all this fuss about Anona was going to help or hamper his finding the Picassos. It could help. It certainly gave him a reason to stay around the Stack House for a few more days. But the police might start poking around, too. And George. Would the old fart ever leave the premises now?

He'd made a quick round-trip flight to Santa Monica, stashed Anona's sketches in his office safe, then called Mario Drago. Drago was his usual terse self.

"Have you found out when the Fritzheim Van Gogh is going to be sold back to the insurance company?"

Drago wouldn't be satisfied until—

The banging on the bedroom door jarred him back to the present.

He looked up to see Robert Duran poke his head into the room.

"Lark. I had the police check the Carmel cottage. Someone left a bottle of Scotch and a glass in the sink. Was that you?"

Lark elbowed himself into a sitting position. "Carmel. Why the hell would I go to Carmel?"

"That's what I want to know. George tells me you've been snooping around the house."

Lark swung his feet to the floor and rested his hands on his knees. "Look, Bob. I don't know what the hell happened to Anona. But something strange is going on. You being pushed off the trail, then the fire at the studio. I'm wondering. Could it have something to do with the Fritzheim Van Gogh? Maybe the thieves are . . . shit, I don't know. Holding Anona because they think you're closing in on them, or . . . something like that," he finished lamely.

The two men stared at each other in a stiffly formal silence for several seconds.

Duran said, "You can stay until I find Anona. In fact, I want you to stay, so I can keep an eye on you. I've got a gut feeling you're involved in this somehow, Jason."

"Don't be silly," Lark protested, cutting the rest of his response off when Duran turned away, slamming the door behind him.

Lark dug his cigarette case out of his jacket pocket and lit up a ready-rolled joint, inhaled deeply, then hissed the smoke out between his teeth. "Prick," he murmured, the target of his curse Robert Duran. If he'd just hit him a little harder at the studio. If the damn fire department hadn't arrived so soon. Duran and Drago. The two thorns in his side. He blew a perfect smoke ring and stabbed his finger through the hole. *If I find the Picassos, I won't have to worry about either of them.*

Johnny Stack downshifted the Porsche and tapped his foot on the brakes. He was just a few feet behind the boxy station wagon that had been hogging the road.

He blinked his high beams on and hit the horn, but the driver of the station wagon held to a steady forty miles an hour.

Johnny saw his chance to pass, gave the horn another blast, then glided into the oncoming traffic lane and accelerated, feeling the wind in his hair and his spine being pressed into the back of the bucket seat. He caught a quick glimpse of the white-faced station wagon driver, then saw the headlights of an oncoming car. He swerved to the right, almost clipping the station wagon's front bumper.

He stuck his right arm up in the air and extended his middle finger in response to the blaring horn. The speedometer flickered between fifty-five and sixty as he negotiated the next turn.

The road flattened out, taking him onto Bridgeway and through the downtown area of Sausalito. At this time of the morning it was deserted—the busloads of tourists, exhausted from a day of shopping and souvenir hunting were all safely tucked away in their dingy motel rooms.

He was still upset about what he'd learned at the meeting at Stack House. Something *had* happened to his mother. He could sense it. He'd never trusted Duran. All those "I want us to be friends" bullshit gestures hadn't fooled him.

Duran was like Jason. A hanger-on. Someone with no real talent of his own, clinging to her, hoping some of the magic would rub off.

He throttled down as he moved through town, past the Sausalito Inn, toward the bobbing masts of the Yacht Harbor, then home, just beyond the World War II site of the Kaiser Shipyards. The eclectic mix of upscale houseboats and old, abandoned derelicts suited him just fine. The fact that only a handful of people knew this new address was a plus. He needed time to himself, to think, to create.

You don't have to paint to be an artist, his mother had often told him.

Johnny had tried painting, sculpting, and writing, but found he had no talent for any of them. Then he tried music, but the tedious piano and guitar lessons quickly bored him. Promoting, that was his forte, finding talent, refining it, showcasing it.

The Bay Area was ripe for a new Bill Graham, and he saw no reason why he couldn't be the one to fill those shoes.

His club, Stack's, was just a start. Just the beginning, he assured himself. He planned to bring in some top name acts to bolster the yet unknowns, his "discoveries."

He notched the Porsche into the carport, turning the collar of his leather jacket up as he walked over the wobbly planking leading to the pier.

The drawback to living in a houseboat came at low tide. The smell of raw sewage wafted over the oily bay waters as he carefully dodged rotting planks and dog droppings.

His houseboat was just that, a small house that had been fitted onto a barge and floated to its berth.

He was definitely going to hire a private investigator. In the morning. Right now he needed a drink. And a smoke. He had scored some high-grade grass at the club. Yes, first thing in the morning, he'd—

Suddenly he saw movement out of the corner of his eye. "Hey, what—"

The first blow caught him squarely between the eyes. He grunted a protest. Then there was a second blow to the top of his head. He fell, his arms dangling uselessly at his sides, his face hitting the decking at full force with a loud, squashy sound.

He felt himself being dragged, the rough wood tearing at his skin. He managed to get a glimpse of his assailant before he hit the water, the shock causing his mouth to drop open. He tried to shout, then the darkness closed over him, the water running into his nose, and finally covering his fear-glazed eyes.

Bob Duran had found it almost impossible to sleep. And so had Andamo. The terrier usually slept on the floor at Anona's side of the bed. Every so often Anona would give in to his begging and Andamo would spend the night with his head snuggled up against his mistress.

Now the dog relentlessly paced the room. Duran finally gave up, took a quick shower, dressed hurriedly, stopping in the kitchen only long enough to raid the refrigerator for a few carrots.

Andamo sat on the Jaguar's front passenger seat, his nose pressed against the window.

The morning sky reminded Duran of one of Anona's paintings. Rolling gray-blue clouds gilded pink by the tip of the rising sun.

He parked the Jag in the area where Chief Saylor said Anona was last seen.

Andamo jumped across Duran's lap as he opened the driver's side door. The terrier was running wildly by the time Duran got out of the car.

He watched as Andamo flitted back and forth, stopping to sniff the ground every so often, then going back into high gear.

"You should be a movie dog, Andamo," Duran said, taking a carrot from his pocket and tossing it among the rows of tombstones. "Find a clue. Show me where Anona's gone. Who took her."

Andamo darted off, coming back moments later with the carrot between his sharp teeth.

Duran began walking, first to the Stack mausoleum, then back to the Jaguar, picturing Anona at work. Absorbed in her work. Someone approaches her. Someone who claimed he was a gardener. Someone who told her that she'd have to leave her dog home.

Andamo clawed at his pant leg and he bent down and ruffled the dog's ears. "Come on, pal. There's nothing for either of us here."

Duran then drove straight to his office. The criminal histories were waiting in the fax machine.

The first two were of the "longer-than-my-arm" type, and Rachel had scribbled a series of question marks and a short note across the top of the page: "What the hell are you into, Peg?"

Angelo Belardi and Anthony "Tony Dope" Viscoti. New York mafioso, both in their seventies now. All of the arrests had taken place in New York—the charges ranging from strongarm, to attempted murder to bookmaking. Neither man had an entry in the last three years. Had they retired? Gone straight? Hired better lawyers? Died?

His inquiries relating to the museum thefts in Houston, Santa Fe and New Orleans had proved inconclusive—the thieves, all first-timers, had served their sentences and hadn't been heard from since, as far as the criminal justice system was concerned.

The owner of the Beverly Hills gallery, Joseph Phelps, aka Royce Breamer, Ron Breamer, Joseph Lally, Sidney Harris, William Morries, William Breener, had arrests dating back to 1958. Breamer-Phelps moved around the map: Delaware, Washington, D.C., Philadelphia. The same sad story followed him—arrests, but no convictions. There was a gap of some ten years between his arrest in Philadelphia and the art fraud charges in Beverly Hills. Duran surmised that the lapse between charges had to be during the time period that Breamer had operated in Europe.

The notation following the Los Angeles County arrest showed he was convicted, given a six-year sentence, then seven months later was extradited to Switzerland.

The next two histories were for Otto and Arlene Kline, the two artists who actually forged the paintings for Breamer.

Arlene Kline had been twenty-six at the time of her conviction, her husband thirty-one. Both had received identical sentences—two years, which normally would mean they'd be out in a year.

The second arrest on Otto Kline's record caught Duran's eye: 4501 Penal Code—Assault with deadly weapon by prisoner. Kline had been given a ten-year sentence for this offense.

There was no mention on the sheet as to whether or not he was still in prison.

Duran massaged his chin. Ten years. Pretty stiff. Was Kline still in custody? Could the additional charge have anything to do with Anona? With him? How? Arlene would have been released years ago. Where was she now?

The computer gave him some of the answers. He modemed into a database and entered the California driver's license ID numbers listed on the rap sheets for both Otto and Arlene Kline.

Arlene Kline's license had expired and showed her as deceased.

Otto Kline's license listed a postal box in Crescent City, California.

Duran switched to another database, checked the state death registrar and found that Arlene Kline had died in Los Angeles County just four months after she'd been sentenced to prison. She had died in prison! On October the twelfth. Almost seven years ago to the day.

Duran rechecked the rap sheets. Otto Kline's assault charge was listed as taking place on October 13th, one day after his wife's death.

He was mulling over the possibilities when the phone rang. The answering machine picked up the call.

"Mr. Duran. This is Jack Healy at the *Chronicle*, I'm calling to check a rumor about your wife. Call me at 555-1111, or I'll drop by and see you later today."

Duran cursed out loud, causing Andamo to awaken from a nap and roar out a string of barks.

The phone rang again. The tired voice of attorney Harry Lawson droned into the answering machine's speaker. "Robert. Harry Lawson here. I just got a call at this godawful time of—"

Duran snatched up the receiver and switched the machine off. "Harry, it's me. What's up?"

"What's up is me, Robert. At a time I'm not accustomed to. The gentleman with 'Sun and Sky' wants to do business. Today. Is that possible?"

Duran was still holding Otto Kline's rap sheet. He didn't want to leave San Francisco now. But if he did go to Los Angeles, he could talk to the police about Kline, and check his file at the courthouse. "Just when are you going to get your hands on the Van Gogh, Harry?"

"This afternoon. If it's a go, I'll have it by two o'clock."

"It's a go," Duran decided.

"Who's going to do the authentification?" Lawson queried.

"I'll let you know at two, Harry."

"Ah. Can't be too cautious in this business, can you, Robert? Say hello for me to Anona and to that delectable secretary of yours."

Duran broke the connection and immediately dialed Wendy Lange's number.

"Sorry to wake you up, Wendy, but it looks like it will be this afternoon for the Fritzheim Van Gogh."

"Ahh," Lange purred. "Outside of having breakfast in bed, I can't think of a better start to the morning."

Chapter 22

The big cat had come back during the night. She had no idea of the time. It was dark, the trees backlit by a thin moon.

Anona had been asleep. Deep asleep. Dreaming again. Bob was swimming in a churning pool of water. He'd take a stroke forward, only to be pushed back by a wave. Then he'd disappear under the foamy water, reappear for a moment, his mouth open. He was shouting. Shouting something she couldn't hear. There was a boat in the hazy background. A big white yacht. People in evening clothes, drinking, dancing. Bob was swimming away from them. He'd stop, tread water, open his mouth and call her name—"Anona! Anona!"—then disappear under water.

When she'd first heard the movement, she'd thought it was the madman. Coming for her again. Then she heard the low, throaty growl, saw the huge almond-shaped eyes glaring in at her through the cutout in the door.

The mountain lion made an abrupt turn and galloped away.

She hadn't been able to sleep after that. And now *he* was back. With breakfast. A cup of cool coffee, two slices of stale, white-bread toast, and a single black-skinned banana.

Anona said, "The lion was back last night," when he pushed the plastic tray through the slot.

His only response was a grunt. He turned and walked away. Anona was tempted to call after him. Call his name, but she held back, sinking onto the bed and sipping at the now cold coffee, taking small bites of the bread.

She heard an engine start up. He was leaving again. Off to where?

Then the engine sound got louder. Anona peered through the slot. A van was bucking its way down the narrow path.

It stopped less than a dozen feet from the SHU. Anona could see the license plate. She repeated the number and letter sequence several times, committing it to memory.

She watched as he exited the vehicle, popped the hood and hooked up a long, coiled wire to the battery.

Anona pressed herself against the back wall. Electricity. Was he going to electrocute her? God, was he—

The grinding buzz of a drill shattered the forest silence. She could hear him grunting with the effort of his work: hammering, drilling.

Silence. For a minute, no longer. Then a raw scraping and a slab of metal was drawn across the door's cutout.

Anona ran to the door, plastering the side of her face against the cold metal, peering out one of the bullet-sized holes.

He was standing there, a self-satisfied expression on his face.

Perspiration broke out on her forehead, slicking the door. Why? Why had he closed off the cutout? The mountain lion? No. It wasn't that, she realized. It wasn't that at all.

The dismal food for breakfast. The sealing off of her view—her window to what little of the world that was available. He was punishing her.

She backpedaled slowly, her hair brushing the bra hanging from the ceiling hook. The cell suddenly seemed to shrink, the walls inched inward. Her legs began to tremble and she collapsed onto the bed, as if a trapdoor had been pulled open under her. Her hands gripped her thighs, the fingernails digging into her flesh. She fought the feeling of hopelessness coursing through her body, fought the smell of fear oozing from her pores. "Find me, Bob," she recited in a whisper. "For God's sake, find me."

Jason Lark forked a chunk of potato into the juice of his breakfast steak, watching it slowly turn pink. He'd just sat down to eat when Robert Duran stormed into the house, with Anona's abominable dog clattering at his heels, shouting to old George that he had chartered a jet to fly to Los Angeles, instructing George to call him on his pager or to contact his secretary if there was any news of Anona.

Duran thundered down the inner staircase several minutes later, shrugging his arms into his suit coat as he walked.

Lark waited a short time, then patted his chin with the starched white napkin and headed to the garage area. Duran's Jaguar was gone.

He slid behind the wheel of the Lincoln. The car's motor rose and fell as he goosed the accelerator during the short trip to the gas station on Lombard Street. Duran flying off to Los Angeles. It could only mean one thing: Fritzheim's Van Gogh.

He used his credit card for the call to Las Vegas.

"It's me. Jason."

"And?"

"Duran is on his way to the San Francisco airport. He's chartered a jet to take him to Los Angeles. He's coming down to get the Van Gogh."

"You've done well, Jason. I'm pleased."

Lark studied his reflection in the phone booth's smudged window. "I think it would be a good idea if Duran is eliminated."

"He's connected you to the Fritzheim job," Drago said flatly.

"I'm not sure," Lark qualified, "but I don't like the way things are going, he—"

"The fire at Stack's studio made the news here. You botched the job, now you want me to handle it, right?"

Lark pressed the point. "If Duran is eliminated, I can go ahead with this other job, the old woman with a house full of—"

"Very well," Drago cut in. "He'll be taken care of."

Lark hung up and rubbed his hands together like a man anticipating a gourmet meal. He still hadn't found the Picassos, but at least Duran would be out of the picture.

Permanently.

"Nice flight, Mr. Duran?" asked the shaggy-haired limousine driver.

"Yes. I've got a tight schedule. First stop is the Los Angeles Police Department headquarters on West Sunset Boulevard."

"Yes, sir. My name's Lenny. No luggage?"

Duran patted his briefcase. "Just this." He settled

into the stretch Mercedes' backseat, opened the briefcase, and fingered the contents.

He had used the phone on the chartered jet to call the Los Angeles Police Department, and made contact with Paul Haber, the lieutenant who had headed the investigation in the Breamer–Kline arrests. Haber had since been upgraded to captain and now worked out of Homicide. Haber agreed to meet Duran in his office.

Duran had decided to keep Anona's name out of their conversation, for fear of Haber contacting Chief Saylor. He was sure that Saylor would advise his fellow policeman not to cooperate with the husband of a woman missing under suspicious circumstances.

The two men shook hands and Duran congratulated Haber on his promotion.

"Thanks, Bob. It's been a long time."

Haber had put on some weight and lost some hair since Duran had last seen him. He gestured Duran into his office, pointed to a chair, then said, "What can I do for you?"

Duran told him everything he knew about the Klines.

"What's your interest in them?"

"The Fritzheim Van Gogh."

"I thought they were forgers, not a burglary team."

"Their name has popped up, Captain. I can't overlook it."

Haber picked up a pencil and ran it through his fingers. "The Klines, and that old scoundrel Breamer. I haven't thought of that case in years. I wonder where Breamer is now? Probably living it up in Zurich or Paris."

"Probably," Duran agreed.

Haber pursed his lips, then got to his feet. "Let me go see what we've got."

He returned ten minutes later carrying a small batch of computer printouts.

"Otto Kline's been a bad boy, Bob. He damn near killed a guard while he was at the state prison in Chino. He got a stiff sentence and was shipped up to Pelican Bay, the toughest prison in the state. Maybe in the whole country. It's up north, by Crescent City, just a few miles from the Oregon border." Haber glanced down at the printouts. "He was released last month."

Duran's back stiffened. "Last month?"

"Right. His wife committed suicide. Right here in the county jail. She hung herself in her cell."

Duran leaned back in his chair, trying to digest the information. "How about a current address on Otto Kline?"

Again Haber went back through the printouts. "No. Nothing. Just the prison postal box in Crescent City."

"Do you know anyone at Pelican Bay?" Duran queried.

"Not personally," Haber chuckled. "I've sent them a few customers since I've been here at homicide. Do you want to talk to someone up there?"

"Very much so," Duran confided.

Chapter 23

Duran used the limousine's phone to call Peggy.

"You got out of town just before the posse, Bob. A reporter from the *Chronicle,* some guy from the fire department, and that Colma cop have been calling. Are you all right?"

"Yes. But somebody's leaked the story of Anona's disappearance to the press." Duran's jaw bunched. "I guess we were lucky to keep them at bay this long. I think your hunch on that old CIA case turned up positive." He told her about Kline's prison experience and his wife's suicide. "I just went through the medical examiner's file. Arlene Kline hung herself in her cell at the county jail. Run a driver's license check on Barbara Linker. She was in the cell with Mrs. Kline the night of her death. Forty-two years of age, born on August eleventh."

"Where are you now?"

"I'm on my way to the cemetery where Arlene Kline's buried."

Peggy moaned softly. "You're not thinking that—"

"No, but it's something to do while I'm waiting for that address on Linker. The medical examiner told me that the usual procedure when a prisoner dies in jail is that the body is cremated, at the state's expense. Otto Kline paid to have his wife buried. I've got a

Los Angeles police captain trying to put me in touch with someone at the Pelican Bay State Prison. Call your buddy Rachel. See who she knows in the prison system. I want to talk to someone up there at the prison, anyone who can give me some information on Otto Kline. Spend whatever's necessary."

"All right. Harry Lawson has called a couple of times. He says he'll be ready any time after two o'clock."

Duran glanced at his watch. It was close to noon already. "Call Wendy Lange. Tell her I want to set it up for three o'clock. Then call Harry back, give him the time schedule, and then call him again at two-thirty with Wendy's address. He'll be sitting on the phone with the Van Gogh cradled in his lap. I should still be able to get to Lange's place before he does." He read off the number labeled on the phone. "Call me as soon as you have anything on Barbara Linker."

Duran stretched out his legs and gazed out the limo's window, not noticing the passing scenery, thinking of Arlene Kline's death. "Incomplete suspension" was the way the attending coroner had described it. She had tied her bra around the bedpost of the upper berth in the two-bed cell. Then, while lying down, she had leaned out and over the bed far enough to compress the blood vessels of her neck and shut off the supply of oxygen to her brain. She'd stuffed a piece of her shirt in her mouth, apparently to keep from awakening her cellmate or drawing the attention of the guards.

It was an incredibly difficult way for someone to kill themselves. No quick fracture of the neck—a long, slow, painful, self-inflicted strangulation. What had driven her to it?

According to the ME's report, Barbara Linker, her

cellmate, claimed she heard nothing and knew of no reason for Arlene Kline to kill herself.

"We're here at the cemetery, Mr. Duran," the driver announced on the speaker.

"Let's find someone who knows where the bodies are buried."

It wasn't much of a cemetery, Duran noticed, once he was out of the limo. The lawn looked in need of a trimming. The grave markers were small, some just knee-high crosses.

"I'm looking for a grave," Duran told a man bent over the engine of an industrial-size lawn mower.

The man straightened up. He was a bonily thin man with long-lobed ears. Dark sweat marks showed at the armpits of his chambray shirt. "You came to the right place, Mister. Any particular grave?"

Duran smiled lightly. "The woman's name is Arlene Kline. She died in—"

"I know the grave. Over that hill." He pointed to the west. "There's a pond, then a small meadow. It's the one with the big new headstone."

Duran was impressed. He slipped on a pair of sunglasses and surveyed the area. The sky was cloudless, with a peculiar yellowish smog almost blotting out the brassy sun. The distant hills looked as if they were shielded behind saffron curtains. "There must be thousands of people buried here. Have you got them all memorized?"

"Nope. I just laid in the new headstone for Mrs. Kline a few weeks ago."

Duran dug out his money clip and pushed out a twenty dollar bill. "Would you mind showing me just where her grave is, Mr. . . . ?"

"Linszky." He waved the money away and hopped onto the seat of the lawn mower. "Follow me."

Duran climbed back into the limousine. "Follow that lawn mower," he said with a tight grin.

Linszky was right. There was just one new headstone. Duran scanned the older stones. Except for Arlene Kline's, the burial dates were twenty and thirty years past.

"This here is a potter's field," Linszky informed him. "Jailbirds. The county don't bury them anymore. They cremate 'em. It's a lot cheaper." He reached out and fingered the polished gray marble slab standing guard over Arlene Kline's remains. "This is the first new one I can remember."

Duran fixed his eye on the tombstone. Arlene Kline's name was chiseled in cursive script, then the words: AT FIRST THOUGHT SWEET.

" 'At first thought sweet,' " he said aloud. "It sounds familiar."

Linszky shrugged. "You got me. That was what was ordered, that's what I put on it."

Lenny, the limo driver, solved the puzzle for Duran.

"It's poetry. John Milton. 'Revenge at first thought sweet, bitter ere long back on itself.' It's from *Paradise Lost.*"

Duran arched his eyebrows in a questioning gesture.

"One thing about my job, I get a lot of time to read," Lenny explained.

Duran turned to Linszky. "Did you ever meet Mr. Kline?"

"Nope. I saw him just once. A few weeks ago. He spent about six hours at the grave. Brought his lunch and everything."

"What does he look like?"

"What's your interest?" Linszky countered.

"I think he may be trying to kill me."

The gardener's eyes widened sharply. "God's truth?"

"God's truth," Duran pledged.

"He's a big, gangly guy. Hair cut real close to his scalp. He didn't look friendly, and I didn't get very close."

"How did he pay for the tombstone?"

"He called on the phone, told me what he wanted. I gave him a price and he sent a United States Post Office money order." Linszky put his hands over his eyes to screen the sun as he peered at Duran. "Why do you think he's trying to kill you, mister?"

The girl who came to the door had long, carrot-red hair that streamed below her shoulder blades. Her eyes were topaz colored and doe-like. She was taller than Duran, thanks to her spiked heels. Her micro-mini, beige crocheted dress hung from a narrow strap looped around her neck.

Duran figured if he had a dollar for every year she was over sixteen he wouldn't be able to buy a Big Mac.

"I'm looking for Barbara Linker. Is she home?"

A scratchy voice called out from inside the apartment. "Who the hell is it, Paula?"

"I don't know," the girl answered softly.

The door was yanked open and a woman appeared, shoving Paula out of the way. Paula's companion was short, her gray-brown hair a tousled shag. Her skin was leathery. She wore jeans and a red-and-black flannel shirt, the sleeves rolled up to show a series of tattoos on each of her thick forearms. "What'd you want?" she challenged.

"I'm looking for Barbara Linker."

"What for?"

"I just want to talk to her."

The woman leaned her shoulder against the door jamb and frisked Duran with her eyes. "You're too fucking good looking to be a vice cop."

"I'm not a cop," Duran acknowledged. "I'd like to talk to Barbara Linker, and I'll pay for her time."

"Just to talk? You can get that from one of those phone-sex operations." She stuck her head out the door and looked down the hallway. "Maybe you want to talk to Paula, huh?"

"No. It's you I want, Barbara. It's about Arlene Kline."

Linker's mouth started to move, then stopped. "Kline? The push that hung herself in jail?"

"Yes. That's the one."

Linker held up a finger. "Wait a sec." The door closed. Duran could hear Linker ordering Paula to go to her room. The door reopened and Barbara Linker waved him inside.

"You said you'd pay, didn't you?"

The walls were covered in black leather, the ceiling mirrored. There were two zebra-striped couches against one wall. A wooden cross with handcuffs dangling from its edges sat in the middle of the room. A cobralike leather bullwhip was coiled neatly alongside the cross.

Duran massaged a fifty dollar bill between his fingers and held it out to Linker.

"Talk's not cheap, honey. Two hundred dollars." She shoved her hand out and wiggled her fingers for the money. "Three hundred, if you want Paula to join in."

Duran reached for his wallet. "Just tell me why Arlene Kline killed herself."

Barbara Linker leaned back against the wooden

cross, sliding her fingers in and out to the cuffs. "That happened a long time ago."

"Yes. And there is no way you could be held responsible. I just want to know why she did what she did."

Linker pursed her mouth in contempt. "Are you one of those kinky bastards that digs snuff films and all that shit? Is this the way you get your kicks?"

"It's a kinky world, Barbara. You know that. Tell me about Arlene Kline."

Chapter 24

Wendy Lange decided a cup of tea was just what she needed to calm her nerves. She had celebrated her thirty-eighth birthday the night before. Perhaps over celebrated. Long-legged, with a shapely figure and eyebrow-length bangs, she always projected an abundance of energy. Today, more so. She was excited about examining the Van Gogh. Just holding the painting, if it was authentic, would be the best birthday present she could have possibly given herself.

Her combination office-residence was a neat, white-brick Regency home on a quiet, tree-lined street in Los Angeles. She had spent most of the day at her computer, researching "Sun and Sky." Her lab was ready and waiting to give the painting a minute examination: ultraviolet, X ray, autoradiography, carbon dating. She entered the kitchen and turned on the tap. No water. She fiddled with the faucet handles, then cursed and checked the bathroom sink. Still no water.

She was reaching for the telephone when the front doorbell rang. She peered through the peephole. A stocky man with a drooping mustache, dressed in a tan shirt and cap was on her porch.

"Yes? What is it?"

"Water Department, ma'am. We've had a rupture up the street. Are you getting any water?"

"No." Wendy slipped the lock. The man had a tool belt sagging at his waist and a City of Los Angeles Water Department logo stitched on his shirt.

"Can you tell me how long this is going to take? I'm expecting—"

"It all depends, ma'am. I looked at your meter connection. You're lucky you haven't had problems before. Come on, I'll show you."

Wendy hesitated. "Just do whatever you—"

The man pulled something from his tool belt. It took Wendy a moment to realize that it was a gun. She opened her mouth to scream.

"Don't do it," he warned. "I really don't want to kill you."

Lange backed slowly into the house. The man waved the gun and nudged the door with his foot. "Turn around and get down on your knees."

She felt helpless. "Listen, I—"

"Just do what you're told, Wendy. I just want the Van Gogh. You won't be hurt."

"But, I—"

"Down," he shouted, as if commanding a dog to obey.

She sank to her knees. There were more footsteps, the door banged shut. Something wet, cold, bitter-smelling, was forced against her face.

The man in the tan shirt turned to his companion. "Grab her arms. She's fighting it."

The wet cloth was ground into her nose, her mouth. Her skin was burning, her eyes were hot and watering. She made a final effort to free herself, then suddenly went limp.

The man kept the towel in place for several seconds, then said, "She's out. Let's drag her into a back room."

"How long have we got to wait?"

"Until Duran shows up. Grab her feet."

He rolled his palm across Lange's breast. "She's kind of pretty. Too bad you put her out. We gonna do her?"

"No. We just do Duran."

"Good. I hate doin' women."

"Sorry about the traffic, Mr. Duran. I can get off the freeway in about a mile and take a back route."

"Do what you think best," Duran suggested. He checked his watch. Three-forty p.m. He had spent a long time with Barbara Linker, but it had been worth it. Wendy Lange would need at least several hours to authenticate the Van Gogh, so there was no reason to hurry.

Harry Lawson knew he could not contract a deal without Duran's approval. He reached for the mobile phone and called his office.

"Nice timing," Peggy said. "I've got you a connection with a guard at Pelican Bay. Rachel's boyfriend has a friend who has a friend, you know how it goes."

"I know. Time and place?"

"The only time this guard can meet you is before he goes to work in the morning. That means you'll have to be up there before seven."

"No problem, Peg. I've still got the chartered jet on standby."

"How are you fixed for cash? The guy you're meeting with will expect a donation."

"How much?"

"Rachel suggests three hundred dollars."

"Okay. Any other calls?"

"The fire investigator, Lieutenant Powers, he was by in person an hour ago. He's not a happy camper."

"What's his problem?"

"Not being able to talk to you. He was threatening to go to the district attorney if you don't cooperate."

"Who else?"

"Chief Saylor and the reporter from the *Chronicle* again."

"Did Saylor say anything about Anona?"

"No. He didn't seem too happy when I told him you weren't around."

"Okay. I'll fly into San Francisco tonight and talk to Chief Saylor and the fireman, then go on up to Crescent City in the morning."

Duran recognized Harry Lawson's pearl-gray Cadillac sedan parked in front of Wendy Lange's house.

Duran rang the doorbell and waited. He rang again, then knocked on the door and shouted out Lange's name. Still nothing.

Duran tried the handle. The door was unlocked. He pushed. Something was blocking the door. He pushed harder, grunting at the effort, calling out first Lange's name, then Lawson's.

The door finally budged enough for him to squeeze his head in. Harry Lawson was sprawled on the floor. A thin line of blood spiraled down from behind his ear, puddling in the crease of his neck and shirt collar.

"Is there a problem?"

Duran's head jerked around. It was Lenny, the limo driver.

"Call 911."

It was nine-thirty that night when Duran watched Captain Paul Haber and the uniformed policeman who had been guarding the door to Wendy Lange's room walk out of the lobby of the hospital.

He rode the elevator up to the seventh floor.

A nurse, gritty eyed with fatigue, called to him from her workstation. "You can't go in there. Ms. Lange is not receiving visitors."

"I'll just be a minute," Duran promised. "Captain Haber forgot a couple of questions."

Wendy Lange was propped up in bed. Her eyes were puffy and there was a raw red circle around her nose and lips.

"I'm sorry about this, Wendy."

"Me, too. I saw my face. I look like the flag of Japan. Any word on the Van Gogh?"

"No. Not yet."

Duran snapped open a folding chair and set it alongside the bed. "How did it go with the police?"

"I told them everything I know, which wasn't much. I just saw the one man, but there were two of them." She reported to Duran just what she had told Lieutenant Haber, including the description of the stocky man with the tool belt. "They were planning on killing you. Just you, Bob."

"You're sure about that?"

"Positive. I heard them. Whatever it was that they used on me, the police think it was some kind of ether, it didn't put me out right away. I heard them. They were discussing whether they were going to 'do me.' One of them was a real charmer. He gave me a little groping, then he said he didn't like 'doing women.' Then the other one told him, 'We just do Duran.' That's what he said."

"What else did they say?"

"The one who came in first, he said he didn't want to hurt me. He just wanted the Van Gogh. They knew about the meeting. Someone had to tell them," Lange said.

Duran frowned with annoyance. "I told the insurance carrier that I had a meeting set up with Harry Lawson. I didn't give them the date or the time."

"Then it had to come from Harry's end. He dealt with a lot of crooks."

"Yes. But he was valuable to them. Why would they kill Harry?"

"Maybe they thought Harry was pulling a double-cross," Lange suggested.

"Maybe," Duran conceded. He got to his feet. "Is there anything I can do for you?"

"Find the Van Gogh, Bob. I'd really like to look at it."

The weary nurse gave Duran a withering look as he headed to the elevators. He pushed the down button and stared at his image in the polished brass elevator doors.

They had planned to kill me. "Just do Duran." Then why kill Lawson? They could have just as easily put him out with ether like they did Lange. Did they mistake him for me?

During his session with the police, Captain Haber had informed him that the killings were done by a professional hit man. "A .22, probably a semiautomatic with a silencer. One shot behind Lawson's left ear. There was no exit wound. A .22 isn't powerful enough to go through the skull, but it ricochets around like a pinball."

The hospital was cool, almost cold, but Duran felt a trickle of perspiration roll down his spine. The notorious Los Angeles freeways had been responsible for an untold number of deaths. But today, the traffic jam had saved his life. If he had gotten to the meeting on time, he would have been killed.

"We just do Duran."

Why? And how was it connected to Anona? Or to the fire the other night?

The elevator pinged open. Two dark-haired men dressed in business suits looked out dispassionately at Duran. He took one step toward the elevator, then stopped, wheeled suddenly and headed for the stairs, the sound of his heartbeat pounding in his ears.

The men in the elevator were probably doctors going off shift, or friends coming from a visit with loved ones. Probably. His feet made sharp cracking sounds on the steps, the words "We just do Duran," echoing in his brain. Kline, Lark, Fritzheim, Harry Lawson, Wendy Lange. The names whirled around in his mind like playing cards flipped in the air by a magician.

Duran flopped into the limo's backseat like a runner whose legs have given out. "Get me to a motel near the airport," he instructed the driver.

Chapter 25

The chartered jet touched down in Crescent City a little before six in the morning, giving Robert Duran time to rent a car and drive out to view Pelican Bay prison. The morning was dark and damp. From the road, the flood-lit prison resembled something out of a science fiction movie: gray concrete walls and dark blue gun towers; razor-tipped wire fences encircled the entire complex. Just looking at it gave him a cold, eerie feeling.

He drove back to town, to the agreed-upon meeting place. Yvonne's, was a glorified coffee shop, adjacent to a Spanish-mission–style motel with a sagging red-tiled roof, which catered to truckers by the look of the parking lot.

Duran slid into an empty booth. He spotted his guest as soon as he entered the restaurant. Junior Erwin looked typecast for what he was—a prison guard. In his forties, short, heavy set, with ruddy, porcine features, his head topped by a high-walled crew cut, no doubt scissored by a trustee at the prison. He was dressed in spotless, heavily starched gray slacks and shirt.

The nature of Duran's job put him in contact with law-enforcement personnel of every stripe: local, sheriff, FBI, Customs, Interpol. Raw recruits, veteran sergeants, world-weary detectives, lieutenants, captains, and chiefs. And he got along well with most of them.

But not prison guards. He had a hard time understanding why a man would voluntarily take a job that placed him behind bars for forty hours a week.

Duran stood up and signaled to Erwin. The guard gave him a wide grin and shambled toward the booth, a cigarette dangling from the corner of his mouth.

"Nice of you to take the time to meet with me," Duran said, gesturing for Erwin to sit down.

The prison guard plopped with a thick-bodied slump into the Scotch-tape–patched booth. "They said you was real anxious to see me." Erwin ground out his cigarette in a coffee saucer, then immediately lit another.

The waitress, a lush-bodied young woman in a snug brown-and-white uniform came by to take their order.

"You want the usual, Junior?" she asked, bending over to pour coffee, giving Erwin a catbird's view of her cleavage.

"Nah. Just a piece of pie, honey."

The waitress questioned Duran with her eyes.

"Just coffee, thanks."

Duran reached into his coat pocket, pulled out a business-size envelope stuffed with fifteen twenty-dollar bills and slid it across the table. It was not the first time he'd offered a civil servant an envelope. A "green subpoena" was the description his first boss at the Centennial Insurance Agency had used to describe the package.

"A little something for your time."

Junior Erwin's ample stomach caused his uniform shirt to stretch open at the navel. He burped lightly, then said, "I appreciate that. What's your interest in Otto Kline?"

"He's involved in a case I'm working on," Duran said vaguely.

The waitress arrived with Erwin's pie, which was covered with a ball of melting vanilla ice cream.

Erwin swooped the envelope into his lap before sampling the ice cream. "Otto Kline. He was a spooky bastard. Hell of a talented painter, though. He did a mural in the guards' mess room." Erwin raised an arm above his head. "Floor to ceiling, all blue sky, sunsets, and trees. It's really something. He did a few things for the warden. Paintings of the beach, waves rolling onto the shore, crap like that." Erwin took a final drag on his cigarette, snubbed it out and dug a fresh one from his shirt pocket. The cigarettes were like a sixth finger, almost never leaving his hand. As soon as one burned down, he'd grind it out and light another one with a red plastic disposable lighter. "I do a little moonlighting, repairing boat engines. I gave Kline a picture from *Field and Stream* magazine. It showed a boat at a dock. I wanted him to paint my name and something like the picture on my beat-up camper shell. Kline taped the picture to the side of the shell and damned if he didn't copy the thing, just about perfect."

"What kind of a man is Otto Kline? Tell me what brought him here to Pelican Bay."

Erwin leaned across the table and winked. "He fucked with a guard. Down in some fruitcake lockup in LaLa land. He choked the guard, kicked him around some. You fuck with a guard in this state, you come to us. You're a member of the Aryan Brotherhood, or some Mex or black jive-ass prison gang, you come to us. We ain't here to rehabilitate these sleazeballs, we punish them, Mr. Duran, that's what we do. We gave Kline some SHU time. A year and a half of it. That always takes all the juice right out of their balls."

"Shoe time?"

Erwin slid the ice cream off the top of the pie with his fork. "S-H-U. Solitary Housing Unit. The boys call it 'the hole,' things like that." He used his fork to saw off a third of the pie, then shoved it in his mouth. "Some guys spend two or three years in the SHU. By the time they get out, they're cream of wheat, tapioca. No visitors, no books, no TV. Nothin'." Erwin belched, then gouged out another hunk of the pie. "Kline, he was scared shitless."

Erwin smiled, showing a ragged set of blueberry-stained teeth. "Hell, they're all scared, but Kline, all a guard had to do was shake a club at his hands and he'd jump out of his skin." Erwin slid his right hand, fork and all, under his left armpit. "Every time you got near Kline, he'd hide his hand like this. I guess it was 'cause he's a painter and that was his paintin' hand. Kline wasn't used to doing time, especially hard time. He'd cry like a baby when I brought him his food. Beg for me to talk to him, that kind of shit. He was always whining about his wife. She hung herself, you know, in some pussy palace, dyke cooler down in Southern California."

Duran took a sip of his overheated coffee while Erwin demolished the last of the pie. "What did Kline say about his wife? Did he blame himself for her death? Or did he blame someone else?"

"Hell, I don't know. I don't pay any attention to their bitching, Mr. Duran. They're all scum. No matter who they are, the SHU changes them, I can guarantee you that. They become zombies. Kline was an exercise nut. Running back and forth in his cell all the time. It was kinda funny to watch. He could only take about three steps one way, three the other; then he was laying on the floor, doing all those exercises. We gotta give the sleazeballs an hour a day in the yard. They're by themselves, of course, and we strip search them before they leave the SHU and when they return. Otto Kline, he spent the whole time out there running around in circles. Except when he was playing at being sick. He was always bitching about headaches."

"So Kline did his time in the SHU, then what?"

"Then he went into the mix with the rest of the prisoners. If you've got some skills, you can get into Level One, meaning you can work. For each day you work, you get a day off of your sentence."

Erwin took a drag on the cigarette, then almost immediately shoveled a spoonful of ice cream into his mouth.

Duran said, "What about friends? Did Kline have anybody special?"

Erwin wiped his sweating face with the restaurant napkin. "You mean a hump? Hell, everyone in there has someone to love. Even if it's only their own hand." He held up his palm, closed it into a circle and made an obscene pumping motion. "You know what they say. 'Close your eyes and this is the girl of your dreams.' But we don't allow no vogues inside."

"Vogues?" Duran queried.

"Yeah. Like the magazine, you know. Models. They make hot pants out of their dungarees, paint their faces, lipstick, makeup, the whole routine." His face wrinkled in disgust. "We don't allow none of that stuff up here. When I was down in Soledad, it was different. You should have seen some of those perverts. You'd have to be pretty horny to get the old cobra up to strike at those babies." He flicked the cigarette in his hand. "These are still as good as money inside. By the time Otto went home, he had a couple of cases of smokes plus."

"Plus?" Duran asked, tiring of Erwin and his prison jargon.

"Yeah, plus. Coming to him. The warden, us guards, we didn't want to give him no money for the stuff he painted, so we gave him smokes."

"So Kline had nobody special."

"Oh, he had someone special all right," Erwin conceded. "Old 'Ramblin' Nose' Firpo."

"Tell me about Firpo."

"Ken Firpo. A tough old bastard. He's spent more of his life inside than outside of prison. He comes from a family of scumbags. His old man died in prison, they say. He's got a big nose, a real honker, broken more than a couple of times. That's how he got the nickname, like the song, you know, 'Ramblin' Rose.' So Firpo's Ramblin' Nose. Though nobody calls him that to his face. At least none of the prisoners."

"What was their relationship like?"

"Real lovebirds. Way I hear it, Firpo paid three cartons of smokes to get Kline when he came out of the SHU."

"Firpo knew Kline then?"

"No. The old bulls, they just like to get pancakes that come out of the SHU and make houseboys out of them. They got along real good, 'cause they were cellmates 'till Kline got released."

"Would Firpo talk to me?"

"Nah, I don't think so. Wouldn't do you much good if he did. He's a D. F. W. as far as the cons go. Don't fuck with. Big bastard. Strongarm man, burglar. He did SHU time. Handled it pretty well. He and Kline used to spend their lunch hour in the sandpit. That's where the exercise equipment is, barbells, that kind of crap."

"How much time has Firpo got left to do?"

"I'm not real sure. A few years, at least."

"Does he keep in contact with Kline? Would he know where Kline is now?"

"I don't know. They're all scum. We treat 'em all like ducks, if you know what I mean."

Duran wasn't at all sure what Erwin meant, and he didn't want to find out. "What does Firpo do in prison? I mean, does he have a job?"

"Oh, sure. They'll do anything to get a job, 'cause like I said, it can cut down their time. Firpo works in the library. Funny spot for a guy like that, but that's what he wanted. Always reading. Even using the computer," Erwin offered, as if there was something wrong with people who did such things.

"I'd like you to question Firpo. See if he's heard from Kline."

Erwin's features creased in apparent pain. "Well—"

"Naturally I'll reimburse you for your time. I'm interested in anything else you can find out about Kline. Especially his address."

Erwin bowed his head down, his voice dropping to a confidential whisper. "That's kind of confidential stuff. You got to realize—"

"I've got another envelope in my pocket. I need that address in a hurry."

"I kind of figured you might." Erwin pulled a crumpled piece of paper from his shirt pocket, unfolding it, and spreading it on the table as if it was a treasure map. "I don't know how good it is, these pukes move around like gypsies, but this is where he's at according to our records and his probation officer. Some half-assed, halfway house, 276 Turk Street, San Francisco."

Duran grabbed the paper, the address seemingly jumping off the page. San Francisco! Kline was in San Francisco.

"Who determines where a prisoner goes? Does his probation officer pick a place, or is it up to the released prisoner?"

"It's up to the puke. Usually they go where they got family or a job possibility."

Duran tossed the second envelope stuffed with money onto the table. "I'd like any information you could dig up about Kline. Why he picked San Francisco. Who he knows there. Any relatives he may have. The names of any visitors he may have seen in prison. And some background on his cellmate, Firpo."

Erwin stubbed out his cigarette in the puddled remains of the ice cream, and hefted the envelope in the palm of his hand. "I'll see what I can do."

"How old is your camper shell, Mr. Erwin?"

"My camper shell? Why? I don't—"

"You get me this information in a hurry, and I'll buy you a new one."

"You shittin' me?"

"No."

Erwin shook a cigarette from its pack, scorching it halfway down its length in lighting it. "I think that Firpo was from Frisco, or some place down that way."

Chapter 26

Jason Lark waved the morning paper at the butler. "Did you see this, George? An attorney was killed in Los Angeles. Duran found the body, and narrowly missed being killed himself. Apparently it's got something to do with the Van Gogh that was stolen from that movie producer. What do you think is going on with Duran?"

"I'm sure I wouldn't know, sir."

"Seems awfully strange, don't you think? First Anona's missing, then the fire at the studio, and now this."

"Very disturbing. Will you be with us much longer, sir?"

Lark ignored the impertinent question. "You're an iron man, George. Don't you ever take a day off?"

The butler pivoted on his heel without responding. Lark silently mouthed an obscenity at George's back, then turned his attention to the newspaper article. He had a good idea what had happened to the phony Van Gogh. Drago destroyed it. He wondered how the thieves who boosted the painting from Fritzheim's house were feeling now. Their stolen painting stolen.

Duran. What did it take to kill the bastard? He survived the fire, and now this. How hard would Duran dig into the Fritzheim theft now? He just wouldn't give up. It wasn't the bastard's nature to give up. Even jiggle-head Danielle Fritzheim had recognized that.

Lark waded through the rest of the newspaper. His call to the *Chronicle* reporter about Anona disappearing hadn't borne fruit yet.

And neither had his search for the Picasso sketches. The fact that no one else seemed to be aware of their existence was encouraging. If he could find them, he could just pack up and run off. The hell with Anona, with Mario Drago, and Duran.

George was the problem. The old fart seemed to be everywhere. He'd caught Lark looking through drawers and closets several times, but he'd been quick to make up a line about looking for old snapshots of the children. And now the jibe: "Will you be with us much longer, sir?"

Duran only wanted him around so he could keep an eye on him. Lisa didn't seem to care if he lived or died. And Johnny. Where the hell was his son?

Johnny wasn't at his club last night. Lark had called the Sausalito houseboat, but all he'd gotten was Johnny's answering machine.

He decided to try the basement again. Those boxes stacked near the luggage. He had to check the unmarked boxes.

The butler's voice boomed out as Lark was within a foot of the steps.

"May I be of some assistance, sir?"

Lark felt the back of his neck redden. "I'm going for a swim, George. I think I can manage that myself."

The address Junior Erwin had given Bob Duran for Otto Kline was located in the Tenderloin, one of the raunchiest districts in San Francisco, dominated by adult movie houses and bookstores, rough and tumble bars, prostitutes, and drug dealers.

Duran slipped his watch, a gold Piaget that Anona had given him on their first anniversary, from his wrist and jammed it in his pants pocket. The watch would be a magnet with the bizarre street parade: trolling, sallow-faced hookers of both sexes, stooped-over old-timers walking off the effects of a night spent sleeping in a doorway, and mean-eyed street dealers who took one look at Duran in his suit and tie and made him as a policeman. Which didn't bother Duran at all.

He kept his eyes straight ahead, weaving between the hostile stares, his shoes making light kissing sounds on the sticky, refuse-strewn sidewalks.

Groups of bright, happy-faced Vietnamese youngsters ran and rollerskated through the mangy crowd as though they didn't have a care in the world.

The building at 276 Turk Street was an old hotel, The Excelsior, that some fifty years ago may have worn a coat of respectability. Now the glass windows were blurred from years of accumulated grime and fingerprints. The lobby was stockpiled with elderly men and women sitting in fissured sofas, bundled up to their chins, staring blankly at the outside world. An accordion-wire gate secured the front entrance. A stout-bodied black man was leaning against the gate. He wore an Australian-style outback coat that stretched to the tips of his shoes and was swinging an aluminum baseball bat back and forth in a slow rhythm.

"Morning, officer," he said with a wide smile. "What can I do for you today?"

"Open up," Duran commanded.

"Who you looking for? Maybe I can help you."

"Otto Kline."

The man's forehead knitted. "Kline? I don't know that name."

"Are you telling me his parole officer lied to me?"

"I ain't telling you that. Just the name don't mean nothing to me." He rested the bat against the wall. The metal screeched as he opened the gate. A redhead in a bare-shouldered, frothy pink dress elbowed her way past Duran. She had long, curvy legs covered with black fish-net stockings. The red wig was tilted at an angle; a five o'clock shadow was beginning to show through the rouge.

"Morning, Justice," the redhead said in a high falsetto.

"Mornin', darlin'. Come on, officer, I'll see what the book says about your Mr. Kline."

Duran followed the black man over to a check-in counter. The top half was wire mesh and extended to the ceiling. There was a horseshoe-shaped arch for the passing of keys and money.

Odors of sour food, spilt beer, and urine hung in the air.

Duran watched as the black man poked a long arm through the arch and grabbed the register.

"Justice. With a name like that you should have joined thc force."

Justice gave a tambourine laugh. "Yeah. Save me a whole lot of trouble if I did. Who you with? I ain't seen you before."

"Homicide," Duran supplied. "Which room is Kline's?"

Justice pulled a pair of glasses from his coat pocket. One bow was missing and he had to hold the ramshackle glasses to his eyes to read. "You know the smoke here, huh?"

Duran had no idea what Justice was talking about. "Remind me."

"The first five floors is for the old folks. The next two are the halfway house. The rest is for off-the-street trade." He moistened a finger with his tongue and turned a journal page. "Oh, yeah. Here's the dude. Otto Kline. He ain't been here but a couple of weeks. Room 704. Now I know the guy. Always drawing people. He's good, too. He did one of me. Made me even better looking than I am," he said with a loud cackle. "What's your interest in Kline? He can't be too bad, otherwise you'd have your partner with you."

"Routine questions," Duran said, realizing he sounded like a TV policeman.

"I can't give you the key, man," Justice disclosed. "You want me to see if he's in?"

Duran nodded his head and Justice picked up the house phone. He shook his head negatively after a minute. "He must have gone out early. I was at the door at nine."

"Is someone on the door around the clock?"

"Nah." Justice craned his neck and peered through the mesh. "The manager's supposed to have somebody there, but he don't. I get off at five, then Sheo, the manager's brother, hangs the door 'till he gets tired of it."

"I thought there were bed checks for the people in a halfway house project."

Justice laughed and slapped his hand on the check-in counter, leaving a moist imprint. "Oh, there is. Once a week they change the sheets and make sure the bed's there."

"I don't want Kline to know I'm interested in him, Justice. Understand?"

"Yes, sir. Officer. I understand perfectly."

He'd decided to wait for Duran near his office on Fisherman's Wharf. He liked the cover of the crowds. The streets were filled with tourists of all sizes and ages, speaking a mishmash of languages—he recognized French, Spanish, the guttural German, but there were other languages that he'd never heard before. He was beginning to attract a following of customers. Yesterday, he'd made over a hundred and seventy dollars doing caricatures of children for their parents—some of whom communicated with him by pantomiming their requests and holding out handfuls of coins and dollar bills.

He hadn't read the morning paper or heard the news, so was unaware of Duran's trip to Los Angeles.

He slipped his right hand under his arm, the fingers massaging the taut skin covering his rib cage, his mind wandering back to the fire at the studio. Jason Lark had almost robbed him of Duran. If Lark tried anything else, he'd have to be eliminated. No one was going to take Duran from him.

He'd seen Duran's secretary show up for work at nine o'clock. Several hours later the policeman from Colma had arrived. The one who'd found the rosary beads. He'd gone into Duran's office, only to come out a few minutes later, and walk a half block away, where he was now, leaning against the fender of his car.

Waiting for Duran. Come on, Duran, he coaxed. Anona is waiting, too. We're all waiting for you.

Chapter 27

Peggy Jacquard heaved a massive sigh of relief when she saw Duran come through the office door. She jumped to her feet, ran over, and gave him a big strong hug.

"You're going to be the death of me," she said when she pulled back. "First the fire. Then that poor old scoundrel Harry Lawson." She blotted her eyes with the sleeve of her blouse. "What's going on, Bob?"

"I wish I knew," Duran admitted. "I'll tell you what I learned in Pelican Bay as soon as I get a cup of coffee."

Peggy ran her hand over his chin. "You could use a shave, too. The phone's been going crazy and that policeman from Colma was by a while ago. He said he'd be back."

"And here I am," Chief Bill Saylor announced from the door.

Duran said, "Any news of my wife, Chief?"

"Anona Stack? No. Nothing yet. I read about what happened in Los Angeles. Trouble seems to have a way of following you around. I had a long visit with a San Francisco Fire Department arson investigator, Tom Powers. He thinks you've been avoiding him."

"I'm not," Duran asserted. "I had to go out of town. What did Powers tell you about the fire?"

"Do you want to talk here, or down at my office, Mr. Duran?"

"That sounds like a threat, Chief."

"It does," Saylor granted. "I want to talk to you. Uninterrupted."

Duran nodded his head toward his office, then said, "No calls, Peggy."

"Why don't we take a walk?" Saylor suggested. "It's a beautiful day."

A strong wind was blowing in off the bay, whipping up whitecaps and fluttering the clothing of the tourists waiting to board the ferry for Alcatraz Island.

Saylor said, "I've had two experts analyze the letter Mr. Stringer received from your wife. They both agree. There's no doubt that Anona Stack wrote that letter."

"She was forced to write it," Duran maintained.

"I've been doing some digging," Saylor disclosed.

"And," Duran responded impatiently.

"I started digging in New York City."

Duran pulled to an abrupt stop and stared at the policeman, whose eyes were shrouded by his tinted glasses.

"What about New York?"

"Your first wife. She died of a aneurysm, like you said, but the coroner's report showed that she had some bruises and scrapes."

Duran took a breath and counted to ten before responding. "The day before she died, Teresa took a spill in Central Park while she was jogging."

"Is that right? Just like you were jogging and then were pushed off a cliff."

"That's exactly right," Duran said angrily.

"I never asked. Were there any other marriages? Between New York and Anona Stack?"

"No. Are you trying to paint me as some kind of a Bluebeard who goes around killing his wives?"

"I'm not a painter, Mr. Duran. I'm a cop." Saylor brushed off a spot on the pier railing before settling his elbows on it. "Lieutenant Powers says that the fire at your wife's studio was definitely arson."

"That's not exactly news. Somebody knocked me out, poured paint thinner all over me, and set the place on fire."

"Yes, they used an accelerant," Saylor said, stressing the last word in the sentence.

Duran tried looking behind the policeman's tinted lenses. "Is that what's bugging Powers? The terminology I used? Accelerant? I handled a lot of arson investigations when I started in the insurance business, Chief. I know the jargon. It's as simple as that."

The ferry horn tooted four times, then the boat started edging away from the dock. A group of youngsters began waving at Saylor.

He waved back. "Everyone loves a uniform," he observed. "Almost everyone. What was in your wife's studio worth destroying?"

"Me," Duran said pointedly.

"You were knocked out, you say. If they wanted to kill you, they could have done it right then and there."

"Someone wanted to make it look like I set the fire and then got trapped inside the building."

"Someone? The same someone who put the rosary beads in your car? And pushed you over that cliff? Would that be the same someone who killed that attorney down in Los Angeles? I'm trying to splice the arson and the L.A. fiasco in with your wife's disappearance. But I just can't seem to do it."

Saylor's head was centered between the massive, fog-capped, terra-cotta-red towers of the Golden Gate Bridge.

"Look, Chief, you won't find any of your answers in New York. I've been checking my old cases. A man named Otto Kline and his wife were convicted of forging one of Anona's paintings. This was seven years ago, in Beverly Hills. They were given light sentences, but his wife couldn't handle prison life. She killed herself."

"How do you know all this?" Saylor demanded.

"I spoke to the woman who was in the cell when she killed herself," Duran explained. "A tough cookie by the name of Barbara Linker. Arlene Kline was a good-looking young woman. Linker and her friends were all over her. When she wouldn't play the kind of games they wanted her to, they made life unpleasant for her—got her in trouble with the guards, told her they were going to fix it so she'd have her sentence extended, that kind of thing."

Saylor shook his head slowly. "And you're suggesting that this Kline guy has been brooding all these years about his wife offing herself in prison, so he grabbed your wife?"

"It's a strong possibility, Chief. Kline is here. In San Francisco. At the Excelsior Hotel on Turk Street."

Saylor straightened up, whisking the sleeves of his uniform jacket. "Who gave you that address?"

"I'd rather not say."

Duran turned toward Jefferson Street. A stream of bicycle-driven rickshaws were showing off the wharf to sore-footed tourists. A man was sketching a youngster in the backseat of one of the rickshaws.

"The only trouble I'm interested in is my wife's, Chief. I want her found."

"I'll check out this Kline character, but he doesn't sound too promising to me. I got a call yesterday, from a reporter asking me about your wife. If she was missing."

"What did you tell him?" Duran asked quickly.

Saylor kicked the remains of a hot dog over the pier and into the oily green bay water. "That as far as I knew she was not. That she had been in contact with her attorney."

"Anona has been kidnapped, damn it."

"So you say. But that's not what her letter says. You're not disputing it's her handwriting?"

Duran shook his head vigorously.

"Then again, maybe we're all just spinning our wheels, and she'll turn up back at the house. No one's called asking for money."

Duran twisted the wedding ring on his finger. "This is not about money."

Saylor settled his sunglasses back on his nose. "If she is missing, I'll find her. And I'll find out who's responsible. You can count on that."

"I'm not counting on anyone, including you, Chief. I'm going to find my wife."

Saylor rocked back and forth on his heels for several moments, then swiveled sharply and marched off toward his car.

There was a hazy, floating circle of light around the boy's head.

"I'm sorry," Otto Kline apologized. "I can't finish this." He ripped the sheet from the sketch pad and handed it to the ten year old sitting in the back of the rickshaw.

"Hey," the boy's father protested. "I'm not—"

"No charge," Kline muttered with annoyance as he started off after Duran, widening his stride to catch up with him.

Duran and the cop had been arguing heatedly. For a moment, Kline feared that the policeman was going to arrest Duran. It was too soon for that. Much too soon.

The pain had been building ever since Kline had spotted the cop near Duran's office. Building slowly, the way it always did before a massive migraine. Throbbing, pulsating, as if his brain was being squeezed by an unseen hand. He had to lie down. Somewhere dark and quiet. He had to.

Chapter 28

The Bentley was missing from its parking spot. Jason Lark slipped the Lincoln into an open slot and hurried into the house, cruising through the vacant kitchen and front rooms. There was no sign of George. Finally, the old bastard had left the house.

Lark returned to the kitchen and selected an eight-inch carving knife, then made his way to the basement. He began going through the unmarked boxes, slitting the neatly taped creases, finding mostly household items such as cookware and linens, until he cut open the last box. It was crammed with papers: scribbled papers. He recognized the stick figures and smiling-face suns, childish, distorted versions of cartoon characters, authored by John and Lisa. He remembered how Anona had encouraged their interest in art.

He sank back on his haunches and scraped the tip of the knife along the cement floor. The Picassos. He had a sudden vision of Lisa and Johnny filling in the master's work with crayons.

Lark climbed quickly to his feet. He'd searched through most of the house. What was left? The west wing—the staff's residences. At one time there had been a full-time cook, several young maids, and butling apprentices working under George. Now there were only temporaries.

Lark silently cursed, fearing that some damn maid or swishy housekeeper had thrown the Picassos in the garbage.

Lark made his way up the stairs. George had always supervised the packing and unpacking of suitcases.

He dropped the knife in the kitchen sink and peered out the window overlooking the garage area. The Bentley hadn't returned. He moved swiftly up the stairs to the third floor, past his "guest" room and into the west wing.

George occupied the corner suite. Lark knocked on the door and called out George's name. He tried the knob. Locked.

He moved down the hallway to the adjoining room. It was vacant, stripped bare of rugs, not a stick of furniture. He went to the window, opened it and leaned out, looking down to the shadowy, dark green mass of the garden. A narrow stone ledge skirted the house's weathered brick exterior wall.

Lark took a deep breath, then carefully climbed onto the ledge, his mind picturing himself as a suave jewel thief about to steal the crown jewels. Once he was on the ledge and inching his way forward, that image quickly vanished, replaced by one of him falling to the tangled hedges some thirty feet below. He kept his eyes tracked on the slowly approaching window to George's room, his head pressed tightly to the wall, the bricks scratching at his ear, his fingers moving jerkily for a grasp on the next brick.

The journey took no more than two minutes, but to Lark it felt like an hour. Finally he was there. The heavy brocade drapes were tied back. He pushed the sash up far enough to allow entry and slipped through the window, falling to the carpet with a grateful thump.

The suite's decor resembled an English gentleman's club—burgundy leather chairs, burgundy carpeting, and a paisley couch in front of a limestone fireplace.

Lark's eyes quickly inventoried the walls—there were several prints, inferior copies of Toulouse Lautrec's music hall and Paris street scenes.

Lark strode into the bedroom—briefly noticing the four-poster canopied bed. The walls were festooned with dozens of paintings and sketches. His eyes were drawn as if by a magnet to the framed drawing hanging over the nightstand. The paper now saffron colored from age—a small residential building on a cobblestone street. Lark gazed lovingly at the address printed along the bottom of the work—11 Boulevard de Liche. An address known by anyone who'd studied modern art. Picasso's studio in Paris! Lark's hands were trembling as he carefully slipped the frame from the wall. George. Stuffy, stodgy, pompous, boring old George. Goddamn George had the Picassos!

"I thought I was going to have to call Rachel and get her to bail you out," Peggy said when Duran returned to the office.

"I don't think Chief Saylor is one of my biggest fans," Duran confessed. "Peg, I want to be certain that the leak about my meeting with Harry Lawson at Wendy Lange's place didn't come out of this office."

"How could it?"

"I don't know. Has there been anyone in here who could have gotten a look at the reports on your desk?"

Peggy shook her head vehemently and a strand of hair fell like a twist of wire across her cheek. "No. And I always lock up when I'm gone, Bob. You know that."

"Somehow they knew I was coming. They were

waiting for me at Wendy Lange's house." He gave her a brief synopsis of his conversation with Lange and the Los Angeles policemen. "They were going to 'do' me. Take the Van Gogh and kill me."

"It must have been someone in Lawson's circle," Peggy insisted.

"Harry was too sharp to let something like that slip out. He went to Wendy's with the painting. He was living up to his end of the bargain."

"They must have been afraid you'd recognize them, Bob. Maybe it was someone we've dealt with in the past."

"No. We've never dealt with professional hit men, and that's what this crew was. Pros. Someone hired them to get the Van Gogh and kill me. The fire here in San Francisco was a totally different thing. I surprised someone in the stuido. No one knew I was going to the studio that night, except George. Someone acted on an unexpected opportunity. The shooting in Los Angeles was planned." He rubbed a hand through his hair, then his over his face. "An entirely different M.O. Different people. Why? It's got to be something that I know, or that I'm likely to find out. But what does it have to do with Anona's disappearance?"

Peggy threw both hands out sideways, palms up. "I can't figure it out!'"

"We've got a lot of work to do. I'm waiting for some information to come from Pelican Bay, and—"

"You mean from the guard, Junior Erwin?"

"Has he called already?"

Peggy grinned and tapped the top of her desk. "He faxed these a few minutes ago."

Duran picked up the papers, which, except for one, bore the letterhead of Pelican Bay State Prison. The complete dossiers on both Otto Kline and Kenneth J. Firpo. The last page was a copy of a magazine ad for a pickup truck camper shell.

Otto Kline clamped his eyes shut and rolled into a fetal position. After fifteen minutes he knew it wasn't going to work. The noise—constant voices in the hallways, shouts, a radio booming out rap music—angered and enraged him.

At least his cell had been quiet. Even the darkness and solitude of the SHU was comforting when the attacks came.

Someone began pounding on his door. He shouted out an obscenity, but the pounding continued.

"Hey, Otto man. It's me. Justice. Open the fuck up."

"Go away," he groaned.

"It's important, man. Some cop was here looking for you."

He dragged his legs across the mattress, struggled to his feet, and stumbled over to the door.

"Man, you look like shit," Justice said when the door opened. "You been doin' some bad acid or something?"

"Headaches. What's this about a cop?"

Justice slipped into the room, grinning like a cat. "The dude said he was a cop, but he didn't dress like one. Man, he had some heavy threads on. And he didn't act like no cop. The more I talked to him, the less I think he is a cop, you know? I tell him you're not in your room and he believes me. He doesn't shove my ass in the elevator and make me prove it. And he's all alone. Cops don't come in here alone unless they're looking to steal a piece from one of the whores. He wanted you, Otto. Said it was 'routine.' "

"What was his name?"

"What you been up to, Otto?" Justice picked up the sketch pad. "Drawin' dirty pictures or something?"

"What was his name?" Kline repeated.

Justice tilted the pad to the light coming from the street. "I like this one. Cute little kid."

Otto Kline jammed his hand in his pocket and pulled out a roll of cash—his take from the day's sketching.

Justice plucked at the money with two forklike fingers.

"He didn't give me a name. Dark hair, tan, blue eyes. Big scar over one eye, like maybe he got hit with somethin'." Justice waggled the aluminum baseball bat. "Somethin' like this, maybe."

Kline felt his throat constrict. "What time was this?"

Justice carried the roll of bills to the window and began uncurling them. "Oh, 'bout noon, I guess."

"I need some help, Justice."

"Yeah, I bet you do, Otto. I bet you sure as shit do."

Chapter 29

"Come in, come in, Lisa," Hugh Stringer said, cupping her elbow and ushering her over to the high-back green leather chair directly in front of his desk. She was wearing skin-tight jeans and a man's charcoal-pinstripe suit jacket—no shirt or blouse. Stringer could just make out the white V of her bra.

"Your secretary said you were busy, Uncle Hugh."

"Never to busy for you, dear," Stringer proffered with a professional smile.

"I'm worried about Johnny. He's disappeared. Like Mom."

"Disappeared? Surely you mean he's just not been around to the house, Lisa."

"No. He hasn't been at his club, either. Eric has been trying to get him to—"

"Eric?" Stringer broke in.

"Eric Marvin. He's Johnny's manager at the club, and a friend of mine. I just don't feel safe at Stack House. I'm moving in with Eric."

"I'm sure John's just visiting someone, or—"

"No," Lisa said adamantly. "He wouldn't stay away from the club."

Stringer flipped a palm back and forth. "Johnny isn't involved with drugs again, is he? I thought that the rehabilitation program I arranged for him had straightened him out, Lisa. If John gets caught using drugs again, I'm afraid he'll end up going to jail."

"I'm really worried, Uncle Hugh."

"I don't think that—"

"First Mom, and now Johnny. And someone's tried to kill Bob. At least that's what he says. Maybe I'll be next."

"Lisa, about your mother's letter. Do you think Anona was going to leave Robert? She mentioned he was violent. Do you suppose that Robert found out about the letter and . . . did something to her?"

"I don't know what to think, Uncle Hugh. He . . . he . . ." She combed her hair with her fingers. "I just don't know anymore."

"I'll check on John if you wish, but I think you're jumping to conclusions, dear. He's probably staying with someone—"

"No," she insisted. "I know Johnny's friends. I've checked with them. He was supposed to meet with Eric two days ago to talk about plans for the club."

"Do you really think John might be in some danger?"

Lisa closed her eyes for a moment and brushed her finger across her lips. "I'm frightened. For Mom. For Johnny. For me. I don't want Bob, or anyone else to know that I'm moving in with Eric."

She got to her feet and jammed her purse under her arm. "I want you to find out what's going on, Uncle Hugh."

"And I shall," Stringer assured her. "I've always taken care of you, Lisa. And your mother and your brother. And I'll continue to do so, believe me. Maybe Jason knows John's whereabouts," Stringer suggested.

Lisa dug her knuckles into the back of the leather

chair. "Jason. Everything's gone to shit since he got here."

"Lisa, surely you don't think your father has anything—"

"I want him out of here," Lisa said adamantly. "Get him out of Stack House, Uncle Hugh. Now!"

The prison records were fascinating to Duran. Otto Kline's life history had been condensed into three pages. Born in Iowa, then schooled in New Mexico, Oregon, and Southern California. A short stint in the army followed by marriage to Arlene Dore. No children. He worked as a painter—a house painter for a short time—then a range of jobs from hamburger flipper to bicycle messenger to waiter.

Duran had found that many artists struggled much the way actors do—taking part-time jobs, making just enough money to keep going, waiting for a break. And, like actors, there was just too deep a well of artistic talent out there for most of them to scratch out a living.

There was a brief reference made by the prison psychiatrist about Kline's wife's background: Arlene Dore—born in Paris, France. Also an artist.

Duran tried to picture the two of them in his mind. The rejections—the sparks, the passions diminished—the realization that they'd probably never really make it big—all those plans, those hopes, taken away day by day until they were reduced to forging paintings for a Swiss con man.

Breamer was probably paying them peanuts, while he himself was living a jet-setter's life.

There was no mention in the report about Arlene Kline's suicide, but Barbara Linker, her cellmate, had described Arlene as a "push." Frightened to death most of the time, an easy mark for the hardcases. Duran remembered his few months in jail. If you let them push you around, you soon found yourself on your knees. Literally. Barbara Linker had made it clear that's exactly what had happened to Arlene Kline.

The medical profile on Otto Kline indicated that after his wife's suicide, he'd spent four weeks in the Southern California prison hospital. Duran had no doubt that Kline had been severely punished after the assault. Following his transfer to Pelican Bay, there were over dozens of scribbled entries, all listing the same complaint—migraine headaches.

There was nothing in Otto Kline's past history to link him to San Francisco. No relatives or past employment.

Kenneth Firpo was another story. He was born in Montara, a sparse, coast-side community some twenty miles south of San Francisco.

Firpo's criminal history was a steady input of felonies: burglary, robbery, kidnapping, rape. As the prison guard Junior Erwin had told him, Firpo was following the family tradition. The report indicated that Firpo's father had died in prison. Alcatraz. And that his grandfather had been killed while running away from the police.

Alcatraz. Duran swiveled his chair around and looked out the office window, across the choppy, gray-green bay waters at the former prison. Once known as the toughest prison in the United States. Now that honor belonged to Pelican Bay.

Otto Kline, whose wife had killed herself in her prison cell, locked up with a lifer whose father died in prison. Kline and Firpo must have had some bizarre discussions.

The prison file cleared up another thing that had been bothering Duran—how Kline had been able to afford to pay for Arlene Kline's elaborate tombstone. Otto Kline had paid for it with a money order. Where had the money come from? A one-sheet "personal assets form" for Kline listed a Seiko watch, leather wallet, dark blue suit, white shirt, tie, and a passbook savings with a Los Angeles branch of Bank of America. Kline had eleven thousand, four hundred dollars and forty-two cents in the account when he was released from prison.

What else would Kline do with the money? Transportation. Duran kicked himself for not thinking of it earlier. A car. He'd rent or buy a car.

He put the computer to work, triggering into the proper database. The DMV files were updated weekly. He clicked in his account number, his password, Kline's name, and x'd the square alongside—Vehicle Registration.

Within seconds the information flicked across the screen. Kline had purchased a 1976 International truck from Honest Ed's Used Vehicles on South Van Ness two weeks ago. Kline's address was listed as a postal box in Crescent City.

Honest Ed nodded toward a truck at the far end of the lot. "Yeah, I remember him. He bought a bread truck. Like that one down there. Only that one's in tip-top shape. Damn nice vehicle. He bought an old, beat-to-shit thing ready for the boneyard. Kline thought he was screwing me on the deal, but I was gettin' ready to ship it out to the junkers."

"Did he say why he wanted the truck?" Duran asked.

"Nope." Honest Ed grinned wickedly. "He paid

cash. He could have got it five hundred bucks cheaper if he knew how to bargain."

"Was he alone?"

"Far as I could see. Skinny guy. Looked kind of like Ichabod Crane—long neck, big Adam's apple."

"What color was the truck?"

"Once it was blue and white. With a checkerboard running around the top. Kilpatrick's Bread. It's all nicked up and rusty now." Honest Ed narrowed his eyes and lowered his voice. "I really dumped that thing on him good. Real good."

Duran thanked him for the information, then walked directly over to the truck the salesman had indicated was like the one Kline had purchased.

The bread company's name had been wire brushed off the sides of the truck, leaving swirling waves of bright steel. Duran walked around the vehicle. Why a bread truck? It was big and bulky, and if left parked in one spot for any length of time was going to draw attention.

He opened the back doors and climbed inside. The racks had been removed—Duran's head almost touched the ceiling. A portable studio? Something he could use to store his sketching and painting materials.

A sudden gust of wind slammed the truck doors closed behind him. Duran swiveled around, hands up in a defensive position. It was pitch black, confining. Like a cell. He hastily pulled at the door handle, jumping out onto the pavement.

He wiped his sweaty hands on his pants legs as he stared into the back of the truck. Like a cell. Kline. The son of a bitch bought himself a prison cell. For Anona! A cell he could drive anywhere he wanted.

Chapter 30

Justice clicked the highbeams on and shifted the van down to first gear. The sun was close to calling it a day and darkness was rapidly closing in over the misty, thicketed landscape. "Shit, Otto, how'd you ever find this place? This is the fuckin' boondocks."

He slammed on the brakes and yanked on the parking brake when he spotted the locked gate.

"Is this it? The end of the line?"

Kline leaned sideways, grimacing as he extracted a ring of keys from his pocket. "Open the gate. It's just a little further."

Justice ripped the keys from Kline's hand, swearing as he used the headlights to illuminate the padlock.

"Keep going," Kline moaned when Justice was back behind the wheel. He peered at the road from the barest of slits in his eyelids. The pain was intense now and the nausea rolled through his stomach every time the van went over a bump. "Up the hill, then left when we reach an opening."

"We'll be lucky if we make it up this hill," Justice predicted. The road was narrow, bordered by expanses of towering trees. It was like driving through a tunnel. He was pissed off at himself for agreeing to drive the goofy bastard. Drive him down to this hellhole. Then he'd have to drive himself back to the city.

The agreement was for him to come back in the morning. Kline had agreed to pay him a hundred and fifty dollars cash for each trip. Which meant Otto had at least that much money tucked away in his pants.

The van bellied into a ditch, the undercarriage making a loud, scraping sound.

"Man, we better get to your spot soon. I'm gettin' tired of this shit."

"Just a little farther," Kline promised, his voice a painful croak.

"What you got? Some kind of withdrawals? Maybe I can fix you up with something."

"No. It's a migraine. I just need someplace dark and quiet."

The ground leveled out and Justice pulled to a stop. Low flying clouds scudded under a watery moon.

"That piece of shit over there?" Justice scoffed. "That's where you're hanging out?"

"Yes. Park over by the cabin."

Justice followed Kline's directions, then shoved the gear shift into park. The dashboard lights barely showed the flash of steel from the knife that Justice slipped from his jacket. "Otto. I got to tell you, you need some help, man. Let me help you."

He was leaning toward Kline's cowering figure when he heard the unmistakable double click of a gun hammer being cocked.

"You must think I'm awfully stupid," Kline whispered, narrowing his eyes, trying to steady the funhouse mirror image of Justice from moving too fast, too far.

"What's you talking about, man, I—"

Justice made a quick, powerful move with the knife, the blade slashing toward Kline's left arm.

Kline pulled both triggers of the derringer, the bullets entering Justice's throat inches from each other.

Justice's head jerked sideways, the knife slipped from his hand and fell harmlessly to the floorboard.

Kline reached over, turned off the van's lights and the ignition, then rolled out the door, landing in a heap on the soft, weather-slicked weeds. Justice's body could wait for the morning.

Anona heard the van's engine, then the gunshots. Her eye was screwed into one of the holes in the door. Gunshots! Oh, dear God, let it be the police. Or Bob.

She saw the beam of a flashlight licking at the trees. Her heart sank when she spotted Kline. He had the flashlight in one hand, the rifle in the other. He was rocking from side to side in a stiff-legged manner that reminded Anona of Frankenstein's monster.

The gunshots. Maybe he'd been hit!

She heard the sound of the locks being undone. The doors groaned open.

"Put these on," Kline snarled, hurling the leg cuffs into the cell.

Anona stood there staring at him. He appeared to be in a great deal of pain. His face was a putty-gray color, glazed with sweat. This could be her chance.

"Put the cuffs on, right now!"

Anona complied quickly. She shambled out of the cell, hands at her side, her razor-sharp nails raking at her denim pant legs.

"I just killed a man," Kline rasped. "You try something now, and I'll kill you here and now!"

He jammed the barrel of the rifle into her back. "Get going."

When Anona was alongside the van, she spotted the bloodied head of the black man hanging out of the driver's side window. Kline's victim. She paused at the foot of the steps to the cabin, but Kline augered the rifle barrel viciously into her kidneys.

"I haven't had anything to eat," she reminded him.

Kline pushed her toward the chair with the rifle. "Sit down!"

Anona hesitated a moment. Kline pulled the trigger. The muzzle flash illuminated the cabin, like an arrow of lightning.

"Do it!" he screamed.

Anona toppled into the chair and snapped on the handcuffs.

Kline wrapped his long fingers around the cuffs, squeezing them until the metal bit into Anona's flesh.

He then scrambled outside, using the rifle as a cane, making the painful journey back to the SHU. He lurched inside, his knees coming into contact with the iron bunk ribbing. He collapsed onto the bare mattress and hugged his knees to his chest. The SHU. He never thought he'd ever be happy to see the SHU again.

The Excelsior Hotel's vertical sign of faded orange lettering had several blank spots so that it flashed X ELS R off and on every few seconds. The darkness muted the graffiti and the neighboring storefronts had a coat of neon makeup.

The chill wind hadn't influenced the dress code: The hookers still wore thigh-high miniskirts, hotpants, and thin, tight blouses or tank tops.

Robert Duran had dressed down for this visit. Cords, and a suede casual jacket—his gold watch safely tucked away in his pants pocket.

The smell of danger wafted through the exhaust-tinged air. A rubied string of taillights cruised the street at loitering speed, the drivers pulling over to the curb, rolling down their windows to conduct their transactions.

Young men with soft smiles and hard eyes were positioned at every other doorway; cliques of two or three of them monitored each corner. Many of them, like Justice, had aluminum baseball bats dangling from their hands. There was a feeling that at any moment someone would say the wrong thing to the wrong person, or that a shoulder would come into innocent contact with the wrong shoulder and violence would erupt.

Justice wasn't working the door to the Excelsior Hotel. A dark-skinned man in baggy pants and a blue hooded sweatshirt was holding down the fort.

Duran turned down a half dozen or more "Hi, how about a date?" queries from the collection of prostitutes on patrol.

He found a girl slouched against a parking meter on Jones Street. She had tightly spiraled, hay-colored hair. Her skin was white and marshmallow soft. Her black leather pants had silver-dollar-sized peephole grommets running up the outside of both legs. Her nipples looked ready to drill free from the glittery, midriff-baring blouse. She was tottering on her platform shoes, shoulders hunched up, hands clasped at each elbow.

Her spiel was the familiar, "Hi, want a date?"

"Do you know the place around the corner? the Excelsior Hotel?"

"Are you a cop?"

"No."

"My name's Candy. Sure, I know it, honey. But I got a better place."

"I want to go there."

She shrugged her thin shoulders. "You'll have to pay extra for the room."

"That's not a problem."

She tilted her head to one side and surveyed Duran. "Okay, I'll have to ask Tyrone."

"Ask him."

"It's a hundred dollars. Plus twenty-five for the room. Up front."

"I'll pay you when we're in the elevator," Duran said firmly.

She hugged her arms to her chest and shivered. "Okay. Let me check."

Duran watched her skip across the street. The window of a bright-red Corvette hissed down an inch or two. Candy leaned on the car's roof for a moment, then came running back to Duran.

"The party's on," she announced.

Candy kept up a nervous line of patter as they walked back to Turk Street. "What's your name? Where you from? What do you like? Do you want me to bring a friend?"

Duran saw her flash a signal to the man in the hooded sweatshirt and baggy pants—first two fingers, then five.

The doorman smiled lazily at Duran. "Have fun, children," he advised, as he pulled the metal gate open.

Candy hurried to the check-in counter and quickly passed a bill to a man who looked enough like the doorman to be his brother.

He slid a key through the cutout, not bothering to look at Duran.

As soon as the elevator doors clanged shut, Candy held her hand out. "You said you'd pay when we were inside."

"Indeed I did. What's the room number?"

She turned the key over and rubbed a bony finger over the engraved numbers. "816."

Duran peeled seven twenty-dollar bills from his money clip, then pushed the buttons for floors seven and eight. "Give me the key. You go on up and wait for me, I'll be right up."

Candy started to protest until she counted the money. "Sure, honey, sure," she said eagerly.

The elevator's walls were battle scarred with initials and obscenities. Candy's overpowering dosage of perfume couldn't disguise the stench coming from the soggy carpet underfoot. It came to a jarring halt at the seventh floor. "See you in a few minutes," Duran said, exiting the elevator.

Candy smiled and waved at him. A good-bye wave. She couldn't believe her luck. Or how stupid the guy was.

Duran heard the elevator grind up a floor, stop, then immediately begin its descent. Candy hurrying back to Tyrone.

He made his way to room 704. The door was warped. The numbers were stenciled in wavy, fading black ink. He leaned his ear against the door for a moment, then rapped lightly with his knuckles.

"Otto," he said in a husky whisper. "Otto."

Duran had thought of bringing a gun. There were still several of Conrad Stack's hunting rifles and shotguns stored in Stack House. He hadn't fired a weapon since leaving the army. He'd selected an elegantly hand-engraved Bertuzzi double-barreled shotgun with exposed hammers. There was something about the exposed hammers that seemed intimidating. The shotgun was now tucked away under a blanket alongside the passenger seat in the Jaguar. He hadn't been able to think of a way to conceal the weapon for his visit to the hotel, so he'd settled for a foot-long pry bar that he'd found in the garage. He slid the bar from his belt and knocked louder. "Otto."

He tried the door handle, his mind flashing back to Wendy Lange's house. It was locked. He tried the key Candy had picked up in the lobby. It slid easily into the lock, but wouldn't turn the cylinder pins.

Over the years, Duran had investigated so many burglaries and museum thefts that he'd become as adept as most burglars at forced entries. He edged the end of the pry bar into the slim opening alongside the lock then gave a quick tug. The door resisted momentarily, then opened with a slap.

He charged into the room, the pry bar cocked at shoulder height. Light imprinted the floor with a shadowy X from the hotel's sign. Duran closed the door behind him and leaned against it, watching the neon X flicker through tattered window curtains. He fingered the wall for the light switch. A pair of naked electric bulbs spotted with fly droppings threw an ugly glare from the ceiling fixture. There was a single bed, the blankets tangled and cascading to the floor. A lone pine dresser, on top of which sat an electric hot plate.

The closet door was ajar. Three shirts and two pairs of pants hung neatly on metal laundry hangers. Duran fingered the clothing. All gray. Heavily starched. Replicas of Junior Erwin's prison uniform. He searched the bureau, reverting to a burglar's technique of starting at the bottom and working toward the top, thus saving the time of closing one drawer before opening on the next. All he found was a collection of socks and underwear, some still in cellophane wrappings.

He tore the blankets from the bed, then raised the mattress. A piece of paper was wedged between the mattress and the wall. Duran picked it up eagerly. A caricature of a young boy's innocently smiling face. In the background was a watchtower that Duran recognized immediately—the Ghiardelli tower at the Cannery on Fisherman's Wharf, located less than a block from his office. Duran remembered his conversation with Chief Saylor that afternoon.

A man had been sketching a youngster in a rickshaw. Could it have been Kline?

Duran rolled the paper into a slim cylinder and slipped it into his pocket while glancing around the room. Something was missing. Justice had told him he'd phoned Kline's room from the hotel lobby. There was no telephone.

Chapter 31

The butler settled the drink tray on the table, then walked off without saying a word.

Jason Lark picked up his Scotch on the rocks. Dispose of George. That seemed to be the only reasonable solution, he decided. The Picasso sketch on George's bedroom wall was the real thing, but obviously George didn't realize that. Or did he? What if George had stashed the rest of the Picassos in his safety-deposit box? Or given them to a friend? Did George have a friend? Lark could not recall George having a family or friends. His life seemed to revolve around Stack House.

Lark had just begun to search George's suite, stopping when he'd heard the sound of a car's engine in the garage. It had been George returning home in the Bentley. And as far as he knew, the bastard hadn't left the house since.

He took a swallow of the whisky. Yes, dispose of George. He was an old man. It shouldn't be too difficult. He could whack George over the head—like he'd done to Duran at the studio, only a little harder, then ransack his room. Or perhaps Mario Drago could recommend someone to him. Certainly not the same ones who had failed in their mission to kill Duran.

Drago was still worried that Duran would link him

to the Fritzheim Van Gogh. But it had been Drago's people who'd screwed up by not waiting for Duran and killing him along with the attorney.

Drago wanted Lark to come to Vegas. It was a trip that Lark feared would end up being a one-way journey. He had to accept the fact that he was no longer an asset to Drago. He owed more money on the inventory in his shop than it was worth. His bank accounts were down to nothing. All he had were the sketches he'd taken from Anona's studio the night of the fire, but he'd have to wait to see what had really happened to Anona before putting them on the market.

He had managed to stall Drago from sending someone to escort him to Vegas, with the promise of a new job: the old woman in Beverly Hills. "I talked to her this morning," Lark had assured the Vegas gangster. "She's expecting me to be there in the next couple of days to finalize the contract for the redecorating job. There's a Renoir, a Rembrandt, and a fantastic Caravaggio, Mario. They're all magnificent." Actually, the old bitch had decided to put off redecorating until next year.

"Call me in two days," Drago ordered. "I won't wait any longer than that."

Lark drained the rest of the drink, then crushed the ice cubes with his teeth. He was drinking too much. He knew it. The cocaine he'd brought with him from Santa Monica was gone.

Surely John would know someone who sold reliable drugs. All those young barbarians who frequented his club looked like they were stoned. Where the hell was John, anyway?

Lark heard a door slam and did a half turn, hoping to see his son. But it was Robert Duran. Looking grim and pissed off.

They stared at each other a moment. Then Duran entered the room and they slowly circled, like boxers waiting for the bell to ring. The physical contrast between the two was strikingly pronounced: Lark, immaculately attired in a tailored, camel-hair sport coat, black cashmere turtleneck, and matching slacks, his hair sprayed helmet hard in calculated disarray. Duran was in need of a shave, his nose and forehead showing bruises and scrape marks, bandages on his wrist, dressed in shirt-sleeves rolled up past his elbows, his suede jacket draped over one shoulder.

"You just missed a policeman," Lark informed him, as if it was painful for him to do so. "Chief Saylor, from Colma. He left no more than fifteen minutes ago."

"Did he have any news of Anona?" Duran asked quickly.

"No. Other than to say he is puzzled over the whole thing. I'm puzzled, too, I must say. And that affair in Los Angeles, Bob. The man who got killed. Harry Lawson. An attorney, wasn't he?"

Duran dropped his suede jacket onto a chair. "Yes. Did you ever run into Lawson, or the appraiser, Wendy Lange?"

"Not my league, not my territory, I'm afraid. Do you think what happened in L.A. has anything to do with Anona?"

"I'm not sure. What about the Fritzheims? Did you ever—"

The butler appeared before Duran could finish his sentence.

"A policeman was here, Mr. Robert, I—"

"Yes. Lark told me. Did he question you, George?"

"Quite thoroughly. Is there something I can get for you, sir?"

"A sandwich and coffee, thanks, George."

Duran waited until the butler was in the kitchen before wheeling around to face Lark.

"Lisa talked to Stringer about you. She wants you out of the house."

Lark set his drink down and jammed his hands in his pants pockets. "She's under a lot of stress. First Anona. And now these worries about Johnny."

"Stress or not, she wants you out. And so do I."

Lark's fingers moved in his pockets as if jingling change. "When I know Anona is safe, then I'll leave."

"Too many things have happened to this family since you showed up, Lark."

"That's a ridiculous statement. It's a coincidence that—"

"I don't like coincidences," Duran said flatly. "You better start packing, Jason. I'll give you one more day. That's it."

"How extraordinarily nice of you," Lark said, half under his breath to Duran's retreating back. He nibbled at one of his carefully manicured nails. One more day. Everyone was giving him ultimatums. Duran's didn't worry him. Drago's did.

Chapter 32

The crowd was three and four abreast and curved from the stairway out to the parking lot. The mix was almost fifty-fifty, male to female, the age group from late teens to mid-twenties.

Robert Duran felt out of place as he skirted the line. A broad-bodied Samoan dressed in a lavender, up-collared Polo shirt, and black tuxedo jacket was working the door.

He eyed Duran's progress and stuck his chin out as Duran approached him. "You got business, brother?"

"I'm Johnny Stack's stepfather. Is he in?"

"I ain't seen him," the bouncer said. "You say you're the stepfather?"

"Right. Bob Duran."

"Well, he better show up soon. He owes me a week's pay."

"Is Lisa here?"

"The sister? Yeah. She's here."

Duran started down the stairs. There was a chorus of boos and catcalls from the crowd. The bouncer raised his arms like a priest granting benediction. "Peace, brothers and sisters. Keep the peace. Your time will come."

The noise hit Duran first—a combination of decibel screaming music and the plangent babble of the crowd. He could understand the line outside now. There hardly seemed space for one more body. He elbowed his way through a sea of denim, leather, and flesh, swiveling his head, hoping to spot Lisa.

The elevated bar took up the entire side of one wall. He'd stepped on several sets of toes, some in shoes, some bare, by the time he reached the bar.

The musty scent of marijuana mingled with the odors of cigarette smoke and alcohol. He waved a ten-dollar bill at a sullen-faced bartender and ordered an Anchor Steam beer. His drink arrived five minutes later and the bartender collected the money, not bothering to return with his change.

A young woman with spiked, tomato-red hair and dark stains under her eyes nudged Duran with her elbow. Duran could see her lips moving, but couldn't hear what she was saying. He leaned down and soon found her teeth fastened on his earlobe. "Want some blow?" she asked, when she opened her mouth again.

"No, thanks," Duran said, thinking that if Johnny didn't hire better security people, the cops would be closing him down. He pushed his way to the end of the bar and stood on the tips of his toes, scanning the dance floor. The music seemed to get louder with every tick of the clock. Strobe lights flashed in random sequences, bathing the dancers in red and blue puddles of color.

He finally spotted Lisa, her head rocking back and forth, her knees bent slightly forward, her hips gyrating in an attempt to keep up with the staccato bursts of the music. She was wearing a black, spiderweb knit dress. Thick silver bracelets encircled her wrists. Her dancing partner was at her back, his pelvis thrust against Lisa's buttocks, hands holding onto her bare shoulders.

Lisa twisted her head, her hair swishing in front of her face as she licked at one of her partner's hands.

They moved in a slow half-circle and Duran was able to catch a glimpse of her partner—Eric Marvin, his narrow face sweat-sheened, his hair lacquered into place.

The music ended in a discordant, measureless frenzy of high-amp clamor. There was a brief moment of silence, then the crowd erupted in foot-stomping applause and shouting.

Duran held his space against the tide surging toward the bar. Lisa and Marvin melted into the throng. He moved in the general direction of where he'd last seen them, finally spotting the pair in a brass-buttoned, red-leather booth near the bandstand.

Their heads were close together, Marvin's mouth on Lisa's neck.

Duran rapped his knuckles on the Formica-topped table. "Lisa, I need to talk to you and John."

Lisa pulled her head away and looked up, her eyes glassy. "Hey, Bob. What are you doing? Slumming?"

Eric Marvin's eyes weren't glassy. They stared daggers at Duran. "We're busy," he snarled. "Go away."

Duran ignored him. "I'm worried about your brother, Lisa. And you, too."

Marvin bolted to his feet. He was wearing designer jeans and a black silk, banded-collar shirt. "Why don't you get the fuck out of here? You're not wanted."

"I'm got something to say to Lisa. And to you, too, Eric. Sit down."

Marvin opened his mouth to say something, then pushed Duran out of the way and swaggered off toward the bar.

"Somehow I get the feeling he doesn't like me," Duran said, sliding in next to Lisa.

She rested her elbow on the table and propped her chin in the palm of her hand. Duran could see she was high as a kite. "He thinks you did something to Mom. And to Johnny. You didn't, did you?"

"No, Lisa. I promise you, I did not." Duran extracted the sketch he'd found at the Excelsior Hotel. "Have you seen anyone around doing sketches, like this one?"

Lisa tilted her head as she examined the drawing. "Is this one of the sketches Jason is talking about?"

"Jason? Has he been here asking you about sketches?"

"Everybody's been here. Everyone but Johnny." Lisa's flushed cheeks dimpled. "A policeman was here a while ago."

"You mean Chief Saylor from Colma?"

A tress of hair dropped down in front of Lisa's face and she blew it away. "He sure looked funny. He was wearing a suit." Her bracelets chimed together as she covered her mouth and gave a soft burp. "No one wears a suit in here."

"Lisa. The drawing. I think the man who drew it may be involved in your mother's disappearance. Does the name Otto Kline mean anything to you?"

"No. Why would he hurt Mom?"

"It's a long story. What did Chief Saylor say?"

Lisa reached out and touched Duran's beer bottle. "May I, step-daddy dearest?"

Duran opened his hand in approval and Lisa grabbed the bottle and took a long swig.

"What did Saylor say?" Duran repeated.

"He asked questions about you, and Johnny. And Jason. And Mom." Lisa put the beer bottle down and buried her hands in her hair. "I don't know where Johnny is. I don't know where Mom is." She parted her hair and peered at Duran through her fingers. "Where is she, Bob? Where's Mom?"

"Look at the drawing again, Lisa. Think. Have you seen anyone around sketching? Where have you—"

Duran felt someone grab his shoulder. He looked up and saw the face of the bouncer from the street.

"Hey, brotha. Eric says you're leaving."

Marvin was standing alongside the bouncer, a triumphant look on his face.

"In a few minutes. After I talk to Lisa." Duran turned back to Lisa, who was having trouble keeping her eyes open.

The bouncer's hand increased its pressure, causing Duran to wince. "Now, brotha."

"All right, all right," Duran said between clenched teeth, climbing slowly to his feet.

Maybe it was the way Eric Marvin was glaring at him, his lips spread apart as if he was ready to spit. Or maybe it was the over-confident look on the bouncer's face, who was twenty years younger, and outweighed him by a hundred pounds, but when Duran tried pushing the Samoan's arm away, only to find the huge fingers digging deeper into his shoulder, he reacted. He raked his heel down the man's shin, and when his shoulder was finally freed from the vise-like grip, he brought his knee up to the bouncer's groin, and followed it with a quick left hook to the head, flinching at the pain shooting through his hand.

The Samoan bent over at the waist and groaned in agony and astonishment. He straightened up and snarled, coming at Duran with both hands open, going for his head, planning to squash it like a pumpkin.

Duran ducked inside and threw two quick left-right combinations to the Samoan's well-padded belly, feeling his hands sink in to the wrist, then put everything he had into an uppercut to the man's massive chin.

He stepped back ready to fire again, but the Samoan's mottled face told him the fight was over. The bouncer sank slowly to his knees, gasping as he tried to catch his breath.

A group of customers had encircled the table. A tall man in a business suit bumped into Duran.

He pointed a finger at the man on the ground. "I think I'm going to get out of here," Chief Tom Saylor announced in a formal voice. "Before he decides to file charges."

"That was a real dumb stunt," Saylor advised Duran, once they were seated in Saylor's unmarked police car, which was parked in a red zone a half block down from the nightclub.

Duran massaged the knuckles of his left hand. "You won't get an argument out of me, Chief."

Saylor flicked on the car's interior light and examined the sketch of Ghiardelli Square.

"So you found this in Otto Kline's room. The door just happened to be open, I guess."

Duran studied the policeman out of the corner of his eye. He looked different out of uniform—smaller, uncomfortable, less menacing, like a football player who had discarded his pads.

"Kline's door was open, Chief. The wood was split. Whoever got there before me did the damage."

"Yeah, sure," Saylor scoffed, folding the drawing in half and dropping it in Duran's lap. "I could have saved you the trouble. I spoke to Kline's probation officer, Al McCarthy. McCarthy says that Kline has been working as a street artist for a couple of weeks. He brought some of his drawings into McCarthy's office. He even did one of McCarthy while he was there. So your breaking and entering his room didn't turn up squat."

"There was no phone in Kline's room," Duran said.

Saylor turned off the light, then dropped both hands down to the steering wheel. "No phone. Gee, that's too bad. Maybe he should move to the Ritz, or the Fairmont."

"The first time I visited the Excelsior Hotel, the doorman, a tall black man named Justice, took me over to the hotel register. He used the house phone—said he was calling Kline's room, and that there was no answer."

"So? Big deal. The man was shucking you."

"He thought I was a cop, Chief."

Saylor inhaled sharply. "You told this man you were a police officer?"

"No. I was dressed in a suit and tie. He assumed I was a cop. He called me 'officer.' "

"And you didn't bother to correct him."

Duran held out his hands in mock surrender. "What are you going to do, arrest me? Some lunatic has kidnapped my wife, tried to burn me to death. I can't find my stepson, and all you're worried about is some doorman who thought I was a cop!"

Saylor made a clucking sound of disapproval. "You forgot to mention breaking and entering, burglary—you had no right to remove that drawing from Kline's room—and roughing up a bouncer. Did I leave out anything else, Mr. Duran? Those are just the local laws you've broken. I'll let the Los Angeles boys figure out what happened down there."

Duran fought to hold his temper in check. "This Justice character lied to me. He probably tipped Kline off that I was by asking about him."

"Did you tell this gentleman your name? Any name?"

"No." Duran ran a finger down the scar alongside his eye. "But I'm not a hard man to describe. Kline would know it was me."

Saylor slipped the key into the ignition and gunned the motor. "Good night, Mr. Duran. Go home. Stay there."

Duran opened the car door and put one foot out on the sidewalk. "Chief, I checked Otto Kline through DMV. He bought a truck. A bread truck."

Saylor shrugged, then raised his eyebrows as an invitation to continue.

"I think he bought it to make a prison cell. A portable prison cell, that he could drive around, move whenever he felt like it."

"That's a reach, Duran."

"Then why the hell else would he buy that damn thing? What good is a bakery truck to someone like Otto Kline?"

Saylor waited until Duran was out of the car, and had slammed the door behind him. He leaned over and rolled down the window. "Kline's due to check in with his probation officer at eleven o'clock tomorrow morning."

"Where?" Duran asked impatiently. "Where's the probation office?"

"At the Hall of Justice on Bryant Street. I'm going to be there, and if you want—"

"I'll meet you there, Chief."

"Not if you're going to pull another dumb stunt like you did in the nightclub, or at Kline's hotel."

"I'll be on my best behavior, Chief," Duran promised.

Saylor grudgingly nodded in confirmation. "I'll see you in the morning."

Chapter 33

He thrust the shovel down into the soft ground. Justice's knife had madc a small gash in his arm, but the bleeding had been minimal. More important, his migraine was under control—a dull ache now, not the fierce, blinding pain of last night.

He had to keep his head clear. Somehow Duran had figured it out, had identified him. He hadn't expected that. He'd underestimated Duran—which meant he'd have to up the tempo on Anona Stack, push her, punish her, maybe hang her by the bra, until she was almost there—almost gone. Let her get a feel for what was coming. And he'd have to be prepared for Duran giving his name to the police. To his parole officer—and he had a meeting at the parole office later in the morning.

Otto Kline tossed the shovel aside and climbed out of the hip-high hole, crossed over to the van and grabbed one of Justice's ankles, pulling him from the vehicle and dragging him over to the makeshift grave.

Justice's black, marblelike eyes stared vacantly up at Kline.

He searched through the dead man's pockets, retrieving the roll of cash he'd given him last night, a collection of keys, and his wallet. The wallet held close to six hundred dollars in cash, several credit cards, and a driver's license in the name of J. Allen Wells. He pushed Justice's body into the hole with his foot, then picked up the shovel, scooped up some loose dirt, then sprinkled it over Justice's face.

When he finished with the burial, he jammed the shovel into the ground, and thought about saying a prayer. When a prisoner died in Pelican Bay, the warden made an announcement over the speaker system, ending with a short, nondenominational prayer.

Kline remembered his churchgoing as a child. The word "amen" concluded each prayer. Ken Firpo had a better ending. "Good-bye, asshole." He missed Firpo.

The morning sunlight slanted through the cabin door. Anona Stack wiggled her fingers to ward off the numbness. Her wrists ached from the handcuffs. She could feel her skin bruising, swelling up. She had been awake most of the night. She'd tried rocking the chair back and forth, but the slightest movement dug the cuffs deeper into her flesh.

Why had he moved her to the cabin? she wondered. Kline had obviously been in pain. But there were no visible wounds. The gunshots. One or two? It was hard to tell. Whatever the number, they had hit their mark. The grotesque head hanging out of the van's window. The dead black man.

What was his part in her abduction? A partner? A policeman? Or just an innocent bystander?

Why had Kline moved her from the SHU? She craned her neck as far as she could to her left. There was a sleeping bag on the floor, near the fireplace. His sleeping bag. So where did he sleep last night? In the van? With a corpse? The van hadn't moved. She would have heard it.

He must have used the cell. The SHU! Why in God's name would anyone want to sleep in the SHU?

Her head jerked up when Otto Kline banged his way into the cabin.

He was no longer pale and sweaty, and he was walking normally. He reached over her shoulders and examined the handcuffs.

"They're too tight," she protested. "My fingers are numb."

He grunted an undecipherable response, then headed into the kitchen area. The sound of the shower running intensified her thirst, and her need to use the bathroom.

When Kline returned, he was wearing a fresh pair of gray pants and gray shirt, his face clean shaven, his hair still wet from the shower. The rifle hung loosely from its strap over his left shoulder.

He unlocked her handcuffs.

Anona rubbed at her wrists to get the blood flowing, then rose slowly from the chair, like an old person afraid that some new ailment had been inflicted during the night, cataloging her pains as she moved. She arched her back, and rotated her neck slowly.

"Come on, you're going back in the SHU," Kline informed her.

"I'd like something to drink," she protested. "To eat."

"I went on a fast once. Five days. Nothing but water. They didn't care. Didn't give a damn. They made jokes, saying they hoped it was a trend that would catch on. That we'd all starve ourselves. They get paid so much for each man, for each meal. Per diem. Just like in the army. All I was doing was saving them money." He waved the rifle stock toward the doorway. "Get going."

"At least let me use the bathroom."

Kline sucked in his lips so that they virtually disappeared. "You're stalling, aren't you? You don't want to go back in there, do you? I used to try that—try and get the doctor to put me in the infirmary, but he wouldn't. He just gave me some aspirin and called the guards. You're going back inside. You're never going to get out of there—until you decide to end it. Just like Arlene did."

Anona folded one hand over the other and massaged her wrists. "I remember Arlene. She was very talented." Her eyes sought out his. "So were you, Otto. Why did you waste your talent like that? Copying others? Why—?"

Kline pounded the butt of the rifle against the floor. "So, you know! You remember me now! I knew you would. I didn't think Duran would. Not so soon, anyway, but it won't do him any good. Duran's going to be blamed for your death. He's going to go to prison. Like I did. All because of you, you bitch!"

Anona stared into Kline's feverish, protruding eyes. A true madman's eyes. His skin was flushed, there was a spasm on the right side of his mouth that she hadn't noticed before. She wouldn't have been surprised if he suddenly started foaming at the mouth like a mad dog.

He brought the rifle up to firing position and pointed it directly at her. "You want to know why we forged your painting? Because we needed the money! We weren't born rich, like you. And we didn't have a name like yours, a name that opened gallery doors. We didn't have the money to buy good reviews. We didn't have rich friends to buy our work! You had it all. Did you read about Arlene's suicide in the paper, and get a laugh out of it? Is that it? Did it amuse you? Something to pepper a cocktail party conversation with?"

When Anona didn't reply, Kline repeated the question, in a loud, anguished voice: "You knew, didn't you? You knew!"

Anona fought to keep her voice calm and steady. "No, Otto. I haven't any idea what happened to your wife."

Kline tilted his long neck to one side, opened his eyes wide, distended his tongue, then made jerking motions with his right hand, as if he were a puppeteer pulling strings, making his head twitch up and down.

"She hung herself!" he wailed. "In her cell! With her bra! Seven years ago, October the twelfth! Just like you're going to do." He prodded Anona's stomach with the rifle barrel, herding her back against the table. "You know there's no escape. No way out. I've been too soft on you. Too easy. That's going to stop. You're going to do it, and your precious husband is going to be blamed."

Kline backstepped away from her, the rifle barrel steady in his grip.

"You're going back inside. Now."

Anona moved with awkward, wooden movements, her feet barely rising above the floor. Arlene Kline. Was what he said true? How twisted was his mind? October twelfth. He was going to kill her that day. She knew it now. One way or the other, she was going to die on the twelfth.

The voice on the other end of the line had a strange, garbled, high-pitched tone.

"Mr. Duran isn't in at the moment," Peggy Jacquard said cautiously. "Who's calling?"

"No. No name. I'll call back. Tell him we want the painting back."

"And which painting are you talking about?"

"Our Van Gogh, lady, 'Sun and Sky.' You tell Duran we want it back."

"Would you like to leave a number where he can reach you?"

"Very funny. You just tell Duran I'll be calling in an hour."

There was a buzz, and the connection was severed.

Peggy tapped the linebar with her fingernail, then touch-toned Duran's car phone number.

"You just got a doozy of a call, Bob. I think it's the guy who stole the Van Gogh from Fritzheim."

"What did he say?"

"He wants 'Sun and Sky' back. He says he'll be calling back in an hour."

Duran checked the Jaguar's clock. "Well, he'll be disappointed. I'm meeting Chief Saylor at the probation office."

"What do I tell him when he calls again?"

"I'll leave that up to your imagination, Peg. But keep the door locked. I'll be back as soon as I can."

Peggy took Duran's advice and double-locked the office door. Back at her desk, she began flipping through the Fritzheim file. It was obvious that the caller thought Duran had the painting. She could almost understand his convoluted thought process: Wendy Lange drugged and tied up. Harry Lawson, his contact, killed. Bob untouched, arriving on the scene after all the damage was done.

All that plotting, planning, scheming. He'd committed the perfect crime, then the Van Gogh was snatched back.

Peggy read through Duran's notes, his fax to Wendy

Lange, the appraisal figures, the logged times of the calls with Harry Lawson. There wasn't much information to go on in the file. She hadn't examined the Nexis search on Fritzheim's property, and wondered if Duran had had the time to look it over.

Simply by entering Fritzheim's name, and then coupling it with Van Gogh, the computer database had pulled up seven pages of stories starting from when Fritzheim had purchased the painting three years ago from a Christie's auction, to numerous articles trumpeting the movie producer's life-style and new home.

Peggy flipped through the printout with little enthusiasm until she came to the top of page six. The storyline jumped from an interview with Danielle Fritzheim to a feature on the construction of the house. It took her several seconds to realize that there was a page missing. Page five. She shuffled the papers again, but it wasn't there. Had Duran found something of interest on page five? Removed it from the file?

She put the computer to work, re-entered the Nexis request and in a matter of seconds the printer began coughing up documents. Again, seven pages, the first four identical to the ones in the file.

She studiously reviewed page five. It didn't take her long to spot the paragraph mentioning that the architect employed by Fritzheim had "used the talents of local interior designer Jason Lark to assist in completing the project."

"Holy shit," Peggy said, loud enough to startle herself.

"Don't try anything," Chief Bill Saylor warned Bob Duran as they entered the Probation Department office at the Hall of Justice. It was a large, L-shaped room. A receptionist sat behind a gray-steel desk, clicking away at a computer keyboard.

Duran said, "I won't. But I want to see Kline. I want to talk to him."

"That's up to his probation officer."

Saylor walked over to the receptionist and showed her his badge.

Duran ran his eyes around the room. There were three modern, turquoise-vinyl, chrome-legged couches and a half dozen matching chairs scattered along the walls, all of them occupied by an eclectic group of men and women—black, white, Latin, and Asian.

He studied their faces, his eyes jerking to a halt at the long-necked man with short dark hair sitting between two beefy Latinos.

Otto Kline! He was sure it was Kline. His right hand was positioned under his armpit, just like the Pelican Bay guard had described.

Duran took a quick peek at Saylor, who was still engaged in a conversation with the receptionist. He sauntered slowly across the room, until he was standing directly in front of Kline.

The back of Otto Kline's neck had gone icy cold when he saw Duran enter the room. He'd fought back the urge to bolt—to race back to the cabin. He squeezed his eyes shut and concentrated on his breathing, bringing his pulse rate down so it was slow and regular, just as he had when he'd been interrogated by the guards.

Duran coughed, and Kline raised his eyes. He gave Duran an indifferent look, then he dropped his chin to his chest.

"Mr. Kline," the receptionist called out. "You can go in now."

Kline pushed himself to his feet, brushing within

inches of Duran. Their eyes met for a fraction of a second.

" 'Scuse me," Kline said innocently.

Duran started to follow him, but Saylor held out a hand like a cop directing traffic. "You wait right there. I'll call you."

A bulky man with a high-bridged nose over a guardsman's mustache was waiting at a door marked PRIVATE. Kline nodded to the man and disappeared through the door, Saylor right behind him.

The probation officer held out his hand to Saylor. "Al McCarthy, Chief. This is Mr. Kline."

Saylor shook McCarthy's hand, then Otto Kline's. Kline's hand was strong, the skin dry.

"Is there some kind of a problem?" Kline asked McCarthy. "I haven't done anything. Why is a policeman here?"

"Let's go in my office and find out," McCarthy suggested.

Once they were all seated in the probation officer's office, McCarthy laid out the ground rules.

"Mr. Kline, you're not accused of anything. The chief is from Colma. He'd like to ask you some questions. If you want to have someone from our legal staff here to monitor the situation, I can arrange it. Or you can contact your own attorney."

Kline slipped his right hand under his armpit. "Where's Colma?"

"It's just a few miles from here, Otto," Saylor said, edging forward as far as he could on his chair, wishing he could move in a little closer, get within three or four feet of Kline, into his innermost "behavioral zone." "Did you recognize anyone outside in the waiting room?"

Kline quizzically raised his eyebrows. "Just the receptionist. She's the same one I've seen before."

"No one else?" Saylor queried.

"No. What's going on, Mr. McCarthy? What's this all about?"

McCarthy tapped a ballpoint pen against his desk. "Do you remember Anona Stack, Otto?"

The questioning went on for fifteen minutes. Saylor was impressed. Kline answered the questions without a pause. There were no delaying gestures, no coughing, taking a deep breath, clearing the throat, scratching the nose. No licking the lips, no defensive gestures, other than his right hand continually creeping up under his armpit.

McCarthy pulled his shirt sleeve back and looked pointedly at his wristwatch. "Any other questions, Chief?"

Saylor folded his arms across his chest and gave Kline a patronizing smile. "No. Thank you for your time."

When Kline started to rise from the chair, Saylor said, "Would you mind talking to Mr. Duran, Otto? He's worried about his wife. Eliminating you as a suspect in her disappearance would be a great relief to him."

Kline slumped back in his chair and looked at McCarthy, who advised him, "You certainly don't have to meet with the man. It's up to you."

Kline's lips rose up over his gums. "Sure. Why not?"

Chapter 34

Anona Stack slipped out of the denim jeans, cursing Otto Kline as her bare buttocks made contact with the mattress.

It was another part of Kline's torture technique. No panties. And no bra. Except for the one dangling from the ceiling. The one he wanted her to hang herself with.

She turned the jeans inside out, fingering the pocket linings. Kline wouldn't notice if they were missing. Or would he? If he did, what more could he do to her?

After their confrontation at the cabin, he'd paraded her past the freshly dug grave of the man in the van.

Then he shoved her in the SHU, returning minutes later with a quart of milk and a packaged loaf of bread. Plain white bread. Bread and milk. She would have preferred bread and water. The semi-sour milk did nothing to quench her thirst.

Kline had made a mistake. He might not have realized it, but when Kline said that he had underestimated Bob, it must mean that Bob knew about him. That Bob was after him. It also meant that he was in danger from Kline.

She knew that her husband was resourceful, and would do everything in his power to find her. Now

Kline knew that, too. He might just go after Bob. Kill him. Or kill her before Bob got close to finding her.

She had to get away. She couldn't wait for Bob to save her. She had to break out of this monstrosity of a cell.

His sealing off the cutout in the door had been devastating. She wondered if that had been Kline's plan all along—allowing her a window to the outside world, then shutting it.

Whether it was his plan or not, she had to admit it was working. Kline had been on target when he accused her of stalling in the cabin, not wanting to return to her cell.

She remembered one of her childhood playmates using a mayonnaise jar, with holes punched in the lid, to capture bees. The trapped insect would batter itself against the jar.

Anona thought it a cruel, sadistic thing to do and had unscrewed the lid and freed a yellow jacket, which had promptly rewarded her by stinging her on the hand.

That's what she had to do. Get out somehow and sting Otto Kline.

She ran her hand along the seams of one of the jean pockets, then carried the garment over to the door, holding it close to one of the holes for light and using her fingernail to saw through the thread, breaking a seam. She then methodically undid the rest of the stitches.

She repeated the procedure until all four pockets were removed, then gently laid each pocket on the mattress, ironing them out with her hands, then folding them in neat bands, approximately an inch in width.

She draped one of the bands around her wrist, directly on the flesh, which was bruised now and swollen by the handcuffs. It wasn't long enough. She tied two of the bands together and tried again.

The band wrapped around with enough room left to fasten the ends together.

She next rolled her shirtsleeve down, buttoning the cuff, covering her wrist.

She squeezed the band hard enough to cause herself to wince. Not thick enough. Damn it! It wasn't thick enough!

The blanket. She could tear off a piece of the blanket.

No, she decided. The bastard checked the blanket, and the mattress, and the pillow. And the bra. He checked those every day.

She rolled up her sleeve, undid the band from her wrist and laid it on the bed again. She'd have to stuff it. Make it thicker. But with what? Something that Kline wouldn't see. Wouldn't miss.

She reached for the loaf of bread, squeezing the plastic wrapper. It was spongy. Like flesh. She smiled for the first time in days. It just might work.

"Otto Kline, this is Bob Duran," Chief Saylor said when Duran entered McCarthy's office.

The probation officer got to his feet and hurried over to Duran.

"Mr. Kline has agreed to talk to you," he advised Duran. "But he's under no obligation to do so. I want you to understand that."

"I understand," Duran acknowledged.

He walked over to Kline, who was sitting casually in his chair, one leg hooked over the other.

"Do you remember me, Otto?"

"Barely. I just saw you once, when you came to Mr.

Breamer's gallery. To tell you the truth, if I saw you on the street, I wouldn't have recognized you."

Duran slipped his right hand under his armpit in a mocking gesture. "Is that right? What about my wife? You remember Anona Stack, don't you?"

Kline rubbed his chin thoughtfully. "I remember her from the trial, but that was a long time ago. A very long time ago."

McCarthy said, "Mr. Kline has answered all of Chief Saylor's questions—to my satisfaction. I don't think there's much point in continuing this meeting, do you, Chief?"

Saylor kept his eyes on Kline while addressing his remarks to Duran. "He says he hasn't seen your wife since he was released from prison and has no idea of where she is at the present time."

"And no real interest in where she's at, either," Kline contended. "I don't know why you're bothering me. I just want to get on with my life."

Duran said, "Why did you come here, Otto? Why come to San Francisco? You've got no friends here. No family. I thought you'd move back to Los Angeles. Where Arlene is buried. I saw her grave. The new tombstone. She died what? Seven years ago, this month."

"San Francisco is a perfect spot for an artist." Kline nursed a pause, then said, "Your wife should know that."

"I've seen some of your sketches, the ones you did down by Fisherman's Wharf. That's where my office is. You know that, don't you?"

"No, I don't," Kline said with a one-sided grimace. "Why should I care where your office is?" He placed his hands on his knees as if getting reading to push himself to his feet. "Can I go now, Mr. McCarthy?"

"Wait just a minute," Duran said, his voice low and razor sharp. "Your room at the Excelsior Hotel. You're not sleeping there. Where are you sleeping, Otto?"

"What's this all about?" McCarthy challenged. "How did you find out where my client is living?"

Duran pulled a face. "Your client? That's a hell of a description. Kline is registered in room 714, but he's never there."

"This is a crock of shit," McCarthy said, biting off the words, making each one sharp and emphatic. "I don't like seeing Mr. Kline harassed for no reason. I want to know how you found out where Kline is living."

"What difference does it make?" Duran protested. "He's not living there—that's what you should be worried about."

Chief Saylor moved between the two men. "Let's calm down, boys." He glanced over at Otto Kline. "Are you still living at the Excelsior?"

"Yes. Certainly. You can check with the manager."

Duran pushed his way past Saylor. "What about your bread truck, Otto? Where the hell is it?"

"It was stolen," McCarthy announced in an irritated voice. "Mr. Kline informed me of the theft last week. He made out a police report. Now, Chief, I'm a busy man, and I'm sure Mr. Kline would like to be on his way, so if you don't mind—"

"I do mind," Duran objected. "You and Kenny Firpo, Otto. What did you do up there in Pelican Bay? What are you trying to—"

"Enough!" McCarthy barked. He reached for the phone on his desk. "Chief, if you can't get Mr. Duran out of here, I'll get someone who can."

"We're leaving," Saylor said, bulldozing Duran toward the door.

Duran jerked himself free. Kline had reacted to the mention of Firpo's name—his head snapped back as if he'd been slapped. "You and Firpo. What did you talk about all those nights, Otto?"

"Outside," Saylor ordered, wrapping his arms around Duran and tugging him through the door.

Duran's parting shot was, "You harm my wife and you're a dead man!"

Otto Kline gave Duran a sneering wink just before he disappeared from sight.

"I'm sorry about that," McCarthy apologized, settling back behind his desk. "Are you all right? You look like you're going to be sick."

Kline took out a handkerchief and mopped his forehead. "I'm okay. It's headaches. I told you about them. When I get upset, I get headaches."

"I'm sorry I let Duran in here. You haven't moved from the Excelsior Hotel? You can't do that without my permission. You should know that."

"Oh, I know. Sometimes the noise around my room gets unbearable and I use one of the vacancies upstairs. That's all right isn't it?"

"I guess so."

Kline said, "That man Duran. He knows where I'm living. Maybe I should move—even if it's just for a few days."

McCarthy began sifting through his address book. "That might be a good idea. I don't know how the hell he found you in the first place. Here. Try the St. Regis. I'll call the manager and let him know about you." He looked up at Kline. "And make sure you stay there until our next meeting."

"Thanks, sir. Thanks a lot."

"Sure." McCarthy sighed, frowning at the stack of folders on his desk. He had over three hundred parolees under his supervision. Half of them could move to Calcutta and he'd never know about it. Or give much of a damn. "Check in with me next week, Mr. Kline."

Chapter 35

"I warned you about making a scene," Chief Saylor said, steering Duran toward the elevator.

"He's got Anona, Chief. I'm telling you, he's got her."

Saylor dismissed Duran's accusation with a wave of his hand. "You've got no proof of that, and nothing he said during my interrogation makes me think otherwise."

"No? Did you see the way he reacted when I mentioned his buddy's name, Firpo? That shook him, Chief. I'm telling you—"

"What is it with this Firpo?"

The elevator opened, but Duran edged away, back toward the probation office.

"Ken Firpo was Kline's cellmate for a few years. Firpo's from Montara. Just down the coast."

"So?" Saylor challenged.

"Ken Firpo's a hard-timer. His father died while serving time in Alcatraz. The prison guard I spoke to said Firpo took Kline under his wing."

"That still doesn't tie Kline to your wife's disappearance," Saylor said, pushing the elevator button again.

"No. But Kline must have learned a lot from Firpo. It gives him the expertise—to go along with his motive. He came back to San Francisco for a reason," Duran argued. "And that reason is my wife."

The elevator door pinged open and Saylor motioned Duran inside. The two men remained silent until they were on the main floor, walking toward the lobby.

"Chief, you've got to help me on this," Duran urged. "Kline's dirty. You could tell that, couldn't you?"

"Go home, Duran. I'll look into Firpo. But you go home. Stay away from Otto Kline."

Duran shook his head resolutely. "No way. Kline's got my wife. I'm going to find her, with or without your help." He shifted his gaze past Saylor's shoulder, toward the bank of elevators. "The seventh anniversary of Arlene Kline's death is October the twelfth. Two days from now. Two days! That may be all the time Anona has left."

Jason Lark sat with the phone tucked between his cheek and shoulder, examining Conrad Stack's collection of leather-bound books squeezed spine to spine along the library walls. He'd gone through most of those books page by page looking for the Picassos.

"Two men were in the shop this morning looking for you, Mr. Lark," Adam Sheehan reported. "Large, disagreeable men."

"Well? Did they tell you who they were?" Lark asked irritably.

"No, just that they were anxious to talk to you."

"Did you tell them where I was?"

"No, but I overheard one of the men say something about San Francisco."

Lark groaned and leaned back in the swivel chair, the creaking of the leather sounding like old arthritic joints, reminding Lark of his own joints and bones—

the ones Mario Drago's goons had no doubt been told to break into little pieces.

"Adam, I want you to make a phone call for me. Call here, to Stack House. George, the butler, should answer the phone. In case he doesn't, ask for him, understand?"

"Yes, but what do I tell him?"

"Tell him that you're the police. The . . . Sausalito police and you want him to come over right away. To John Stack's houseboat."

"But why would—"

"Just do it, Adam. It's important. If George questions you as to what it's all about, just tell him that you'd rather not talk about it on the phone. Do it, Adam. Right now. There's a bonus in it for you. Do it as soon as I hang up, okay?"

Adam's response was an unconvincing "I guess so."

"Do it," Lark urged. "Then go into my office. The key to the lower-right desk drawer is taped under the phone. You can have all of what's there, Adam. But first make the call."

He hung up and then leaned forward, elbows on the desk, waiting for the phone to ring. Would Adam call right away, or would he sneak into the desk and help himself to a few of the ready-rolled joints first?

The phone chirped. Lark watched the button designating the houseline blink. When the ringing stopped, he picked up the phone, cupping the speaker with one hand.

On a scale of one to ten, he'd give Adam a strong eight. He'd identified himself as "Captain Smith" to George. Not a very inventive name, but he'd carried it off. The fish had bitten, the hook was well set. George told Captain Smith that he would "depart immediately" for Sausalito.

"Depart immediately" took no more than five minutes.

Lark watched the Bentley purr out of the garage and onto Broadway. Then he sprinted up the stairway to George's room. The door was locked again. He moved swiftly to the adjoining room and retraced his earlier route, out the window, along the ledge, and into George's suite.

Upon entering the bedroom, he took Picasso's drawing of the studio in Paris from the wall, then began combing through the places he wasn't able to search on his first visit, his fingers clawing at shirts, socks, underwear. Then the closet, fingering suits, jackets, and several shoe boxes.

He was panting like an animal after a race. There was a chest of dark wood banded by iron at the far end of the closet. He pushed the hanging garments out of his way and dragged the chest out of the closet. He unlocked the hasp and raised the lid. It was jammed with multicolored papers. There were more of Johnny and Lisa's crayon drawings, old photographs, and stacks of letters rubber-banded together.

Lark burrowed through the maze, then spotted the brick-colored packet. Claude Bresson's packet! It had to be!

He yanked the packet free, his trembling fingers undoing the ribbon, folding back the lid, carrying the contents over to George's bed.

He spread the sketches across the bedcover. The first was a one-dimensional rendition of Bresson's chateau. The next an equally bad Paris street scene. Then the women! He arranged the five sketches in a neat line. Five young women. Three showed only their faces, the other two were full-figured nudes. *Cinq putains.* He'd found them!

Lark turned the five sketches over, his eyes narrowing as he tried to decipher the French inscriptions. Then the initials. PRP. Why hadn't Picasso signed his name? Was it because the models were whores? Had he intended to give them to the women? Perhaps as payment for their services?

He slipped the sketches back into the packet, then tidied up the chest, sliding it back into the closet, and giving the room a quick once-over. He considered whether or not to take Picasso's drawing of the Paris studio, then reluctantly placed it gently back on the wall. George could keep that one, he decided.

He rushed to his room and packed his suitcases, slipping the packet with the Picassos into the smaller of the two bags. Then he used the phone, dialing information for the number of Yellow Cab and United Airlines.

He promised the dispatcher he'd give the driver a twenty-dollar tip if the cab showed up in less than five minutes, then called the airline.

"I need to get to New Orleans in a hurry."

"There's a flight leaving at five forty-five," he was informed.

Lark glanced at his watch. More than enough time. "Is there anything available in first class?"

Peggy Jacquard jumped when she heard the clicking of a key in the office door's lock. She quickly got to her feet. She relaxed when she saw the familiar profile of Robert Duran through the slanted window shades.

Duran slammed the door behind him and stalked over to his desk.

"What happened?" Peggy asked.

"I blew it. I had Otto Kline in front of me, right in front of me, and I blew it."

He gave Peggy a quick rundown of the meeting. "I waited for Kline, but he must have gone out a back way. Now I don't know where the hell he is."

"What about the police chief? Does he think Kline has Anona?"

Duran fell into his chair with a thick-bodied slump. "I don't know, Peg. Saylor says that Kline had all the right answers. Kline claims he's paid his dues, done his time, now he just wants to be left alone." He pounded the desk in frustration. "Kline looked me right in the eye and said he wouldn't have recognized me—that he barely remembers Anona. Shit! And I let the cat out of the bag about the Excelsior Hotel. Kline won't go back there now. You should have seen him, Peg. Sitting there, cocky as hell. Sure of himself. He didn't even bat an eye when I mentioned his wife's grave. He's creepy, Peg. When I mentioned his cell-mate, Ken Firpo's name, I hit a nerve. It got Kline sweating. I have a gut feeling about the anniversary of his wife's suicide, October twelfth. He's got something planned. I'm sure of it, but his probation officer wouldn't let me near him."

"What are you going to do now?"

"I don't know," Duran admitted scornfully. "The hotel is the only lead I've got. Maybe I can bribe the doorman, Justice. Maybe he knows something. You haven't heard from Erwin, the Pelican Bay prison guard, have you?"

"No. The only call was that strange one, the man asking about the Fritzheim Van Gogh."

"Did he call back?"

"No, not yet. Did you ever look at that Nexis report I did on the Van Gogh?"

"No, Peg. That's the least of my problems."

"Well, you better look at it now, Bob."

She handed him the Nexis report. "I found a page missing from the original report. Someone removed it. I ran it again. Look who turned up."

Peggy had highlighted Jason Lark's name in yellow. Duran thumped his forehead with his fist. "*Menso,*" he said, the gutter-Spanish word for idiot somehow popping into his mind. "Lark has had the run of the house. He must have gone through my room, found a set of spare keys. He'd have keys to the office, the Jaguar, and Anona's studio. Christ, why the hell didn't I think of that earlier?"

"After reading that article, I thought of it, too. I called a locksmith. He's coming over to change the locks."

"Great," Duran grunted, remembering how he had criticized Alan Fritzheim for locking the barn up after the horse was stolen.

"Jason must have been involved in the Fritzheim theft," Peggy asserted.

Duran snapped his fingers nervously. "Yes. He was involved all right. He broke into the office and saw that file, saw his name in the Nexis search. And he saw everything else, my letters to the insurance company, my fax to Wendy Lange, and the notations of the calls to Harry Lawson. Lark was the leak. He set me up."

Duran's shoulders suddenly slumped in dejection. "Let's back up, Peg. We're missing something here. Lark is working at the Fritzheim house. He sees the Van Gogh. Tells his accomplices about it. Tells them the Fritzheims' schedule: The husband is always away at the studio, Danielle is out denting the cash registers in Beverly Hills most afternoons. He tells them that the maid is usually alone in the house. Lark's buddies pull off the heist. They have the painting. They want to sell it to Pacific Indemnity. They contact Lawson. Everything is working out perfectly. So why would they want to kill me? Why kill Lawson?"

"Maybe Lark's partners double-crossed him," Peggy suggested.

Duran pinched his lower lip between thumb and forefinger. "The maid, Eleana, said the two men who came to Fritzheim's door were both tall, young, *flaco*, skinny, and looked enough alike to be brothers. Wendy Lange heard two men talking, but she just saw one of them. She describes him as short, heavy-set.

"Both jobs were done by two men. But with completely different M.Os. Eleana said that they treated her *suavemente*, gently, told her not to cry, made sure that the ropes weren't too tight, apologized for having to gag her, promised her that they wouldn't harm her in any way. They brought along the ropes to tie her up with.

"Wendy got a faceful of ether, then was trussed up like a steer with strips of sheets from her bed. One of the men made a comment about her being pretty, and it being too bad they had to put her to sleep, as if he planned to rape her."

"A gun was used in both instances," Peggy reminded.

"Yes, a *grande pistola* according to Eleana. Like a cowboy's gun. The LAPD says that a twenty-two was used to kill Lawson. A professional killer's gun. Probably with a silencer attached. There were two different teams on those jobs, Peg. I was the target at Wendy's studio. They wanted to kill me. And now this guy who took 'Sun and Sky' from Fritzheim's bedroom wall thinks I've got the Van Gogh."

Peggy's eyebrows cocked in a questioning arc. "You think that Lark told them—"

The chirping of the phone cut her off. She picked it up, then cupped her hand over the receiver. "It's him," she told Duran. "The man with the strange voice."

He nodded, reached over and pushed the phone's speaker button. "This is Bob Duran. What can I do for you?"

"Give us back our painting," was the off-pitch reply.

Duran gave an exasperated sigh. "I don't have the Van Gogh, and it isn't yours in the first place. It's Alan Fritzheim's."

"We want—"

"I don't have what you want. Why don't you ask Jason Lark?"

There was a long pause. "Who?"

"Your partner."

"The only partner I have is standing three feet from me. Cut the shit. You set up Harry Lawson. Harry had a lot of friends. Friends who aren't happy about what happened."

"Harry was a friend of mine, too," Duran exaggerated. "And I couldn't do business without him."

Another long pause, then: "We've done business together before. Through Harry."

Duran wasn't surprised at the admission. "And I've always played straight. I don't have the Van Gogh and I had nothing to do with Harry's murder. You can believe that or not, I really don't give a damn."

His finger stabbed at the phone, breaking the connection.

Peggy said, "That voice. It was one of those electronic gadgets, wasn't it?"

Duran nodded in agreement. A voice changer, originally developed by law enforcement to protect witness identification. As usual, the crooks found it suited their purposes just as well.

Peggy said, "He sounded like he didn't know about Jason Lark."

"Yes, he did," Duran agreed. "So what's it mean? Lark wasn't involved in the theft from Fritzheim's house? He had to be. He was there, he had access."

"Maybe the man on the phone stole 'Sun and Sky' before Lark could get to it."

"Maybe. But then . . ." He curled his tongue against his teeth and whistled softly. "What if Lark did steal the Van Gogh—then it was stolen again?"

"You're losing me," Peggy confessed.

"What if Lark had replaced the Van Gogh with a forgery while he was on the job at Fritzheim's house? Then the forgery was stolen. He couldn't afford to have me get the painting authenticated. Wendy Lange would know it was a forgery. I'd find out about his being Fritzheim's decorator. Hell, he's probably pulled this scam before. It fits Lark to a T."

Peggy sucked her lips inward. "But what does it have to do with Anona, Bob? What's the connection? This Otto Kline is a forger. Did he paint the phony 'Sun and Sky' in prison?"

"No. Junior Erwin told me that Kline was only allowed to sell paintings to the guards. For cigarettes. And to reproduce something like 'Sun and Sky,' he'd have to have some very good photographs to work from. No. Not possible."

"Then what's the connection?" Peggy asked again.

Duran got to his feet. "That's exactly what I'm going to ask Jason Lark."

Chapter 36

Anona Stack was as elated as she usually was at the completion of a painting. She swabbed her sweating forehead with the back of her hand. The bread slices she'd molded were stuffed between the jeans pocket linings, which were tied around her wrists and covered up by the shirtsleeves. They padded out her wrists almost an inch, but they were soft and spongy. When the handcuffs were snapped on, she'd have room to maneuver, to wriggle her hands free, undo the leg shackles, and get out of there—and into the woods. Disappear.

The trick was getting back into the chair, without Kline being there, hovering over her. Like last night. She chastised herself for not thinking of the bands earlier.

Would she get another chance like last night? Would Kline take her out of the SHU again? Sleep there himself?

She shuddered at the thought of voluntarily spending a night in this clammy, suffocating steel cage.

What had driven Kline into the SHU? The pain, he was in obvious pain. The medicine—the pills he constantly took—some type of headache. A tumor? A brain tumor? That would explain his being . . . crazy, a madman. The killing of the other man—the black man in the van—was that what set him off? Drove Kline over the edge? Was there a way for her to drive him over the edge?

She had to get into the cabin again. Had to get cuffed to that chair.

Anona lay down on the steel floor and began doing some stretching exercises, concentrating on her legs, keeping them loose and flexible, her eyes fixed on her bra hanging from the ceiling.

She worked steadily on the exercises, until her muscles screamed for a break, then got to her feet and tugged at the bra.

Kline had tied pieces of rope to each end to make it longer—long enough to accommodate her hanging.

She looped the bra around her neck, feeling the nylon bite into her skin, thinking of Arlene Kline.

God, what a way to die.

Anona dragged the mattress over, then rolled the blanket around the pillow and placed it on the mattress, directly under the bra, and again fastened it around her neck. She began experimenting, tieing knots with the free end of the rope.

If the wrists bands didn't work, she'd have to try something else.

Bob Duran descended the broad Stack House stairway slowly. Grimacing, he brought his hands together in one quick, derisive clap. Jason Lark's bedroom was empty—he'd packed his luggage and taken off.

Andamo nipped playfully at Duran's pant cuffs, then raced down the steps, made an abrupt U-turn and raced back to him.

Duran sat down on the steps, picked up the terrier and ruffled his fur.

The slamming of the front door startled them both.

George Montroy strode into sight. Duran had never seen the butler look so upset.

"What's the matter, George?" Duran called out.

George froze in his tracks, then swiveled to face Duran. "I received a call from someone who identified himself as a Captain Smith with the Sausalito Police Department. He asked me to come right over to Mr. John's houseboat."

He raised his fist and extended a finger. "There is no Captain Smith in the Sausalito Police Department." He raised a second finger. "No one from the police called this house." A third finger shot out. "Master John has moved his houseboat, three docks over. I wandered around for half an hour before I found its new berth. He is not onboard. His neighbors have not seen him in days, though his Porsche is parked in its allotted space."

Duran released the dog. "When did this call come in?"

"A few hours ago."

"Was Jason Lark here?"

"He was in the library."

"Could the voice on the phone have been Lark's?"

George took a few seconds to respond. "No. It could not have been Mr. Lark. The voice was much different, and there was only one telephone line in operation—the one I was on."

"Who else was in the house?"

George said, "Just Maria."

Duran sprinted toward the kitchen, Andamo snapping at his pant legs again. Someone wanted George out of the house. The only reason Duran could think of was so that they could get in and plant something. Anona's ring, her watch. Would Kline be that bold? So soon after being questioned by the police?

The cook was at the stove. The rich aroma of sauteeing onions and garlic wafted up around her.

"Maria, *momentito, por favor.*"

He questioned her in Spanish. She was positive that no one had entered the house since George had left. Jason Lark had driven off in a taxi cab approximately an hour ago. Maria had been in front of the house. She'd heard Lark give the cab driver his destination: "*Aeropuerto.*"

Duran tugged at an earlobe. The airport. Lark was suddenly in a hurry to get away from Stack House. All of his "not leaving until Anona is found" vows forgotten.

What had caused the change in his plans? The airport. There were planes departing every half hour for Southern California. He might already be airborne. Still, it was worth a chance.

He spun around, finding the butler blocking his path.

"Lark went to the airport. I'm going to try to catch him before he takes off."

"I'll drive," George volunteered. "It will save you the time of parking your car."

"Good idea," Duran agreed, almost tripping over Andamo in his haste to get to the garage.

He scooped up the terrier. "You might as well come along for the ride, pal."

The airline clerk, a slim, elfin-faced woman in her twenties, said, "I'm afraid that there's a problem with your Visa card, sir."

Jason Lark managed to look offended. "You must be mistaken."

She gave him a tired smile. "They won't accept the charge on the flight to New Orleans."

Lark smiled ruefully and pulled out his wallet. "I've been out of the country so much lately, I guess my accountant has screwed up. Here. Try American Express."

Lark kept a confident look on his face, while he fumed inwardly. His feet were bracketing his carry-on case with six-million-dollars' worth of Picassos in it, and the lousy credit card couldn't handle a nine hundred and ninety-seven dollar, one-way, first-class ticket to New Orleans.

"That did it sir," the clerk said with a professional smile, handing Lark back his American Express card.

She hummed softly to herself while she wrote up the ticket.

"Have a nice trip, sir. Your flight number is 372, leaving from gate 86 in an hour and ten minutes."

"Where's your VIP lounge?" Lark queried.

He sucked in his breath when the carry-on was placed on the conveyer belt and scuttled through the X-ray machine.

He didn't feel comfortable until the bag was back safely in his hands. As soon as he picked it up, someone bumped into him and he clutched it to his chest like a fullback recovering a fumbled football. He needed a drink. His first-class ticket awarded him entry to the airline's VIP lounge, a large, narrow room with smoked-glass windows and polished chrome-and-leather furniture.

A ping-pong-sized table groaned under the weight of dozens of bottles of liquor, wine, and platters of unappetizing-looking hors d'oeuvres.

Lark helped himself to a generous measure of Johnny Walker Black Label and collapsed into a chair near the windows.

He wedged the bag between his shoes, took a large

sip of the whisky, and relaxed. He had made it. Another hour and he'd be in the air. Then New Orleans.

It had been years since he'd been there. He tried to recall the name of the top hotel. Senestra? Something like that, right on Bourbon Street. Brennan's was the restaurant to go to back then. He wondered if it still was.

"Do you mind if I sit here?" a voice asked.

Lark's eyes twitched open. The woman had sultry, chocolate-brown eyes. Her long, sable-colored hair framed a perfectly formed face. She wore a smartly tailored green dress with a velvet collar.

She wet her lower lip with the tip of a very pink tongue and said, "That man across the room, the big fat one, thinks he's Romeo and I'm Juliet."

"Be my guest," Lark offered. He looked over to the bar and saw a heavy-set man in a safari jacket with bulging pockets. The man gave him a strained look, then did an about-face and marched out of the room.

"It looks like you scared him away." The woman beamed. She offered her hand. "Jessica Savant."

"Jason Lark." Her hand was satiny feeling. The diamond ring on her finger looked to be at least two carats.

"He was behind me when I checked in," she explained. "Unfortunately I think he's going to New Orleans, too. If his seat assignment is next to mine, I may ask for a parachute."

"I'm going to New Orleans. Maybe we can arrange to sit together," Lark suggested.

"That would be wonderful." She looked at the glass in his hand. "The least I can do is get you a drink. What's your poison?"

"Scotch. Black Label."

Lark watched her saunter to the bar. Firm body. Nicely dressed—not flashy, but there was no doubt that there were a hundred and ten pounds of goodies under the expensively wrapped package. Jessica Savant. It had a theatrical sound. Movies. TV. Commercials. He could bring up Alan Fritzheim's name to give her a charge.

"Here you are, kind sir," she said when she was back with his drink, a glass of white wine nestled in her other hand.

"Cheers." Lark sampled the Scotch. "You're so beautiful, you must be in the movies."

"I was about to say the same about you, Jason," she said playfully. "What is your game?"

"I'm an art dealer."

"How fascinating."

Lark told her just how fascinating it was for a few minutes, then he noticed her features start to blur. His lips were feeling numb.

It appeared that she was moving in slow motion when she reached out and took his glass.

"I . . . I'm not feeling . . ."

She put her lips together and made soft kissing sounds. "Not feeling well? Poor baby." She leaned closer, her voice barely a whisper. "I wasn't kidding when I asked you what your poison was, Jason. To tell you the truth, I can't remember its name—some new designer drug, but they say if you have to go, this is the way to do it."

Lark fought to keep his eyes open as she got to her feet, leaned down and kissed him lightly on the head, then, as an afterthought, slid the bag from between his legs.

"Mario said to say good-bye, so good-bye, darling."

Chapter 37

Junior Erwin ran the tip of his baton across the cell bars. "Hey, Firpo. Are you missing your old buddy, Otto Kline?"

The prisoner lay stretched out on his bunk, hands behind his head, a passive expression plastered on his face as he responded to the big-bellied guard. "Not much."

"I got a paintin' job for Kline. Know how I can reach him?"

Firpo swung his legs onto the floor and reluctantly got to his feet. What was Erwin fishing around after Otto for? "He didn't tell me what his plans were."

Erwin's baton thunked out a ribbon of notes against the bars. "That's too bad. How you like bein' alone? We was talking about you. We think it's about time to get you another roomie. Some of the guards was sayin' they'd like to see Jumbo move in with you. What do you think of that?"

Firpo shrugged his heavily muscled shoulders. Jumbo Garcia was the leader of the prison's Latin community, a scar-faced killer who hated white men. "It might be a tight fit."

"More ways than one, huh?" Erwin winked. "You two old bulls would probably kill each other. Then again, I hear there's a pancake getting out of the SHU next week. Just twenty-four years old. Cute little feller."

Firpo gauged the threat. "What kind of job have you got lined up for Otto?"

"Oh, it's a good one. He'd make some big money, and be doin' me a favor." Erwin slipped the baton into its belt holder. "And maybe I can do one for you, Kenny. I hear this pancake is going to need a lot of nursin'."

Firpo laced his fingers through the bars. "Kline told me something about going down to San Francisco."

"I know about the halfway house. I just thought you might have some other ideas—like where he was goin' to look for a job, or some friends of his he might visit."

Firpo squeezed his fingers around the bars and stared into Erwin's piggish eyes, then relaxed his grip. Otto was gone. And he had four more years to serve. He'd never make it if they shoved Garcia in his cell. They'd end up at each other—and it didn't matter who'd win. That was the beauty of the system as far as the guards were concerned. They had everyone by the balls. A fight would automatically extend your sentence and both the winner and the loser would do SHU time.

"What's the pancake's name?"

Otto Kline gulped four pain pills and washed them down with a sip from the bottle of fruit juice.

He needed a drink. A real drink. Whisky. But alcohol wasn't allowed in the hotel room—and its painkilling effects only lasted an hour or so. Then the headaches got even worse.

He stretched his legs out, his heels riding over the edge of the mattress. The St. Regis was worse than the Excelsior. It was just as dirty, just as noisy, the room just as small. The view from his window looked out all of six feet to the brick wall of an adjoining building. It was hot, muggy. Someone had turned the central heating up.

He wanted to get back to the cabin. Back to Anona Stack. But he didn't want to risk getting his probation officer ticked off, so he'd have to stay the night. The hotel manager told him that one of the other parolees made bed checks at eight o'clock, then again at six in the morning.

Kline was sure that he could bribe the man, just as he had Justice. But not on the first night. He'd have to feel him out first.

He wondered how Anona was doing. This was her longest stretch of time in the SHU. It was ironic: He was being forced to spend the night in the hotel room, and Anona ended up being the one who was punished—no yard time today. No hot meals.

He thought about the meeting at the probation office. Duran had looked frazzled—like he'd wanted to take a swing at him. In front of the policeman. Duran! The bastard! He'd gone to Arlene's grave. He had no right to do that!

And he knew about Firpo. Who told him about Firpo? It had to be the policeman—Saylor. Did he talk to Ken? Ken would never tell him anything. Never.

Kline had anticipated Duran waiting for him somewhere in the Hall of Justice, probably near the main exit.

He'd taken the stairs to the basement and going through a door marked POLICE PERSONNEL ONLY, found himself in an underground garage. No one had paid any attention to him as he walked up the ramp and out onto the street.

Saylor. Dull eyes, dull questions—but he was persistent. Why had he brought Duran to the probation meeting? Were they working together?

Kline rolled off the bed and began pacing the room.

He stripped off his shirt and threw it at the cracked, cloudy mirror on the wall, then kicked off his shoes and pants and shorts and flopped back down on the bed.

He draped his forearm over his eyes and took himself back, back to Pelican Bay, back to his cell with Ken Firpo. Firpo naked, doing pushups—fingertip pushups, a hundred at a time, sweat oozing out on his broad shoulders, his back and streaming down to the crack between his buttocks.

You wouldn't tell, Ken. You wouldn't, I know that.

This was when he missed Firpo most. At night. For all his strength and roughness, Firpo could be gentle. His hands had a way of massaging the pain away, of making—

A loud knock on the door brought him out of his reverie.

The door creaked open. A wide-faced man with a shaven head, long sideburns, and an enormous walrus mustache, smiled at him.

"Hi. Just checking. I'm Ronald. You're Otto, right? First night here."

Kline shifted over on his side. "That's right." Ronald's shaven head reminded him of Firpo's. "Do you check me out in the morning, too?"

The man smiled, his teeth barely visible through the mustache. "Yeah. Around eight. Why? You wanna sleep in?"

"No. I was hoping to get an early start."

Ronald retreated into the hallway, looked both ways, then popped his face back in the door, his gaze coasting down Kline's naked body. "Maybe we can work something out. You feel like a little company, Otto? I'll be through with my rounds in about fifteen minutes."

"Well, I—"

"I've got a couple of cold beers in my room. I'll bring 'em over."

"I could use a beer," Kline said.

"Looks like we both could, Otto," Ronald replied softly, then shut the door.

Kline stretched out, his fingers wrapping around the metal bed frame. It was going to be all right. Ronald was going to be easy. Like Justice. Only Justice wanted money; this one wanted sex. He let his mind drift back to Pelican Bay and Ken Firpo.

Firpo had nursed him back to life after those eighteen months in the SHU. Nursed him along slowly, gently. The guards had made jokes. Raw, crude jokes.

"You wouldn't talk to Duran, Ken. I know you wouldn't," he whispered to himself.

The building dated back to the late nineteenth century. "Historic" Old Molloy's. Its history included several bare-knuckled prizefights involving the likes of the great black heavy weight champion Jack Johnson, Battling Nelson, and Jack Dempsey.

The frenzied strains of a Dixieland band greeted Chief Saylor as he approached the bar. Six intense senior citizens, decked out in red, candy-striped shirts and straw hats were finishing an upbeat version of "Sweet Georgia Brown."

The crowd gave them a rousing cheer, then turned its attention back to the bar.

Saylor spotted his target, Dave Cassel, at his customary table, shuffling a deck of cards. Cassel had been the chief of the Colma Police Department when Saylor joined the force as a rookie almost twenty years ago.

Cassel was in his eighties, a lean, stringbean of a man with parchment-colored skin stretched over his hawklike features.

"Hi, Chief," Saylor said genially, sliding into the hardback chair next to Cassel. "How's it going?"

"As long as it's going, it's good, Bill. How's the law business?"

"Confusing at times," Saylor admitted. "I thought I might pick your brain if you've got the time."

Cassel grunted. "Man my age has nothing but time in some ways, and no time in others. Whatcha need?"

"Ever hear of a family of crooks that worked on the coast, last name of Firpo. The father supposedly died in Alcatraz. The son, Ken, he's in his fifties now."

"Firpo," the old man snorted. "Miserable bunch of cusses, and it goes all the way back to the grandfather. He was big in the moonshine business."

"Moonshine? I thought that was something they did in Oklahoma."

Cassel riffled the edge of the deck of cards. "They did it here, too, son. Big time. Dan Firpo had stills hidden all over the coast. They raided him once in a barn in El Granada. One of his stills had blown. They found 12,000 gallons of mash whisky hidden in a nearby cave. Firpo got away that time, but they caught him with a truckload of bourbon, chased him to San Bruno. He lost control and the truck rolled over and killed the bastard."

"We're talking ancient history," Saylor said.

Cassel began shuffling the cards slowly. "Nineteen twenty-eight. Then the kid, Dan's son, I can't think of his name, he was another rotten apple off the same tree. He was into drugs. The boats would bring the stuff up from Mexico, and this Firpo would go out and meet them, bring it ashore. He smuggled more than dope, too. People. Mexes and Chinamen. Sold 'em like cattle. He shot a fed. Customs man. That's what sent him to Alcatraz."

"There was one more rotten apple on the tree," Saylor reminded him. "Ken Firpo, he's doing time now in Pelican Bay."

Cassel dealt out a solitaire hand, then said, "I remember that bastard, too. What's all your interest in this?"

"It might have something to do with a missing person's case I'm working on, Chief. Anona Stack. The lady might be more than missing. She could be dead. I've got a suspect, her husband, Robert Duran. The woman's wealthy, and she sent a letter to her attorney telling him her husband was violent and that she wanted a divorce."

"Sounds reasonable. It usually is the husband in these cases."

"Duran's story is that his wife was kidnapped. She testified against a man named Otto Kline and his wife in a criminal case. They went to jail, convicted on a forgery charge. The wife killed herself while in prison. This Kline guy reacted to the news by beating up a guard, that's why he was sent to Pelican Bay. He was Ken Firpo's cellmate. Kline's out now, living in some flophouse in San Francisco.

"I met with Kline this afternoon, at his probation

office. He's a cool customer, I couldn't budge him. But I got that feeling. You know what I mean."

Cassel ran a playing card across his stubbled chin as if it was a razor. "Yeah. I used to get that feeling a lot myself."

"If Kline did kidnap Anona Stack, he'd have to take her somewhere, hide her out."

"Maybe he's already killed her and she's six feet under the ground, Billy."

"It's a possibility," Saylor agreed. "Kline's not from around here. He wouldn't know the territory."

"So? You're thinking Firpo told him where to go? A hideout?"

"It's a possibility," Saylor said again.

"Well, son. You got some looking to do. Them Firpos had caves all over the mountains."

"But they didn't live in the caves, did they, Chief? They had to have a house—a home somewhere."

Cassel slapped a red jack on a black queen. "I don't remember nothing like that. But I think they had some kind of a shack up off San Vincente Road."

"Do you think—" Saylor's beeper went off, the mini screen flashing the coded message: 10–36. Emergency notification.

"Back in a minute," Saylor said. He went out to his unmarked police car and used the radio to contact the station.

"Thought you'd like to know, Chief," the police dispatcher announced, "a Jason Lark is an 802 down at SFX. Isn't he involved in the Anona Stack case?"

"Ten-four," Saylor responded irritably. He didn't like his dispatchers using case names on the air. "I'm enroute to the station."

Jason Lark. Dead at the airport. It was just last night that he'd spoken to Lark, at Stack House. Lark was an aging peacock. But a healthy-looking peacock. Not the kind to die of a heart attack at the airport. He'd have to contact the airport police to get the cause of death, but he was willing to bet a month's pay that it wasn't from natural causes, or a suicide.

Chapter 38

Duran circulated through the Tenderloin area until almost one in the morning, dispensing money to various grifters in and around the Excelsior Hotel. No one had seen Justice, or Otto Kline. Kline's room was still vacant, the damage to the door unrepaired.

He kept an eye out for a converted bread truck—just in case Kline had made a mistake, knowing full well that the jails would be empty if the criminals didn't make mistakes. Would he keep it near the hotel? Or was it parked in some remote spot and moved around every day?

Kline had to have transportation of some kind. Anona's Land Rover. Would he be stupid enough to hang on to the Rover? Duran had rechecked with the Department of Motor Vehicles—Kline hadn't purchased any other vehicles. He then ran a credit check on Kline, coming up with a complete blank—no credit cards under his name. No car rentals. His best guess was that Kline had stolen a car.

He thought about waiting out the night in Kline's room, but decided to go home, and, if possible, get a few hours of sleep before resuming the hunt in the morning.

The sight of Chief Saylor's unmarked car parked in front of Stack House caused his stomach to roll.

George's doleful face waiting at the front door had the opposite effect—his stomach tensed, waiting for a body blow.

"Is it Anona?" he asked, brushing by the butler.

"No, sir. Mr. Lark. He's dead. Apparently murdered."

Duran froze in his tracks, then did a slow about-face. "Jason? Where?"

"The airport." The butler waited for the words to take effect, then added, "Chief Saylor is waiting in the living room."

Duran found the policeman, back in uniform, standing with his hands clasped behind his back, his head angled to one side, examining Anona's painting "Leaves in Transit."

Saylor turned his head slowly in Duran's direction. "Did your wife paint this?"

"Yes."

Saylor looked back at the painting. "How much would it sell for?"

"It's not for sale, Chief. George just told me about Jason Lark."

"And George told me that you were at the airport this afternoon. About five o'clock. The coroner places Lark's death around that time."

Duran moved his head in a quick, negative gesture. "Christ, you don't think that I killed Lark, do you? At the airport? In broad daylight?"

"Someone did," Saylor pointed out. "George says you went into the airport by yourself. That he stayed in the car."

"That's right, but hell, I didn't see Lark. I couldn't find him."

"Someone did," Saylor said again. "Did you see anyone at the airport who would recognize you?"

Duran waved a hand vaguely. "Ticket clerks, the people at the boarding gates. I was all over the place. How did Lark die?"

"He was poisoned. In United's VIP lounge. I imagine someone like you, you probably travel a lot. You probably have a pass to the VIP lounges."

Duran ignored the remark.

"Why were you so hot to see Lark?" Saylor pressed.

"I found out that Lark had worked on the Fritzheim house in Santa Barbara. He was involved with the stolen Van Gogh, one way or the other. I also think that he broke into my office, went through my files, and then notified the people who killed Harry Lawson that I was coming down to Los Angeles. Lark set me up for the killing."

"Sounds like that gives you a hell of a motive for getting rid of Lark."

"I didn't kill Jason Lark," Duran said, his voice growing hoarse with anger.

"Who did?" Saylor countered. "Otto Kline? Is that where you were tonight? Looking for Kline?"

"I was looking for my wife."

Saylor's voice was flat, as if he was reciting something from a book. "I'm going back to the airport to meet with the investigators handling Lark's case. I'm sure they're going to want to see you in the morning. I wouldn't want you going anywhere."

Duran grimaced and frowned. "Don't leave town. Isn't that the standard warning? What's next? You read me my Miranda rights?"

Saylor tapped the breast pocket of his uniform jacket. "I've got my Miranda card right here, Mr. Duran. Always handy. Be here in the morning."

* * *

A cold, howling wind was knifing through the trees and shrubs outside the SHU. Anona Stack bundled herself up in the blanket and went to the door, tilting her head so she could position her right eye directly in line with one of the small holes.

She missed the cutout. Missed it badly. All she could see now was a murky circle of blackish mist stream by.

Where was Kline? He hadn't been by to check on her. Or to bring her any food. She hadn't heard the van return, but the way the wind was howling, he could have come back without her hearing him.

She was frustrated at not knowing what time it was. It could be anywhere from midnight to five in the morning. She had no idea how long she had slept—she wasn't even sure if she had slept in the last few hours. Time seemed to be playing games with her mind.

She settled back onto the mattress and closed her eyes. Sleep. She needed sleep—needed to be alert when Kline came back. Needed to be ready for him. She'd gone over her plan dozens of times in her mind—and in her mind it worked very well. What would happen when it was time to do it? Will I have the guts to really do it? she asked herself for the hundredth time.

I've got to. No matter what. I can't wait for Bob. I can't wait for anyone.

She fingered the wrist bands under her shirt cuffs. Her fingernails were razor sharp now. And if they failed, there was the bra. As a last resort, she'd use the bra.

Those were her only weapons. Now she had to get to sleep! She had to be ready for him!

She closed her eyes and prayed. Prayed to be allowed to go to sleep. Is that too much to ask, God? Just a few hours sleep.

His full name was Ronald York, and he insisted on buying Kline breakfast at a nearby coffee shop on Leavenworth Street.

York had two more months of probation time on a vehicular manslaughter charge. "The son of a bitch gave me the finger and I pulled alongside him. He panicked and drove into a telephone pole. He makes a dumb mistake and I ended up doing twelve months."

York was fascinated by Kline's gruesome tales of life in Pelican Bay State Prison.

Kline mopped up the last of his pancakes as York went to the bathroom.

The man on the neighboring stool finished his breakfast, leaving the crumpled morning newspaper behind.

Kline smoothed out the front section, paying little attention to the headlines regarding another bombing in the Middle East, and a tornado in Kansas. He was reaching for his coffee cup when he spotted the story.

The cup slipped from his hand, sending hot coffee cascading across the countertop.

"Otto! Are you okay?" Ronald York asked, sliding back into his seat, pulling a clump of napkins from the chrome holder and blotting up the coffee.

Kline read the article twice, his upper lip riding up over his gums.

"What's so good?" York queried. "What is it?"

Kline carefully folded up the paper and slipped it under his arm. "Someone I know was killed."

"Oh, that's a shame. A good friend?"

"He is now," Kline said, sliding from the stool and heading for the door.

“See you tonight,” York called after him.

Kline didn’t hear him. His mind was on Anona Stack. How would she react to the article? Jason Lark dead. And her son missing. Duran. It had to be Duran. Duran was making it easy for him. Almost too easy.

He pulled up short, quickly bringing the newspaper up in front of his face, veering back into the coffee shop. A dark green Jaguar was coming down Eddy Street.

Chapter 39

Duran's eyes felt gritty, the lids leaden, half closed. He'd been circling the blocks of the Tenderloin since a little before seven a.m. It was half-past eight now. Andamo was dozing, curled like a pretzel in his lap. He scratched the dog behind the ears.

Andamo responded with a low growl.

He'd widened the search area, block by block, hoping for a glimpse of Kline or Justice, monitoring the parked vehicles for a beat-up old bread truck or Anona's Rover.

A few minutes past nine, he gave up and headed for Fisherman's Wharf.

When Saylor wanted him, he could damn well come to the office.

Gulls circled aimlessly under a gunmetal gray sky. The street-side restaurants were stoking up their crab pots and the strong scent of boiling shellfish hung heavy in the salty air.

Andamo strained at the leash when he heard a band of sea lions bark for breakfast from the early-hour cliques of tourists.

Duran yanked the dog's leash, half dragging him into the office. He started a pot of coffee, then once again went through Kline's criminal file. There was nothing there that gave even a hint as to where Kline would have taken Anona. Duran dropped the file in disgust, leaned back, massaged his eyes with the heels of his hands, then picked up the prison report on Ken Firpo.

Firpo's last arrest was on a rape charge in Pacifica. His address was listed as a postal box in Montara.

What did Duran know about Montara? Only that it was on the coast. The population was probably no more than five or six hundred. There was an old Coast Guard lighthouse nearby.

He accessed a real estate database and checked the name Firpo through San Mateo County records. Fourteen hits—none under the first name Ken and none in Montara, or anywhere closeby.

The office door opened and his head snapped up, half expecting to see Chief Saylor and his troops.

Peggy Jacquard waved a morning newspaper at him. "You know?"

"Oh, yes. The cops will probably be here anytime to third-degree me." He gave Peggy a capsule version of his last conversation with Chief Saylor.

Andamo's tail beat out a welcome and he began licking at Peggy's shoes. She shooed the dog away and perched on the edge of Duran's desk. "What do we do now?"

"You better put your bail bond friend Rachel on standby. I can't afford to spend any time in jail now."

"What about an attorney, Bob?"

"Yes. But I don't want to use Hugh Stringer. Call Mike Malone. He's the best—"

The phone rang. Peggy's hand reached tentatively for the receiver. "What if it's the police?" she asked.

Duran turned up his palms. "I can't hide from them."

Peggy picked up the phone and identified herself. Her worried frown turned into a smile.

"Jut a second please." She leaned across the desk, punched the speaker button, and cradled the receiver. "It's Junior Erwin."

"Hi, there, Mr. Duran. How you doin'?"

"Just fine, Junior."

"I did what you asked. Talked to old 'Ramblin' Nose' Firpo."

The line was silent for several moments. "And?" Duran prompted.

"I'm at the sporting goods store. Sports World. I was just looking at this electronic fish-finder. Damnedest thing. It's like sonar on a submarine. You trail it in the water and the fish show up on a screen. Can't miss with these suckers."

"If what Firpo told you is of any help to me, you can put the salesman on the phone and I'll charge it on my credit card right now."

"I think it'll help," Erwin said, trying to sound casual. "Firpo says he and Kline used to talk a lot about his grandfather, and his father, the one who died in Alcatraz. Grandpa was a moonshiner down there. Some place called Montara."

"What does all this ancient history have to do with Otto Kline?"

"Well, Firpo says his father kind of kept the family business going for a while. Switched from moonshine to smuggling drugs, even some Chinamen once in a while. Firpo's father made a mistake of getting in a shootout with the cops. Wounded one of them. That's what landed him in Alcatraz. The thing is, Grandpa Firpo kept his stills spread out all over the place in these caves up in the mountains down there. Hold on a minute."

Duran could hear the rustling of paper. "San Vincente Creek Road. Firpo's family owned the property. It went for taxes years back. The state sold it to some lumber company. Only thing is, there's a moratorium or some damn thing. They can't cut down the trees. Firpo says the land is vacant. Not much good for anything. 'Cept hiding stills, I guess."

"This doesn't sound very promising, Junior," Duran objected.

"Well, there was one particular spot that Firpo says he told Kline about. Got a pencil?"

Duran reached for a pen. "Go ahead."

"You drive south on the Cabrillo Highway. Turn on Sixteenth Street in Montara, just when you get to the lighthouse. Then turn right on San Vincente Road. You go for two-point-two miles. You go over a couple of rickety bridges on the way. There's a bunch of small dirt roads off to your right. You turn up the one with a big crescent-shaped boulder. Follow it up for about three quarters of a mile. Firpo says that's where the caves are. Dozens and dozens of 'em, honeycombed all over the place. And the cabin."

Duran dropped his pen in disgust. "Junior, no disrespect intended, but Firpo was pulling your leg."

"No, sir," Erwin blurted belligerently. "He wasn't. Firpo was lying low there 'fore his last arrest. He says he knows for sure the cabin is still there. I got the feelin' that he's sent some people there since he's been in Pelican Bay."

"What makes you think any of this is true?"

Junior responded with a coarse laugh. " 'Cause I gave him two choices for his next cellmate. A young baby, a pancake just out of the SHU, or the toughest, ugliest Mexican in Pelican Bay."

Duran leaned back and pondered the information.

"Okay," he finally said, "put the salesman on." He snapped his fingers to get Andamo's attention, then said, "Peg, I'm going to check this out. Pay the man whatever he wants."

Anona had heard the vehicle's deep-throated engine roar up the hill, then come to a sudden stop. He was back. But that had been some time ago. At least an hour by her estimate, though she knew she couldn't rely on that anymore.

She ate the last two pieces of bread and finished the remains of the milk, then used the awful toilet in the corner of the cell.

When he finally came down the trail, he was whistling. Anona couldn't make out the tune, but Kline was whistling. As if he was happy about something.

She edged to the back of the cell as he unlocked the door. He stood there, silhouetted against the pine trees, the rifle cradled in one hand. He tossed the leg restraints at her feet.

"Yard time," he barked.

Anona went quietly through the procedure of snapping the restraints on her legs, then shuffled slowly outside, exaggerating her pain.

"You don't look so good. Tough night?"

"The cuffs hurt my ankles. And my wrists are still sore."

"Tough shit," he grumbled nastily. "I guess you want to take a shower."

"No. No, I don't need a shower."

He smiled, exposing his gums. "There was a guy named Leo. He hated to shower. Just wouldn't do it. He was kind of pretty. I guess he was afraid. They finally gave him a scrubbing. A real scalding-water and hard-brush scrubbing. He got second-degree burns. Yeah, Leo was a real mess after that."

"I want something to eat," Anona said quickly.

She was disappointed with the weather. The wind had died down and the fog had dispersed. The sky was nothing but endless gray clouds. Should she wait? Wait another day for the wind to come back, the fog, maybe even some rain, something to give her cover.

"Oh, you're going to get something to eat this morning. Bacon and eggs. Coffee. And the morning paper. Yeah, you're going to enjoy this meal."

Anona swallowed hard. "This meal." The last meal? She did a pigeon-toed walk through the cabin door and over to the chair, obediently snapping on each of the handcuffs, making sure the encircling metal was resting on the bread-pocket bands around her wrists.

Kline watched her with an amused grin on his face.

"My, my, you are getting the program, aren't you?"

He tested the handcuffs.

"Not too tight," Anona pleaded. "My wrists are really sore."

"Quit bitching," he ordered, squeezing each cuff while he stared into her eyes. "You don't handle pain very well, do you?"

Duran followed Junior Erwin's directions. Once he was on San Vincente Creek Road he kept an eye on the odometer and the Jaguar maneuvered around the narrow gravel road, and across the rickety bridges Erwin had described.

Two-point-two miles clicked by and there was no crescent-shaped boulder. He mumbled a silent curse. Junior Erwin was probably out on a lake with his new fish-finder, laughing at him. Then there it was. Almost covered by a thicket of ferns. The crescent-shaped boulder.

Andamo's ears perked as they turned on the dirt trail. Duran kept the Jaguar in low gear, negotiating the trail cautiously, his head half leaning out the window, one hand on the steering wheel, the other on the stock of Conrad Stack's double-barreled shotgun,

He coasted to a stop in front of a metal gate, exiting the Jaguar, shotgun in hand, Andamo right at his heels.

The gate was old and rusty. There were fresh gouge marks in the dirt, indicating that the gate had been swung open recently. He spat on the padlock, then rubbed at the thin layer of patination with his thumb, slowly revealing a circle of bright shiny steel.

"The lock's new," he said to Andamo, who was on his haunches, looking up expectantly at him.

Duran snapped his fingers. "Back in the car, Andamo."

The terrier had a mind of his own. He scooted around the gate post and darted up the trail.

The pounding on the door caused Peggy Jacquard to flinch, and the pencil in her hand to fly over her shoulder. She reached for the phone, ready to dial 911, then noticed the outline through the blinds. The police chief.

"Where's Duran?" Saylor demanded angrily, when she opened the door.

"He left just a little while ago, and—"

Saylor pushed her out of the way and stomped into Duran's office.

Peggy was right on his heels, her face flushed with anger. "I told you he's not here, and I don't appreciate—"

Saylor turned and stared at her. "The Coast Guard found John Stack's body floating in Richardson Bay an hour ago. Where the hell is Duran!"

Anona waited until Otto Kline was in the kitchen and out of sight before testing the cuffs on her hands. She tried her right hand first, tugging slowly at first, seesawing back and forth. The metal cuff slipped off the wrist band. She stretched her fingers out, squeezing them together, as the circle of steel rode tightly over the back of her hand, riding up against her knuckles. It was working! It was working!

She could hear Kline clattering around in the kitchen. The thick scent of frying bacon and perking coffee drifted in the air.

Now, she told herself. Now!

Otto Kline came back into the room, his lip peeled back over his gums in that smile that she had come to loathe.

"Here's something to read while you're waiting for breakfast."

He placed the newspaper on the table, tapping the bottom right corner of the front page with his finger. "Take a look at this. It'll do wonders for your appetite."

Anona leaned forward and began reading.

> Jason Lark, former husband of artist Anona Stack, was found dead in the United Airlines VIP lounge at the San Francisco Airport last night. A preliminary investigation indicates that Mr. Lark was poisoned.
>
> Robert Duran, Stack's current husband, was recently involved in a homicide investigation in Los Angeles. This reporter has learned that John Stack, son of Anona Stack and Mr. Lark, is missing, and that

Anona Stack herself has not been heard from in
(*See page 8, column 3*)

"God damn you!" Anona screamed. "You killed Jason. What have you done to Johnny? You son of a—"

Kline backhanded her across the face. "Shut up, bitch! I didn't do anything to your precious son, or that asshole Lark. It was Duran! Don't you see? Your husband is a killer!

Anona's head was ringing from the blow to her face. And the story in the paper.

"No, no—"

Kline clamped his hand across her mouth.

"Shut up," he rasped.

Anona strained her jaw muscles, trying to maneuver her teeth so she could bite into his hand, then she heard it. A dog. A dog barking.

Kline released her, scurried into the kitchen, coming back with the rifle.

"You open your mouth and I kill you right now, hear?"

Anona jerked her head rapidly up and down.

Kline racked a cartridge into the carbine and moved toward the cabin door.

Duran watched Andamo scurry into the woods. The terrier seemed to have picked up a scent.

He kicked his way through a tangle of brush. Andamo's barking increased in intensity. Anona. Had he picked up Anona's scent?

As soon as Kline was out the door, Anona wiggled both her wrists furiously. Her right hand slid free first, and she used it to yank the cuff from her left hand.

She quickly unbuckled the leg restraints and bolted out of the chair, racing into the kitchen. She paused for a second to snatch a knife from the counter, then jerked the back door open and ran as fast as she could toward the trees. She'd done it! She was free!

Chapter 40

The weeds were ankle high. Duran had to keep one hand in front of his face to protect himself from low-hanging tree branches.

Andamo was still ahead of him, barking wildly. The trees and shrubs thinned out as he approached a narrow trail and what appeared to be fresh tire prints. He followed the trail, Andamo's barking getting louder with each step.

As the trail broadened, there were deep ruts in the dirt, then he saw a flash of bright metal. Kline's SHU! The doors were spread wide open.

He cocked both barrels of the shotgun and approached cautiously.

Andamo leaped into the back of the bakery truck, spun around, and jumped out, almost colliding with Duran. There was something dangling inside the truck. A bra. Jesus Christ.

"Freeze," Otto Kline yelled. As Duran started to turn around, Kline pulled the trigger, sending a bullet tunneling into the dirt at Duran's feet. He jacked a round into the chamber. "Drop that shotgun or I'll blow a hole in your back."

Duran crouched down and laid the weapon gently on the ground.

"Where's my wife, Otto?"

"Up at the cabin. Reading this morning's paper. That story about you killing Jason Lark. And her son. You're a real bastard, Duran. I'd rather you went to jail, but I'm going to have to kill you now."

"Is this Ken Firpo's place, Otto?" Duran asked in a controlled voice. "Where his grandfather hid his stills?"

"How do you know about that?"

"Firpo told me. He told me all about it. I met with him up at Pelican Bay."

"Ken would never talk to you," Kline shouted. "Get in the SHU!"

"You've made too many mistakes, Otto. That fire at Anona's studio. You left your prints on the paint-thinner cans."

"Nice try," Kline scoffed. "That wasn't me. I saved your ass. I called 911. I wanted you alive, so you'd know what it's like to lose your wife. Tomorrow's the day, Duran. Tomorrow. October twelfth. You and Anona will die together. Now get moving!"

Duran stood his ground. "Firpo traded me the information about you for a new cellmate. Someone like you were. Just out of the SHU."

"You're lying! You never talked to Ken!"

"Yes, I did, Otto. He's an ugly bastard with a big, rambling nose. He told me everything."

Kline brought the carbine to his shoulder and stared at Duran over the barrel. "You're a liar."

"How do you think I found this place? Junior Erwin, the prison guard got me to Firpo. Firpo also told me about your time in the SHU, Otto. And Firpo told me about Arlene. How she died. I saw the inscription you had put on the tombstone. I saw it all. And I told the police everything, Otto. They know about this place."

The tip of the rifle sank slowly until the barrel was pointed at Kline's feet.

"Firpo's new cellmate. A 'pancake' is what Erwin called him. Just out of the SHU, like you were, Otto."

Kline shook his head slowly. "Ken would never talk about me, he would never—"

Duran kicked the shotgun as hard as he could. Both barrels went off simultaneously, a portion of the buckshot hitting the truck's steel doors, flattening into jagged-edged discs and spraying out in a deadly pattern.

Duran felt his knee being ripped apart. He crashed into the dirt, grasping at his leg, spinning around in pain, his eyes searching for Kline.

A cluster of the shotgun pellets slashed across Kline's abdomen, knocking him backward, his head smacking against the tufted trunk of a redwood tree.

Duran tried to get to his feet, but his legs wouldn't hold him. He started to crawl, jamming his elbows into the turf, using them like ski poles to propel himself toward Kline. He reached out, grasped Kline's foot, and twisted it savagely.

Kline clasped the rifle in both hands and swung at Duran's arms. "Let go!" he screamed. His left hand groped at his stomach, feeling the sticky ooze of his own blood.

Duran joined his fists together and brought them down as hard as he could into the bloody mass at Kline's belt line.

Kline howled in anguish, swung the rifle around and pounded the barrel against Duran's skull.

Duran grabbed for the weapon, twisting the barrel viciously, hearing a cracking sound as Kline's fingers snapped.

The intense pain acted like a surge of adrenaline to

Kline. He kicked himself free of Duran's grasp, pulling his battered and broken fingers from the rifle's trigger guard. He rolled on his back and aimed his heel at Duran's head. Feeling it make solid contact, he kicked out again, then again, stopping only when he saw Duran quiver and go limp.

Kline lay still for a moment, staring up at the braided tree branches. He held his right hand in front of his eyes. The index and middle fingers were broken, the bones slanted in unshapely angles, the flesh torn, bleeding, the knuckles turning a deep, purple blue. His painting hand!

He inched over to Duran. The vein on Duran's neck was beating out a slow, steady pulse. He wrapped his left hand around Duran's windpipe and began to squeeze, feeling his nails burrow into the muscles and tendons. He slowly released his grip. It was better if Duran was alive. He wanted him to see Anona. See his wife, before he killed her.

Kline flopped back on his side. He looked at his mangled fingers again and began sobbing.

Anona Stack scrambled through the woods, careening off tree trunks and thorny bushes. She paused in midstride at the sound of the shot. A rifle shot. Kline's carbine! The dog had stopped barking. Now he started again. It sounded like Andamo. Could it be Andamo? If it was, then Bob was here! Something small and tan moved in a dark patch of trees to her right. A small cat appeared. No. Not a cat. A cub. A lion cub.

The cub's tawny-skinned mother slithered out from the treeline, snarling menacingly, baring its fangs.

Anona held the kitchen knife out in front of her in a white-knuckled grip. It was a scaling knife, the blade five or six inches long, and sharp. But not long enough or sharp enough to do her any good against a mountain lion. Dear God, she prayed, not this. Not now. Not after all I've been through—

The lion lowered its head and crept toward her.

Anona retreated until she felt her back bump up against a tree.

The double blast of the shotgun startled them both. The lion turned gracefully and leaped into a stand of trees.

Anona sank to her knees, screaming out when a furry object suddenly jumped up on her.

Andamo! She picked the dog up and hugged him. He wiggled against her chest, his pink tongue licking at her face.

Otto Kline leaned against the cabin's door frame, staring at the empty chair in disbelief. The bitch was gone! The leg restraints were on the floor, the chair cuffs dangling free. He cradled the rifle under his right arm and examined the handcuffs. They were still locked. How had she slipped free? He lumbered to the kitchen, bellowing incoherent curses when he saw the back door was open.

Anona circled back toward the cabin, Andamo tucked under her arm, while one hand held the knife and the other kept her pants from falling.

There had been no more gunfire. Just the rifle shot, then the twin blasts from the shotgun. She had done enough shooting with her father to know the difference. Kline had the rifle. Bob must have used the shotgun. One of her father's? The shotgun fired last. Bob got in the last shots.

She threaded her way through the forest. Andamo squirmed free just as she got a look at the cabin.

Kline's van was still there. No other cars. Where was Bob's car?

Andamo was galloping across the open area. Toward the SHU. She ducked back into the treeline, and—

A shot rang out again. A rifle shot. The sound was coming from behind her. Away from the cabin. Another shot. Kline! She hung back for a second, then ran after Andamo.

The loud snarl gave him time. Time to spin around and see the big cat perched above him in the tree. He pulled the trigger instinctively. The bullet caught the mountain lion in mid-leap, a blotch of blood mushroomed on the whitish hair of the animal's chest.

The impact knocked Kline to the ground. He landed on his back, the lion on top of him. Kline struggled free, dragging the rifle with him.

He lay there, at eye level with the lion, who was bleeding heavily from its mouth.

The lion was still breathing—her sides bellowing rapidly. Kline climbed to his feet, cocked the carbine again and placed it between the cat's eyes and pulled the trigger. The animal's blood spurted out, arcing onto Kline's shoes.

Kline tilted his head back and howled like a wounded animal. Anona Stack. He'd lost her. All he had left was Duran. Tears streamed out of his eyes as he staggered back toward the SHU. Kill Duran. That was all he had left.

Chief Saylor followed the directions Peggy Jacquard had given him, wondering if it was just a stall, and he'd been sent on a wild goose chase. If so, Jacquard was going to see the inside of a cell, because he—There it was—the crescent-shaped boulder.

Saylor veered onto the narrow dirt road, both hands firmly on the wheel as the car bumped and heaved its way up the grade.

He slammed on the brakes when he saw Duran's Jaguar. He was halfway out of the patrol car when he heard the rifle shot. He stayed motionless for several moments. Another shot! He leaned into the car and yanked the microphone free from the dashboard. "All units, all units, this is Colma one. I have a 217 in Montara, off San Vincente Road. Request for backup. All units . . ."

"Oh, sweet Jesus," Anona cried when she saw her husband's body. His head was a bloody mess. One leg was twisted at an awkward angle and bleeding heavily. She knelt quickly, her fingers caressing his face, sliding down to his carotid artery.

It was beating!

She ripped her shirt off and wrapped it gently around his head. She had to get help. Had to get him out of there before Kline came back. Had to—

A car engine turned over. The van? Kline?

She picked up the shotgun, broke the barrels and ejected the empty shells, then bent down, digging through Duran's pockets for cartridges. There were none!

The engine was racing now. Kline was coming! She dropped the shotgun, started to run, then stopped. She couldn't leave Bob. He'd kill Bob!

Anona took a deep breath and strode purposefully into the SHU.

Chapter 41

The van slewed and yawed down the trail, sliding to a halt at the base of a redwood tree. Otto Kline dropped his head onto the van's steering wheel for a moment. It seemed to take all his strength just to raise it back up. He peered out the windshield at Duran's body.

Kline's blood-smeared left hand slipped off the door handle twice before he was able to leverage it open. He literally slid out of the blood-slick driver's seat. He reached back for the carbine, then lifted his head and looked up at the cement-gray sky. It was like a prison. Another prison. The whole world was a prison.

He recognized the small dog sitting next to Duran. The terrier. The bitch's terrier. He laid the carbine's barrel on the van's sideview mirror and snapped off a shot.

Andamo barked and ran into the woods.

Kline drew in a chest-rattling breath, then pushed himself off the van and staggered forward.

He dropped to his knees, his left hand clutching his bloody stomach. Duran. His head. Someone had wrapped it in a shirt. Her shirt! Anona! She'd come back!

His head reeled back and forth, then he heard a noise. A groaning noise. He looked at the SHU and fell back on his heels. He smiled, his teeth laced with bloody foam. She'd done it. He crawled over to the SHU. She was hanging from the hook, the bra wrapped around her neck, the mattress and pillow under her feet—her back naked, her pants half hanging over her buttocks.

He got to his feet. He had to see her face. See that beautiful face all purple, black, and blue, like Arlene's must have looked.

He reached out with his left hand, feeling the still warm flesh of her back, sliding up to her shoulder. Too late he noticed that her feet were planted flat on the pillow.

Anona whirled around and plunged the kitchen knife into the bloody target of Otto Kline's stomach. She slipped her head free of the bra-noose and pushed Kline toward the bed.

Kline's eyes were bulging from their sockets. He was pulling at the knife handle, falling backward.

Anona gave him a final shove, pounding on the protruding knife handle with her palm, then leaped outside, and slammed both doors shut, slipping the locks in place. She leaned forward, hands on her knees, breathing deeply for several seconds. Then she straightened up and peered through one of the door holes into the SHU. Kline was sprawled on the floor, the knife firmly embedded in his stomach, his teeth bared, eyes glazed, his right hand jammed under his armpit.

"Are you Anona Stack?" a voice boomed out.

She jerked around and saw a policeman. "My husband!" she cried. "Help my husband."

Chapter 42

Hugh Stringer cautiously answered the knock on the door to his apartment. The building doorman hadn't buzzed to tell him anyone was coming.

His eyebrows raised in puzzlement when he saw his visitor.

"George. How did you get in here?"

"The tradesman entrance," George Montroy disclosed. "May I come in?"

"Yes, yes, certainly," Stringer said with little enthusiasm, noticing that the Stack House butler was dressed in a dark blue blazer and gray slacks. It was the first time he could remember not seeing him in a dark suit.

George had a walking stick in one hand. Stringer recognized it immediately. Conrad Stack's ivory-headed, mottled-brown Malacca cane. Stack had willed it to the butler. Not much, Stringer granted, but more than the old bugger had left him.

"I'm surprised to see you, George. What can I do for you?"

"A brandy would be appreciated."

Stringer hesitated a moment, then said, "Certainly," and walked over to the liquor cabinet.

"Is Stack House about shut down?" he called over his shoulder. "The last I heard, the realtor hasn't been able to find a buyer." Stringer had agreed with Anona's decision to sell Stack House. She'd stayed in the hospital just one day after her ordeal in Montara. Bob Duran had remained in a hospital bed for a full week. He had a severe concussion and the wounds to his leg had required two surgeries. They had flown to Hawaii to get away for a while. That was ten days ago. Stringer hadn't heard a word from them since. "Have you spoken to Anona recently?"

"Yes. And Mr. Duran."

Stringer reached for the thirty-year-old Couvoisier, then pulled his hand back. Christian Brothers would do for George.

Montroy studied the attorney, who was wearing a dark cardigan sweater over a white shirt, with a red scarf at his neck, then surveyed the room. A curving, cantilevered stairway was silhouetted against a background of shuttered windows. The carpeting was of yellow and red fleur-de-lys. Two embroidered chairs sat alongside a white-tiled fireplace. Dark, brooding baroque portraits of bearded men in ruffled collars dotted the soft beige walls.

Stringer passed George his drink, then said, "Well, what are you going to do with yourself now? It must be difficult for you. You've spent most of your life in Stack House."

"Actually, I was thinking of purchasing Master John's houseboat."

A bemused smiled settled on the corner of Stringer's lips. "Houseboat? You? I'm amazed. You just don't seem to be the houseboat type."

"I know. It . . . it just seems the right thing to do. I've only been there once. At the christening. You were there, also."

"Yes," Stringer agreed. "I remember Anona smashing a bottle of Dom Perignon on the damn thing. A waste of good wine."

"It seemed in good condition. Very comfortable. You've seen it since, haven't you?"

Stringer waved a hand vaguely, then poured himself a glass of port. "I went over there to check on John for Lisa. It makes me sick to think that he was dead in the water, just a few hundred yards away."

"Yes. Indeed," George agreed. "You didn't get inside, did you?"

"No. It was locked."

"And it was still in that same spot? Next to that garish boat that looks like a Chinese junk?"

"Yes," Stringer responded irritably. "It's none of my business, but I don't think you'd be happy there, George. It's more of a younger crowd."

George sighed deeply, then took a letter from his jacket pocket and passed it to Stringer.

"This arrived a week ago. I thought you should see it."

While Stringer examined the letter, George sniffed the brandy, took a small sip and settled the snifter on the coffee table.

"I don't understand this," Stringer protested. "I never spoke to anyone at the Gerhow Gallery in Switzerland. Never."

"We didn't really think so," George disclosed.

"We? Who is we?" Stringer asked, going back to the letter.

"Miss Anona, Mr. Robert, and I," George confided. He raised his cane level to his chest and pointed to the shuttered windows. "Does that lead to the balcony?"

"Yes," Stringer said angrily. "But neither Anona or Robert mentioned this letter to me."

George caned himself over to the windows. "It

didn't seem necessary, Mr. Stringer. We're quite sure that Jason Lark was the one who spoke to Mr. Gerhow."

Stringer clenched his teeth. "Using my name! The shit. He got what he deserved."

"Perhaps more than he deserved," George concluded. "Mr. Lark found the drawings mentioned in the letter in my room. In a trunk in the closet."

"You had these Picassos in your room?" Stringer asked incredulously.

"I was unaware of their value," the butler explained. "Or that Mr. Picasso was the artist. Mr. Bresson gave them to Miss Anona many years ago. They were in her luggage when she came back from France. I did mention them to her, but she was quite upset at that time. She had decided to divorce Mr. Lark. She told me to keep the sketches. I have quite a few of her old drawings. And those of Miss Lisa. And Master John," he added sadly.

"What happened to the Picassos? Who's got them now?" Stringer slapped the letter against his leg. "They're worth a fortune!"

"Mr. Robert isn't sure. But I believe he will find out. Whoever killed Jason Lark no doubt took them."

"It had to be that lunatic Kline," Stringer said adamantly. "If Robert can find them, it would be something, wouldn't it?" He smiled benignly. "The rich get richer, eh, George? Anona's worth millions and she falls into something like this."

"Actually, if the drawings are found, they will be mine. Can we step outside?"

"Yours? Who told you that?"

"Miss Anona." George unlocked the glass sliding door and walked out onto the balcony, which was eight feet wide and stretched out over twenty-five feet.

There were potted plants and glass-topped iron furniture scattered about. The city's jagged skyline, punctuated by the TransAmerica tower twinkled in the distance.

Stringer followed him outside.

"I wouldn't get my hopes up too high about those Picassos, George. I know the police didn't find them among Otto Kline's possessions."

George leaned over the balcony railing and looked at the street, twenty-five stories below.

"Kline didn't kill Jason Lark. Or Master John."

"The police think he did," Stringer said sternly.

"Both Miss Anona and Mister Robert are sure he did not. If he had, he would have boasted of it."

"Ridiculous." Stringer snorted. "The man was a homicidal maniac. There's no telling how many people he killed."

The butler reversed his grip on the cane, holding it from the narrow end, swinging it lightly back and forth as if it were a golf putter.

"I've been getting things in order at Stack House. Going through everything, arranging for the moving people. I've gone over the financial records. Miss Anona's financial records."

Stringer looked offended. "That's a little out of your boundaries, George."

"A little out of my field of expertise. That's why I hired an accountant. And an attorney."

Stringer's face crimsoned. "You've no right to do any such thing, damn it! You're a butler!"

"An honest butler, sir. Not a crooked attorney."

Stringer jerked his thumb over his shoulder. "That's enough from you. Get out!"

"You were clever, Mr. Stringer. Very clever from what I've been told. The stock churning, the real estate sales. We were able to trace the property transfers—your selling Miss Anona's holdings here and in Mexico and Hawaii. The buyer, your corporation, acquiring them substantially below their market value. The accountant estimates that you swindled the family out of at least two million dollars. Unfortunately, there may be no way to charge you criminally." He shook his head slowly, as if it weighed a ton. "And Miss Anona trusted you so."

"I said get out!" Stringer roared, grabbing the butler by his coat sleeve.

"Even in a civil court of law, I've been advised that you would most likely be acquitted."

Stringer was surprised at the ease in which George wrenched his arm free. "And the cost of a civil suit. More attorneys. I imagine Miss Anona would have let you off the hook. Not even bothering to prosecute you."

"You're talking rubbish, and I'm going to tell Anona exactly that as soon as she gets back. Now get out of my house."

"It's an apartment," George corrected. "Or, if you prefer, a condominium, not a house."

Stringer gestured impatiently toward the sliding-glass doors. "Go! I've got things to do."

"And places to go," George said calmly, then lashed out with the cane, the carved ivory ball striking Hugh Stringer in the nose.

Stringer rocked back on his heels. His hand went to his face.

George's next blow caught the attorney in his left knee. He dropped to the cement floor with a thud.

"Master John moved his houseboat, Mr. Stringer. I know, because I had to search half an hour for it. It seems his former neighbors were complaining about the noise. So he moved three docks over. That was months ago. Miss Anona didn't know of the new location. Neither did Mr. Robert. Even Lisa was kept in the dark. Nor Eric Marvin, John's manager at the club. You remember Eric, don't you?"

"No. I don't keep track of John's friends or business associates," Stringer said, his labored breath exploding like little clouds in front of his face.

"Eric remembers you. He remembers you coming to the club. Arguing with John about his decision to hire an investigator to locate his mother—to see if Mr. Robert was plundering the estate. It was quite a heated argument, according to Eric. John's parting words to you were, 'Go shit in your hat.' Was that when you decided to kill John? Did you follow him to Sausalito? Or did you wait for him, near where he parked his car, then assaulted him on the dock and threw his body into the bay?"

Stringer pulled his bloodied hands away from his face. Blood was spurting from his mangled nose. "You're mad!"

"Yes. Very mad. Very mad indeed."

"I'm telling you, you're crazy. I—"

George slammed the cane over Stringer's head, breaking it in half in the process. He squatted down so that he was at eye level with the attorney. "You didn't want John to hire an investigator, did you? A professional digging into the financial records. I suspect you originally intended Mr. Robert to be blamed for John's death. You must have been relieved when this Kline creature showed up. Miss Anona kidnapped, perhaps murdered. With John gone, there was just Miss Lisa left. And you no doubt thought you could control Miss Lisa." He squeezed Stringer's red jowls. "The police would never have enough evidence to prosecute you for John's death. And, I'm not going to mention this, the fact that you murdered him, to Miss Anona. She's been through enough."

He grabbed Stringer by the back of his neck and hoisted him to his feet and shoved him hard.

Stringer staggered, his arms flailing, fighting for balance, his weight carrying him forward until his stomach rested on the railing. For a moment he teetered back and forth, like a child's seesaw.

"No," Stringer blubbered though bloody lips. "Don't."

George fastened his hands on Stringer's trousers, hoisting him up over the railing.

"Stop! It . . . it was an accident, George. I went to see John and . . . he took offense to my wanting to help him. He slipped. Slipped on the dock." His hands made a desperate grasp at the narrow, dew-slick, metal balcony posts. "An accident. I swear."

George hooked a hand under Stringer's knees and heaved. He got a last look at the attorney's face, which was upside down, on the opposite side of the balcony posts. Their eyes met briefly. Stringer opened his mouth to say something, then he was gone, cartwheeling down into the blackness.

Chapter 43

Las Vegas
New Year's Eve

"You can go," Mario Drago told the big man in the ill-fitting tuxedo. He gestured to the chair in front of his desk. "Have a seat, Mr. Duran."

Duran limped across the room, which was tennis-court size. The carpet was snow white. Duran sank slowly into the eighteenth-century, Lancet-back, elbow chair. He leaned back, noticing the ceiling was parchment colored and covered with a map of the world, looking like a beautiful old globe that had been flattened out. One wall was entirely taken up by rows of TV screens—the casino's ceiling cameras focusing on the blackjack, craps, roulette, poker, and baccarat gaming tables.

The other walls were festooned with an eclectic mixture of elaborately framed paintings. Duran spotted a Gauguin Tahitian beach scene, a Van Eyck cathedral, a Vermeer portrait, a John Singer Sargent landscape, two Roy Lichtenstein pop comic strips, a Helen Frankenthaler abstract, a Manet nude, a Seurat dotted beach scene, and a Joseph Albers square amongst the mix.

"All reproductions, I can assure you," Drago said with a wide smile.

"The same artist who copied Van Gogh's 'Sun and Sky'?"

Drago's smile stayed frozen in place. "I'm not familiar with that one." He leaned his hands on his desk, a Swedish Empire mahogany with gilded, winged sphinxes.

"You picked a bad time to come. New Year's Eve is our busiest day of the year."

"Then let's come right to the point. I want the Picassos."

Drago slid his finger along the polished surface of the desk, stopping at a thick white business envelope. "So you said in your letter, Mr. Duran." He picked the envelope up, balancing it in his hand, like an assayer weighing gold. "You're making a lot of wild accusations."

Duran stared directly into Drago's arrogant eyes. "You stole the Fritzheims' Van Gogh, as well as several other paintings that Jason Lark switched for you. You had Harry Lawson killed. Then you killed Lark and took the Picasso sketches that he'd stolen from a friend of mine."

Drago slipped back into his chair and wrinkled his brow thoughtfully. "Jason Lark. I read his name in your letter. I don't know the man."

Duran shifted uneasily, his hand going to his knee. "I've got Lark's phone records. He made a couple of dozen calls to you in the last six months."

Drago's eyes were in constant motion, flicking around the room from the paintings to the TV screens. "A man calls a casino in Vegas. That's no big deal."

"Calls to your personal number, Drago."

The gangster held out his arms, like a priest granting

benediction. "I don't have a personal number. Maybe this Lark guy, he comes to Vegas once in a while. Maybe he was calling for a room. I can check our guest list for you."

"I've got your phone records, too. The calls you made to Lark. Including one to Stack House two days before he was killed."

Drago took a few seconds to respond. "If you've got those records, and I say *if,* because they would have to be subpoenaed to be used in court, and if they were subpoenaed, my attorney would know of it, but let's say you have something like that, then maybe I did know of this Lark guy. Maybe he lost some money in the casino. There are hundreds of guys like that. I can't keep track of all the names. Maybe I was calling him to get the money." He slipped the pocket handkerchief from his tuxedo pocket and wiped his lips. "There's no crime in that." He flexed his arm, consulted his wristwatch. "Like I said, this is a busy time, so if you've got nothing else—"

"I've got another name for you," Duran said with the calm of a man who was holding four aces. "Peter Rodash."

Drago made a rolling gesture with one hand, inviting Duran to go on.

"He's your forger. He's good. Very good. He did 'Sun and Sky,' and the others. He's a happily married man, his daughter just presented him with his first grandson. He doesn't want to go to jail. He's been very cooperative."

Drago's hand crept toward the telephone.

"You make the wrong call," Duran said calmly, "and you're a dead man."

Drago's voice dropped to a deadly whisper. "Do you know who you're threatening?"

"Yes. A casino manager for the 'Tony Dope' Viscotti family in New York. You should have stuck to skimming the take, Mario. Viscotti isn't going to like it when he finds out about your hobby." Duran smiled guilessly. "Or maybe I'm wrong. Maybe you're sharing the forged painting money with Viscotti. I'll have to ask him about that."

"You're bluffing," Drago said with a hard edge to his voice.

"No, I'm not," Duran responded calmly. "Give Viscotti a call and check me out. Or give me the Picassos."

"What's so special about these Picassos? The insurance company won't pay off?"

"They're not insured."

"Ah," Drago sighed. "They were yours, huh? Or your wife's? And Lark stole them. So that's why you got this bean up your ass."

"They belong to a friend of mine. A friend who did me a big favor."

"Let's play 'what if.' What if I was able to find these Picassos you're talking about? And what if I gave them to you?"

"Then I'd give them to their owner and everyone would be happy."

The two men stared at each other in a stiff, formal silence, then Duran pushed himself painfully to his feet.

"Yes or no, Drago?"

"How'd you get to Peter Rodash?"

"Your phone records. It was a lot of work, but Rodash was the only other person you called in the Los Angeles area from your personal line around the same time you called Lark."

"You're bluffing again. None of this would hold up

in court. You obtained the phone records illegally. They're useless."

"You're not the only one with influential friends," Duran replied stiffly. "Harry Lawson had a lot of underworld connections. They're not going to be very happy when they found out you had him killed."

Drago started to say something, then swung his chair around and walked to the Gauguin oil. He slid the painting aside, revealing a steel-faced safe.

"When I got your letter, I started asking around," he said, while spinning the safe's combination dial. The door opened with an oily click. He extracted a brick-colored manila packet from the safe, then closed it, and slid the painting back in place.

He held the packet out to Duran. "I had nothing to do with the murder of Harry Lawson or Jason Lark, and nothing you can say or do can prove otherwise. But, I'm an admirer of your wife's work. And I know you and her have been through a hard time, so here. You take these and we'll call it quits. How's that?"

Duran slipped the packet under his arm without opening it. "If these are forgeries, I'm going to pay a personal visit to Tony Viscotti."

"They're legit," Drago assured him. "I've got to give you credit, Duran. You've got balls, writing that letter, and coming here to see me. This friend of yours, the guy who owns the Picassos, he must have done you a real big favor."

"He killed a man," Duran disclosed, then limped out of the room.

We invite you to preview
Jerry Kennealy's
next exciting thriller:

S.F.P.D. Police Inspector Jack Kordic
(last seen in *The Conductor*)
returns to face an international terrorist
in *The Hunted.*

Coming soon from Signet books.

Jack Kordic was hurrying across the plush lobby of the Savoy Hotel, a shopping bag in tow, his new raincoat draped over one shoulder when he heard a familiar voice inquire: "New suit?"

Kordic wheeled around, his mouth dropping open when he spotted the sardonic expression on the face of the Israeli Mossad agent Anatoly Weeks.

"Anatoly, what the hell are you doing here?" Kordic beamed. "Have they come to their senses and decided to give you the award instead of giving it to me?"

Weeks held up his good right arm. "Thank God, no. You take the glory. I'll stay in the background."

Kordic stepped back to get a better look at his friend.

Weeks had taken a bullet in his left shoulder, during those last frantic minutes before Kordic had killed the terrorist Rene Santos. The intelligence agent didn't look much the worse for wear: a full crop of steel-wool hair, his skin tanned the color of tree bark. It wasn't until Weeks walked closer that Kordic noticed that his left arm hung straight down, motionless along his side.

"You're looking good, Anatoly. How's the arm?"

Weeks gave an unintelligible grunt, then reached over and ran a thumb and forefinger along the lapel of Kordic's dark blue suit jacket. "Not bad. You've been doing some shopping, huh?"

"Yes." Kordic laughed. "Orders from my new partner."

"Are you and Mary Ariza still seeing each other?" Weeks asked.

"No." Kordic frowned. "She's moved down to San Diego. We still talk, but . . ."

Weeks shrugged his good shoulder. "Hey, a cop and

an attorney. That's a tough combo. I hope you're not going to give a long, boring speech at the banquet tonight."

"You'll be there?"

"Why not?"

Kordic grimaced and shook his head. "How about a drink?"

"Absolutely," Weeks accepted. "Let's go to the Grill."

Weeks led Kordic around the High Tea in the Thaymes foyer, with its tailcoated waiters and tuxedoed pianist, who was playing a soft Cole Porter medley, then into the renowned, yew-paneled Savoy Grill.

There was a line of impatient diners waiting to be seated. The maître d' greeted Weeks with a raised eyebrow.

Kordic wasn't sure what the Mossad agent whispered into the man's ear, but whatever it was, it got his immediate attention. They were quickly escorted to a corner table.

When they were seated, and had their drinks in hand, the two men brought each other up to date on their current activities.

Weeks gave Kordic a quick rundown on the latest terrorist activities plaguing his homeland.

He took an appreciative sip of the vodka martini, then said, "I've got something that's connected to your neck of the woods, Jack. Does the name Phillip Bovard ring any bells?"

Kordic sampled his beer before responding. "Bovard. No, should it?"

"Probably not. He's ex–Swiss Intelligence."

"Switzerland has an intelligence service?" Kordic asked, grinning a little.

"Indeed. Two of them actually: a very efficient military unit, and their banks. Don't knock the Swiss. We molded our army after theirs. The army has 650,000 troops—ten percent of the population. Civilians who spend one day out of every ten in uniform. Most of them march around the alps with top-flight American weapons at the ready. The bankers handle most of the intelligence work—when they're doing their army time and when they're back behind their desks at Credit Suisse. That's when the real work gets done. Those bankers have access to stuff your CIA and FBI would kill to get their hands on." Weeks gave a wolfish smile, then added, "Us, too. They do their own recruiting. Friends recommend friends, who recommend friends. It's run like an English gentleman's club. Only these guys ain't no gentlemen.

"Bovard left Switzerland fifteen years ago. He describes himself as an arbitrageur. A financial wizard who plays both ends of the currency markets and somehow makes a buck. A very large buck."

"Sounds legitimate enough," Kordic said warily. "Since you're interested in him, he must have some other bad habits."

"He does indeed, but we've never been able to prove it. When there's a catastrophe of some kind, a bombing, a plane crash, an assassination, the financial markets react. Bovard always seems to be on the right side of the street at those times."

Weeks leaned across the table. "Did you read about the plant at Hamerling Industries in Germany blowing up last month? They're the outfit that had been shipping some high tech stuff to the Iranians?"

Kordic shifted uncomfortably in his chair "Yes. The spin the newspapers gave was that your people may have been involved."

"We weren't," Weeks responded hotly. "But you're

right. The papers did spin it that way. Because there was evidence planted that made it look like we were dirty. Just like it looked as if Iran blew up that British Airways jet, or that Baghdad was behind the dam bursting in Turkey."

"And you think this Bovard character did all this?" Kordic asked skeptically.

"Yes. And a lot more, Jack. He's an evil *momzer.* He works mainly out of London. Big office on Old Broad Street, near the London Stock Exchange. Dozens of phones with brokers buying and selling stocks and currency all the time. Boring stuff, but we've got a wire on his private office line. Calls come in, but no real names are given, just short, cryptic messages, asking Bovard to contact them. The telephone numbers left are always to a pay phone.

"Three days ago someone, male, middle-aged, American accent, calls from a Laundromat on Larkin Street in San Francisco." Weeks pulled an ordinary looking ballpoint pen from his coat pocket. "Get a load of this," he said, then clicked the pen three times and handed it to Kordic.

Kordic listened to the recorded message: "Tell him his old friend from America wants to talk. I'm at 415-555-9995."

"The voice means nothing to me, Anatoly," Kordic said, admiring the pen. "But I like this gadget."

"Not bad, huh? You can even write with it while your taping some schmuck. We didn't have time to put a tap on that telephone line, but we did find out that it's a public phone in the Laundromat. The next day another call came in. Just click the pen," Weeks instructed.

Kordic clicked the pen and the miniature tape recorder activated:

"This is his old friend. I'm at 415-555-4210."

Kordic said, "It's the same voice."

"Right. Another Laundromat. This one's in San Francisco too, on Chestnut Street. You know why he uses Laundromats, Jack?"

"I haven't a clue," Kordic admitted.

"Coin machines. He loaded up on quarters to pay for the international calls. He's a very careful man."

Kordic handed the pen back to Weeks. "I can check out both places when I get back, but I don't think it'll do much good."

"Neither do I," Weeks confirmed. "So, tell me, how does it feel to be a hero?"

"Believe me, I wanted nothing to do with it," Kordic assured him. "The new mayor is a publicity hound. He ordered the chief to send me. So here I am."

Weeks rolled the olive around in his glass. "Are you doing any real police work, Jack?"

"Some," Kordic sighed. "Nothing as exotic as what you're used to. My partner called me with the preliminary results from the medical examiner on a new homicide case. The victims were a madam and two girls in their early teens."

"There's a lot of that going around," Weeks granted glumly.

"Here's a twist, something I've never run into. They found bits of *Solanum tuberosum,* plain old raw potato, in all three of the victim's bullet wounds."

"The potato's nothing new, Jack. An 'Irish silencer.' The IRA used them all the time before they got the real thing from Qadaffi and those other *shtarkers.*"

Kordic had picked up quite a bit of Yiddish slang from Weeks while they worked together chasing after Rene Santos. He knew *momzer* was bastard, but this was a new one to him.

"*Shtarker,* a strong man, a big shot," Weeks explained. "What do you know about the kids that were killed?"

"Not much," Kordic admitted. "Both were caucasian, one dark, the other light-skinned and blond. The killer took the madam's computer base, and all its paraphernalia. We found a hidden metal box in the bedroom. It was empty, but there were computer disks laying alongside it. I don't know yet what was on the disks yet, but I'm hoping it's the madam's john list."

"Sloppy killer," Weeks said, then drained what remained of his drink and signaled to a waiter for a refill.

"You've got a pretty big Irish community in San Francisco, don't you?"

"Well, look for a Harp hit man. The potato. That's definitely one of their old trademarks. And the one-shot kills on the woman and the one kid, then the coup de grâce to the second kid. Sounds like a real pro to me. You ready for a refill?"

Kordic picked up his half-finished glass of dark beer. The butterflies were already dancing in his stomach in anticipation of his giving an acceptance speech at the banquet.

"Why not? Are you going to be at the head table tonight?"

"No. I'll be way in the back. One of my bosses, Ira Heiser, will be presenting you with your award. Just do me a couple of favors, Jack. Don't mention my name in your speech, and don't spill any wine on Heiser, okay?"

Although Jack Kordic had paid what he considered to be an outrageous price for his off-the-rack suit from the London tailor Maureen Connah had recommended, he felt considerably underdressed as he approached the dais in the conference room at the Savoy Hotel.

The majority of those in the audience were in black tie, as were most of the men Kordic would be sharing the dais with.

He had met many of them at a welcoming breakfast that morning and now he nodded his hellos, finessing names he didn't completely remember.

Kordic recalled once reading a magazine article in a dentist's waiting room. The author's premise was that the two things Americans feared most were public speaking and death—in that order. He'd been amused at the time. But not now. He was nervous, more nervous than he'd ever been testifying at a murder trial. He'd worked for hours on his speech, the results tucked away on three-by-five index cards in the inside pocket of his new suit.

"You look like you need a drink," a short man with an unruly black beard said, thrusting a glass at Kordic.

"Ira Heiser," the man announced. He wore gunmetal-rimmed glasses. One lens was noticeably thicker than the other. "Anatoly told me you might be feeling a bit nervous. Champagne's just the thing for the nerves."

Kordic accepted the wine gratefully, holding the glass out to see if his hand was shaking.

"Weeks told me to be careful not to spill any of this on you."

Heiser barked out a loud laugh. "Anatoly's been a little testy lately. He's been chained to a desk for several months."

There was a loud gong sound. Kordic looked around and spotted one of the hotel staff pounding a mallet against a large circle of brass.

Heiser drained what little champagne was left in his glass. "The dinner bell, I'm afraid. Come on, Inspector. You're sitting next to me."

The meal was elaborately prepared and formally delivered: a soup Kordic couldn't recognize, and was too ill-at-ease to ask about. A poached fish dish, a salad swimming with prawns and scallops and a slab of rare roast beef as thick as first base. The sommelier arrived at each serving with a different wine, announcing its vintage and heritage in the hushed tones of a priest giving the last rites to his bishop.

Heiser was sitting on Kordic's left. He cut his food with the precision of a surgeon and kept a running conversation on a variety of subjects.

The man on Kordic's right was named Gilbeaux. The scent of gin drifted over the table when he explained his position in the Belgian government.

A waiter tapped Kordic on the shoulder as dessert was about to be served.

"A call for you, sir," the waiter advised. "In the lobby. From the San Francisco Police Department. They say it's urgent."

Heiser looked up at Kordic with a twinkle in his eye.

"You're sure this hasn't been staged just to get you out of giving your speech, Inspector?"

Kordic pushed his chair from the table and got to his feet. "I wish I had thought of that," he granted, before taking off after the waiter.

Do I tip him for this, or not? Kordic wondered when the waiter escorted him to a spacious phone booth. He dug in his pocket for a pound coin, hoping it was an adequate amount.

He picked up the receiver and said: "Hello."

At that moment there was the thunderous sound of an explosion.